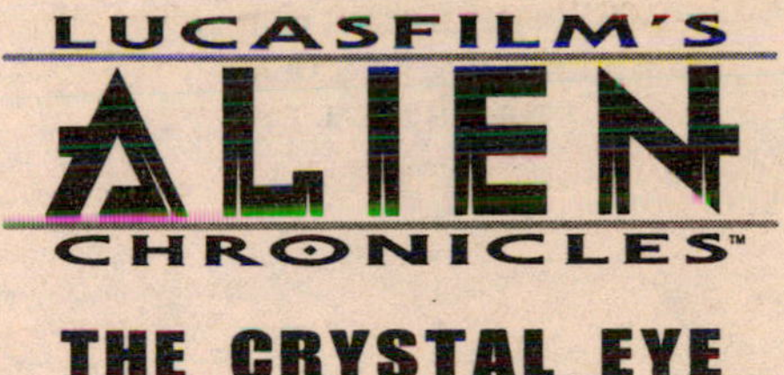

THE CRYSTAL EYE

Lucasfilm's Alien Chronicles™ by Deborah Chester

THE GOLDEN ONE
THE CRIMSON CLAW
THE CRYSTAL EYE

THE ALIENS OF

LUCASFILM'S ALIEN CHRONICLES™

THE VIIS . . . A race of seven-foot tall, beautifully reptilian creatures. Their physical attractiveness has convinced the Viis that they are the most important, godlike creatures in the universe. This has led to an underground race of the "uglies"—Viis that were cast off as unacceptable, worthless spawn . . .

THE AAROUN . . . The race of Ampris are powerful, golden-furred creatures with sharp teeth. They have long been kept by the Viis as slaves, or as in the case of Ampris, pets.

THE KELTH . . . A submissive, doglike race with stiff, bristly coats and simian hands. Because they are so easily intimidated, Kelth are considered unreliable to handle important tasks. They are not to be trusted.

THE MYAL . . . Renowned for their insight and memories, Myal stand barely three feet tall and are usually poets, musicians, and historians. They control the archives of the Viis empire.

THE ZHRELI . . . They are filthy, noisy, foul-smelling, and socially repulsive creatures. Yet they are unequaled at maintaining and repairing quantum hardware (the only reason to tolerate them).

THE SKEK . . . Less than two feet high, furry, multilimbed, and quick, the Skek live like rats in the ducts and garbage of the Viis. It's a common slave belief that if you dropped one Skek in a barrel, the barrel would explode with Skek offspring within a day.

Continued . . .

THE TOTHS . . . Big, stupid, and brutal, Toths roam the ghetto streets as thugs, but they are also used by their Viis masters as hired enforcers and brownshirts. Nearly as tall as the Viis, they have massive heads covered with thick mats of dirty, curly brown hair. Flies usually buzz around their long, floppy ears. Their faces are broad and flat, with wide nostrils, and their eyes are small and cruel.

THE CRYSTAL EYE

Deborah Chester

ACE BOOKS, NEW YORK

LUCASFILM'S ALIEN CHRONICLES™: THE CRYSTAL EYE

An Ace Book / published by arrangement with
Lucasfilm Ltd.

PRINTING HISTORY
Ace edition / August 1999

The Penguin Putnam Inc. World Wide Web site address is
http://www.penguinputnam.com

Check out the Ace Science Fiction & Fantasy newsletter
and much more on the internet at Club PPI!

Visit the Alien Chronicles Web site at http://www.lucasaliens.com

ISBN: 0-441-00635-3

ACE®
Ace Books are published
by The Berkley Publishing Group,
a division of Penguin Putnam Inc.,
375 Hudson Street, New York, New York 10014.
ACE and the "A" design are trademarks
belonging to Penguin Putnam Inc.

PRINTED IN THE UNITED STATES OF AMERICA

10 9 8 7 6 5 4 3 2 1

CHAPTER ONE

Panting in the heat, Ampris dragged her harvest basket to the end of the row. She looked around warily, staying alert for the first sign of trouble, but no one was paying attention to her. Lugging her heavy basket, she walked over to the sorting bin and joined the end of the line, where workers were waiting to dump the contents of their baskets.

The sorting bin shook and hummed noisily, vibrating all over. Its belts screeched, in need of maintenance. Slaves stood on a platform above the bin, tipping the contents of baskets into its maw. Mechanical teeth and rollers shook the globular grain heads, each one as large as Ampris's fist. They bounced through openings that determined grade and rolled along an open chute that fed them into the cargo hold of a parked transport. The heads too small to make grade went rolling out a side chute into a smaller bin.

Ampris hunched her broad shoulders and kept her head low to make herself look smaller. The line shuffled forward, and she dragged her heavy basket on her left side to conceal her limp. She wore a ragged jerkin, belt, and conical straw hat with a torn brim to protect her from the brutal sun. She looked exactly like every other slave at work in this stelf field. But she was no longer a slave; she did not belong here; and if all went as planned neither the guards nor the overseer would notice her.

She moved forward again, glancing ahead at a lean Kelth with grayish-brown fur and a slim, pointed muzzle. Wielding a long-handled rake, he was pushing the grain heads along the chute into the transport hold. Garbed in a coat with both sleeves torn off, its color long since faded to a nondescript gray, Elrabin snagged any grain heads that were too bruised or rotten to go to processing. As Ampris watched him from beneath her ragged hat brim, Elrabin raked out two deformed heads, then slyly snagged a plump, perfect one. He dropped the deformed ones into the stinking basin that encircled the base of his platform and with a flick of his wrist tossed the good one into the basket he had concealed in the weeds.

Ampris drew in a satisfied breath and lowered her head. All was going perfectly. She and Elrabin had slipped into the fields just after dawn, when the security nets were turned off. They had come down from the foothills in the dark, taking cover and waiting until morning. Ampris had watched the operations of this farm for several days, while she formulated her plan.

She knew the slaves were carted to the fields on the decrepit old grain transports, but once they were unloaded they were left unrestrained while the transports were parked and other machinery was set up. The guards all seemed to be Toths, which meant they were both stupid and lazy. They seldom bothered to do more than make sure no slave bolted for freedom into the hills.

With such a lax operation, it was simple to emerge from cover and join the slaves. Once inside the field with everyone milling around, Ampris and Elrabin found it easy to blend in.

Right away, Elrabin had climbed onto the sorting platform and talked a worker into letting him handle the job, probably saying he was ordered to take over. Ampris picked up a basket and a slicer along with the others, unremarked by the guards handing out equipment.

It was risky, what they were doing. If they got caught, they would be hanged from the boundary markers at one corner of the farm. Ampris had seen such dangling corpses. Now, despite the fact that the plan was working smoothly, she couldn't help but think of death. She shuddered and stepped forward in line, telling herself to stop worrying. She wasn't going to get caught, and she wasn't going to be hanged.

A dirty haze of pollution obscured the sky, and the air held a faint stench of smoke. Sneezing, Ampris supposed one of the Viis cities was on fire. Maybe far away in Vir the abiru folk had finally rebelled against their cruel Viis masters and were burning the capital city. For a moment Ampris let her mind drift over her old dream of freeing all the abiru races. Years ago, she had been a rebel dedicated to the cause of freedom. She had established the Freedom Network and worked hard to unite the abiru into one cause. She knew that if they could ever be persuaded to work together, they could overthrow the Viis yoke. But those old days of rebellion were long since over. Ampris no longer traveled the length and breadth of the empire as she had when she was a champion gladiator. She no longer had contact with other members of the underground. She no longer plotted and schemed to bring down the Viis empire.

Instead, she lived free in the wilderness areas of Viisymel with her half-grown cubs and a little band of abiru folk. She spent her time hunting, trying to make sure she and her cubs did not starve.

When she led a raid these days, it was in the name of survival, not rebellion.

Sighing to herself for a past that had long ago ceased to matter, Ampris stopped gazing at the smoky sky and shuffled forward again in line.

A Toth guard strolled by, swinging his stun-stick and looking bored. Flies swarmed his matted, dark brown hair and collected at the corner of his right eye, which looked diseased. The Toth rubbed his face, grumbling to himself, and glanced up at Elrabin just as the Kelth raked another prime grain head out of the chute.

Ampris gripped her basket in alarm, her heart thudding in her chest. Just like that, they were caught. Her risky plan was over, and they were done for. She panted harder, tensing her muscles to spring to Elrabin's aid.

But Elrabin never hesitated. "I'll get it!" he shouted over the screeching clank of the machinery. He jumped down off his platform and rooted around on the ground in the tall, scraggly weeds before bouncing upright again with the grain head clutched aloft in his hand. "Got it!" he announced, while the Toth glared at him suspiciously.

The Toth flipped his drooping ears back and forth and slid his thick tongue up into first one nostril, then the other. He said nothing while Elrabin climbed onto his platform and tossed the grain head back in.

Elrabin yipped nervously and grinned. "Made a mistake," he said to the guard. "Thought it had blight spots on it, but it's just a little dirt."

The guard's small, stupid eyes stared at Elrabin for another moment, then he walked on without a word.

Ampris let out her breath in a long sigh, drained with relief. Up on his platform, Elrabin looked at the Toth's departing back and let his narrow jaws part in a grin before scooping out two plump grain heads and dropping them out of sight.

Ampris grinned to herself and ducked her head lower.

The slave behind her prodded her in the back to make her move forward. She hoisted her heavy basket up with a grunt to workers who dumped its contents into the main sorting bin and handed her empty basket back to her.

Ampris glanced around to make sure no other guards

were close by and circled around the base of the machinery to where Elrabin's small basket stood concealed in the weeds.

It was nearly full of stolen grain. She poured it into her own basket. The basin holding the rejected produce was half-full of black slime, with blighted grain heads floating on top. The sickly sweet stench of rotting grain nearly overpowered her sensitive nostrils.

Trying to breathe as little as possible, Ampris gathered a few of the blighted heads and put them on top of her stolen ones. The slaves were allowed to gather all the rejected grain they wanted for their own consumption. The fact that the blight usually rendered the grain poisonous seemed of no consequence to the Viis landowners.

She hoisted up her basket with a grunt and balanced it on her hip before glancing up at Elrabin, who stood on the machinery platform looking the other way. She pinched the back of his heel.

He threw another blighted head into the garbage with a splat. Ampris dodged to one side and whispered, "I'll cut one more row."

Elrabin raked out another deformed head and twisted around to drop it. As he did so, he shot her a warning look and muttered, "Got enough, Goldie. Don't get greedy."

"We need another basket," she insisted.

He backed his ears. "Ain't worth the risk—"

"One more," she said and walked away with her laden basket.

He snarled behind her, but Ampris limped over to a rusting shed that housed the irrigation well pump and circled around behind it. No one seemed to be looking.

At the rear of the shed was a low, slanted lean-to attachment of polyfibe boards that were brittle and decaying from age and no maintenance. One of the boards was hinged to allow access to the interior, and the lean-to had probably been designed to hold tools for servicing the irrigation pump. It was now empty, except for Ampris's hoard of stolen food.

Kneeling, she pried open the hinged board and swiftly dumped in the contents of her basket. The space beneath the little lean-to was almost full, and as she lowered the board back in place Ampris's sense of satisfaction faded momentarily.

Maybe Elrabin was right, she thought. Maybe they should thank their good luck at what they'd gotten so far and get out of here while they could.

But then she thought of the hungry mouths back in their little camp up in the foothills rising above the east side of this dusty field. She thought of how she'd hunted all day yesterday and brought in no game. Neither had anyone else. The long summer drought had driven them here into the semiarid Seren region, but they had not fared well in the move. Last month they had lost Morlol, a big Aaroun male who was their best provider, in a hunting accident. Elrabin worked hard to bring in food, but while he might be quick, clever, and streetwise, even twelve years of living off the land had not managed to make a good hunter of him. Paket, one of the Kelths who had escaped with her from the Vess Vaas Laboratory years ago, was getting old and stiff. Robuhl, a Myal, was so ancient his mane had turned white. Blind and senile, he had to be watched constantly so that he didn't wander away from camp and get lost. Tantha was pregnant and still grieving for her dead mate Morlol. Normally she would be as strong and tireless as Ampris, but she was near her birthing time and needed to stay as inactive as possible. Velia was a timid Kelth female, mate to Elrabin. Long abused before she gained her freedom from her Viis masters, she would not leave the camp by herself and usually took on the main domestic tasks of cooking, mending, and watching over Robuhl. The two Viis Rejects, Luax and Harthril, could hunt successfully if there was any game to find, but they did not always bring home enough to feed the entire camp and tended to take care of their own dietary needs first. Ampris's cubs, Foloth and Nashmarl, had begun to shoot up in growth. They were nearly as tall as Elrabin now, and constantly, voraciously hungry.

No, Ampris decided, thinking of the many responsibilities resting on her shoulders; she could not take the safe course and steal only enough for them to eat one or two meals. Ampris was determined to take enough to supply their needs for several days. She wanted to dry the grain and pound it into flour. They needed to move on from this region, perhaps venture closer to Vir by the end of summer. With old ones and cubs soon to be born, they would need a warm, fairly gentle climate for the winter months. Relocating was hard work, involving difficult travel on foot and the need to scout ahead to make sure they ran into no trouble or encountered no settlements where their presence might be reported to the authorities. Hunting would be harder than ever. Therefore, she needed to get as much food as she could today before the work ended.

At night the uncut harvest was guarded with electronic sensors that protected it from theft. Her only chance was to cut the produce boldly today, in full sight of the guards.

Once cut, the grain heads would keep for three days before they began to rot. This field would be harvested by the end of today or early tomorrow. As soon as it was cleared, a mechanics crew would come to cap off the well and remove the pump starter. Thus locked down, the field and well would be abandoned until next season's planting time. No longer would the security nets be activated. It would be a simple matter for Ampris to come back under cover of darkness and collect her cache of food.

Ampris had not been born a thief, but she had learned to do whatever was necessary to survive.

Rising to her feet, she clipped her empty basket to her belt and unsheathed her slicer. As she limped back into the field, heading for an uncut row of the waist-high stelf, she saw a skimmer approaching at such speed the driver's clothing billowed out behind him.

He circled the field once, then twice, the metal sides of the skimmer flashing in the sun. A static-filled loud-speaker blared:

"Everyone, work faster! Faster! This field must be cleared by midday."

Holding her slicer in her hand, Ampris stood gawking at the skimmer, which was driven by an obese Gorlican. He must be the overseer, she thought, but why was he in such a hurry? She looked at the amount of grain yet to be cut. There was a full day's work ahead of them. They couldn't possibly finish in a couple of hours.

The overseer flew his skimmer to the sorting bins, where he gestured at Elrabin and the other workers. "Stop sorting!" the Gorlican shouted. "Dump everything into the holds. Faster! There is little time."

Ampris watched Elrabin move to shut off the noisy machinery, and for an instant quiet settled over the field. The slaves were still staring in disbelief.

Then a whip cracked across Ampris's shoulders without warning. The pain knocked her to her knees, and she cried out before she could stop herself.

A Toth guard towered over her. "Work," he said, his small brutal eyes holding no mercy. He whipped her again before she had a chance to regain her feet. "Work fast. Bantet has ordered it."

Ampris scrambled upright, clutching her basket and slicer. Her hat had fallen askew over one eye, and she tipped it back. The pain across the back of her shoulders burned like fire, and she could hear her own breath keening raggedly in the back of her throat. Realizing it, she forced herself to stop making the sound.

She straightened, remembering long-ago days when pain and whippings had been commonplace. Across the field, other slaves were being whipped back to work. Ampris knew it was time to get out of here, but the guard was still glaring at her. She got busy.

The stelf plants were bushy, with coarse, jagged gray-green leaves that rustled dryly in the hot, steady wind. Each plant produced several thick stalks, and on the tip of each stalk grew a single, globular head. When dried and processed, stelf produced the flour that made Quixlix, the staple food of the empire. Quixlix could be flavored to taste like anything, even meat. It was fed to the abiru population and consumed by the middle-class Viis population as well. Colony worlds grew the more exotic hybrid strains preferred by the Viis aristocracy, but the semibarren, depleted soil on Viisymel itself would grow only the original varieties, which were weak and susceptible to blight.

Scorn filled Ampris as she thought about how the Viis had practically ruined and poisoned their own planet during the past century. They were users, depleters. They had no concept of conservation. They used a resource until it was gone, then they went out and conquered another world and took all that it had. They wasted so much and created lack where there could have been plenty.

Another whipcrack sounded, making Ampris flinch. Annoyed at herself, she steeled her nerves. If the overseer wanted speed, she would show him speed.

Humming softly to herself, Ampris gripped a grain head and swung her slicer expertly and cleanly. It had been a long time since she'd done blade work. Remembering her days in the arena, when she'd been gladiator champion and famous across the empire, Ampris imagined herself back in training, honing and perfecting her swings and thrusts. She'd been a master of the glaudoon, the glevritar, and the parvalleh. All the ancient weapons of war.

But today, she was just a thief, wielding a slicer in need of sharpening. She cut the heads efficiently, dropping them into her basket as she went, and harvested a row of stelf twice as fast as any of the other workers.

By the time she reached the end of the row, her basket was heavy and heaped high. She wiped her face beneath her hat brim and started toward the bins, but a Toth blocked her way.

He thrust an empty basket at her. "Leave that. Cut."

Ampris took the basket hesitantly. If she could get to the sorting bins, she had a good chance to slip away. With the guard right on her, however, she had little choice but to turn and start cutting another row.

When she finished, another guard intercepted her with an empty basket. "Cut," she was told.

Panting and tired now, Ampris continued to work. But inside she felt a growing sense of desperation. The workers were still being harried constantly. Anyone who flagged was beaten.

The overseer's skimmer hovered here and there at various points around the field. The sorting bins had been disassembled and loaded. As soon as they were filled, the big transports lumbered away. Ampris could not understand this sudden urgency. She knew that if the blighted heads weren't separated from the good ones, the whole harvest would be contaminated. What was going on?

Never mind, said a voice inside her head. *Get out of here as soon as you can.*

She panted, dry for water, but she carried no water skin because none of the slaves were allowed them. Anyone who paused for any reason was whipped, and Ampris went on cutting despite the burning ache of fatigue now spreading through her arms and shoulders.

Her crippled leg was tiring too. Soon it would begin to hurt.

Two rows over, a female Kelth emitted a soft moan and dropped in her tracks.

Concerned, Ampris put down her basket and hurried to help.

The Kelth lay on the hard-baked ground, not moving. Ampris knelt beside her and lifted her head, feeling for a pulse in the fur at her throat. She found it, far too fast and thready. The Kelth's nose was hot and dry. Her eyes were rolled back in their sockets, and her tongue hung slackly out one side of her mouth.

Unable to rouse her, Ampris took off her hat and fanned the Kelth with it. The heat was still increasing. Ampris felt like she was being roasted inside an oven. She could see heat waves shimmering atop the stelf, and even the steadily blowing wind was hot, bringing no relief at all.

A shadow loomed over Ampris. She squinted up at the guard and said quickly, "This female is ill. She needs water or she will die."

Without a word the guard unclipped the water bottle at his waist and poured its contents over the Kelth's face and head. She moaned, half-rousing, and feebly tried to lick some of the moisture.

"To drink," Ampris said angrily. "Give her some of it to drink."

The Toth replaced the bottle on his belt. "Go to work."

Ampris rose to her feet and glared at him. "Dead slaves can't cut anything. Give her water and some rest in the shade, and she'll be able to resume work in a short while."

The guard pointed at the row she'd left. "Go to work."

"Not until you give her water to drink," Ampris said.

The guard swung his inactivated stun-stick at her. He

aimed the blow at her head, but Ampris saw it coming and spun out from under it. The stick whistled past her, glancing off her shoulder instead of cracking her skull.

Growling, Ampris gathered herself to spring.

"You there!" shouted a voice from overhead. "Guard Eight, clear that corpse from the field. Aaroun in the hat, come here."

Both Ampris and the Toth looked up at the scanner floating over her head. Its mechanical voice blared again, "You in the hat, come here."

Ampris tilted up her head to stare at the scanner, while her breath tangled in her throat and her heart thudded so hard she felt dizzy. She backed her ears, panting fast.

"You," the voice blared at her again. "Come here. Guard Eight, follow orders."

The Toth grunted something rude and slung the unconscious Kelth over his shoulder. Straightening with his burden, he gave Ampris a shove and pointed at the overseer's skimmer, which was bobbing on park at the edge of the field.

"You go," the guard said gruffly.

The scanner floated down the row toward the overseer. The last thing she wanted to do was follow the scanner, but again she had little choice. She was almost in the middle of the field, in the wrong position to try to make a break.

Ampris walked slowly, trying to conceal her limp. She wanted to exhibit no distinguishing characteristics. Elrabin was always telling her to blend in, to bring no attention to herself. It was important that she be just another anonymous Aaroun worker.

Her hands were shaking as she cleaned off her slicer. Inside, she was berating herself, realizing she had worked too fast, too efficiently. She shouldn't have tried to help the Kelth. She shouldn't have defied the guard.

The overseer had only to run a scan over her to learn she lacked a registration implant. Maybe that wouldn't matter, especially if the Viis owner of this farm wasn't particular about where and how he acquired his slaves. Sometimes slaves had their registrations removed if they were stolen property or sold illegally through the black market.

The Gorlican was the fattest one of his kind she'd ever seen. Bulges spread out past the edge of his orange and black-spotted torso shell. His scaled arms were thick and puffy. Behind his mask, his yellow eyes stared at her with cold interest.

Ampris's heart sank. She stopped next to his skimmer and stood there with her head lowered, not in humility but to conceal her features beneath her hat brim. This overseer was likely to know the faces of the slaves in his care.

Her mind raced in all directions. Should she run? Should she attack him and use him to hold the guards at bay? Should she stay calm and try to bluff her way through this? At her side, her right hand clutched the slicer so hard her whole arm trembled.

"Off with hat," the Gorlican said. His accent was thick; his tone was harsh.

Despair sank through Ampris. She hesitated, dreading the confrontation that would come as soon as the overseer realized she did not belong here.

A guard came up on her right side, stun-stick in hand. Ampris considered the odds. If she caught him unawares, she could probably bring him down, but she would have to make sure she stunned or killed him. With her bad leg, she couldn't outrun him.

"Off with hat!" the Gorlican said to her more sharply.

The guard knocked it off her head.

Ampris backed her ears and slowly straightened herself to her full height. She looked the Gorlican right in the eyes.

His gaze swept over her, and his eyes widened. "Not ours. I knew it."

Ampris let no expression appear on her face. Inside, however, she was still calculating how to get out of this. The Gorlican was smart and clearly good at his job. He would be hard to fool.

"No ownership ring," he said.

"I lost it." She kept her tone flat and defiant.

"Shut up!" the guard said. His fist crashed against her temple, making her stagger sideways. "No speak till ordered."

"Not one of ours," the Gorlican repeated. "What you doing here?"

"I'm on loan," Ampris replied.

Again the guard hit her. This time it hurt, and she snarled at him.

"We don't share slaves," the Gorlican said. His voice was low and intent. "You a runner."

Over the years, Ampris had learned a lot from Elrabin. "I belong here," she said. "I belong to this farm."

"Not ours," the Gorlican insisted. "I know every slave."

"Been here three years," Ampris said, knowing the lie was outrageous. She couldn't hope to succeed, but she had nothing to lose. Maybe her story would distract the Gorlican just long enough for her to break away. Maybe she could hope for a cloud to fall from the sky and rescue her, too.

"You running from where?" he asked. "Zafelil Farms? Tuluath?"

"Right here," Ampris said. "I've been here three years." She twisted around and pointed at one of the slaves. "That's my mate, over there. The big one, with stripes."

She didn't see the Gorlican give a signal, but the guard hit her again. She took the blow across the side of her head and staggered to one knee. Her head rang, and for a moment the world spun around her. There was no pain yet, only a cold clamminess and a sense of being unable to find reality.

Somehow she managed to hang on to consciousness. Blinking hard, she pushed herself upright again and stood there, swaying while little black spots danced in her vision.

"Now, answer with truth," the Gorlican said. "From where?"

She met his eyes with all the disillusion life had taught her. "Why do you care? You won't return me."

The Gorlican's yellow eyes narrowed for a moment, then from behind his mask came a peculiar, snuffling sound.

Ampris realized he was laughing. Her spirits rose slightly. Maybe Elrabin's lessons on how to bluff were going to work after all.

"Best worker I find all year," the Gorlican agreed, still snuffling. "Best worker on farm. Master will be pleased to have you. Not care where you running from, even if you dropped from sky." He laughed again, then gestured at the guard. "Put restraint on her, then back to field."

Desperately, Ampris tried one last gambit. "If you put me in restraints, I can't work. You're in a hurry here, aren't you? Got a little problem perhaps? Time of the essence? I'll work hard and fast as long as I'm free, but—"

The guard's stun-stick buzzed as it was activated. Ampris saw no response in the Gorlican's eyes, no relenting.

She spun around, wielding her slicer like a glaudoon, and caught the guard across the wrist as he swung.

He bellowed with pain and dropped his stun-stick, staggering back from her and clutching his bleeding wrist.

The Gorlican shouted with alarm and started calling for help over his hand-link.

Ampris paid him no attention and instead tackled the guard. Before he could lumber to his feet, she knocked him down again and kicked him viciously in the head. With a Toth, the only hope of winning a fight was to play dirty. She kicked him again, making him bellow, then rolled away from him and reached for the stun-stick lying in the dirt.

Just before she could grab it, he caught her by her ankle and pulled her back.

Roaring with frustration, she turned on the Toth, but his fist struck her like a hammer between the eyes.

The world went black, as though she'd been sucked into a hole.

Her next cognizant sensation was one of motion. She could feel her body moving, could hear the dry rustle of stelf, could smell the hot, kicked-up dust of the ground. Her eyes would not open, but after a moment she realized she was being dragged by her legs, her cheek raking the hard ground as she went.

She opened her eyes and found herself being dragged by the Toth guard, downwind of his stinking, unwashed body. She'd been stripped of her slicer and belt, and she was being dragged facedown along the edge of the field opposite the foothills. In the distance she could hear an odd, muffled sound, deep and steady. It made no sense to her right then, and she dismissed it. What was more important was getting free of the Toth before he put her in restraints.

Her hand raked over a clod of dirt, hard as stone. She was past it before she could grab it. In desperation she grabbed another, but it crumbled in her fingers. She grabbed another, then found a stone as big as her fist and clutched it instead.

Twisting around as best she could, she readied her

aim to throw the stone at the back of the Toth's matted head.

But that deep, muffled sound came suddenly loud and close, filling the air. The Toth stopped dead in his tracks and stared, openmouthed, at the sky. Ampris looked too, and saw a blinding flash of silver off the hull of a sleek shuttle. Six of them came flying over the field, booming exhaust, then they circled and landed right in the middle of the crop. Their jets blew some plants up by the roots, sending them tumbling away. Their landing tripods flattened whatever was still standing upright. The slaves scattered desperately to get out of their way.

The overseer's skimmer zipped past Ampris and her captor, the Gorlican shaking his fist and screaming something that could not be heard over the shuttle engines.

Ampris seized the opportunity she'd been given. She threw the stone and caught the Toth on his temple. He toppled over without a sound, and Ampris scrambled upright, panting in triumph.

She looked around to get her bearings, and saw the black insignia painted on the side of the shuttles. For a moment she didn't know whether to be puzzled or alarmed. What were patrollers doing here?

Shuttle hatches popped open with hisses of escaping air. A loudspeaker blared a message in abiru: "All workers will leave the fields immediately."

"No, no!" the overseer protested, flying his skimmer in and out among the parked shuttles. "No blight here. No inspection needed."

The patrollers waved him over. As soon as he stopped, a patroller yanked him out of his skimmer and forced him to kneel on the ground with his thick hands clamped on top of his head. The patroller stood over him with a drawn weapon.

Ampris grinned slightly to herself.

More patrollers in their distinctive black uniforms and

helmets spread out through the stelf, sweeping it with handheld scanners.

She understood then why the overseer had been trying to get as much harvest cut as possible. He must have been warned that the patrollers were coming for an inspection. Ampris snorted to herself. Of course the plants were infected. Anyone with eyes could see the telltale whitish fuzz on the leaves or the spots on the round grain heads themselves. But she supposed the scanners would make the verdict official.

Meanwhile, what the patrollers did wasn't her business. Despite the ache in her leg, Ampris quickened her pace and hurried to join the disorganized stream of slaves exiting the field. In the general confusion, no one seemed to have missed the guard she took down. The other guards were approaching rapidly. For a moment, Ampris thought they were coming for her, then she realized that they were simply moving to intercept and round up the slaves, who were trying to scatter in all directions. Ampris kept walking purposefully, angling in the direction of the hills while she resisted the panicky urge to run.

She had to get out of here fast, while the patrollers were distracting the guards, but if she ran someone would chase her.

At least Elrabin had had the good sense to duck out of sight and get away the moment the overseer had shut down his job.

If only she'd listened to him and quit while she had the chance.

Growling, she shoved self-recriminations away. She'd had good reasons for staying. Now she would just have to get out of this situation.

She veered even farther away from the others, but one of the Toth guards bellowed at her to turn back.

Ampris backed her ears and kept going. She'd nearly reached the edge of the field now. Beyond the shed housing the well pump there were perhaps twenty meters of cleared ground to be crossed before she could reach the gnarled scrub and thicket that covered the hillside. Above her, the hills themselves rose in rough, ascending layers, looking wrinkled, bald, and brown, with green thickets filling the canyons.

So close, yet the refuge offered by the hills might as well have been leagues away.

She glanced at the other slaves, noticing that they were bunching together as they reached the edge of the field. The Toth guards herded them, yelling at them to close ranks.

Ampris knew that if she let herself be rounded up with the others, any chance she had to get away would be gone forever. Snarling, she made up her mind to run for it, even if they shot her down.

Behind her, there came a loud belch of sound, followed by a roar. Startled, Ampris glanced back and saw one of the shuttles shooting flames across the field.

The dry stelf caught fire and began to burn, sending clouds of black smoke into the sky. Now Ampris understood why the sky had been hazy with smoke all day. The patrollers were apparently burning one field after another.

"This field is condemned," came the announcement over the speakers. "All grain harvested from it is now confiscated and will be destroyed."

A distant wail rose from the overseer. The slaves yelled and swore in disgust. "Too bad patrollers didn't come 'fore all this work we did," one of them shouted.

A shove from behind nearly knocked Ampris off her feet. She stumbled and turned around, finding herself looking up at the Toth with the diseased eye. Flies buzzed around his face, and he looked brutish and mean.

"Get moving," he told her, pushing her over to join the rest. "Transport coming to take you."

A ragged little cheer rose up among the slaves. "Hey,

good!'' a Kelth youth said with enthusiasm. ''We don't have to walk back to quarters.''

''Shut up, you fool,'' a grizzled Kelth female snarled at him. ''Burning the harvest means the master won't pay taxes.''

''I don't care—''

''You better care,'' she said, baring her teeth at him. ''No taxes paid means this farm gets taken by the government. That means we end up sold.''

The youth shrugged. ''Sold is sold. Old master or new master, what's the difference?''

Their argument went on, but Ampris couldn't listen to it. Fear robbed her of breath. She couldn't be caught like this. After twelve years of living free, she couldn't go back to slavery. She *couldn't.*

The guard shoved her again, making her stagger. He was staying close to her, keeping her right in the bunch. ''Get moving!'' he ordered. ''Stay with the others.''

She snarled, desperation breaking down her caution. Whirling on him, she attacked, throwing herself at him in a tackle that should have brought him down but didn't.

He stood like a rock under her assault, until her claws raked his side, then he bellowed and knocked her away from him.

She fell sprawling in the dust, and tried to scramble up, but he kicked her bad leg out from under her, and she fell again. Rolling to one side, she eluded his grab at her arm and scrambled again to her feet. She would run. Bad leg or not, she would run as though the wind carried her.

She turned and leaped, making two good, strong strides, picking up speed, the old speed that she'd been famous for; then her leg faltered and she stumbled. She was gripped from behind.

Snarling, Ampris spun around and ducked under the Toth's arm. She tried to twist free of his grip, but he hung on grimly. She tilted her head and bit his arm, crunching down hard on bone and sinew.

He bawled and slung her around, but Ampris's jaws didn't turn loose. She tasted Toth blood and smelled Toth stink. Fear, fury, and old memories of the Toths who had injured her mother and abducted her filled her mind. She raked him again with her claws, her jaws crushing harder, and had the satisfaction of seeing his small, dark eyes widen in panic.

Clawing again, Ampris shifted her feet, pushing him off balance while he bellowed in pain.

Then thudding footsteps came up from behind her. She started to turn, but the sizzle of a stun-stick filled the air. She heard it before she felt it—the jolt to her spine that felled her in her tracks.

Gagging and snarling, she lay there in the dust. In her mind she heaved and struggled with all her strength, but her paralyzed body did not move.

For a moment there was silence, broken only by the moaning of the Toth she'd injured and the harsh breaths of the Toth who'd stunned her. Heat and smoke rose over the field, coming their direction as the fire spread rapidly.

Ampris lay there on the ground, half-smothered in the dirt, and tried again to make her body move. Disbelief and despair warred inside her, but there was nothing she could do.

One of the Toths laughed and planted his foot possessively on her back. "Bad slave," he said, grunting his words. "Make you wish this day never come."

CHAPTER TWO

Elrabin pulled himself out of the canyon, climbing the rocks and scrambling through scrub that scratched and tore at his fur. He was panting hard, his tongue hanging out, and his upright ears swiveled forward and back almost constantly, listening for sounds of pursuit.

Getting too old for this, he was. Getting tired of living like a Skek, scavenging whatever he could find, running for his life as soon as trouble reared up.

And today plenty of trouble had hit. Elrabin shuddered and paused a moment to catch his breath. He was near the summit of the second-highest hill, and he turned to stare down at the checkerboard of fields below him. Slaves and guards moved about like insects. Flames consumed the stelf, and smoke curled high into the air.

Elrabin's nostrils flared in repugnance, and he sneezed. Worriedly he rubbed his muzzle with both hands, over and over, until he realized what he was doing and stopped himself.

Ampris was caught. What to do? His mind circled endlessly, too stunned and worried to think. All he'd managed to do was get himself away, but she was back there, a prisoner, a slave again. As soon as the overseer ran a scan over her, he would learn she wore no registration implant. That would immediately brand her as a renegade, an illegal. Her old record would be called up, and she'd be identified. Then the authorities would know that Ampris hadn't died in the explosion that destroyed Vess Vaas Laboratory twelve years ago. She'd be executed as an outlaw.

Stop it, Elrabin told himself sternly, putting a halt to his inner hysteria. This was no time to go soft in the brain and panic. He had to think, and think fast. He knew better than to run into camp, shouting his bad news. No, he had to have something in mind, some solution on hand to suggest, when he told the others what had happened.

Elrabin whined in the back of his throat, still watching the moving figures and burning fields. The slaves were loaded on board a decrepit old transport, which lumbered off in the direction of the farm compound.

"Ampris, Ampris," he said, moaning her name.

He crouched on his haunches until he stopped panting, then wearily he resumed his climb. Ampris was his best friend, the one individual he truly admired and respected. Beyond that, she was a natural leader, and Elrabin liked to follow her. Although sometimes she came up with outlandish schemes, she was always more concerned with the welfare of the group than with her own. She'd kept them alive through that first terrible winter after she and the other inmates escaped from Vess Vaas. Despite having suffered horrible torture and experimentation at the hands of the Viis fiends who called themselves research scientists, Ampris had found the strength to keep going. Her hope and optimism had never wavered even when they were nearly starving and lost.

Thanks to Ampris's courage and determination, the little group of Vess Vaas escapees had found a tiny village of free abiru, who took them in and gave them shelter. They learned how to hunt and live off the land. But in time, game in the area grew scarce and it was time to move on. The village divided itself and parted ways. Besides Ampris and her cubs, two of the original escapees—a Kelth named Paket and a Myal named Robuhl—still remained with her. The others had long since left to take mates and join other groups, or had died of illness or accident. In their stead, new abiru folk joined. Velia, Elrabin's mate, had been a warehouse loader in Lazmairehl. When Ampris led a raid on the food stores in the warehouse, Velia had been liberated in the process. The two Rejects currently in the group had been with them for less than a year. Luax, grievously injured, had been dragged into the wilderness by her companion Harthril to die. But Ampris, when she came across the two Viis Rejects, had insisted on nursing Luax back to health, even though it delayed their migration to a better hunting region. Harthril had never talked about what had driven the two from civilization, but thus far they'd stayed with Ampris's small abiru band.

Elrabin lowered his head and snarled to himself. Ampris and her big, soft heart. Always she was worrying about the group, taking all the burdens onto her broad shoulders. It had been her idea to go down and steal from the stelf harvest today. A good idea, up to a point. Elrabin told himself for the umpteenth time that he should have insisted on going without her, maybe taking Paket along as a helper. Thieving came easily to Elrabin. He'd practically been born into the life, especially with the da he'd had. But Ampris insisted on going, insisted on staying too long, insisted on showing off once she got a slicer in her hand. Now she was caught and chained, smack in the middle of everyone's worst nightmare. She'd said more than once that she would die rather than be a slave again.

"Don't give up yet, Goldie," he muttered aloud. Somehow he'd find a way to free her, and fast.

Rising to his feet, he climbed higher until the hill leveled off. Finding the faint trail that led toward the camp, Elrabin strode through a stand of trees, until without warning a bulky figure with beige-spotted fur burst from the underbrush to block his path.

Elrabin's heart jumped, and he nearly yelped in fright.

Gulping for breath, he bared his teeth at the tall, pregnant Aaroun. "What you doing, scaring me like that? I lost growth here."

"Never mind," Tantha said with a growl. Her brown eyes locked intently on him. "You get the food?"

Elrabin sighed. That was Tantha, always thinking about her stomach, which grew larger every day. Elrabin had a bet laid with Paket that she was going to bear four cubs at least. Or maybe five, although Ampris said that was rare. Tantha herself said she was carrying three, and Elrabin figured she should know.

But looking at her now, he told himself that if only three cubs came out of her womb, they would be very large ones indeed.

"Food!" Tantha insisted, her growl deepening. "Three days now . . . nothing we eat. Are we supposed to gnaw bark like the—"

"Keep your fur on," Elrabin said with annoyance. "We got more important things to—"

She gripped his thin shoulder, letting her claws dig in. "Nothing more important than we eat. If you bring us nothing, then we—"

"Ampris got caught!" Elrabin said desperately.

Tantha fell silent and stared at him with her eyes wide and serious. "Caught," she echoed at last. "Dead?"

"Not yet," he said, rubbing his muzzle. "Got to get her out of there, see?"

Tantha said nothing as she stepped aside. Elrabin strode past her without a glance and Tantha hurried to keep up with him.

"Elrabin," she said, "what will you say to the others?"

"Just what I told you," he said, not understanding her question. "Why?"

"You say it too harsh. You will worry her cubs."

His ears swiveled back impatiently. "Foloth and Nashmarl *should* worry. They could be orphans by dawn—"

"Do not say such things!" Tantha said in outrage. She gripped his coat from behind, slowing him down. "You are cruel."

He glanced over his shoulder and met her gaze. "No, just realistic. I see things how they are. And right now they ain't good."

Growling in her throat, Tantha released him. Together they hurried on. Situated in a clearing surrounded by trees, the camp was small and rudimentary, consisting of five crude shelters made from cut branches and circling one old, much-patched tent that belonged to Ampris and her cubs. No fires were lit because the camp had been left on standby alert in case something went wrong, but Elrabin noticed that every shelter's outdoor cooking circle had firewood laid in readiness. Their meager collection of pots and kettles stood filled with water.

Paket stood in front of his shelter, squinting against the sunlight. His shoulders were stooped and twisted with age. All his joints were swollen, and it was painful for him to move.

But he came limping forward, his eyes shining eagerly until he saw Elrabin's empty hands. Then the light died in his face, and he tipped down his white muzzle in disappointment.

"Elrabin," he said. "The plan did not work?"

Elrabin whined softly in his throat, and for a moment did not know how to answer. "It worked fine," he replied at last. "We got food waiting down in the field for us, if we can get to it."

Paket's lips skimmed back from his teeth in a grin. "Good. We'll do that. Ampris said after dark the security nets won't be on."

"Yeah, but there's a problem."

Paket's grin vanished. ''With the food?''

''Look, forget the food, see?'' Elrabin said, losing patience.

At his side, Tantha growled.

He shot her an irked glance. ''Going at this easy ain't going to work.''

''What?'' Paket asked sharply, stepping forward. ''What happened?''

A movement behind him caught Elrabin's attention, and he saw Velia emerging from their shelter. As always his breath jerked a little in his throat at the sight of her. Slender and tawny brown in color, Velia was young and the most beautiful Kelth female he'd ever seen. Just a look from her tilted golden-brown eyes had the power to render him speechless.

But he saw the hope in her expression, clouded swiftly by disappointment. He panted, feeling ashamed of his failure. He couldn't bear to see Velia hungry like this. He couldn't bear to have her think him incapable of providing for her.

''Something's gone wrong,'' Paket said. ''What? Why won't you answer? Is it Ampris?''

''Yeah,'' Elrabin replied, his worry a knot inside his chest. ''Where are her cubs?''

''Out hunting with the Rejects,'' Velia said. She pushed past Paket and slid next to Elrabin's side.

He embraced her and gave her a quick lick on the side of her muzzle.

''He brings no food,'' Tantha said, her voice deep and scratchy. Her ears were flat to her skull. ''And there is worse news.''

Velia tightened her grip on his arm. ''Trouble?''

Hating to see how swiftly fear still came to her, Elrabin rubbed her fur in swift reassurance. ''Trouble for Ampris,'' he said. ''She got caught. We have to go back and free her before—''

''You can't go back!'' Velia said shrilly, gripping his

arm now with both hands. Her eyes grew wide, and she panted. "You can't!"

"Hush," he said softly, trying to calm her. "I wouldn't have left her, but I—"

"No, no, no!" Velia said. "I won't let you risk yourself for her. You must think of yourself first. You must think of me."

"He already thought of himself," Paket said with a growl. "He's standing here, safe and sound."

The criticism burned Elrabin. He turned on Paket with a snarl, but held his tongue. After all, the old one was right. What could Elrabin say?

Velia bristled at Paket. "My mate is not a coward. He came to protect us. Will the Viis come here for us? Do they know about us?"

"Always think of yourself, Velia," Tantha said. "You in no danger. I smelled no Viis on our hill."

"Lots of smoke though," Paket said. "Why are they burning the fields?"

"Blight," Elrabin answered.

Velia whined and put both hands to her muzzle. "Then the grain is ruined, poisoned. We can't eat it."

"Nothing to eat," Tantha said gruffly. She glared at Elrabin. "Left it behind, like he left Ampris behind. You valued your hide first, Kelth."

Elrabin had had enough of her criticism. He glared up at her. "Hey, back off, Spots. I came to get some help. I know when the odds are against me. Paket—"

The old Kelth tried to straighten his crooked spine and pricked his ears. "I am ready."

"Good. We need Harthril."

"Gone hunting," Tantha said before Paket could answer. "Told you already."

"Yeah, but we still need him," Elrabin said. He was thinking rapidly, trying to ignore Velia's frightened panting in his ear as she pressed closer. "I figure we'll slip into the compound at nightfall—"

"No!" Velia said with a yip. "It's too dangerous. You'll be caught."

Elrabin grinned. "As good as I am? I can break into anything, slip past any security system. I am Elrabin the Quick."

"You are Elrabin, full of wind," Tantha muttered. "Why you so brave now?"

Elrabin glared at her a moment, then without a word he ducked into Ampris's tent. It took a second for his vision to adjust to the shadowy interior. As usual the cubs had scattered their meager possessions carelessly on their side of the tent. Ampris's side showed only a neatly tied bedroll, a battered portable vid player that needed recharging the next time they ventured near a city, and a small box of personal items. Elrabin glanced around swiftly, then untied her bedroll. From the center he pulled out a pair of hand-links—one of which he tossed to Paket, who was hovering at the entrance—and a side-arm whose safety mechanism was as long gone as its registration number.

Holding the weapon in his hand, Elrabin drew a deep breath and steeled himself, then stepped outside.

He faced Tantha with the side-arm aimed at the ground and waited while she looked at it, her eyes growing wide.

"Yeah," he said quietly. "I can be brave now, when the odds are going to be more even. What you want me to be, Spots? Stupid? You want me to charge unarmed into a nest of Viis patrollers and Toth guards and get myself caught too? What good would that do?"

Tantha said nothing. She kept her gaze down as though ashamed.

He stared at her good and hard, then nodded. "Now. Paket and I will go down there and—"

"No," Velia said. She began to keen. "Don't risk yourself like this. She isn't worth it. She isn't—"

"Quiet," he said, angry and half-embarrassed.

"I won't be quiet," Velia said. Slender, tawny, and young, she was beautiful except when afraid. Now her eyes were wild, and she bared her teeth. "Ampris knew the risks when she went to the field. Why should you risk yourself and Paket for her?"

Elrabin felt something precious turn sideways inside him. He shook his head, not wanting to hear what she was saying. "Stop," he said with a growl. "It has to be done. You know why."

"You'll be caught, both of you. Then the Viis will know there are more of us up here. They'll come for all of us. How can we run from them? You put all of us in jeopardy."

He didn't want to hear what she was saying, but she had a point. Elrabin looked at the weapon in his hand and felt his shoulders sag. What was the best thing to do? Save Ampris? Or protect the group? What would Ampris want him to do?

Doubts and uncertainty crowded him for a moment, clouding his mind. He closed his eyes, longing for the old days when no responsibilities had chained him, when he'd lived by his wits on the streets of Vir. *Yeah,* muttered a sarcastic voice inside his head, *the good old days when you were young and stupid and starving most of the time, taking all the risks for Da while he gambled and sniffed dust.*

Growling to himself, Elrabin opened his eyes and faced them all. His grip tightened on the weapon, and he tucked it grimly into his pocket. He was no killer, never had been. But he could do what he had to, if it meant survival for himself or those whom he loved. And he loved Ampris, as a friend, as family, in a way that Velia still could not understand. Ampris would want him to take care of the group and her cubs, but Elrabin knew that Ampris was an excellent leader, the best they could ever have. Without her, the group would suffer.

He met Paket's gaze. "We're going after her."

Approval filled the old Kelth's eyes, and he nodded at Elrabin, who felt relief at having made the right decision.

But Velia's eyes grew stormy. "Fool," she said sharply. "I might as well start mourning now."

He didn't want to argue with her in front of the others. Embarrassed, he gestured for her to step aside with him. Taking her inside the shadowy interior of their small shelter, he ducked his head to keep his ears from brushing the roof poles and cradled Velia's muzzle between his hands.

"Have a little faith in me," he said softly, his hurt evident in his voice. "I been around a long time, see? I can take care of myself."

Her hands gripped his, and her breath puffed warm against his palms. "But who will take care of me if I lose you?"

"You ain't going to lose me," he said.

She whined softly. "I am afraid for you. You take terrible risks, and I cannot live without you."

His heart softened and he gave her a gentle lick between her ears. "Ampris would do the same for me."

"But she has no family, no—"

"She has her sons."

Velia pulled back her head in scorn. "Those creatures! They are monsters—"

"Hush," he said, gripping one hand around her muzzle and giving her a tiny shake. "That ain't Ampris's fault. And that ain't got nothing to do with the problem in front of us right now. Time's getting away. I gotta go."

She clung to him, holding him tight as she wept against his chest. Sighing, Elrabin circled her with his arms. How he'd hoped that with time, Velia would grow stronger, would find courage. But at every crisis she fell apart. He knew she'd been badly abused before he met her, but at times like this he felt powerless to help her.

Ampris kept saying that he should give Velia time. But right now he had to go.

"Here," he said softly, digging into his capacious pockets. He pulled out a plump grain head and placed it in Velia's hand.

She stopped weeping and pulled away from him. "Food!" she said in astonishment, her tears forgotten. "But I thought you failed. Why didn't you tell us at once you had some food? Robuhl has been crying. Twice today I grew dizzy and thought I would faint. Tantha has been half-wild with hunger."

Elrabin shifted away, uncomfortable. He thought about the numerous basketloads of grain Ampris had concealed behind the shed. They would have feasted beyond their imaginings tonight if all had gone as planned.

Instead, here they were with the scant amount he could stuff into his pockets as he'd run like a coward from the first sign of trouble.

"Never underestimate me, my love," Elrabin said. He pulled out three more heads, each one of them large and heavy. "If you can stretch 'em right, there should be enough to feed everyone tonight."

"Oh!" Velia said, cradling them happily in her arms. "I have some chuffie roots that Tantha found this morning, and there are still a few greens. If I use the last of the pepfrike for seasoning, and boil these until they can be mashed, I can—"

To stop his mouth from watering, he slid his muzzle against hers in a final caress and ducked out of the shelter.

Blinking in the light, he saw that Paket had taken the opportunity to fill a water skin and sling it across his crooked shoulders by a leather cord. The old Kelth had armed himself with a rusty slicer that he'd found half-buried in the ground several days ago. He'd been trying to clean the rust off it without much success ever since.

"Ready," Paket said and held up his slicer with a grin.

Tantha also stood there, holding a water skin and carrying her hunting sling. "Ready," she echoed. "Let's go before the Rejects come back with the cubs and there is much trouble."

Elrabin glared at her impatiently. "Slack yourself, Spots. Ain't no way we're taking you."

"Of course I will go," Tantha declared.

He sighed, hating the way she always tried to take charge when Ampris was absent. Elrabin felt that Tantha ought to be sitting quietly somewhere, weaving swaddling cloths for her unborn cubs, instead of demanding to be included in the action. But at least she wanted to help, unlike Velia, who had to be bribed and distracted with food.

Looking up at Tantha, Elrabin tried to keep his annoyance out of his voice. "You can't go," he said.

Her hand clamped hard on his shoulder, the claws digging in slightly. "I will go. I am strong. You need me with you, not tending a cooking fire."

Elrabin met her fierce eyes and didn't back down. "You're near your time. You can't run and if we hit any trouble, you won't be able to fight."

She bared her teeth and held up her sling. "I can fight! I have good aim with this."

"And if there's shooting?" he asked, hoping Velia didn't overhear this. "A sling and some stones up against stun or worse? No," he said sharply. "Sorry, Spots, but you'll just slow us down."

She growled at him, but he held up his hands, refusing to relent.

"I wish we could take you. We need you, but you ain't no good for this."

"I can do what is necessary," she said fiercely. "I want to kill Viis."

"Yeah, and what if they kill you?"

She backed her ears in disdain.

"Or what if you start birthing? We gonna all get caught or killed 'cause we got to stop and carry you? What if you lose those cubs? They gonna be all you got left of Morlol. You lose them, and you got nothing. Is that what you want?"

She snapped her teeth together and turned away, but not before he saw the stricken hurt in her eyes. Hunching her shoulders, she strode away without another word.

Silence fell over the camp for a moment. Elrabin stared after Tantha unhappily. He hadn't wanted to hurt her. But she was so stubborn she had to be hit between the eyes to get her to understand. Still, he felt bad about it.

Velia emerged from their shelter, still holding the grain, and shot him a look of reproach that told him she'd overheard every word. "Oh, Elrabin," she said softly. "That was harsh."

"But necessary," Paket said in his gruff way. "Tantha has no sense sometimes."

"That doesn't mean she should be treated cruelly," Velia said.

"Wasn't trying to be cruel, see?" Elrabin said. "I just—"

She reached up and gripped his muzzle to silence him. "I know," she murmured. "But she wants so much to be active. Otherwise she thinks too much about Morlol, and her heart breaks inside."

He nodded, understanding, wishing these females could understand too. "Better Tantha gets hurt this way instead of with plasma slugs. Now be careful. Light just one cooking fire, and keep it small. They ain't going to smell that with all the fields blazing. If any shuttles fly this way, everyone hide in the canyon past the stream. Promise me."

Velia nodded seriously. Her eyes filled with fresh worry, and she began to pant.

He recognized the signs and turned away. "We're going."

Collecting Paket with a look, he strode out of camp before Velia could fall apart again. Paket hurried along beside him.

Elrabin glanced at the old one. "Females," he said with exasperation.

Paket winked at him. "Right," he said with feeling. "Got their uses though."

Refusing to laugh, Elrabin snorted, but his annoyance faded. Together they headed along the trail as fast as Paket's stiff old legs would go.

Halfway down the hill, they veered off the trail and dropped into a shallow canyon. Thereafter, the going was slow, for they had to push their way through the thick undergrowth. Elrabin could hear Paket's hoarse panting, but the old Kelth never complained and never asked to stop.

It was Elrabin who called a halt at last so the old one could rest. Wheezing for air, Paket sank down on a boulder with wispy golden grass growing at its base, and closed his eyes.

Worried, Elrabin watched him a moment, but didn't make the old one waste his breath in explaining how he felt. It was obvious anyway that he was in considerable pain.

Guilt touched Elrabin, but he shoved it away and turned his back on Paket to peer ahead down the slope. They were upwind of the fields, so the smoke was blowing in the opposite direction. Still, the stench was enough to choke Elrabin's nostrils.

He squinted and swiveled back his ears, calculating. It had been maybe two hours since Ampris had been captured. The guards would take her back to the compound's slave quarters first. There, her missing ownership ring and lack of a registration implant would give her away. Then the Viis owner would probably be consulted. Being a Viis, he would not want to turn her in as he was supposed to according to the law on runaway slaves. He would probably keep her.

But she would be in chains, confined, under orders. She'd been free long enough that the pierced hole in her ear had grown together. They'd have to punch a new one so they could fit an ownership ring through it.

Elrabin snarled silently to himself. He had worn both ring and collar himself. How well he knew the feeling of degradation.

His greatest worry was that Ampris would fall into despair over her capture. She might do something foolish, might risk death, might invite death, might fight until her captors were forced to hurt or kill her.

Think of your cubs, who grow tall but still need you, Elrabin thought her way. *Do not lose heart, my old friend.*

Behind him Paket lurched to his feet with a groan he tried to conceal. "Wasting time," he said.

Elrabin looked at Paket and swiveled his ears in fresh worry. Paket looked winded still, despite the rest. Perhaps it would have been wiser to bring Tantha instead.

But as soon as the thought crossed his mind, Elrabin dismissed it. Tantha couldn't follow orders, and Paket could and would. End of second thoughts.

"We'll get there," Elrabin said aloud, to reassure both Paket and himself. "Got to wait until dark anyway."

Paket limped steadily along. "You think the patrollers will be gone by then?"

Elrabin knew why he was asking. Most of them had possessed the usual registration implant, but Paket had been a worker in the quarries before he was condemned to Vess Vaas. The quarries branded their workers with an ion-release tattoo that couldn't be eradicated. So Paket was still traceable if he crossed paths with the authorities. Bringing him was a very big risk, except that

Elrabin figured the patrollers were already long gone.

"I've seen how the patrollers on ag duty operate," Elrabin answered finally. "Check a field for blight, condemn it, and set the fires. Then they go. Got no reason to hang around. They ain't here looking for runaways. Their scanners won't be calibrated for that kind of check."

"Yeah," Paket said bravely. "I figured that."

Again guilt touched Elrabin and he ducked his head while he quickened his pace. He'd been lying his whole life. What was one more falsehood now?

The truth was, a bounty lay on the head of every runaway, whether that individual was wanted dead or alive. Sometimes when he happened to be in a city, Elrabin would tap in access on a public vid link just to check to see how big his reward had grown. Galard Stables was still operational, although no longer the undisputed champions of the arena circuit. And the bounty reward for Elrabin's death still stood on record. Ampris was believed to be dead, so no reward had ever been posted for her, the lucky creature. Sometimes when times got lean, Elrabin was tempted to turn himself in so he could collect a percentage of the reward. But he couldn't figure out how to work the scam so he didn't get himself taken prisoner in the process.

The patrollers were Viis individuals as hard hit by the economic troubles of their empire as any of the other citizens. All patrollers had scanners with an infinite number of missing registrations programmed into them. Whether they drew duty on the city streets, or agricultural details, or merchant guards, or the Bureau of Security, they checked anyone and everyone, always hoping to score lucky and collect a reward.

Taking Paket anywhere near the vicinity of a patroller was suicide. Elrabin knew he was risking getting the old one killed. If Paket had any sense he would know it too.

But to save Ampris, Elrabin was willing to let almost

anyone become expendable. That wasn't the way Ampris wanted it. She'd tried for years to reform him, to turn him into someone as honest as she was. But Elrabin knew the truth didn't always get you where you needed to go.

Still, he felt guilty and unsure. To distract himself, he started talking.

"I figure we'll circle around and not head toward the compound until nightfall. We want it good and dark before we leave cover. I'll have to pick the security system, fuse it some way."

"But that will cause trouble," Paket said worriedly. "The guards will be alerted. They will come after us."

"Yeah, but by then we won't be there," Elrabin said, rolling his eyes at having to explain the obvious to Paket. Too old for this, he really was. "We'll be at the slave quarters instead, pulling Ampris out."

"You make it sound simple," Paket said, panting hard. "But nothing ever is."

"Yeah, well, we just have to make up the rest of our plan as we go," Elrabin muttered. "I had enough doubts coming my way from Velia. Let's think positive, see?"

"Think positive. We're going to break into a Viis compound, complete with guards and security nets, just the two of us, with nothing but one old side-arm and my slicer." Paket snorted. "Yeah, I'm positive."

Put like that, it sounded worse than foolhardy. Elrabin flicked back his tall ears. "So what you be doing loping along with me?"

He made the question a challenge, but Paket didn't falter. "I was condemned to the quarries, and I survived them. I was condemned to Vess Vaas, and I lived to see that place of horrors destroyed. You think I don't believe Ampris can find a way out of a farmer's slave quarters?"

Elrabin yipped. "Yeah, same figuring I had. She's—"

He heard a faint rush of sound and turned his head,

glimpsing motion from the corner of his eye. Alarmed, Elrabin flung up his hand and started to call out, but he was tackled from the side and knocked to the ground.

The impact hurt. His shoulder hit the ground first, jolting sharp pains up into his neck, then his head thumped hard. He bit off a yelp and squirmed violently beneath the weight of his attacker. Whoever it was didn't weigh much. Elrabin threw him aside and scrambled dizzily to his feet, swaying and cursing while he drew the side-arm from his pocket.

"Stop!" It was Paket who spoke, Paket who gripped his arm and deflected his aim.

But by then Elrabin had seen the identity of his attacker. Glaring at the thin, gangly figure swathed in a hood of coarse cloth, Elrabin did not fire. Instead he pocketed his weapon and slapped dirt from his coat. "Go home, Nashmarl," he said in disgust.

The cub strutted around him once, then twice. Nashmarl was the number two son of Ampris's single litter, born of genetic experimentation deep in the horrific recesses of Vess Vaas Laboratory. Neither Aaroun nor Viis but instead some tragic combination of the two, the youngster was skinny and awkward, with long limbs and bony shoulders. His skin was a pale cream color, showing through a fur pelt so thin it resembled down. On his face and head he had no fur at all, and his skin tended to burn if exposed to the sunshine. Now twelve years old and more than half-grown, he was as tall as Elrabin, with an ugly flattened face lacking more than a vestigial muzzle. He had no visible ears, and his forehead curved in a dome above two deep set eyes of Viis green.

Now blocking Elrabin's path, he parted his jaws in a grin, revealing Aaroun-sized fangs. "I got you, Elrabin!" he said triumphantly. Glee danced in his green eyes. "I got you good. Hey, Paket! Did you see how I got him?"

Paket's ears were flat. He said nothing.

Elrabin glared at the cub. "Go home."

Nashmarl skipped and strutted back and forth in front of them. "Admit it. I've been following you all the way down the mountain, and you didn't know it, Elrabin. Neither of you knew it. I could have taken you anytime."

Elrabin locked eyes with the cub. "Sure, you attacked me, but you ended up on the wrong end of business." He patted the pocket that held his weapon and looked hard at the cub to make sure he understood how insignificant his accomplishment actually was. "Now, go home."

Nashmarl's grin faded and he came closer. "What are the two of you doing out here in the hottest part of the day?"

"Hunting," Paket said with an impatient growl.

Elrabin gestured at the old one to stay quiet, but Nashmarl noticed the signal. His green eyes were quick. "What's going on?" he demanded. "Paket, you'll tell me the truth, won't you?"

"Nothing's going on," Elrabin told him before Paket could answer.

"What are you doing with Mother's side-arm?"

"Paket told you. Hunting."

Nashmarl's gaze narrowed. His mouth pinched down tight and suspicious. "You don't hunt with a side-arm, not game you don't. What are you up to? Where's Mother? You were supposed to be—"

"Look, forget the questions," Elrabin broke in impatiently. "We're busy, see? We got no time to stand here jawing with you. Ain't you supposed to be hunting with Harthril? Yeah, you are. So what's the news? You find game? You got something to contribute to the pot tonight? Or ain't you doing whatever Harthril told you to do?"

The last question hit its mark. A dull blush of red

darkened Nashmarl's facial skin. His green eyes grew bright with anger.

Elrabin nodded, not giving the cub time to answer. "Thought so. You ain't never going to learn nothing, you keep slipping off from your lessons."

"I don't have to do what Harthril tells me," Nashmarl said, lifting his head very high. "He's just a stupid Reject."

"He ain't no Reject with us," Elrabin said angrily. "You know that. Your mother done made that clear to everyone."

Nashmarl's thin nostrils flared, but he said nothing.

"So what are you supposed to be doing?" Elrabin asked.

Nashmarl didn't answer.

Elrabin grimly reminded himself that Ampris had given birth to this green-eyed brat and tried to be patient. "I asked you a question."

Nashmarl's gaze shifted away. Sullenly he said, "Harthril told me to watch the mouth of the top canyon. He was going to flush out some grassens, and I was supposed to hold the net."

Paket growled, very softly.

Elrabin thought of plump grassen, a fowl with tasty white flesh, and his mouth started watering. He thought of the folks in the camp, hungry and waiting. He glared at this spoiled youth who couldn't seem to get the concept of responsibility through his bony head.

"You and Harthril found grassens," he said, keeping his voice low and quiet. Inside, his heart was thumping hard and violently, shooting his pulse through his veins.

Nashmarl shrugged. "We found them, a whole flock. Have you ever realized how stupid they are? Harthril couldn't drive them anywhere. They just panic and start running in circles."

"Defense mechanism," Paket said with a growl.

"Stupid," Nashmarl said. "I could hear Harthril in

the brush, but he never got them herded to the nets, so I left. It was boring anyway. At least when Mother goes hunting, she takes a sling and brings them down on the wing with one good shot. Boom!'' He smacked his fist into his palm.

Elrabin's anger was pumping red into his vision. He felt almost nauseous at the thought of Harthril's hard work wasted because of this careless, heedless cub.

''Harthril can't use a sling,'' Elrabin said in the Reject's defense. ''He has a crippled shoulder.''

''Yeah, the same old excuse,'' Nashmarl said, tipping his head back to look at the sky. ''Is something burning?''

Both Elrabin and Paket ignored his question. Paket's teeth were bared, and Elrabin wanted to bite Nashmarl so bad he almost didn't dare trust himself.

''So you left Harthril,'' Elrabin said. ''You left the net.''

''Sure. I heard you go up to the camp, puffing like you were going to pass out.'' Nashmarl tipped back his head and laughed. ''You're getting old, Elrabin. Old and out of shape. So I followed you. I wanted to show you I can track and stalk, as good as anyone in the camp. Proved it too. Tackled you before you knew I was coming.''

''Shut up,'' Elrabin snapped.

Nashmarl's laughter died away, but he stared at Elrabin with devilment still dancing in his eyes.

Elrabin glared back. ''Harthril has spent how long hunting those grassens?''

Nashmarl shrugged. ''Who cares? It was boring. It was taking too long.''

''You little fool! It takes time and skill to drive grassens into a trap. Harthril is a master at that. No one else among us can do it.''

''So?''

''So we would have had a whole flock held captive.

We could have eaten them for several days. Instead, you just walked away. You got tired and bored, and you quit. We could starve because of you—''

''No way,'' Nashmarl said, although his green eyes grew wider. ''You and Mother were supposed to bring home lots of food. So where's yours? I don't see any. You goof up, Elrabin? You think you can blame your failure on me? It was your responsibility to get food today, not mine.''

Elrabin's temper got away from him. Before he could stop himself, he stepped forward and cuffed Nashmarl hard where his ear should have been.

The cub squalled and cowered down, putting his arms over his head. ''You hit me!'' he said, his voice raw with fury and disbelief. ''That hurt!''

''Shut up. You ain't been hurt. You don't know what hurt is.''

Nashmarl glared at him. ''You'd no right to do that.''

''When your mother isn't here, I'm in charge,'' Elrabin said harshly. He wanted to hit the cub again, wanted it so much the emotion scared him inside. ''Everyone in our band has a responsibility to bring home food, every day. You know that! It's the cardinal rule of the camp.''

''Rules,'' Nashmarl said scornfully, still rubbing his face where Elrabin had smacked him. ''Your rules, maybe, but I don't—''

''*Our* rules, you little fool!'' Elrabin said, wanting to shake some sense into him. ''Don't give me any more of that. You've known the rules since you were crawling. They go equal for everyone. You deliberately blew 'em off. When Ampris hears about this, she'll—''

''I was getting too hot,'' Nashmarl said, switching his defiance into a whine. ''My skin was burning. I'm not supposed to be outside when the sun is this hot.''

''Then what you be doing out here right now?'' Elrabin asked him through gritted teeth.

Nashmarl blinked. "I thought you'd be proud of me. I wanted to sneak up on you and show you how much I've learned."

Elrabin could barely listen to him. The cub's insincere flattery annoyed him even more than he already was. "Yeah, you showed me. You showed me you ain't willing to think about anyone but yourself. Now you go back to camp and apologize to Harthril, then maybe you'll learn something."

Again, Nashmarl's face reddened. "Apologize?" he echoed. "Never! I don't owe that Reject any—"

Elrabin came at him again with his hand upraised, and with a cry Nashmarl cringed away from him.

"Shut up," Elrabin said in disgust. "Get back to camp and lie in the shade. You be spoiled and lazy—"

"I am not!"

"You be useless."

Outrage flared in Nashmarl's eyes. "You can't talk to me like this—calling me names, insulting me. You aren't my—"

"I'll talk to you like I want," Elrabin said. "You done put the camp at risk, see? You got to be punished."

"No one's going to punish me," Nashmarl said. His green eyes narrowed with all the arrogance of a Viis. "Certainly not you."

Elrabin pointed up the hill. "Get out of here. Go!"

"I will not go. I will not do anything you say. You can't make me."

Elrabin bared his teeth, tempted to seize the cub by his scruff and drag him back into the camp. But there wasn't time. He'd wasted enough of it with this young fool already.

"Fine," he said shortly. "When your mother gets back, we'll deal with it. Now, get out of my way."

"I'll tell her," Nashmarl said, making it a threat. "I'll tell her what you said to me. I'll tell her you hit me."

"I'll hit you again if you don't get out of my way,"

Elrabin growled. He pushed past Nashmarl, who scurried out of reach, and strode on down the hill with Paket at his heels.

"Street trash!" Nashmarl called after him. "You think you're someone important because Mother likes you, but you're really—"

With an oath, Elrabin swung around, but Nashmarl vanished from sight into the underbrush. Seconds later, a rock came sailing out of the thicket and struck Elrabin on the shoulder.

His temper snapped completely. Growling, he started into the brush, but Paket grabbed him by his coattail and held him back.

"Let him go," Paket said.

Elrabin panted with anger. "He needs his hide skinned."

"Later," Paket said. He yanked harder on Elrabin's coat. "Later."

Growling, Elrabin bared his teeth. Slowly he pulled his emotions under control. Giving himself a shake, he moved away from Paket's restraining hand and rubbed his muzzle. He hated losing his temper. Only Nashmarl could make him go crazy like this, where he lost track of everything except the desire to attack and punish. The cub had a talent for irritating him. Elrabin knew he ought to stay iced, not let Nashmarl get to him, but every time he looked at the cub he could see so much potential, so much promise. And it infuriated him to see what Nashmarl was growing into.

The faint echo of the cub's jeering laughter carried down the hill on the hot breeze. Elrabin heard the noisy progress as Nashmarl pushed through the thicket, and he sighed to himself. He knew Nashmarl was making the noise on purpose, just to irritate him even more.

With a shrug, Elrabin turned around and resumed walking.

Paket puffed and struggled along beside him. "That

cub is getting too full of himself. Has no manners. Has no brain. Someone's got to tell Ampris."

Elrabin's exasperation boiled over. "Tell her what?" he demanded. "You want to get in her face with criticism of her son? He's got the prettiest manners in the world when his mother's around. Gah!" Elrabin slapped a branch out of his way, letting it whip viciously behind him. "She got a lot of smarts, Paket, but when it comes to her cubs she's blind, *blind*!"

"The mother love of Aarouns," Paket said with a sigh. "We Kelths are much smarter."

Elrabin thought of his own mother, stressed and thin, working too hard to support her lits, too tired to share much affection. Twitching his ears, he angrily slammed old memories away. Time to think of the here and now.

He shot Paket a glance. "Nashmarl ain't my problem, see?"

"You get mad like he is."

Elrabin fumed. "Going to get his mother out of trouble, I am," he muttered. "Then she can deal with him."

"You know we got another rule in camp," Paket said quietly, ducking a branch that Elrabin had heedlessly let whip back. "Anyone who gets to be a problem can be shunned."

Elrabin snorted to himself. "Yeah, sure. You going to shun Ampris's cubs—"

"Not both of them. Foloth's all right."

Elrabin looked over his shoulder and met Paket's gaze. "Foloth ain't all right. One cub's as bad as the other. Just in different ways. Which don't mean they can't be straightened out."

"Who's going to do that?" Paket asked him.

Elrabin shrugged. "So you going to shun them, and you think Ampris won't fight it. I want to see that."

"I'm not saying we will," Paket said earnestly. "I'm saying we can."

"We need her," Elrabin said, getting angry again.

"We be nothing without her. Don't you forget that."

"I know what I owe Ampris," Paket said in a low voice. "I wouldn't be following you here and now if I'd forgotten."

The rebuke made Elrabin flatten his ears. "Yeah, yeah," he said and squinted ahead where the hill began to flatten out. The fire had already burned up the field and was now dying out with huge billows of black smoke. He saw that the shed where Ampris had concealed their cache of stolen food had also burned. His spirits plummeted. All that hope and risk for nothing.

He slowed down and glanced at Paket, then decided not to mention the grain they'd never eat. It seemed to be a bad omen, but he shook the thought off.

Feeling bleak, he coughed as the smoke gusted their way.

"So what do you think?" Paket asked him. "How far to the compound from here?"

"Another hour, maybe more if you can't keep the pace."

Paket bared his teeth. "I can keep up. I ain't slowing us down."

"Got to have something left when we get there."

Growling, Paket shouldered past him and moved out into the open between the underbrush and the charred edge of the field. "Let's can the gab and save our breath for being heroes." He shot Elrabin an impatient glare. "Come on."

Elrabin hesitated, reluctant to leave the safety of cover. "We better go around—"

"The long way won't help us." Paket waved at the empty, smoke-filled sky. "We'll take the road. No one's going to pay any attention to us."

"If we get buzzed by a patroller—"

"They're busy burning stelf," Paket said. "My legs be too old to take the long way. You go whichever way you want. I'm taking the road."

He marched off, and Elrabin groaned to himself. If he wasn't having to deal with Ampris getting greedy and staying in the field until she got caught, he was busy trying to knock some sense into her offspring. Now Paket had thrown caution to the winds. The old one had to be losing his mind.

Elrabin hadn't lived this long by being reckless and crazy.

Except once in a while. This seemed to be one of those times. Sighing to himself, he left the safety of the thicket and trotted into the open, following the old Kelth, who had set his muzzle grimly to the south.

Together, they headed for the compound.

CHAPTER THREE

The sun was setting, spreading huge rays of copper and gold across a sky smudged indigo and charcoal. The air smelled of smoke. With twilight, the breeze had shifted directions, bringing coolness for the first time all day.

Within the farm compound of a Viis landowner whose name Ampris did not know, she waited with the other field slaves inside a circular holding pen located between the barns and the ramshackle quarters which housed the slaves. It had been a long time since Ampris had found herself pushed down a loading chute and held prisoner inside a pen of wire mesh. The pen was fitted with a security field that delivered stinging electric shocks to anyone who touched the wire.

"Prisoner" . . . the very word conjured up old memories of hurt and cruelty that Ampris did not want to relive. She fought to hold back the panic that kept rising inside her. She was not someone who lost her head in a crisis. She was too experienced for that. Fear had to be held down and controlled. But no matter how hard she tried, it kept getting away from her and filling her with cold surges of worry that made the fur around her neck bristle.

Most of the other slaves had clustered in the center of the pen. They crouched on their haunches, murmuring softly among themselves and pointedly ignoring the heated conference going on among the Viis standing in the garden. The garden's wall was no more than waist-high and served not as a barrier within the taller walls of the compound but instead as a demarcation of private space reserved for use by the landowner's family only. Right now, the landowner himself stood among his shrubs and flowers, with his wife wailing softly behind her veil and the fat Gorlican overseer standing a short distance away. A delegation of patrollers in black uniforms, helmets tucked beneath their arms, faced the landowner. Arguments in Viis flew back and forth, furious and heated, but too far away for the words to be clearly overheard.

Ampris stayed at the perimeter, continually circling the pen. She was unable to keep still, unable to remain passive. All her instincts warned her to stay alert, to seize the smallest chance to escape.

She watched the argument, wishing she were close enough to hear better. She had managed to retain her fluency with the Viis language and had taught as much of it as she could to her sons. The other members of the group disliked her doing that, saying she was teaching her sons to become Viis, to become the enemy. Only Elrabin understood her reasons and gave her his approval. Many Myals of course understood Viis, especially those who worked in areas of research and historical preservation, but Ampris knew of no Aaroun besides herself who was fluent in Viis. She could even read and write it. In an age when so many of the abiru folk could not always speak their own native language and instead knew only the multilingual abiru patois, Ampris's level of education was both unique and remarkable. She wanted Foloth and Nashmarl to have the same advantages and knowledge base she had, so that when they grew up they could deal with the Viis both intelligently and resourcefully. But teaching them was difficult at best. Foloth was willing but slow to pick up abstract concepts. Nashmarl had a brilliant mind, but he was too impatient to work hard.

Thinking of her sons, growing so tall yet with so much still to learn, Ampris's sense of urgency increased. She had to get out of here.

Panting, Ampris halted and leaned as close to the wire fence as she dared. The current in it crackled in warning, but she went on peering intently across the compound at the landowner and the patrollers. She believed that everything depended on the outcome of their discussion. Not just the landowner's fate, but hers as well.

The Viis wife wailed again, more loudly than before, and staggered away with her hands pressed to her face.

Ampris strained her ears and heard the word "taxes," then "enforced sale of all assets now under confiscation."

The landowner was ruined. Growling, Ampris drew back. She was not concerned about him or his family, but his ruin meant serious trouble for her too. If the patrollers had been satisfied to simply burn the fields and leave, Ampris figured she could have gotten away the next time the slaves were taken out to work. But if the government confiscated not just the harvest, but also the land, equipment, and slaves, then she had to get out of here before she found herself shipped to Vir's slave auction.

Her growl grew louder, and determination hardened inside her. Never again would she go through that humiliation. She was a person, free, not an object to be possessed or purchased.

"What is it?" asked a deep, rumbling voice from behind her.

Ampris jumped and spun around to find herself looking at the striped Aaroun male. He had not been friendly earlier that day when they were all crammed inside the broiling interior of a transport and hauled here. But now he looked at her in open inquiry, and worry filled his eyes.

She hesitated, not certain what to answer. Not all Aarouns could be trusted. She'd learned that the hard way.

"You understand what's going on over there?" he asked, pointing at the patrollers.

Ampris glanced that way and saw the landowner handing over his seal of warranty. Her heart sank inside her. Time was running out.

"Your Viis master just lost his farm to government confiscation," she said. "He has surrendered his seal of warranty."

The Aaroun looked at her without understanding.

Ampris backed her ears impatiently. "The seal is a symbol of his ownership, like a title or a deed to the property. It was probably given to one of his ancestors long ago. Now he's giving it back. He doesn't own this farm anymore."

The Aaroun shrugged. "Oh. Nothing about us, then."

He started to turn away, but Ampris sprang after him and gripped his arm. "Are you crazy?" she asked. "You belong to the farm, all of you," she said, sweeping all the slaves with her gaze. "So you now go to the government. You'll be transported to the nearest city and auctioned off for whatever profit you can bring."

Consternation rippled through their huddled ranks. Several rose to their feet.

"I told you," a Kelth female said shrilly. "I told you we'd be sold."

Someone started to ask a question, but one of the younger Kelths yipped gleefully.

"Good!" he said. "I'm tired of breaking my back over stelf. Now we can do city work, live the easy life."

"Easy!" Ampris echoed, amazed by his naivete. "What makes you think city workers have it easy?"

"Sure they do," he said, rising to his feet and brushing himself off. His fur was a tawny hue, and his upright ears were tipped with black. "They ain't out here, grubbing weeds and hauling—"

"No," Ampris broke in scornfully, "instead most of them work the docks, unloading cargo off the shuttles. Or they go on deliveries and unload those. Or they break their backs hauling construction stone. Or they stand waist-deep in the city sewers all day, never seeing the sky, while they scrape out the built-up sludge from the tunnels. Or they go wash out the contaminated tanks in factories, never mind how many die of chemical poisoning. Instead of choking on dust, they breathe industrial pollution. Instead of living in quarters behind the barn, they live in decayed tenement buildings, crammed in tiny spaces too small to hold their families."

The brown Kelth blinked at her with his narrow jaws agape.

It was the striped Aaroun male who said softly, "Least they can have families. They live in their own place they can call home. They ain't chained and whipped."

"You want a home that leaks, that has no heat, no sanitation, sometimes no running water?" Ampris replied. "And do you want to have little ones, only to see them kidnapped in raids to be sold on the black market? I was taken from my mother at birth, and never saw her again. I do not even know her name or clan. We were still in the birthing hut, and I never even saw my father to have a memory of him."

The Aaroun dropped his gaze from hers, looking abashed, while the other Aarouns in the group came up to surround her.

"What is your name?" one of the females asked.

"Ampris."

Her name brought no recognition until the striped Aaroun lifted his head. He stared hard at Ampris, as though trying to remember something.

"Kuma?" one of the others asked. "What is it?"

The striped Aaroun went on staring at Ampris and said nothing.

Another female tapped Ampris on the arm. "Kuma was born in Vir. He and his litter mates were sold for farm work when he was very young."

Pity filled Ampris. She shot him a look of compassion. "I'm sorry I spoke so harshly. You understand what I—"

"Yes," he said. His gaze flickered to the young Kelth with the tawny fur. "Moska here is always looking for a way to escape field work. He thinks anything else must be better."

Moska's black-tipped ears twitched nervously, although the look he sent Ampris was sly. "I don't believe—I *know,*" he said arrogantly. "There is nothing worse than here."

Ampris wanted to laugh at him. In some ways he reminded her of her sons. "No matter how low you go, there is always something worse," she told him.

"And what do you know about anything?" he shot back. "Who are you anyway? Some kind of spy?"

"Why do you ask?" she answered. "You got something to hide? Something that needs spying *on*?"

Moska glared at her, but the Aaroun male shoved him aside. "No," he said before Moska could speak. "We are simple field slaves. We tend the crops. We harvest the crops. That is all we do and know. But you are no common field slave, Ampris. That is plain to see."

She blinked in surprise. Years ago, when her golden fur was sleek and beautiful and her muscles rippled gracefully in perfect condition, yes, she had stood out from the others. But she was older now, had survived experimentation and abuse, had lived in the wild for many years, had grown thin and rough. Today she was dressed in rags, like the others in this pen with her. What was so different or remarkable about her?

"Years ago, there was a golden Aaroun named Ampris who fought in the arena,'' Kuma said. ''I heard my father speak of her. He used to bet his wages on the competitions, and my mother would get very angry. But when he bet on Ampris, he always won.''

A gasp ran through the group. They stared at her with widened eyes, while Ampris glared back with her ears flattened.

''A gladiator,'' Moska breathed, his eyes shining. He stepped closer to her and pointed at her crippled leg. ''Those scars . . . from fighting?''

Involuntarily she glanced down at where her fur had grown in white over the scars on her leg. Denial seemed pointless. ''Yes,'' she said.

They gasped again, and some drew back from her in fear.

She didn't understand their reaction. She stood among them, unarmed and civilized. Did they expect her to turn on them like a savage?

''What are you afraid of?'' she asked.

Instead of answering, they drew back as far as the pen would allow. Only Kuma and Moska stood their ground near her.

Ampris looked around in exasperation. ''I won't hurt you.''

''Killer,'' someone in the crowd murmured. ''Abiru slayer.''

Shame touched her then. But she had long ago come to terms with what she'd been forced to do in the arena. ''Yes, I killed many,'' she said with her head high. ''All had been condemned—''

''—The standard excuse,'' Moska muttered.

''—and I could obey my Viis master or be executed in the arena myself,'' Ampris finished grimly. ''How many of you have never been forced by your master to violate all you believe in and hold sacred?''

They fell silent. Many stared at the ground and would not meet her eyes.

"Anyone?" she asked, making it a challenge. "No? Then I need offer no excuses or apologies for my past."

As she spoke, it struck her as absurd that she should finally be defending her actions to a bunch of ignorant field slaves on a remote farm.

A shout in the distance caught her attention. Ampris turned aside to look and saw one of the patrollers waving as he spoke into a hand-link. Moments later, a shuttle flew over the compound wall and landed near the barns, throwing up a fierce cloud of dust.

Turning away to shield her eyes, Ampris coughed, then straightened as the shuttle engines cut off. She watched the activity a few more seconds to confirm her worst fears before she turned back to her fellow prisoners.

"Kuma," she said, "we must form a plan."

The striped Aaroun looked at her in amazement. "What?"

She pointed. "Look at what they're doing. They're raising an imperial flag over the compound. In a few minutes they'll start loading property, the important and perishable items first, which means any valuables owned by the family, their stores of food, and us."

Kuma's eyes still held no understanding. "The Viis will do what they will do. What do you expect of us?"

"We must make a break for it," Ampris said urgently. "The chance, when it comes, will probably be while they are loading us, or perhaps when the guards unlock this pen. We'll have to—"

"You're saying escape?" Moska interrupted. He twitched his black-tipped ears and looked at her in disbelief. "Run away?"

"We'll be shot," Kuma said.

The others behind him murmured agreement.

Ampris looked at their fearful faces in exasperation. "Don't be so docile," she said. "This is a chance to take charge of your lives. You could be free, live as you please—''

''Free to do what?'' Kuma asked her. ''Starve?''

''We can't survive on our own,'' one of the Aaroun females said.

The others nodded.

Ampris backed her ears in exasperation. ''Of course you can. I and my friends will show you—''

''You mean you been living free?'' Moska asked her with open skepticism. ''No master?''

''Do I wear an ownership ring?'' Ampris asked him. She held up her arm and parted the fur across the back of her elbow. ''See this scar? It's where my registration implant was cut out.''

Kuma came forward and peered curiously at the small scar, but the others hung back, exchanging glances.

''You're a renegade, an outlaw,'' Moska said.

Ampris faced him with pride. ''I am.''

Someone gasped in admiration, but Moska yipped loudly. ''That means a reward's on your head. I'm going to tell the—''

In two limping strides Ampris reached the young Kelth. Gripping him by the throat, she lifted him so that his feet almost left the ground and propelled him backward at the electrified fence.

Clearly he thought she was going to shove him into it because he closed his eyes and yelped shrilly.

''Let him go!'' Kuma said, moving to intervene, but Ampris blocked his ineffectual grab at her arm.

She throttled Moska expertly, letting him feel his own mortality in her hands. When he began to gasp and pant, his tongue lolling out, she released him.

His legs wouldn't support him and he dropped to the ground, coughing and sputtering.

Ampris stood over him and growled. ''Never threaten me,'' she said harshly. She swung around to glare at Kuma and the others. ''We are abiru, kindred brothers and sisters all. We do not betray each other. Is that clear? The Viis are our enemy. We should not be enemies among ourselves.''

No one replied. They stared at her with wide eyes.

She looked at them in rising exasperation. ''Where is your spirit?'' she asked them. ''Have you no yearning to be free?''

''We are slaves,'' Kuma answered at last. ''Born slaves. Will die slaves. We obey. We do our work. Sometimes we are treated well. Sometimes we are not. It is the way of life.''

''No,'' Ampris said hotly. ''It is not the Aaroun way. It is not the Kelth way. It is not the Myal way. We were born free. Our ancestors lived on their own separate worlds. We did not always have Viis masters to grind our faces into the dust. Everything possible lies before you, if you will only find the courage to reach for it.''

''Freedom Network,'' said one of the older Kelth females from the rear of the group. ''That was you.''

''Yes,'' Ampris said. She craned her neck, trying to see the female who was speaking, but they were bunched too closely together behind Kuma. ''Long ago, I worked for the cause. You know it. Were you a part of it?''

''No,'' came the voice with too much haste. ''I saw the messages. I heard the slogans, but nothing came of it. In the end, there was nothing to fight for. There never is.''

Her pessimism annoyed Ampris, who glared at them all. ''The Viis were lazy and disorganized when I lived among them. I can't imagine they have improved. You could be free anytime you want.''

''That is a lie,'' Kuma said flatly.

Ampris's ears went back flat against her skull. She glared at him through narrowed eyes and bared her teeth. ''If you remain a slave, it is because you wish to be.''

His mouth fell open, but it was Moska who jumped to his feet in outrage. ''Not true!'' he said shrilly, holding his throat. "We didn't choose to be slaves."

"Then what have you chosen to be?" Ampris asked him.

He snarled at her. "You make fun of us, but you are prisoner too. If you value freedom so much, why don't you take it for yourself?"

"I will," Ampris said.

As though she had been overheard, a spotlight stabbed through the darkening gloom and illuminated the pen with blinding force. Ampris squinted and put her hands to her eyes to shield them.

"Attention, slaves!" came a Viis voice over a loudspeaker. "Move to the rear of the pen now. When the gate is opened, you will come out one at a time with your hands on your head. Obey now."

In silence, the slaves moved to do as they were ordered.

Ampris squinted past the blinding spotlight at the figures silhouetted in black. She could smell the sour Viis stink, and her nostrils wrinkled in repugnance.

"You, Aaroun!" came the harsh voice over the loudspeaker. "Move back with the others."

Slowly Ampris backed up. Her fur bristled on her neck and stood up in a ridge down her spine. She kept her jaws closed, but a constant growl rumbled in her throat.

Kuma reached out and gripped her wrist, making her jump violently. She turned on him with a snarl, but he glared at her, close and furious.

"Make no trouble," he said in a low voice. "Bring no harm to us."

It was death for any abiru to strike a Viis. Ampris knew that if she attacked and was defeated, the slaves would all be executed as accomplices. At least that would be the official word put out on the planetary newscast, but in reality the slaves would be sold for whatever profit the patrollers could get.

She met Kuma's eyes, trying to find some spark of defiance or courage in their depths. "There are four patrollers, armed only with stun-sticks. Their side-arms are not drawn," Ampris said softly. "We number twenty-three. We can take them."

His grip tightened on her arm. "No! You will get us killed."

"It's dark. We take them, put out the spotlight, and slip out through the back gate of the compound. By the time we are missed by the others, we can be well-scattered."

"Their scanners will find us in minutes," he said.

"Ah." She drew in her breath with a sharp hiss. She'd forgotten about their implants. "Some of you will get away," she said. "They won't have time or fuel enough to hunt down everyone. It's worth a try, Kuma."

"No."

"Kuma!"

He snapped at her muzzle, making her jerk her head back to avoid a bite. "No!" he said fiercely.

The fence buzzed, then went dead. The gate swung open with a shriek of rusty hinges. "Everyone, out," one of the patrollers ordered. "Single file, hands on your heads."

Ampris hung back when Kuma stepped forward. He was the first one out of the pen, and Ampris heard rather than saw the click of restraints being locked onto his wrists. Past the spotlight, she saw him walk up the ramp into the belly of the large shuttle. Regret filled her. She wished she had worn her Eye of Clarity today. Perhaps it would have helped her make these slaves understand what freedom could offer them. But they were afraid of uncertainty. They did not know how to take risks or turn dreams into reality. Wishing, by itself, was not enough. Action had to be taken if anything was ever to be accomplished.

One by one, the slaves filed past her, exiting the pen

and standing in docile acceptance as restraints were locked on them.

Ampris growled softly to herself. She would not be docile, and she would not go quietly.

When half the slaves were gone, she joined the exodus, moving into the center of a small bunch.

At the gate, they tried to go through in a wad, but the patrollers shoved them back.

"Single file! One at a time."

Ampris let herself be shoved back, but she grabbed the wrist of the patroller who pushed her. She yanked with all her strength, using his own impetus to send him sprawling on the ground. She twisted his stun-stick from his grip as he fell.

He yelled something in Viis, but Ampris found the button and activated the weapon. She stunned him and spun around just as another patroller came through the gate at her.

She stunned him too, and with a strangled yell, he fell at her feet.

The other two patrollers jumped back. One of them drew his side-arm while the second one started calling for assistance on his hand-link.

Snarling, Ampris hurled her stun-stick at the patroller drawing his lethal weapon. Someone jostled her from behind, however, and spoiled her aim. The stun-stick went flying off into the darkness, and the patroller fired his weapon.

When Ampris saw the flash in the darkness, she was already diving for the ground. She heard a scream next to her and smelled blood and burned fur. One of the slaves fell across her legs, and Ampris frantically squirmed free. By the time she reached her feet, the spotlight had swung in her direction, pinning her in place.

The other few slaves still in the pen screamed and shoved each other, milling in panic. The patroller fired again, shooting down another Aaroun. Realizing they would all be killed, Ampris launched herself at the fence. She bounded halfway up and climbed swiftly, flinging herself over the top and letting herself drop.

A shot blazed over her head, missing her by scant centimeters. She hit the ground hard enough to jolt her bones. Pain shot up her crippled leg, and she grunted, staggering to one side and clutching the throbbing limb.

The spotlight was swinging around again, coming toward her.

Ampris looked around frantically at the shadowy outline of the barns and the open expanse of the compound. Ducking low beneath the sweep of the spotlight, she scrambled forward to the shuttle and dived beneath the ramp as the spotlight swung back.

"Where is he?" one of the Viis patrollers demanded, mistakenly. The gate banged shut, and the slaves still in the pen screamed in fear. "Get the light on him, fast."

Panting for breath, Ampris grinned briefly to herself. So they thought she was male. When would the Viis learn anything about her kind? The females were generally more aggressive than the males, although all Aarouns could fight well when they had to.

The spotlight swung around again, and she heard a noise at the compound's main gate. More patrollers were streaming in, weapons in hand. Lights snapped on, and a scanner was released into the air. It began to fly back and forth, beeping as it went.

A shot burst from the low wall of the gardens. A patroller cried in anguish and fell.

Startled, Ampris whipped her head around, trying to see who was out there. Another shot originating from the garden took down a second patroller. They milled around, activating body armor and aiming their weapons. A barrage of return fire blazed red along the garden wall.

Still concealed beneath the shuttle ramp, Ampris could see small chunks of stone flying into the air.

"It's the family!" a patroller officer shouted from where he had taken cover near some farm machinery. "They have turned traitor. All weapons on the house."

Another barrage broke out. Windows in the sprawling house burst, and flames caught in the draperies. Orange light from the fires filled the darkness, and Ampris could hear shrill screams from inside the structure.

She looked around frantically, knowing she couldn't stay pinned here under the ramp forever.

She didn't want to head for the barns. They were under security net, and the wall stood at its highest behind them. But she couldn't go toward the house and gardens. And the main group of patrollers was between her and the gate.

Picking her moment, she crawled out from beneath the ramp and hobbled toward the shadowy corner of the slave quarters. Pain stabbed through her crippled leg with every step, and she was gasping and whimpering by the time she reached cover.

She sank down into the shadows, not sure she could keep going.

A hand gripped her arm, and she jumped with a roar of alarm that was cut off as another hand clamped itself around her muzzle. Her heart was thudding inside her chest, but already she smelled a scent she knew as well as her own.

"Goldie?" a familiar voice whispered to her. "It's me."

The hand came off her muzzle. She sighed in relief, trying to get her breath back.

"Elrabin," she whispered. "I nearly took your head off."

"Yeah, I know it," he said while the firing continued. "We got to get out of this, and fast. They ain't going to keep shooting up the house forever."

Ampris grinned in the dark. "You fired the shots from the garden."

"Hey, I be getting a better shot all the time," Elrabin said proudly. "So where's the back gate?"

"Behind the house."

He swore. "That's all?"

The firing abruptly stopped, and a ringing silence followed it.

Ampris and Elrabin clutched each other, both of them frozen while the patrollers ventured cautiously from cover and headed for the burning house.

"Out of time," Elrabin said against her ear.

She nodded and pointed at the shuttle.

"No way," he whispered. "You going to—"

A movement behind him made Ampris jump. She started toward it, but Elrabin blocked her with a swift grab at her arm.

"Paket," he whispered.

She sagged against him, wiping the fur around her eyes. "Who else?" she asked, then felt a sudden stab of alarm that Foloth or Nashmarl might be here too.

"Just us, see? Tantha wanted to come. I told her we couldn't play no midwife in the middle of a rescue."

She grinned, but they were losing their opportunity. She tapped him on the shoulder, then Paket, and pointed at the shuttle.

"You serious?" Elrabin asked her. "Who be flying that?"

Ampris pointed at him.

He started to yelp in protest, then cut off the sound. She could hear him making a faint, strangled noise. He shook his head. Exasperated, she pointed at herself, then yanked him onto his feet by the front of his coat.

"Let's go. Paket, stay close."

"We ain't going to make this," Elrabin said, but Ampris was already moving at a half-run, limping badly.

In a moment Elrabin was beside her, gripping her arm and using his strength to partially support her. She threw him a grin of gratitude, and glanced over her shoulder at old Paket, who was gamely shuffling behind them.

They reached the ramp and were climbing it when a shout rang out.

Elrabin raised the side-arm, but one of the patrollers fired first. Paket grunted and fell against Elrabin, nearly knocking him off the ramp.

He juggled the weapon in an effort to catch the old Kelth, and Ampris grabbed the side-arm from his hand and fired over his and Paket's heads.

A patroller screamed and went down.

She fired again, and gave Elrabin a shove. "Get him inside. Now!" she ordered.

Elrabin dragged Paket bodily into the shuttle, and Ampris followed.

Return fire caught her in the arm, spinning her off balance. She staggered into the shuttle and hit the closure control.

The ramp lifted with a whir of gears, and one more shot made it inside the shuttle, the slug of hot plasma nocking one of the struts while the slaves ducked and yelled in fear.

Ampris knelt beside Elrabin, who was cradling Paket on the floor. The old Kelth's eyes were closed and sunken. His breathing was labored and raspy. Grief filled her. She gripped Paket's shoulder. "Not you, my old friend."

Elrabin shouldered her back and bent over Paket. "He's okay," he said roughly. "Just knocked out, see?"

"Is that all?" Ampris tried to peer over Elrabin's shoulder. "But he's been hit."

"He's fine. Just do whatever you got in mind, and do it fast."

Blows sounded on the hull, making her start. She rose to her feet, ignoring the frightened cries of the slaves around her, and climbed up the ladder into the cockpit.

Fitting herself into the cramped space, she glanced around swiftly. The array of controls bewildered her.

She had no piloting skills. What was she doing here? What did she think she could do, fly this shuttle out of the compound and somehow elude pursuit? She must be insane.

All she'd done was gain them a temporary respite, and that would last only as long as it took the patrollers to force open the hatch.

Fiery pain spread through her arm. Growing aware of it for the first time, she winced and peered at her wound. Just a graze, but it hurt.

More thuds rocked the exterior of the shuttle.

"Goldie?" Elrabin's voice rose shrilly from below. "They're coming in!"

Jolted, Ampris threw off her inertia, and her mind cleared again. Even if she didn't know how to fly, she could at least move this shuttle out of the compound. That was all she wanted to accomplish.

She looked around the cockpit again, trying to summon up old memories plus anything she'd observed in years past while watching vids. When she was a cub, living in the imperial palace as the pet of the young sri-Kaa Israi, Ampris had often flown when her mistress was taken on trips. Usually the pilot would treat the sri-Kaa to a visit to his cockpit, and Ampris was allowed to look at the controls too. Israi loved to fly and always begged to take the controls.

Ampris closed her eyes, ignoring the thuds now steadily rocking the shuttle, and tried to summon up that long-ago lesson. Although she was not wearing her Eye of Clarity, she pretended that it hung around her neck. She curled her fist on her chest where the pendant normally rested and forced herself to concentrate.

Slowly her mind cleared and reached back, back into her cubhood. As though she were watching a vid, she visualized the pilot's green, pebble-skinned hands. He touched the three main levers directly in front of the pilot's seat and said that they were the primary flying controls. Forward and to the right was the engine start-up array. To the left were fuel and pressurization gauges, plus other safety features.

Ampris opened her eyes and drew a deep breath as though surfacing from a pool of water. Suddenly she grew aware of shouting and screams from below, punctuated by the shriek of tortured metal.

"They're cutting us open!" Elrabin was shouting.

Without more delay, Ampris hit the engine buttons in rapid succession, not in any particular order.

The engines fired, sputtered, and caught. They roared much too powerfully, making the parked shuttle buck.

From below, Elrabin cheered, and Ampris grinned nervously to herself. She experimented, almost killed the engines, then managed to boost power enough to lift the shuttle.

Something whined ominously, and a red light flashed on. She figured out that the park setting must still be on, but she didn't know how to turn it off.

She managed to slew the shuttle sideways, and heard muffled commotion and some bumps outside. Again she grinned to herself, hoping she'd just flattened some patrollers.

The screens weren't on. She was moving blind except for what she could see through the front port.

She turned the shuttle around until she could see the compound gates, then she gunned the engines and sent the shuttle in that direction. The craft was flying no more than a meter above ground, and it remained tilted to one side, but at least they were going in the right direction.

In frustration she tried to figure out how to get out of park. She pushed some controls at random. The interior lights flashed off. Swiftly she turned them back on. The steering lever was sensitive, and she inadvertently tilted the shuttle sideways just as it went through the gate. The shuttle slammed against the wall, nearly rolled, and lurched in the opposite direction.

Sweating, her heart hammering hard against her ribs, Ampris backed her ears and hung on. At least they were now outside the compound. If she could only pick up some speed, they might have a chance.

Through the port, she could see another parked shuttle ahead of her. She steered clumsily to the side of it, and saw its exterior lights flash in patterns as it lifted off the ground. It swung around and came after her.

Ampris's heart sank. She glared at her controls, cursing them. Then her old arena training came back to her. She reminded herself that panic led to mistakes and missed opportunities. She had to calm herself, had to trust herself. She could figure out this puzzle if she gave herself a chance.

Steering around another parked shuttle, she looked at the controls again and tried to utilize logic. This time she noticed a tiny button on the side of her steering lever. She pushed it, and the shuttle suddenly lurched upward as though catapulted.

Startled, Ampris grabbed the levers too hard, and the shuttle dived, nearly crashing into the ground before she pulled it up. She got it leveled, and blinked sweat from her eyes, sitting tense in her seat with her hands frozen on the controls. After a few rigid seconds, she began to slowly relax.

She was flying, actually flying a shuttle. Triumph soared inside her, and she let herself grin.

Then something rocked them from behind, throwing her sideways again. The shuttle squalled in protest, and Ampris could hear the engines straining. She pushed something, and the engine thrust decreased slightly. Instantly the shuttle leveled off on its own, and Ampris realized she'd been accelerating too hard.

Again they were rocked from behind. She could only see in front of her, but she suspected the other shuttle was on their tail, trying to bring them down.

Grimly Ampris steered her craft toward the hills, raking over a treetop before she saw it in time. She needed to be able to see better where she was going, but she didn't dare take both hands off the controls in order to try and switch on the screens.

Static crackled over a speaker, startling her so that she sent the shuttle skidding to one side again.

"Shuttle four-one," came a Viis voice, "land your craft immediately. You have one warning. Failure to comply will result in destruction."

Ampris didn't answer. She didn't figure she was expected to. Besides, she was too busy looking at her controls. She had a plan now.

"Elrabin!" she called. "Hey!"

"Hey, what?" he replied.

"I'm going to put us in a canyon. It'll be a rough landing."

"No fooling?" he called up caustically. "The way you drive? I'd never guess."

She grinned, and peered through her port. In the darkness it was hard to be sure where she was, but if she strained her eyes enough she could just make out a darker ribbon of shadow on the approaching hillside which she figured indicated trees and a canyon.

"Get ready," she said. "You got their restraints off yet?"

"Oh, sure. I been picking locks like a—"

Something exploded around them. The shuttle seemed to stop abruptly in midair, then plummeted.

Ampris tried moving her steering control, but it no longer worked. Nothing she attempted stopped their fall. Fear swelled in her throat, but she refused to give up. She knew they had only seconds now.

From the port she could see bright orange tongues of flames licking the sides of the shuttle. Ampris stared for what seemed like an eternity, then she saw the rush of ground coming at her.

"Elrabin!" she screamed. "Brace for impact! When

we hit, open the hatch. Everyone is to get out and scatter.''

''You crazy!'' he yelled back. ''We're crashing and you want us to—''

She stopped listening. She had just spotted a lever across the narrow cockpit marked EMERGENCY in Viis symbols. Releasing her useless controls, Ampris threw herself bodily across the space and pulled it hard.

The falling shuttle jerked violently, as though it had been caught by the hand of a giant. They spun crazily, slamming Ampris against the wall, but their plummet to the ground had slowed.

Dazed, she righted herself as best she could while the shuttle spun one way and then another. The nose thudded into the ground with a jolt that snapped her teeth together, then the body of the shuttle settled down on its side.

She took only a moment to comprehend that they were on the ground and intact. Praying they hadn't landed on the side where the hatch was, she pulled herself over the canted seat toward the ladder.

''Elrabin!'' she called. ''You okay?''

No answer. From the hold she could hear moaning and weeping. She looked sideways down the ladder and saw a tangled mess of bodies. Most were moving. People were trying to sit up. She looked for Elrabin and Paket, but saw neither of them.

Fear made her cold. ''Elrabin!'' she called again, more sharply this time.

Nothing.

She scrambled down the ladder as best she could and dropped into the hold. To her relief, the hatch was now overhead. She pushed her way through the others, stepping over those still on the floor, and jumped until she managed to hit the hatch release over her.

With a grinding groan of tortured metal, it opened

partway and stopped. The sweet smell of mountain air, tainted with smoke, reached her nostrils.

She turned around and saw someone she recognized. "Kuma!" she called to the striped male Aaroun. "You climb out first, then help the others as I boost them."

His restraints were off, and he was rubbing his wrists. "No good," he said. "They're right on top of us. We got no chance."

"Shut up!" she said angrily, giving someone a shove. "Just do as I say and *try.* All of you, listen to me. Get out and run in different directions. Scatter; don't stay bunched together. Hide in the undergrowth and keep moving. They can't get all of you. Now, move!"

Moska, streaked with grease, came bounding through the confusion. He pushed past Ampris and jumped for the semiopen hatch, catching the edge with his fingers and swinging there. She boosted him from beneath.

"Now, wait there and help pull up the others," she said.

Moska eeled himself on top of the hatch, peered down at her briefly, and vanished without a word.

"Moska!" She snapped shut her jaws angrily and didn't waste her breath trying to call him back. "One out. Come on, the rest of you! Move!"

Kuma shoved a Kelth female ahead of him and lifted her up. She squirmed and struggled, but finally made it out.

Her scream paralyzed them all. "The patrollers are here!"

The glare of a spotlight outlined the edges of the hatch. Ampris gripped Kuma's arm, jolting him on purpose.

"Keep them moving."

"They'll kill us, pick us off one by one as we come out," he said.

She glared at him. "You fool! You're more valuable to them alive. Now get out of here and run for it."

Others moved past Kuma, struggling and boosting each other. But the big Aaroun continued to stare at Ampris, fear plain to see in his eyes.

"If we get free, how will we live?" he asked. "Without a master, who will feed us? What will we do?"

"I'll teach you," she said in exasperation. She was still looking around for Elrabin and Paket, and at last she saw them, crumpled together against a storage bin.

Forgetting Kuma, she rushed to them and knelt beside Elrabin. A gash on his head bled freely, but he was breathing. She patted his face gently, trying not to weep with relief.

"Elrabin," she said, "wake up. You must wake up."

He moaned but didn't open his eyes. She checked him swiftly for other injuries, finding no broken bones.

Paket, however, was dead. Sprawled there, his body was already growing cold and stiff. She saw the wound that Elrabin had concealed from her and knew that Paket must have died almost instantly, perhaps before she even got the shuttle off the ground.

Grief filled her. She sobbed once, and choked it back. Paket had been so sensible, so good. He had worked hard, helped everyone, supported her loyally. He had come here tonight to help rescue her, and he had lost his life in the process.

She bowed her head, keening in her throat. Not like this. He was old. His life had been hard. He should have been allowed to die peacefully in his old age, surrounded by his friends.

A loudspeaker blared outside, ordering the slaves to surrender. Ampris looked up, coming to herself. With a sniff, she tried to put aside her emotions.

Elrabin was coming around, blinking groggily and holding a hand to his bleeding head. "Somethin' blue ri' for us," he mumbled, not making any sense.

She focused on him, realizing he needed her help. There was nothing she could do now for Paket.

Swiftly she pulled Elrabin up on his feet and put her shoulder under his arm. His head lolled and he mumbled something else she could not make out. Then he went limp, nearly dragging her down.

She hoisted him up again, patting his face. "Elrabin, come on!" she said urgently.

Only two other slaves were not yet out. Kuma boosted a Myal up, then turned to Ampris.

He held out his hand. "You go up. I'll lift him to you."

She nodded, grateful for his help, and after she sat Elrabin on the floor, where he immediately slumped over, she stepped into Kuma's hand and let him boost her.

She caught the edges of the hatch and pulled herself out on top into the warm night air. The spotlight no longer shone on the hatch. Instead, she could see it sweeping back and forth as the shuttle flew in pursuit of the scattering slaves. The patrollers were working to round them up, but while a few slaves had stopped and surrendered, most of them were trying to run in all directions as Ampris had suggested.

She grinned, knowing some would make it. Once the patrollers gave up and left, she would try to find the escaped slaves and help them. They would need to be trained in survival skills. Freedom was not easy. From experience she knew some of them would die in the wilderness. Some would give up and turn themselves back in. Others would make it, as she and her little group had.

"Ampris!"

It was Kuma.

She looked down and saw him struggling to lift Elrabin's unconscious body. Bracing herself, she reached down and grabbed the Kelth under his arms. She lifted, feeling the strain in her back and shoulders, while Kuma kept boosting from below. Finally she managed to pull

Elrabin out and roll him over onto the side of the shuttle. Then she reached down to Kuma.

"Give me your hand," she said.

He jumped, clasping her hand, and she pulled with all her might.

Kuma came scrambling out and perched there beside her, puffing hard. "Not much time," he said.

Ampris heard the muffled roar of the shuttle engines as the craft started back in their direction. She snarled at it and reached for Elrabin.

Kuma pushed her gently back. "Get on the ground and I'll lower him to you."

"Thanks."

She slid down the metal and dropped lightly to the ground. Kuma lowered Elrabin's body to her, and she hugged the unconscious Kelth in her arms, supporting his weight while Kuma slid down.

"This way," she said.

But the shuttle was close, sweeping the spotlight back and forth. Kuma draped Elrabin across her shoulder.

"You go, while you can," he said.

"That way," she said, pointing toward a stand of trees. "There's a canyon not far from here. I was heading there when we crashed. We can—"

"No," Kuma said. "I will distract them, while you take your friend to safety."

"We stick together."

"Do not argue," he told her. "You do not give the orders here."

"But, Kuma—"

"Our paths do not lie together," he said. "I have been a slave all my life. I do not hate it. I would be lost out here, without work, without order."

"But, Kuma—"

"Ampris, go," he said.

He started away from her, and she tried to block his

path. "We can make it," she said urgently. "You must try."

"Why?" he said harshly, glaring at her as the shuttle came closer. "You believe in freedom? Then give me freedom to make my own choice. Go!"

He shoved her, and Ampris bit back her protests. Swiftly she turned and hurried away as fast as she could carry Elrabin's weight. Hobbling and snarling over the pain in her bad leg, she was attempting to make cover when the spotlight caught her in its bright glare.

She kept moving, refusing to freeze in place, and expected a shot to take her down at any moment.

Kuma shouted and went running out into the full glare of the spotlight. Waving his arms, he stopped and gestured at the shuttle, then placed his hands atop his head in surrender.

The spotlight swung his way, and orders blared from the loudspeaker.

Ampris reached the trees and melted into the undergrowth, taking cover swiftly. She looked back only once, in time to see a net of restraint rope settling down over Kuma, imprisoning him while he stood there passively.

Grief mingled with anger filled her. Her vision blurred, and she blinked the tears away. Setting her face in the opposite direction, she hurried away with her burden. She would never understand someone like Kuma, someone who wanted to be cared for at the awful price of being a slave. Never, never would she understand it.

CHAPTER FOUR

At daybreak, Ampris came staggering into camp with Elrabin hanging over her shoulder. Exhausted and aching, she halted and drew in several ragged breaths before letting Elrabin slide gently to the ground. He was still unconscious. The gash in his head had finally stopped bleeding, but he looked terrible, with blood dried across his face and splattered on his coat. He had not regained consciousness in the last few hours, and Ampris was extremely worried about him.

She crouched beside him, and gripped his slack hand. "Stay with me, old friend."

He lay there, unmoving, his mouth open. Flies buzzed about him, and she shooed them away before standing up with a muffled groan. Holding up her arms, she stretched her tired muscles.

Before she'd come into camp she'd known it was deserted. The place was too quiet. All the scents were old and fading. But now she wandered around, studying the evidence of hasty departure. Dirt had been thrown on the cooking fires, the stones scattered. Their shelters still stood, but had been cleared of possessions.

Ampris limped over to Elrabin's shelter and checked it, but Velia had left nothing behind, not a scrap of cloth or a blanket or a crudely made cup of bark. Sighing,

Ampris entered her tent, noticing that a mended place had come unstitched again. The wind was pulling at the tear, widening it.

Looking around, she saw that her sons had been less than thorough. Belongings lay scattered. They had left behind spare clothing and the cooking pot. Her vid player had been taken, along with her bedroll. But her little wooden box of treasures remained, tossed carelessly on the ground.

Picking it up, Ampris opened it and saw the clear stone of her necklace inside. Breathing out in relief, she slipped the Eye of Clarity around her throat, and clutched the stone in her hand. At once she felt calmer, more in control of herself. She rubbed her head in weariness, resisting the need to lie down and sleep.

Instead, she picked up the tattered blanket her sons had abandoned and carried it outside to spread over Elrabin. She had left him lying beneath the shade of a cetex tree, and she saw no reason to move him now.

She carried her cooking pot to the nearby stream, which gurgled and splashed over the boulders, filled the pot with cold water, and took it back to Elrabin. She tried to trickle some of the liquid into his mouth.

He swallowed some of it, then let the rest spill. Ampris settled herself beside him and began washing the dried blood off his face. She was almost finished when a shift in the wind brought her a smell that made the hair on her neck bristle.

Sniffing, she stood up and turned in that direction. With only a single glance back at Elrabin, she limped swiftly out of the camp into the trees and climbed to a mossy knoll a short distance away.

Stopping there, she glanced around, casting for the scent. It was strong here, but confused. She noticed the ground had been scuffed up, as though a struggle had gone on. A wadded cloth lay beneath a bush.

Ampris studied it, then straightened. "Tantha?" she called softly.

A growl came from behind some bushes on her right. Ampris approached cautiously. The birth smell was fresh. She knew Tantha would be sore and exhausted, but still very dangerous.

"Tantha?" she called again, keeping her voice quiet and gentle.

The growling grew louder, warning her away. Ampris parted the bush and peered into a small hollow, where a bedraggled Tantha lay curled around her newborn cubs. Ampris counted four, plus another—clearly dead—lying off to one side beneath some leaves.

Ampris went to it first and carefully scooped up the poor creature. Tantha had made an effort to clean it, but the little one was not properly formed. Probably it had been born dead. Cupping her hands around its tiny body, Ampris bowed her head and whispered the Aaroun prayer of grieving, then she carried it away and buried it.

When she returned, Tantha was sitting up, looking wild-eyed and afraid. She blinked when she saw Ampris.

"You!" she said in her gruff way. "I thought I dreamed you here."

Ampris reached out and rubbed Tantha between her ears. "No," she said with compassion. "I have buried your dead cub."

"Ah." Tantha's eyes filled with tears, and her lips drew back in a snarl. She began to rock from side to side, grieving in silence.

Careful not to touch the living cubs, Ampris embraced her. "Do not grieve," she said. "Do not grieve. The little one is safe. You have others to care for now. Think of the living, who need you, *chenith-fahn.*"

Tantha lifted her face and sniffed. Tear tracks streaked the fur of her muzzle. "What does that mean?"

Ampris smiled at her. "New mother."

Tantha began to weep again. "I miss Morlol. He would have held me now. He would have named our cubs."

"Hush, hush," Ampris said, holding her closer. "This is a day to be glad, not to weep. They look strong and healthy. How many of each?"

"Three females and one male," Tantha said, still weeping. She rubbed her face and lifted her drenched gaze to Ampris's. "How will I feed them? How will I—"

"We will all help you raise them," Ampris assured her. "There will be enough. We are all one family."

Tantha growled and flattened her ears. "Who?" she demanded. "They are gone, all of them! They ran like fehtans, the moment there was trouble."

Ampris stiffened. "Trouble, here?"

"No, but the patrollers were sweeping the lower hills all night. We heard them. We saw the lights. Velia wanted to run at once."

"That's the rule," Ampris said.

"I would have fought," Tantha declared, baring her teeth.

"But you were too near your time. It is sometimes best to be cautious."

"They left me!" Tantha said, spitting the words. "We were fleeing together, and then my birthing pains came. No one would stay with me. If the patrollers had come up this far, they would have found me and killed me."

"Hush! It didn't happen," Ampris said quickly, trying to calm her.

One of the cubs began to mew.

When Tantha didn't immediately respond, Ampris took her clenched fist and forced it down to the cub, which rooted blindly against it.

"Let her learn your smell," Ampris said.

Slowly Tantha's fist uncurled. The fierceness in her eyes faded. Gazing down, she caressed her tiny spotted daughter, and her rigid muscles relaxed. When she began to croon softly to the little ones, Ampris backed away.

Tantha's head snapped up in fresh alarm. "Ampris!"

Ampris turned back immediately. "I won't leave you. I promise," she said. "I must check on Elrabin. He's hurt."

The fear vanished from Tantha's eyes. "Hurt? How bad?"

"I don't know yet," Ampris replied truthfully. "Let me make sure he doesn't need anything, then I will return."

"I must move my cubs back to camp," Tantha said. She tried to stand up and shuddered, sinking down again.

Ampris hurried to her side and gripped her shoulders. "Stay here," she said firmly. "You are not well enough yet to move."

"But I—"

"We will move your cubs to the camp. We will take care of them, and they will be fine," Ampris assured her. "I will help you. I promise. Now stay here and rest until I come back. You must gather all the strength you can. Will you do that?"

Tantha met her eyes, still looking rebellious, but after a moment she nodded. "I will."

"Good." Ampris gave her a pat. "Rest and do not fear. I will take care of you."

By evening she had Tantha and her cubs settled in their shelter. She boiled water and helped Tantha wash herself so that she could rest better. As twilight gathered in dark indigo shadows beneath the trees and closed in on the camp, Ampris picked up Elrabin and moved him into his shelter. He had fever and muttered restlessly, tossing about. She tried again to give him water. After a few swallows he quietened for a while. Ampris doused her fire and settled herself to rest a short time. She was so tired she could not hold her eyes open. Yet after a couple of hours of deep sleep, she jerked awake and listened.

The noise came again, a muffled whimper.

Ampris rose immediately and checked on her patients. She found Tantha sleeping with her cubs, but Elrabin's fever seemed higher. He was sitting up, staring into the darkness.

Ampris coaxed him into lying down again and spent the rest of the night sitting beside him, doing what she could to ease his fever and misery, and dozing in between times.

By dawn, her neck was stiff and sore, and she hurt all over. Her own graze was not healing well. It looked puffy and her arm felt hot. Ampris went off to the stream to clean it properly. She knew she could not afford to fall ill herself. Her cubs had taken her hunting sling, so she went off to hunt without it.

She did not mean to venture so far or be gone so long, but when she finally came climbing up out of the canyon and ascended the trail into camp, she carried a plump grassen hen by its feet. She had snared it at the hen's main nesting place, where she'd managed to steal some eggs as well, which were carefully placed inside her pocket. She was coated with dust and had twigs and leaves tangled in her fur, but tonight she and her patients would eat well.

Before she reached camp, she caught the smell of Viis. At once her neck fur bristled and her lips drew back in a silent snarl. Keeping to cover, she slipped up to the clearing. But it was Harthril who emerged from her tent, not patrollers. The tall Reject wore a tattered jerkin and hood that concealed his features. His hunting axe hung at his belt, along with his water skin and a serviceable knife. Whatever he'd been searching for, he evidently had not found it, for his hands were empty.

Ampris stepped out from the trees and said, "What are you looking for, Harthril?"

He spun around, his hand reaching for his knife before he recognized her. Straightening, he stared, shoving back his hood to reveal his mottled rill and scrawny neck.

His blue eyes swept over her, noticing the grassen dangling from her hand. He gave her a tiny nod of approval. "Thought you were dead."

"I'm not." She'd never distrusted him since he and Luax had joined their group, but Harthril could be unpredictable at times. "Where are the others?"

"Safe."

She allowed herself to savor the momentary luxury of relief. Since her return she'd kept busy in order not to let herself worry too much about Foloth and Nashmarl. Still, Harthril was never one to talk much. He answered only direct questions and volunteered almost nothing. She had to make sure.

"Are all of them well?" she asked. "Everyone accounted for?"

His tongue flickered out, but he did not evade the question. "No. Tantha left behind. But she is here."

"Yes, and very angry at being abandoned," Ampris said. "Did you lose anyone else?"

"No."

"My cubs?"

He hesitated a moment. "Safe."

"Any trouble?"

Harthril's blue eyes stared at her a long moment. "I found Elrabin, much hurt," he said, evading her question. "Where is Paket?"

Her shoulders slumped. "Dead."

His rill rose up behind his head, but he displayed no other emotion. "This is a great loss to us."

Guilt mixed with grief washed over her. "The patrollers shot him while we were escaping. He should have stayed here in camp."

"Velia says he volunteered to help rescue you. Elrabin would not wait until my return."

Ampris nodded. "And now Paket is dead and Elrabin is hurt. I feel responsible. They should have both stayed here."

But as she said it, she knew how relieved she'd been to see them.

"We now have others to feed," Harthril said, shifting the conversation.

She lifted her gaze to his. "Others? You mean some of the field slaves?"

He gestured assent.

"How many?"

"Too many to feed."

She sighed. "We'll manage. Once they learn to hunt—"

"More patrollers in the fields today. Maybe come back into hills with sniffers," Harthril said. "Too close. Too risky. Fires drive game away maybe. Not much game left to hunt anyway. We must go."

"I agree. But we must wait until Elrabin and Tantha are well enough to travel. Is anyone else hurt?"

"Robuhl fell and hurt leg."

She backed her ears. "Can he walk?"

"He cries."

Pity touched her. The poor old creature had outgrown his own wits. Now he was as helpless and simple as an infant. "We'll have to carry him."

"Carry Elrabin too?"

"Maybe. He has fever, and I'm not sure if he will recover."

Harthril's tongue flickered out. He stepped closer and rested his hand briefly on Ampris's shoulder, surprising her again.

"You cured Luax of the wasting sickness. You will cure Elrabin," he said with assurance. "Stay here. I will bring others tomorrow. We will talk then of where to go."

Ampris watched him leave the camp and melt into the

undergrowth with smooth expertise. She wished she could share his confidence.

Tantha appeared in the doorway of her shelter, cradling one of her sleeping cubs on her shoulder. "Is he gone?" she asked, her voice a husky growl.

"Yes."

"Good. I will forgive none of them!"

"Tantha—"

"You have food. Good. I am hungry."

Tantha vanished inside her shelter. Ampris backed her ears but decided to say nothing at the moment. Tantha had been hard to deal with ever since her mate died, but she needed to remember she wasn't the center of the universe. Still, Ampris remembered how she'd felt during pregnancy and after giving birth. She found a wellspring of sympathy for Tantha and went off to clean and cook the grassen.

Tantha came outside, pacing back and forth while the grassen finished cooking. Delectable smells filled the air. Ampris's mouth was watering. She could barely keep herself from grabbing the fowl off the fire and tearing it into pieces. But eating an underdone grassen was like chewing wood.

Mewing sounds of curiosity caught her attention. She turned her head and saw the cubs venturing past the doorway of the shelter. Their eyes had opened today, and now they came crawling out, wobbly and adorable. All were spotted except the little male. His coat was light brown in hue, but it had no markings of any kind.

Ampris left her cooking fire and went to scoop him up. Cuddling him close, she smiled into his wide eyes and slid her finger beneath his tiny chin. He snuggled closer to her, but Tantha appeared at Ampris's side and grabbed him. Draping him behind her neck, she gave Ampris a brief but hostile glance of warning and walked away to gather up her other wandering cubs.

Baring her teeth, Ampris snarled silently at Tantha's

back and went back to her cooking. She worked busily, collecting the sizzling cooking juices in a small brass pot. It helped distract her mind from the welcome sensation of holding a tiny cub in her arms again. There was nothing equal to the joy of motherhood, nothing as precious as those first few days of communing between mother and infant: learning each other's smell, discovering deep and tender mutual love. Over the years, there had been a time or two when Ampris would have taken a mate, but the male Aarouns could not tolerate the physical ugliness of Foloth and Nashmarl enough to accept them as family. Both her sons needed a male figure in their lives, someone with brute strength to back up his authority. Elrabin tried his best to help her raise them, but they were now the same size as the Kelth and they refused to respect him as they should.

Her busy hands slowed and grew idle. She stared past the fire, caught by a feeling of intense loneliness. She missed her sons, missed their arguments and bickering, missed how clumsy they were, all elbows and feet, missed them surrounding her with hugs and growls, complaining constantly about how hungry they were, or begging her to get the portable vid player recharged so they could watch it. They were growing up semiferal, their manners rough except when it suited them to remember her instructions. Often she feared for them, feared what kind of world they would find when they grew up. They fit in nowhere except here, yet this was not the kind of life she had envisioned for them. What would the future give them, when they were neither Viis nor Aaroun, but instead some terrible mixture of both? Already they had often known the stinging cruelty of rejection and insult. She prayed nightly for them, while they snored on their side of the tent, asking that they might grow up strong and healthy, that they might grow into wisdom and good sense. For they would have to forge their own paths, would have to make their own place in a world that might not ever accept them.

"Goldie?"

Her name was spoken by a voice so weak she barely heard it.

Startled from her reverie, Ampris looked around and saw Elrabin leaning against the doorway of his shelter. Beneath the crooked bandage swathing his head, his bloodshot eyes stared at her.

"Elrabin!" She jumped to her feet and hurried over to him. "You shouldn't be up. Let me get you back to bed."

He tried to protest, but he was too weak to resist her. By the time she lowered him onto his blanket and covered him, he was falling asleep again. She sat beside him, holding his hand, until she was certain he was settled.

Returning to her dinner, she lifted the grassen off the fire and laid it on a flat, washed rock to cool. She mixed warm water with the cooking juices she'd collected and when the mixture was cool enough she awoke Elrabin and fed the broth to him.

He sipped eagerly, too weak to even hold up his head without help, and he fell asleep again before he finished all the broth. Ampris tucked the blanket around him and watched over his sleep a few moments longer. He seemed to be mending at last, and she was thankful to see this improvement.

When she emerged from his shelter, she found Tantha sitting on the ground, gnawing on the cooked grassen.

Ampris roared in outrage and rushed at Tantha. She knocked the food from Tantha's hands, and Tantha swiped back with an angry roar of her own. The rake of her claws across Ampris's wounded arm broke the last seal on Ampris's temper. She grabbed Tantha in a headlock and flipped her onto her back with enough force to knock the wind from the spotted Aaroun.

Tantha lay there, wheezing for breath. Ampris stood

over her with ears back and teeth bared. Tantha tried to sit up, but Ampris planted her foot on the Aaroun and held her down.

"I hunted that food," she said furiously.

Tantha's eyes held both anger and desperation. "I have cubs to feed."

"We were to share it," Ampris said. She moved her foot and stepped back, letting Tantha up. "Always I have shared. If you had any doubt you could have asked. There is no need to steal behind my back."

Panting, Tantha looked from Ampris to the food lying on the ground and said nothing.

"We are not barbarians," Ampris said. She picked up the grassen and dusted the grass and dirt off it. Expertly, she tore the still-warm carcass in half and tossed a share to Tantha.

The other Aaroun caught it and resumed eating, tearing off chunks of the white, juicy meat and almost gulping them whole.

Ampris waited, but it seemed Tantha had no intention of offering an apology. Disappointment sank through Ampris. After her kindness toward Tantha, she was hurt that Tantha could be so selfish.

Yet it had long been the tradition among slaves of all kinds to stand alone, to not help each other. The Viis encouraged this, wanting the abiru to betray and distrust each other so that never again would they unite and become a force to be reckoned with. Ampris had thought that among her own small community this trait could be changed, but it took only a crisis or the threat of starvation to tear all her progress down.

She ate slowly, unable to taste her meal while Tantha polished off every morsel and even crunched the bones to suck the marrow from them. When she finished, Tantha buried the bones neatly and walked away in silence.

Still fuming, Ampris put out the cooking fire and

cleaned up, then she went back to sit by Elrabin.

She was there, an hour or so later, holding his hand and softly singing over him when a figure appeared in the doorway of the small shelter.

"So," Velia's shrill voice said, "this is where I find my mate, in the arms of another female."

Ampris backed her ears in annoyance. She did not like Velia and had always considered her a poor choice for Elrabin, but she had never spoken against her, even when Elrabin occasionally asked her advice. Now she rose to her feet and silently pushed Velia outside.

Twilight was falling over the camp, and it seemed everyone had returned. From the corner of her eye she saw Foloth squatted on his haunches outside their tent, unpacking his pouch. Nashmarl, his hood thrown over his shoulders, was rushing back and forth among the crowd of familiar faces and strangers. He had Ampris's hunting sling in his hand and he was whirling it around his head recklessly. She hoped he had no stone in it, or he would surely hurt someone.

"You have no right to push me out of my own home," Velia was saying in Ampris's face, giving her no chance to rush off to greet her sons. "How dare you—"

"Elrabin is badly hurt," Ampris said. "Didn't Harthril tell you?"

"Yes, of course he told me," Velia said. Her golden-brown eyes glared at Ampris. "That's why we came back tonight. I knew Elrabin would run into trouble. It's your fault he's hurt."

"Yes," Ampris said calmly.

Velia blinked as though she hadn't expected Ampris to agree with her. She drew a deep breath, and tried to push past the Aaroun.

Ampris pushed her back, refusing to let her enter the shelter.

"Get out of my way!" Velia said shrilly. "You can't keep me out of my own—"

"You can go in when you calm down," Ampris told her. "Elrabin needs peace and quiet."

"He needs to be told how big a fool he is."

"I am very grateful to him," Ampris said. "He helped me get out of a bad situation."

Velia glared at her, firelight glinting off her eyes. "But you got him into that bad situation. *You,* Ampris. Always *you* thinking up something to cause us trouble."

Ampris backed her ears at the criticism. "I thought up the raid on that warehouse in Lazmairehl too, Velia. The one that set you free. Or have you forgotten that?"

Velia's tall ears twitched nervously. She hugged herself and would not look directly at Ampris. "You have no business tending my mate. I will take care of him."

Sighing, Ampris figured Velia's worry was making her act this way. Velia was usually in a bad mood, but tonight she acted worse than usual. She wasn't often this openly critical.

Ampris stepped aside and gestured at the shelter. "When he wakes up, I'm sure he'll be glad to see you. His fever has gone down. He only regained consciousness a short time ago, but he is sleeping again."

Muttering to herself, Velia pushed past Ampris and ducked into the shelter.

Glad to be rid of her, if only temporarily, Ampris turned her attention to more important matters. "Foloth!" she called, hurrying to her firstborn son.

At the sound of his name, Foloth rose to his feet and turned around. His dark eyes lit up and he ran to embrace her. "Mother!" he said in excitement. "We have had such adventures. Harthril made us break camp and we have been hiding from patrollers. Then we hunted, and then we caught these wandering slaves. They don't know anything," he whispered solemnly. "They can't figure out which berries to look for, and they don't even know how to pluck the feathers off grassens.''

While he spoke, Ampris was busy stroking the thin, downy fur on the rounded back of his misshapen head. She nuzzled his neck and jaw, breathing in the scent of him, finding reassurance that he was safe and sound.

''They can't do anything,'' he finished.

''Yes, of course they can,'' she said mildly, hoping no one had overheard what he said. Foloth was entirely too serious for his own good. He saw things in black and white, and had little patience in considering other points of view. She rubbed the top of his head, where his fur was almost nonexistent. He had the pebble-grained skin of a Viis, and did not burn in the sun the way his brother did. ''Foloth,'' she said, ''you cannot expect them to have the same skills that you do. Their life has been very different from yours, until now. We will have to teach them to be self-sufficient here in the wild.''

''A waste of time,'' he said dismissively. ''Where did they come from, anyway?''

''I helped free them,'' Ampris replied. She noticed that most of the newcomers were staring at her now, and turned around to face them. She kept her arm around Foloth's shoulders and smiled. ''Welcome to our camp,'' she said.

A few smiled back, but most looked uncertain and wary. She counted about seven former slaves. All of them were Kelths, predominantly female. Moska, she noted, was not among them, and she wondered if the youth had escaped or been captured.

''You have met my companions,'' she said to them, giving nods to Luax and Harthril, who stood slightly apart from everyone else. Old Robuhl had seated himself on the ground with his long, prehensile tail curled around his neck. His rheumy eyes shifted and glimmered in the firelight while he muttered to himself. ''We are a small group, dedicated to living free of Viis rule. Our way of life is not easy. We have no luxuries, no conveniences. We live far from vids or government-supplied food. But we can speak our own language and teach our young our own histories. We work for ourselves and call no one master.

"If you will live peaceably among us, if you will contribute your share of work to the group, then you may stay with us as long as you wish. We are nomads, forced to move whenever the game grows scarce. We seldom venture too close to cities or towns. If at any time you wish to leave us, you are free to do that. You are free to do anything you want, as long as you bring no harm to us. Any questions?"

The ex-slaves exchanged glances. One of them murmured to another, and a gray-furred Kelth female stepped forward. "I be called Frenshala."

"Welcome, Frenshala," Ampris said formally. "What is your question?"

"You be leader here?"

Ampris hesitated. After Velia's unexpected hostility and Tantha's foul mood, she felt a certain tension in the air. Even Luax and Harthril were hanging back more than usual. She glanced around for Nashmarl, but the cub had vanished.

Facing Frenshala again, Ampris replied, "Yes, I am leader, after a fashion."

"What work will we do here?"

"That is your choice. Everyone has chores to do."

"What will be *our* work?" Frenshala insisted.

Ampris realized she probably had never been without orders before. "At first, you should probably help with cleaning the camp area, mending clothing, and helping to prepare food. As you learn your way about, we will give each of you lessons in how to hunt. We all take turns in minding this old one." She gently touched Robuhl's white-maned head as she spoke.

He looked up at her with a smile. "Ampris!" he said proudly. "Savior of the people!"

Slightly embarrassed, she gave him a pat and looked at Frenshala. "Anything else?"

"Where are our quarters?"

"Tonight you will have to sleep in the open," Ampris said. "We will help you make your own shelters tomorrow—"

"No," Harthril said, stepping forward. His blue Viis eyes shone in the firelight like jewels. "Not tomorrow. We go. Break camp quick."

Ampris looked at him. "Do you think the sniffers will come this far into the hills?"

"Maybe. They come back for more searching today. Could mean trouble for us."

Luax raised her hand. She was extremely thin, even for a Viis female. Her head seemed too large for her spindly neck, and her skin had pronounced streaks of pink variegated with green. She talked even less than Harthril, but now she, too, stepped forward. "Cut out their implants," she said.

Agitated yipping broke out among the ex-slaves, and even Frenshala became alarmed, drawing back into the group with her arms held tight against her.

"That is their choice," Ampris said hastily, afraid Luax was going to frighten them into fleeing. "Always we have let people choose."

"Not now," Luax said firmly, making a chopping gesture with her hand. "Not when danger comes close."

"You can't!" Frenshala said fearfully. "You will kill us."

Ampris backed her ears and looked at the Kelth in dismay. "Are you saying you have ion-release tattoos?"

"Paket has one," Foloth said beside her. "It can't be eradicated."

She felt the loss anew and searched the crowd for a glimpse of Nashmarl. Since the days when Nashmarl had crawled about Vess Vaas with only a ball made from rags to play with, he had been fond of the old Kelth. Had Harthril not told them that Paket was dead?

She looked at the Reject, but he was puffing his air sacs in and out, looking very serious indeed.

When he said nothing, she prompted him. "Tattoos or implants? Have you looked?"

Harthril's rill stiffened about his head. "They would not let us."

"You will hurt us," Frenshala said.

Some of the Kelths began to wail and yip louder.

"Hush that noise," Ampris said, aware that their shrill voices could carry a kilometer or more if they really got wound up. "We have no intention of hurting you. Once we know what kind of registration mark you have, we can decide what to do."

"You lie," Frenshala said, baring her teeth. "You said that we decide, that there be nothing we don't have to do. Now you say different. Better we go back to master."

Ampris took a step forward. "No, please—"

They backed away from her, glancing at the dark trees beyond the circle of firelight. Exasperated, Ampris tried to figure out what to say that would calm them.

Tantha appeared from the gloom with a suddenness that made several Kelths jump. "You aren't going anywhere," she said to them, growling fiercely. The spotted fur around her neck stood out in a ruff. "You run back to your master, and you'll betray us to save your own miserable hides."

Ampris glared at the Aaroun. Threats weren't going to help. "You have no master to return to," she said, trying to keep her voice calm and reassuring. "He has lost his farm to government confiscation. I told you that when we were penned."

"We know about life out here, life in the wild," Frenshala said. Her eyes shifted back and forth nervously.

"Plants that be poison. Wild animals that kill. No water. No food. No shelter. We will die, and you—"

"I have lived in the wilderness for twelve years," Ampris said. "I have raised my cubs out here without modern conveniences. You will be safe once you learn how to hunt and what to gather. The drought has made it harder to find clean water, but we—"

"We want to go," Frenshala said wildly. "We want to go *now*!"

"You will betray us," Tantha said, her eyes agleam.

The Kelths backed away, clearly getting ready to dash into the darkness. Once out there, Ampris knew, they could get lost or they could fall into a canyon and be hurt or they might wander all the way down to the base of the hills and likely run into patrollers.

Anxious to stop them, Ampris held up her Eye of Clarity so that the firelight caught it and flashed through the clear center of the stone. "Look at this!" she ordered.

Some turned their backs on her, but one or two, Frenshala among them, glanced her way.

"This stone is called an Eye of Clarity," Ampris said, letting her voice ring out. "Have you ever heard of it? Do you know what it is?"

Frenshala shuddered and flattened her tall ears to her skull. "Mind-catcher. No one look at it!"

"It's perfectly safe," Ampris said. She let it spin, flashing refracted firelight. "It is a symbol from the past, when all the abiru folk were free, living on their own planets. It is a symbol of peace, harmony, and strength."

She talked, keeping her voice steady and persuasive. From her old training as a gladiator she had learned how to pitch and modify her voice, for her past masters had used certain voice commands to work her into a killing frenzy. But if the voice could be used to awaken savage instincts, it could also be used to persuade and pacify. She had learned, through long nights when her young cubs suffered nightmares and could not sleep, how to channel calm through her voice. If she held the Eye of Clarity it seemed to amplify whatever emotion she was trying to instill in others.

She used that self-taught skill now, calming the Kelths, making them listen to her.

"Sometimes, the Eye is considered a symbol of our hope that all abiru may live free," she said to them. "We have no intention of harming you. That is not our way. We have welcomed you among us. We offer you a community where no one is master, but all are equal. Before you run back to Viis oppression and cruelty, at least consider what we offer you."

The Kelths were all staring at her now with solemn, intent expressions. Silence lay over the camp, except for the sound of Ampris's voice.

"It is our way to discuss all the options open to us, but no decision is made until we vote on it. We were discussing removal of your implants for your own safety, but you will not be forced to do anything against your will." Ampris met Frenshala's wary eyes. "This I, Ampris, do swear by the life of my own sons."

She lowered her arm and slipped the pendant back over her head. No one spoke.

Then Harthril held out both of his hands, palms up. "We mean no harm to you. I swear by the life of my mate Luax, whose life Ampris saved."

Luax raised her rill halfway and also turned her palms up. "With us you be welcome."

It was Tantha's turn to speak, but she only stood there and growled.

Frenshala glanced at her companions. They whispered among each other for a few moments, then Frenshala walked over to Ampris. "For us, trust is not easy. We did not ask for freedom. We do not think it such a good thing."

"You will learn to cherish it," Ampris said to her.

"Maybe. For now, we stay. But no more talk of cutting us!"

"All right," Ampris said, giving in. She glanced at Harthril, who flicked out his tongue.

"If no remove implants, then we go," the Reject said. "Must go."

Ampris nodded. "Yes, tomorrow or the next day we should break camp and—"

"No," Harthril said, more urgently. "Go tonight. Go fast."

Ampris blinked at him in surprise. "Why?"

"Because the patrollers are still searching," Velia said, emerging from her shelter. "Because Harthril thinks they will set their sniffer range to maximum, and it might pick up our presence here. Because, thanks to you, we aren't safe anymore."

"We have wounded," Ampris protested. "We should wait at least until daybreak—"

"What happened down there?" Harthril asked her. His blue eyes bored into hers. "Why they so determined to get you back?"

Ampris hesitated a moment, stunned by his question. "No one recognized me," she said. "They want all the slaves. The group would bring good prices at auction—"

"Patrollers raid, search a little, then move off," Harthril broke in. "Don't keep searching and searching. Something else is reason now."

"I don't know what it is," Ampris said.

He gave her a flat look of disbelief.

Ampris's puzzlement grew. Something in the air seemed wrong. The tension she had sensed earlier was stronger. She broke away from Harthril's gaze to look at the others.

Nashmarl's face peered at her from behind the Kelth newcomers. Foloth crouched on the ground beside Robuhl, petting the old Myal absently. The look in Foloth's eyes made her back her ears suspiciously.

"What is going on?" Ampris asked.

Velia came up to her. "You have become a problem for us," she said without preamble.

"What?"

"You," Velia said, pointing. "It was your idea that we come into this region in the first place."

Ampris glanced around again and saw their faces, harsh with criticism and blame. The newcomers were wide-eyed spectators. Velia's attack would only unsettle them more, but then Velia had never known when to time anything.

In annoyance, Ampris squared her shoulders and faced Velia again. "We all agreed to come," she said. "We discussed it. There was no game left where we—"

"But it was your idea to come here," Velia insisted. "Here, nearer to Viis settlements, where trouble is close to us all the time."

"But we—"

"And it was your idea to raid the fields," Velia said. "We all thought it was too risky, but you insisted. Elrabin told me you had enough grain stolen early in the day, but you wanted more. Your greed got you into trouble, and you dragged Elrabin and Paket into it. Now look what has come of it. We are all in danger."

"Yes, I made a mistake," Ampris said. "But the plan was working—"

"We have no food," Velia said. "Where is all the stelf we were supposed to be eating? Elrabin brought us four heads. Four! To feed all of us. And at what price? Paket's death?"

"Enough!" Ampris roared. She glared at Velia, then at the others. "Yes, the cost was too high. I grieve for Paket. I blame myself for what happened to him. But—"

"We must leave tonight," Harthril interrupted her.

Ampris looked at him with her ears flat against her skull. She looked at Velia. She looked at her sons, watching her in wide-eyed silence. "Traveling at night is dangerous," she said.

"You are no longer a good leader for us, Ampris," Velia said. "You should no longer give orders."

"And who should lead us instead?" Ampris retorted. "You?"

Velia pivoted and pointed at Harthril. "Him. At least he is not wanted by the patrollers. They know who you are. They must know. Otherwise, they would go away."

Ampris snarled at her and shook her head, but inside she began to have her own doubts. Maybe the fat overseer had recognized her. He'd been too interested in her all along. If Kuma remembered who she was, others probably would as well. For years she had hoped she was believed killed in the Vess Vaas explosion, but perhaps there was still a reward for her.

"Now you see, Ampris," Tantha said. "They betrayed me. Now they turn on you. Fine family we have."

"We vote now," Velia said, her eyes fierce and excited. "Harthril or Ampris."

In moments it was settled. Ampris stood there, swallowing the sting of rejection, and telling herself perhaps it was better if Harthril took over.

The tall Reject came forward into the firelight and swept his blue gaze around at them all. His rill was flushed a faint pink, but otherwise he appeared as calm as ever. "Hah," he said. "We pack up camp now. We go."

Despite herself, Ampris had to speak up. "What of our wounded? Elrabin is hurt. Robuhl is hurt. Tantha has just given birth and is not yet strong. Is anyone else injured?"

Nashmarl came to her then, tugging at her arm.

"Mother, I'm tired," he said. "I don't want to walk all night."

Harthril overheard and his rill stiffened, turning a darker shade of red.

"I'm not trying to undermine your authority," she told him. "I just want to know how we're to carry the injured—"

"Not care how it is done," Harthril broke in harshly, flicking out his tongue. "Just that we go fast. We go now."

"But—"

"Ampris," he said with exasperation. "I make decisions now. Keep your place."

CHAPTER FIVE

Daybreak dawned hot and still, with not even a stir of the usual hot, dry wind to offer them relief. Following a long, arduous climb, they reached the top of a broad mesa while the brassy sun was rising above the horizon. Harthril called a halt, and with groans of relief, the group sank down to rest.

Ampris sat next to a scratchy bush whose leaves were curled and dead. Foloth and Nashmarl joined her without having to be called. Foloth crouched beside her on his haunches, but Nashmarl flopped flat on the ground and flung his arm across his eyes.

"I'm thirsty," he complained.

"It isn't time yet for another sip," Ampris said to him. Tipping back her head, she inhaled deeply and sifted through the mixture of scents that filled her nostrils. "There's no water source up here. We must be conservative."

Foloth closed his eyes, yawning.

Nashmarl sat up and glared at Ampris as though it were her fault. "Figures," he said and turned his back on her.

She ignored his complaints. Both cubs were exhausted, and she felt drained by weariness. They had walked all night, the adults taking turns carrying Elrabin and Robuhl. Now in the rose-gilded light of early morning, they needed a good, easily defended camping spot where everyone could rest during the hot hours of the day. But this mesa offered no site that Ampris considered suitable. There was no running water that she could smell. Without water, there would be no game to hunt. The flat ground looked scorched and brown. Almost no vegetation grew except the low scrub, and even most of it looked dead. She could see for kilometers in every direction, as though she'd reached the top of the world. Which meant anyone else who searched here would see them. Why Harthril had chosen to bring them up here, she could not understand.

But she was no longer the leader. No longer the one who made the decisions.

Ampris sighed, telling herself to rest. But she could not. Although she sat there quietly while her cubs slept, her mind continued to work over their problems. She turned her weary, burning eyes in Harthril's direction, wondering what he meant to do now.

The Reject stood a short distance away, his back to Ampris. The rising sun cast a long spindly shadow from him. Deep in conversation with Luax, his mate, Harthril did not seem tired. His rill stood extended behind his head, and his gaze remained locked on his mate. Luax was pointing across the mesa and gesturing vehemently. Nodding, Harthril listened and occasionally flicked out his tongue.

A few minutes later, the word was passed along: They had to get up. They were going on.

Some of the Kelths yipped and wailed in protest. Ampris heard the disturbance as though from far away, then blinked herself from her doze and forced herself to her feet.

She bent over Foloth and Nashmarl, tugging at them. "Wake up," she said. "Wake up now and gather your gear."

Foloth opened his dark eyes and grimaced in mute protest.

"We're going on," Ampris told him. "Get up."

Foloth obeyed her, grumbling to himself, but Nashmarl lay on the ground with one arm still across his eyes. He refused to move.

Ampris nudged him harder with her toe. "Nashmarl," she said firmly. "Now."

He snarled. "I'm asleep. Go without me."

"Get up."

He snarled again and would not move.

Ampris glanced at Foloth, who shrugged. "Don't look at me, Mother. If he wants to stay behind and live on his own, we'd all be better off."

She swallowed the involuntary growl that rumbled in her throat. Bending down, she gripped Nashmarl by his clothing and hoisted him bodily to his feet.

Nashmarl's eyes flew open, and he yelped in startlement. But he was on his feet. Ampris released him, and he staggered to catch his balance.

Glaring at him, she pointed at his belongings. "Get your gear and move."

Anger brightened his green eyes. He opened his mouth, but Ampris turned away from him, too tired and grouchy to deal with his protests.

Around them, others were getting to their feet and picking up their crude pouches and bedrolls. Ampris saw Velia coaxing Elrabin. The Kelth looked shaky and unwell. He stood there, swaying, with one hand to his head. Compassion filled Ampris. She hated seeing her friend like this. He needed rest and care, not this forced march.

Wanting to help him, Ampris started in his direction, but Velia took his arm and gently got him walking. Ampris halted, backing her ears. Her mixed feelings confused her.

"Mother!" Foloth said sharply from behind her. "Nashmarl's got the water skin!"

Ampris swung around and saw Nashmarl clutching their precious water skin to his chest as he raced away.

"Nashmarl!" she called after him. "Come back!"

But he ignored her and darted all the way to the head of their scraggly column, positioning himself at Harthril's heels.

Ampris saw him tug at the Reject's sleeve and say something, but Harthril ignored the cub and lengthened his stride.

"Mother, he isn't supposed to have that," Foloth said huffily as the line formed and the Kelth ex-slaves shuffled past them. Foloth circled her, indignant. "He'll drink all our water and won't share it. You know how he is."

"I know," Ampris said wearily.

"You have to do something," Foloth insisted. "Make him bring it back."

Grimly she picked up her pack and slung it over her shoulders.

Foloth grabbed his bedroll and kicked Nashmarl's pack aside. "The idiot will be sorry tonight that he left this behind."

"Don't call your brother an idiot," Ampris reprimanded him automatically. "Take his pack for him."

"I won't!" Foloth said in outrage. "It's his responsibility. He took our water. Why should I carry his things?"

Ampris started counting to herself, trying to keep her temper. "Because I asked you to."

"Well, I won't do it," Foloth said. "It isn't fair. You're always taking his side."

Ampris picked up the pack that Nashmarl had abandoned. It was very heavy, and she wondered what he had put inside it. Nashmarl was apt to fill his pack with rocks and leave his clothing behind, if he wasn't watched. Resisting the urge to look inside, Ampris slung it over her shoulder.

Foloth watched her critically. "If you won't go get him I will," he said. "I'll make him behave, since you won't."

He started past her, but Ampris reached out and snagged his arm. Holding him back, she looked into his dark resentful eyes, Aaroun eyes that seemed so foreign in his Viis-like face. "You will join the line," she said firmly. "I'll take care of your brother."

Leaving him, she limped toward the head of the line, already panting from exertion in the heat.

Several of the Kelths glanced up as she passed them and muttered among themselves, but Ampris ignored them. She passed Velia and Elrabin, who was marching grimly along with his head down, saying nothing in response to Velia's constant chatter. For a few moments Ampris kept step with Tantha, who had her mewing cubs bundled in a blanket which she carried on her back.

The younger female Aaroun walked steadily, with her muzzle wrinkled in a snarl that betrayed her exhaustion. Ampris eyed her, knowing a forced march in this heat could render her unable to feed her cubs. She wanted to ask Tantha how she was doing, but in the end said nothing and hurried on.

Nashmarl was still skipping along at Harthril's and Luax's heels. Ampris could hear his nonstop chatter, which the Rejects ignored. In her heart, Ampris felt a pang of sadness at her poor, unlikable son. He never seemed to understand when his company was welcome and when it was not. He wanted so much to be liked and accepted, yet he could not be depended on. He was forgetful, irresponsible, and impulsive. He tended to say whatever popped into his head, whether appropriate or not. And he was both stubborn and willful. Ampris could see so many faults in him, yet she saw his potential too. Nashmarl was more sensitive than Foloth, more aware of people around him. His heart could be tender, and his passions ran deep. But, oh, he had so much yet to learn, so much growing up to do.

The Rejects were setting a hard pace, their long Viis legs seemingly tireless. Limping behind them, Ampris realized she could not catch up. "Luax," she called.

The female Reject glanced back and stopped at once, waiting until Ampris caught up with her. Nashmarl saw his mother, and defiance filled his green eyes. Tucking the water skin beneath his arm, he hurried on at Harthril's side.

"A well day be yours," Luax said formally, giving Ampris a nod.

Panting, Ampris smiled back. "A well day be yours too," she said, returning the Reject greeting. "It's already a hot one."

Luax let her rill droop upon her shoulders as she fell into step beside Ampris. "I was about to scout ahead for water. Can you smell any?"

"No. The mesa is dry," Ampris said. "And if there's no water, there'll be no hunting."

Luax flicked out her tongue. "This we feared. Better to keep going, keep moving fast."

"We can't force-march long in this heat," Ampris said. "Elrabin—"

"He is walking," Luax said without much sympathy.

"But that will sap his strength further. He needs—"

"Elrabin is Velia's worry," Luax said.

For a moment the two females locked eyes. Ampris was the first to look down. Her tongue felt dried inside her mouth. She had nothing else to say when Luax put it like that.

Then she saw Nashmarl taking a long drink from the water skin. Her frustration came boiling to the surface.

"Nashmarl!" she said sharply, hurrying to catch up with him.

Eluding her, he darted ahead of Harthril and pranced along, tipping back his head for another drink. Ampris broke into a hobbled run, favoring her bad leg, and caught him by one thin arm.

Shaking him, she jerked the water skin from his grasp, spilling a trail of the precious liquid in an arc across the ground. It darkened the dusty soil for only a few seconds, then dried up.

"You spilled it!" Nashmarl said angrily, twisting out of her grasp. "Not me. You did it."

She stoppered the skin firmly, then turned on him. She was furious with his behavior, but she didn't want to reprimand him in front of the whole group. "Come with me," she said.

"I don't want to."

"Nashmarl—"

"I don't want to!" he screamed at her. "This is where I always walk. Right behind the leader. You go back and eat dust all day. I'm staying here."

Growling, she gripped him by his shoulder and marched him off, giving him a little push every time he stopped or tried to protest.

"You can't make me walk back here with you," Nashmarl said as they joined Foloth at the rear of the line. "I don't belong here."

"Shut up," Foloth said. "You belong buried in a hole."

The cubs glared at each other and exchanged insulting grimaces.

Ampris didn't waste her breath arguing with him. She forced him to walk beside her, and pulled his hood up over his rounded head to protect him from the hot rays of the sun.

Nashmarl pulled his hood down again. "I don't want to wear this. It's hot. I'll smother back here in the dust."

"Shut up," Foloth said to him in a quiet, fierce voice. "You have no right to walk up there at the head of the line, now that Mother's been shamed."

Ampris turned on them both. She was aware of many

sets of ears flicked back in their direction, listening avidly to the scene they were creating, but the cubs had forced her to the limits of her patience. "Wait right there," she said sharply. "What do you mean, shamed?"

Neither cub would meet her eyes.

"I have not been shamed," she said.

"They canceled you as leader," Nashmarl burst out as though he could no longer contain himself. "They won't follow you anymore. They won't take orders from you."

"The vote was fair," Ampris said, understanding now why he was in such a bad mood. "We've had different leaders before."

"A long time ago," Foloth muttered. "Not since you took over."

"You killed Paket," Nashmarl said to her, blame and resentment burning in his voice. He glared at her. "Thanks to you, we—"

"Nashmarl, you will not speak to me in that tone," Ampris said, cutting him off. "My actions are not for you to judge."

"But if you hadn't gotten Paket in trouble, he wouldn't be dead." Nashmarl glared at her. "Everyone says so."

Nashmarl's words made her heart feel sliced open with fresh grief. Hiding her emotions, she met her son's hot, accusatory gaze. "Paket made his own decisions. He came to help me of his own free will."

"But you—"

"A patroller shot him," she said sharply, too sharply. "I didn't. Stop talking to me as though I did."

Nashmarl's mouth opened, but he said nothing else. His pale skin flushed pink from his jaws to the top of his skull.

At once, she was sorry for her harshness. She reached out and touched Nashmarl's shoulder, but he shrugged away from her. "I know you loved Paket," she said quietly. "I loved him too. I shall miss him deeply."

Nashmarl's green eyes blazed in his flattened face. "I don't love nobody," he muttered. "And nobody loves me."

Quickening his pace, he moved forward.

"Nashmarl," Ampris called after him. "You must stay with us."

Nashmarl ignored her and defiantly positioned himself in the middle of the line, among the Kelth newcomers.

Sighing, Ampris let him stay there. Some battles, she realized, could not be won. Her moody, temperamental son had no reason to feel ashamed on her behalf, but she never knew what was going to upset him. Now she limped along and stared ahead at the rounded back of her son's head, wishing he would stop being so stubborn and put up his hood. If his skin burned today, he would whimper and cry all night in pain.

When she glanced at Foloth, she saw the elder cub keeping pace with her easily. His wide mouth was set in a disapproving line. From time to time, he flicked a contemptuous glance her way.

"What is wrong with you?" she asked him finally.

"Nothing," he replied coldly.

"Are you sure?"

He looked up at her then with a flash of the anger he seldom unleashed. "You spoil him! You let him get away with everything."

I spoil you both, she thought. *Too much.* "Why must you be so jealous of each other?" she asked. "Nashmarl is grieving for Paket. Leave him be."

"See?" Foloth said in a what's-the-use tone. "You always take up for him. What about the water he wasted, and the—"

"Let me worry about that," Ampris said.

"But—"

"Foloth," she said in warning, and he fell into mutinous silence.

By mid-morning, the sun was a bronze orb in the sky that tried to bake the life from them. Trudging along in the heat, Ampris panted heavily and resisted the urge to relieve her thirst from the water skin. She felt as though her brain were melting. Beside her, Foloth lagged, clearly in physical distress, but saying nothing.

Finally Harthril called a halt, and they stopped. In any direction Ampris looked, she could see only the flat vista of the mesa with the sky arching overhead. No clouds, no trees, nothing to cast any shade. Still worried about shuttles, Ampris watched the sky. It remained empty. She smelled no smoke on the wind today, and felt slightly reassured. If the patrollers had finished burning all the fields, perhaps they were gone for good.

Luax, out scouting ahead, returned and conferred with Harthril, who then came and addressed them all.

"The edge of mesa is close, very close, if we go that way." He pointed in a direction perpendicular to the one they'd been headed. "Very steep off side. Very hard. Luax found trails, thinks we can follow if we be careful. Come. We get off mesa, then we can make camp and rest well. Come."

With moans and complaints, they climbed to their feet and started trudging in the new direction that Luax indicated.

But there was more noise now coming from the middle of the line where the Kelths walked. In a few minutes, raucous yipping broke out, which was swiftly silenced. Nashmarl left them and came loping back awkwardly to Ampris, his flattened face flushed with outrage.

More shrill yips of laughter came from the Kelths, and Nashmarl whipped his head around to glare at them, then took his place beside Ampris.

He would not look at her, but he stayed close at her

side. She gazed down at her ill-formed cub, so stiff and anguished, so obviously once again the butt of ridicule. With all her mother's heart she wished she could gather him in her arms and comfort him the way she had when he was small.

But Ampris did nothing, said nothing, knowing her questions would drive him away again. Instead, she pulled up his hood to protect his tender skin from the sun. Nashmarl growled and jerked it off immediately. After a moment, however, he pulled it up and retied the ends around his throat.

She sighed silently, wishing she knew why Nashmarl made everything harder for himself. There seemed to be nothing she could do to help him.

"Those Kelths," he said, muttering low as though he couldn't hold back the words any longer. "Those *slaves.*"

"They're not slaves now," Ampris corrected him gently.

Nashmarl shot her a look of green-eyed fury. "Ought to be, as stupid as they are."

"Frenshala is not stupid."

"Oh, her," he said with a blink. "I'm not talking about *her.* Steegin is so—"

"Which one is Steegin?" Ampris asked.

"The dirty one," he said with loathing. "The one with all the scars. She *looks* at me, Mother."

Ampris's heart sank, but she kept her outward calm. "Yes? It's no offense to look at each other."

"You always say that," he retorted scornfully. "But no one makes fun of *you.*"

Ampris let her ears droop. What could she say? It was true.

"She doesn't belong here with us," Nashmarl muttered, kicking the ground with every step. "She has no right to say—"

"What did she say?" Ampris asked. "If necessary I

will speak to Frenshala tonight and ask her to—''

''That won't do any good!'' Nashmarl said impatiently. ''You always want to talk, but you never *do* anything!''

''What do you want me to do?'' Ampris asked him.

He stared up at her, meeting her gaze for the first time. His green eyes blazed with a combination of anger, indignation, hurt, and something darker, something she did not want to see.

''I want you to make them go away,'' he said, his voice rough with intensity. ''Make them leave us. *Shun* them from our camp.''

Ampris blinked in dismay. ''They can't be left on their own. Not until they are taught to hunt and—''

''I knew you'd say that!'' he broke in furiously. ''I knew you'd take their side instead of mine. You always do!''

''But, Nashmarl, be reasonable. It isn't taking sides to—''

''Never mind!'' he shouted at her, his face a dull crimson beneath its sparse fur. ''I'll deal with this myself.''

Before she could stop him, he hurried away, glancing back only once to yell, ''No wonder you aren't leader anymore!''

Ampris watched him go, his elbows jutting out awkwardly, his head stuck forward on his thin neck. He was fuming, endearing, and hopeless. She didn't know whether to go after him or to leave him alone.

''You should have handled this, Mother,'' Foloth said softly.

She met his critical dark brown eyes. ''You and Nashmarl are growing up. It's time you both learned how to manage on your own. If I handle everything for Nashmarl, he will never acquire the social skills he needs to get along with others.''

Foloth's eyes narrowed. ''He has no social skills. He

never will. He'll only make things worse. He always does. Then I'll get to suffer the consequences."

"Nashmarl's problems with Steegin have nothing to do with you," Ampris said sharply.

"Don't they?"

"No, they don't," she said.

He opened his mouth to argue, but she silenced him with an upraised hand. "Enough, Foloth," she said with her ears back. "Your brother does not need your interference."

By now the group had reached the edge of the mesa. They paused there, staring down at a steep and treacherous descent. "No!" Tantha said fiercely. "That is no trail. Only a fehtan could go down this way."

Luax reached out as though to touch her shoulder. "I will help you with your cubs—"

Tantha snapped at her hand with a savage snarl, and only Luax's quick reflexes saved her from being bitten. With ears back and teeth bared, Tantha glared at her. "Get away from me! Why help me now? You did not care before."

Luax's rill turned indigo in anger. "Liar," she said with equal fierceness. "You would not let yourself be helped when you were birthing. You were crazy, dangerous. You snapped and tried to bite everyone until we were forced to leave you."

Tantha blinked at this denial. For a moment she looked bewildered, as though she did not remember. Ampris watched her with compassion, knowing Luax was probably telling the truth. At her best, Tantha was edgy and unpredictable. During her birthing, she must have been a monster.

"Enough rest," Harthril said, breaking the tense silence. "I will show you the trail. Come."

He started down the treacherous descent, followed by Luax. One by one, in single file, they all followed, picking a slow, careful way along a steep switchback. The footing of loose shale shifted and rattled, spinning off stones that plummeted deep into canyons far below.

Gritting her teeth as she lowered herself, uncertain whether her bad leg could support her, Ampris wanted to grab both Harthril and Luax by their rills and shake some sense into them. A lone and desperate hunter might take such a dangerous trail into the rough, precipitous terrain falling below them; but to bring a group of this kind, burdened with newborns, elderly, and the injured, along such a trail was madness.

Elrabin and Velia could not keep their place in line. The other Kelths stepped around them and kept going. Elrabin sank to his haunches, his head hanging low.

Worried about him, Ampris stopped and gripped his shoulder. "Hey, old friend," she said lightly to mask her concern. "Are you trying to make camp here?"

Velia hovered on the trail just ahead of Elrabin, teetering a little and looking frightened. Her fur was matted with sweat and dust. Her light brown eyes looked dull with exhaustion. "Why must we go this way?" she whined. "I don't like it. We can't do it."

Elrabin was rubbing his head beneath his bandage. Gently Ampris took his hand and forced it away from his wound.

He lifted his gaze to her and quirked her half a smile. Despite his obvious exhaustion, his eyes held some of their familiar sly gleam. "Yeah, yeah, can't be camping here," he said in response to her teasing remark. "You're right, Goldie. Bad spot."

"Better keep going," she said gently.

Velia struggled with their bundles, one of which slipped off her shoulder, and nearly lost her balance. Crying out, she flailed her arms and teetered dangerously on the narrow trail before she managed to steady herself.

Ampris hurried to her. Gripping her arm firmly, Ampris stripped the bundles off Velia's shoulders and crouched on the ground while she untied their laces.

Velia bent over her in instant fury, snapping at her ears. "What you be doing?" she demanded. "You leave our things be!"

"Velia, hush," Elrabin said wearily. "Ampris is helping."

"Don't need her help. Don't need—"

"Velia," he said with more sharpness, and his mate fell silent.

She continued to hover over Ampris, her sharp teeth close to Ampris's ear, her breath hot with suspicion. Ignoring Velia, Ampris retied the bundles into a more efficient shape and lashed them together.

"Now," she said, holding them out to Velia. "You won't be pulled off balance."

Velia took her things with reluctant gratitude. "It *is* better," she said grudgingly. "Thank you. I didn't know how to do that."

Ampris smiled at her. "You're welcome."

"Might learn a lot, if you decided to be willing," Elrabin said. Clutching the back of Ampris's belt, he pulled himself to his feet and swayed a moment.

Ampris moved to steady him, but Velia darted between her and Elrabin, fitting her shoulder under his arm and glaring at Ampris possessively.

"Guess you don't need more help," Ampris said mildly, backing away.

Over Velia's head, Elrabin met Ampris's gaze and rolled his eyes with a comical waggle of his ears. That, more than anything else, assured Ampris he was definitely on the mend. Hiding a smile, she let them struggle on without her.

Most of the group had now passed her. Automatically Ampris looked for her sons. Nashmarl was well ahead on the trail, once again in the midst of the Kelth newcomers. Not pleased to see him there, Ampris backed her ears. He was asking for trouble by pestering ignorant, ill-educated slaves who found his appearance repugnant, but she couldn't reach him now. Once they were safely down, however, she would have a more forceful talk with him.

As for Foloth, he was helping old Robuhl pick a tottery way down. Satisfied that Foloth was being useful, Ampris went to Tantha and offered warily to carry one of the newborn cubs. Tantha accepted, surprising Ampris, and even bared her teeth in a brief smile.

"You, I can trust," she said loudly, looking around to make sure she was overheard.

Mindful of the precious bundle cradled in her arms, Ampris rubbed the sleeping infant between her ears and started down with her. It was not easy keeping her footing. The rocks tended to shift underfoot, and the drop on one side was steep and long. Refusing to look into the depths of the precipice, Ampris focused her gaze strictly on where she was going.

Halfway down, they reached a wide ledge that formed a sort of shelf. Here, Harthril called a halt and let everyone rest.

Returning the spotted cub to Tantha, Ampris allowed herself a small sip from her water skin, then shared it with Foloth. While he drank, Ampris gazed out into the far distance, absently clutching the Eye of Clarity. She was still puzzled as to why Harthril had chosen this difficult trail when out to her left she could see where the northern point of the mesa sloped down in a far more gentle fashion into a forest. Had they gone that way, they would not have been risking their necks every moment.

But their direction instead aimed them toward a mountain range that rose sharply almost from the very foot of the mesa. Heavily forested, the mountains stood in jagged formation ahead of them. South of the mountains spread a wide, arid brown plain half-obscured in the haze of heat and lingering field smoke. Recognizing the geography with an unpleasant jolt of foreboding,

Ampris lifted her muzzle and drew in a deep breath.

"Harthril!" she said sharply.

The Reject looked her way, but he was talking to Frenshala and did not come over. Ampris felt a spurt of annoyance, then realized she would have to go to him. She did so, glaring at Frenshala without really seeing her.

"I must interrupt," she said without apology and took hold of his tattered sleeve to turn him so that their backs were to the others.

Frenshala growled. "We not be finished—"

Ampris backed her ears and glared at the Kelth female with such fierceness Frenshala's protest died in her throat. "I must interrupt," Ampris said, and Frenshala backed away.

Harthril pulled his ragged sleeve free of Ampris's fingers. "What?"

"We're going the wrong way," she said, keeping her voice as low as she could. She did not want to undermine his new-gained authority by saying this where the others could overhear, but neither would she remain silent. "This mountain range is Kreige mal-Hahfra. Its forests contain imperial lands. We can't go there."

Harthril stared at her through his brilliant-hued Viis eyes. His rill was halfway extended, but otherwise he showed no expression. "Good hunting there."

"No!" she said. "We can't risk crossing a boundary marker."

Harthril's rill extended more. He pointed at the bluff rising above them. "You saying to climb back up there?"

"Of course we can't climb back the way we just came," she said irritably, knowing the exhausted group would never make it. "But if we go into those mountains, we'll be heading for greater trouble than we left."

A sharp yelp and the sounds of a scuffle made her break off and turn around. Harthril turned with her.

At the opposite end of the ledge, Nashmarl was shoving the Kelth Steegin, who snarled an insult at him and snapped her teeth right in his face.

Harthril hissed, flicking out his tongue in anger, but a growling Ampris was already limping in her cub's direction. She saw Nashmarl shove Steegin again, pushing her dangerously near the edge. This time, Steegin's yelp held a distinct note of fear. Growling, the other Kelths rose to their feet and closed in on Nashmarl as a pack.

In mingled annoyance and growing alarm, Ampris roared, freezing all of them in place. "Nashmarl!" she yelled angrily. "You—"

But she never finished her sentence. From over the top of the mesa came a thundering boom of sonic pressure and the blinding flash of sunlight off metal. Two high-velocity, scout-sized warships came screaming over the rim of the mesa and barreled down right above them. The ships' noses were aflame, and their jets spewed contrails of white exhaust. The noise of their engines deafened the world, making the ledge itself tremble beneath Ampris's feet. Small rocks dislodged and went tumbling, then the ships went plunging down toward the far-off Plains of Filea, gone in the blink of an eye, with only the stink of exhaust and the boom of their engines echoing off the cliffs and canyons.

Ampris, although she had ducked instinctively like everyone else, was the first to recover. She jumped upright. "They didn't see us!" she said, her voice ringing out over the panicky babble. "Stay calm, everyone. They couldn't see us."

Velia was in hysterics, her hands clawing the air over her head. "This close!" she said over and over. "This close! Could touch us. Had to see us."

"No way," Elrabin said. He gave Velia a shake and she fell silent, standing beside him wide-eyed and shaking, her hands clamped around her muzzle. "Those be spaceships, messengers, coming in on autopilot control. Slack yourselves. We be fine, see?''

The other Kelths weren't listening. Yipping shrilly, they ran about, grabbing up their meager bundles and shoving each other.

''They'll report us,'' Frenshala said, as wild-eyed as Velia. ''We'll be taken back and flogged.''

The confusion increased as they yelped and milled about. Frustrated, Ampris could not make herself heard. Elrabin tried to shout above the noise they were making, but gave up.

Harthril, however, pushed his way through and waved his long arms. ''Follow me!'' he ordered. ''Move fast. We go now!''

He started off the ledge, with Frenshala right on his heels. The other Kelths crowded them, still yipping and sobbing, refusing to calm down. Trying to back out of the general confusion, Ampris looked around for her sons and belongings.

Then a scream pierced the air.

Turning that way, Ampris saw Nashmarl teetering on the edge of the precipice. Horrified, she rushed to him, knocking someone out of her way, and dragged him back to safety. She clung to him a moment, feeling him tremble against her, and sent up a silent prayer of gratitude that he was safe.

''Look!'' someone shouted.

A fresh babble of voices broke out, and Nashmarl squirmed from her arms to look over the edge.

Ampris stared down far below at Steegin's sprawled, broken body. Sickened by the sight, she closed her eyes.

Wails rose up from the Kelths.

Ampris stepped back, forcing herself to look deep into the stricken green eyes of her son. ''Nashmarl,'' she whispered.

He was wide-eyed with shock. His usual defenses had crumbled. Ampris saw the lonely, frightened, deeply insecure cub that lay behind his moody facade.

"I *didn't,*" he said, his voice airless and squeaking. "She shoved me, and I pushed her back. Then her foot slipped, and she just fell." His mouth opened and closed several times. "She just fell."

Ampris said nothing. Her heart went out to him, and she wanted to fold him back within the safety of her arms. But he remained rigid and unmoving, resisting her comfort.

Foloth rushed up to them, his dark eyes blazing. "You *fool*!" he said to his brother. "If you had to push her, why couldn't you do it when no one was around to see you?"

Shock hit Ampris hard. She stared at Foloth, unable to believe what she had just heard.

Before she could react, the Kelths mobbed them, snapping and hitting, jostling the three of them dangerously close to the edge.

"Killer!" they shouted. "Monster! Freak!"

Ampris grabbed her sons by their arms and pushed forward through the pack of Kelths. She snarled, baring her teeth, and bit anyone who blocked her way. Reluctantly the pack parted to let her through.

A small stone came out of nowhere, hitting Nashmarl in the shoulder. He cried out in pain, and another stone hit him.

"Killer!" someone shouted shrilly.

Ampris lost her temper. Drawing herself to her full height, she spun around with the old speed that had once made her champion of the gladiatorial arena and roared with a ferocity that silenced them. Swiping with her claws, she chased one of the Kelths into the safety of the crowd. "Nothing is settled here!" she shouted at them. "Nothing!"

Another roar joined hers, and suddenly Tantha bounded to her side. The two Aarouns snarled at the Kelths, who quietened and backed away uneasily.

Tantha bared her teeth and shook her head from side to side. "Come on and fight, if you want a fight!" she taunted them.

But Elrabin came hurrying forward to stand between them. Holding up his hands, he peered at first one side, then the other, from beneath his rakish bandage. "Slack yourselves," he said sharply. "This ain't the way."

"I told them this will be dealt with below," Ampris said, fury still growling through her voice. She stared at the Kelths through a red haze of emotion, the old, long-dormant fighting instincts roused within her. "Or I can deal with it now, one by one."

"I will help break bones," Tantha said with relish.

"Killers!" yelled a Kelth voice from the safety of the crowd.

"Shut the gab!" Elrabin snapped fiercely. "All of you! We ain't judging this now."

"Steegin be dead!" Frenshala said in anger. "She be dead *now*—so we *deal* with this now!"

"You got no say in when we judge our own," Elrabin told her. "Cool off and get down the trail. Move!"

His fierce orders did the trick. Obviously the Kelths were still conditioned to do as they were told. One by one, they turned aside and went down the steep trail—even Frenshala, although she was the last of them to go. She glared at Ampris as she went. "Liar," she snarled. "Better off we be with Viis master than Aaroun."

Ampris opened her mouth, then closed it without reply. Her anger was cooling now, and she was ashamed of having lost her temper. She had come very close to actually attacking some of them, and that was not the way to live peaceably with her comrades, as she had sworn long ago to do.

She and Elrabin exchanged glances, and the sad, pitying blame in his eyes deepened her hurt. She dropped her gaze from his, and turned around to look at her cubs.

Nashmarl's head was hanging. His breathing was ragged and audible. "Mother—"

"Hush," she told him. "Not now. This will be settled tonight in council."

Foloth shot his brother an icy glare. "Fool," he said so contemptuously that Ampris backed her ears.

"Foloth, don't," she said.

Her oldest son's dark eyes snapped to hers. "He'll get us shunned."

Her heart squeezed in fresh worry, and she admitted to herself that Foloth might be right. Rubbing her muzzle, she told herself not to believe it. Something could be worked out.

"Shunned?" Nashmarl said, his voice shaky and uncertain. "We can't be. Mother is too important."

Foloth bared his short fangs in disgust. "*Was,* you mean," he spit out, turning his scorn toward her. He was so young and inexperienced, yet so swift to judge harshly, Ampris thought with a sigh.

She backed her ears and pushed both of them to the rear of the line. "You will both stay silent," she said. "No more talking."

"But I did nothing wrong," Foloth said.

She wanted to shake him. "Quiet," she snapped, and to her relief he obeyed.

In grim silence the group descended the rest of the treacherous slope. Several times while she waited for the person ahead of her to scramble over a dangerous spot, Ampris gazed across to the easier descent of the mesa. From this angle she realized now that had they gone down that, they would have ended up on the northern side of the mountain range instead of here on the southern side, where the vast Plains of Filea began.

Her suspicions grew, and she wondered what Harthril was up to.

Steegin's body lay wedged in the V of a deep, narrow fissure, impossible to reach or bury. The Kelths wailed as they passed her, but a sharp order from Elrabin silenced them. After that, no one spoke at all. An unpleasant tension filled the air. Ampris could smell hostility and anger simmering in everyone except poor befuddled Robuhl, and she feared for her sons. Young and foolish, they had yet to show good judgment—either of them, although Foloth was far more responsible than his brother. She sighed to herself, grimacing as the climb over a boulder put too much strain on her crippled leg. Perhaps this tragedy, she mused, would help both cubs grow up.

By the time they reached the bottom, long shadows coated the rough terrain. The sun was sinking behind the bulk of the mesa, bringing respite from the day's heat. Overhead, the sky glowed lilac streaked with coral and gold. Kreige mal-Hahfra loomed over them like a bad omen, its sides looking black and heavily forested. Ampris could smell the sharp tang of narpines. It would be cool up there in the mountains. It always was. There would be plentiful game as well.

For a moment, she stood gazing at the forests, the breeze ruffling the fur of her muzzle, her nostrils filled with old scents and memories of long ago. Sahmrahd Kaa, that resplendent, bronze-skinned sovereign, had hunted the forests of his imperial lands with great pleasure, coming back to the lodge on soft evenings such as this with his blue eyes gleaming and his jeweled collar brilliant with the reflected fires of sunset. Splattered with mire, his fine clothing smelling of narpine sap, Viis sourness, and blood, he would stride inside the lodge ahead of a noisy retinue of hunters, casting aside gloves and weapons before spreading wide his arms for little Israi, who always ran to him in greeting while Ampris tagged behind, watching and envying her mistress such a magnificent father.

"Ampris."

The voice recalled her from the past, with all its pleasures and deep pain. Ampris slammed the door on her memories and turned to find herself staring into the sympathetic eyes of Luax.

"We camp here tonight," the female Reject said. Her pink and green skin was dusty. Her eyes looked tired and worried. "Is not close enough to water, but folk too tired to walk more. When eat, will be time for council."

Ampris stared at Luax through the twilight shadows, her breath tangled in her throat. Again she had to control an onslaught of fear and worry, had to remain calm, had to cling to the hope that she could successfully defend her son's innocence.

"You hear?" Luax asked her when she said nothing. "We have the council after we eat."

"Yes," Ampris forced herself to say. She clutched her Eye of Clarity for comfort, wishing she could tap into the font of wisdom legend said it contained. "Thank you, Luax."

The Reject flicked out her tongue. "Not time for thanking yet," she said in grim warning, and left Ampris alone.

CHAPTER SIX

Nashmarl stood among the trees in the darkness, his face mutinous in the light of the tiny fire Ampris had kindled. "I won't do it," he said.

She glared at him with a mixture of exasperation and alarm. "You must. It is the law—"

"Law!" he shouted. "We don't have laws. We're savages, living in the wilderness. We can do anything—"

In two swift steps, Ampris was on him. She snapped her teeth right in his face, wishing he had visible ears so that she could nip one. Instead, she gripped him by his neck and shook him the way she had when he was younger. "Shut up!" she growled at him. "Don't say that. They will hear you, and believe you really did kill Steegin."

His green eyes flared wide. "But I *didn't*!"

Foloth laughed. He was sitting by the fire, tending it with small twigs that he fed into the flames one at a time. The firelight danced orange across his flattened features, making him look impish. "You are so stupid, my little brother. Mother, aren't Aaroun females supposed to have visions when they give birth, visions that tell the future of their sons and daughters? Why didn't you look into Nashmarl's eyes and see that he was doomed to be a fool? You could have snapped his neck and saved us all this trouble today.''

Old grief and rage engulfed her. With a roar, she released Nashmarl and turned on Foloth with a savagery that wiped the smirk off his face and made him shoot to his feet.

''Silence!'' she shouted at him, wanting to shake him, to claw him to ribbons. Trembling with rage, she came at him with her teeth bared, and Foloth scrambled back, nearly tripping over the fire.

''Mother, don't!'' he said in fright. ''I'm sorry. I didn't mean to say that.''

Another growl rumbled through her throat. Her ears were plastered against her skull, and she gave him the flat, merciless glare she had used when she was a professional killer. ''Never say that again,'' she said. Her voice was hoarse and unsteady. She pointed at him with her claws extended. ''Do you hear me? Never say anything like that again.''

''I was just joking,'' Foloth replied sullenly. He glanced at Nashmarl, then back at her. ''Trying to lighten the situation.''

Her rage flared higher. ''A joke?'' she repeated, unable to believe what he'd said. ''Do you think I am a fool, Foloth? I am your mother. I am not worthy of your disrespect.''

''It's Nashmarl I don't respect,'' Foloth said. ''Not you, Mother.''

She looked into his dark eyes and saw only deceit and self-interest there. Her grief over all that had recently occurred welled up again, intensified by her profound disappointment in both her sons tonight. Her throat filled with emotion, and she found herself unable to speak.

''Goldie?'' Elrabin's voice called softly from behind her. The Kelth came up to their small, private campsite, looking serious indeed. He was moving more slowly than usual, and he looked gaunt and tired. ''It be time.''

She couldn't cope with it, not just then. Nashmarl wasn't prepared. He wouldn't listen to her. He wouldn't even try to save himself. Foloth was being so . . . so impossible and cruel. The past flooded her with unwanted memories, of a day so dark she'd hoped to close it from her heart forever.

"Goldie, you hear me?" Elrabin said more loudly. "Council is sitting. Got to take Nashmarl and—"

"I won't go," Nashmarl said in a defiant whine. "They all hate me. They won't listen to anything I say. Mother should go and speak for me."

"Your ma can't speak for you, cub," Elrabin said curtly. "For once, you got to face up to what you did."

"They've already judged me," Nashmarl said. "They threw stones at me."

"Ain't the only thing that should be done to your young hide," Elrabin muttered.

Ampris bowed her head. She was shaking all over. Worry consumed her. Where had she gone wrong in raising her sons? She had loved them with all her heart from the first inhalation of their newborn scent. She had given them all she could, loving them doubly because of their poor sister. She thought of her one daughter, so tiny and new, with her flat little face and wobbly, misshapen head. Only a short span of life, only a few hours to hold and caress that little one before she was gone forever. A piece of Ampris's heart had died with her daughter that day, leaving a small empty void that never healed. She closed her eyes, listening to her sons argue and bicker, and wished the rest of her could be as numb.

"Goldie," Elrabin said quietly, coming up behind her. His hand touched her shoulder, and she started. "You okay?"

Tears streamed down her muzzle. She put her hands to her eyes, unable to answer.

"Hey," he said in concern, coming around to face

her. "You can't defend the cub like this. You got to be more hopeful."

She lifted her drenched eyes to Elrabin's, unable to take his comfort. "I can't lose another cub," she said. "I can't!"

He opened his mouth, but she could bear no more. She darted around him and started for the trees, but Elrabin grabbed the coarse cloth of her jerkin and pulled her back.

"You ain't running off now," he said. "Ain't the time. Nashmarl needs your help."

"What other cub?" Foloth asked sharply. "What does she mean?"

Ampris stared at the ground, knowing Elrabin was right, but unable right then to pull herself together.

"You can't fall apart on us," Elrabin said. "We need you, Goldie. Not just the cubs, but the whole camp."

"I let them down," Ampris said. "I let everyone down, especially Paket."

Elrabin's tall ears swiveled back and he wrinkled his lip. "Nah. You ain't believing that. Paket knew what he was getting into. You think he didn't have the choice of staying behind? Lose the pity, Goldie. Ain't no room in this life for it. You got other things to do."

It was the kind of pep talk he used to give her after a brutal day in the arena. Ampris soaked up his encouragement now, knowing that part of her tears came from fatigue. She nodded, wiping her face.

"Here." Elrabin lifted her hand and closed her fingers around her Eye of Clarity. "You hold on to that a minute and find yourself. I got to shake sense into a couple of cubs."

Ampris nodded again, clutching her pendant. Already she was calmer, although whether it was from Elrabin's good sense, or some quality in the stone she held, or simply that her emotions were now spent, she couldn't say.

He turned away from her and glared at the cubs. Nashmarl stood wide-eyed and silent. But Foloth had his head tilted to one side, and he was staring intently at Ampris.

"What other cub?" he asked again. "What did she mean by that? Aren't we her only—"

"No, you ain't," Elrabin said gruffly.

Ampris lifted her head. "No," she said. "Elrabin, don't."

He looked at her over his shoulder. "Ain't no good keeping secrets."

"What secrets?" Foloth asked eagerly.

Ampris backed her ears. "It is not a secret. Elrabin, I don't wish it discussed."

"You just working up their curiosity now," he said and glanced at Foloth. "You had a sister. She died at—"

"Elrabin!" Ampris cried.

"—birth," he said and looked at her defiantly.

The band of alarm constricting her heart released its grip, and Ampris found she could breathe again.

Both cubs looked at her blankly. "That's it?" Nashmarl asked finally.

"Why keep that a secret?" Foloth asked.

Ampris turned away from them. She could not explain further. She wanted them to never know about the horrors of Vess Vaas Laboratory or the cruel scientist Ehssk who had taken her daughter away for dissection. Neither cub seemed to have vivid memories of their early days in the lab, and she wanted it to stay that way. For their sakes. They had enough to bear already.

"Oh," Foloth said after a moment of silence. "My joke was bad, wasn't it? That's why you lost your temper with me."

She sighed and made herself face him. "Yes, my darling. It was in very bad taste. But you didn't know. You—"

"Ain't the time for jokes, whether old times be known

or not,'' Elrabin broke in. ''Goldie, you got to take Nashmarl before the council now, or they'll be voting without you.''

She blinked, remembering the crisis at hand, and reached out to Nashmarl.

He glared at her, looking both defiant and scared. ''I won't go! You go for me.''

''I can't,'' she told him.

''You mean you won't.''

''No,'' Elrabin said to him impatiently. ''She can't. You be the one in trouble, cub. You be the one who's got to stand before the council.''

''The council is stupid!'' Nashmarl cried. ''You're all stupid! I didn't push Steegin. Why won't anyone take my word for it?''

''Maybe they will, if you show up to explain your side, see?'' Elrabin said.

''Nashmarl, we are trying to help you,'' Ampris said, her worry rising up afresh. ''Why won't you cooperate?''

''Maybe he's really guilty,'' Foloth said.

Ampris glared at him. ''That's enough from you!''

Elrabin also turned to face Foloth. ''You know something? See something? Or you just making this up?''

Foloth did not immediately reply, and Ampris felt herself turning cold. Nashmarl came to her side, staring at his brother as though he could not believe it.

''Foloth,'' he said hoarsely, ''what are you doing?''

Foloth's dark eyes held nothing at all, then a slow smirk spread across his mouth.

Ampris let out her breath, and at that moment could have watched him being skinned alive.

Nashmarl clenched his fists and ran at his brother, but Elrabin stepped between them, holding them apart.

''That's not funny, Foloth!'' Nashmarl shouted, swinging ineptly and almost hitting Elrabin instead.

''Stop it! Both of you!'' Ampris grabbed Nashmarl

and pulled him back before he hurt Elrabin, who was far from well. "I am ashamed of you both," she said, shaking Nashmarl until he wrenched away from her. She glared at him and Foloth.

"You'd better be nice to me, my brother," Foloth said, still taunting Nashmarl. "Or I might decide to be a bad witness."

"You weren't there! You didn't see what happened."

"Enough!" Ampris said sharply, silencing them. She was so exasperated words almost failed her. Nothing she did or said seemed to get through their thick skulls. "Foloth, you will stay here. Put out the fire and go to bed. That is an order, not a request."

"But I'll miss the decision," Foloth said. He shot Nashmarl another icy glare of contempt. "You mean I have to wait until morning to know if I'm to be shunned because of my stupid brother?"

Growling, Nashmarl started for him again. Ampris pulled Nashmarl back and gave him a quick nip on his nape. He hissed, and she spun him around and put her finger in his face.

With her teeth bared, she said, "I will give you no more warnings. Behave, *now.*"

Nashmarl was breathing hard. His face had turned pink, and his green eyes seethed with resentment and fear. "You always take his side," he muttered.

"When you stop rising to the bait, he will stop tormenting you," she said. "Now be quiet."

With Nashmarl glaring at the ground in momentary silence, Ampris turned on Foloth. He deserved punishment, but she was out of time. "Not one more word from you," she said to Foloth.

He smiled a tiny, satisfied little smirk, gone as fast as quicksilver. "I've said all I need to."

Ampris pointed at the fire. "Do your chores and go to bed. When this is over, if you say anything to torment or tease Nashmarl, I will flog you with a stick. Is that clear?''

He looked at her with a blink, unsure.

She never let her gaze waver. ''I can, and I will. There is a first time for everything, and if you think you are too big for punishment, remember that I am bigger.''

Foloth said nothing, but she knew he believed her threat. That was sufficient for now.

''Goldie,'' Elrabin said into the quiet, ''you be late.''

''I know.'' She sighed and gripped Nashmarl's arm. ''Let's go see if we can straighten out this mess.''

As they walked through the trees toward the large fire where the other members of the camp sat waiting, Ampris pulled Nashmarl closer to her and murmured into his ear, ''You must realize there is more at stake than our being shunned.''

''Sure,'' Nashmarl said in a sullen voice. ''Having to put up with Foloth's—''

''*No*!'' She pinched his arm to make him listen. ''If it is ruled deliberate murder, Nashmarl, your neck will be broken.'' She paused long enough to hear Nashmarl's startled intake of breath. ''Or we can choose the shunning, to be cut off forever from any contact with free abiru. I did not want your brother to hear this.''

''But, but—''

''Are you telling me the truth?'' Ampris asked him. She stopped and gripped his face between her hands, wishing she could see his eyes in the darkness. ''Are you?''

''You wouldn't let anyone kill me,'' Nashmarl said, but he did not sound sure.

Sadness curled around Ampris's heart. ''No,'' she admitted. ''I would not.''

He gave a little bounce and pulled back. ''Then there's nothing to be—''

''Nashmarl,'' she said sharply enough to get his attention. She wanted him to understand this very clearly.

"If you really did push that female to her death, if you really did it deliberately, then I would not let Harthril break your neck."

He chuckled in relief. "I knew you wouldn't—"

"I would do it myself."

He froze in the shadows, and Ampris smelled his fear. He gulped audibly, suddenly panting. Ampris waited for what he would say.

Behind her, Elrabin gave her a nudge. "They ain't going to wait much longer, Goldie."

Ahead, through the trees, she could see Tantha on her feet, prowling restlessly. Harthril's rill stood out stiff with annoyance. Velia and Frenshala were talking together in shrill voices. Ampris's heart sank. No, it was not good to antagonize the council by keeping everyone waiting. Delay only made Nashmarl look guilty, but she had to have her answer first.

Nashmarl's silence now left her awash in doubt.

"Well?" she demanded.

"What do you want me to say?" he burst out, sounding panicky. "I've told you the truth, but you keep asking and asking me. Don't you believe me? Do you want me to die?"

She waited, but he said nothing else. The straight answer she'd wanted for reassurance was not going to come. All she had was what he'd told her on the ledge, and she hoped with all her heart that it was indeed the truth. But hope was never the same as certainty.

Elrabin prodded the back of her shoulder, and she trudged forward with Nashmarl in tow, coming into the firelight that filled the small clearing where the others waited to pronounce judgment.

In the imperial palace in Vir, Israi Kaa paced alone in the darkness on the balcony of her private apartments. Although it was night, the breeze flowing across the river held little coolness. It ruffled her gossamer-weight gown and scarves, and with a sigh she turned her face into it for a moment before resuming her pacing. With every step, the tiny silver bells adorning her slippers tinkled musically. Overhead, the city lights reflected off the night sky, obscuring the spangle of stars that had once marked the vast empire of the Viis. At the foot of the palace walls, the Cuna Da'r flowed sluggishly, its brown waters low from the continued drought. She could smell the stench of mud and dying fish from her balcony despite the cloying bouquets of flowers arranged everywhere to mask the unpleasant river smell.

Israi did not often leave the banquet hall early. She did not often find herself unable to sleep. But she had a decision to make, and it was not coming easily. From all her progeny, she needed to choose a sri-Kaa, her official heir. She was in the twelfth year of her reign, and the pressure to secure the line of succession was steadily increasing from her chancellors and court.

Her illustrious father, Sahmrahd Kaa, had been in the tenth year of his reign when he chose her to succeed him. This morning, she had learned that he selected another sri-Kaa before her, one that had died soon thereafter of some chunenhal fever. When Israi was born a few years later, she became her father's next choice. This information had been most unwelcome, almost a shock to her. In her mind, she had always been her father's favorite. To think that once he had doted on and adored another chune—even one who had died before she was ever born—upset her every time she thought about it.

Impatiently, she paused in her pacing and gripped the stone balustrade. Below, in her personal garden, the guard was changing, performing the required rituals with voices muted to avoid disturbing the imperial rest. Israi watched without seeing the cloaked figures. Her mind was far away, coiling around the problem.

Her chancellor of state had spoken with unaccustomed

bluntness this morning, informing her in the privacy of her study that she could no longer delay making a choice. The populace was suffering many afflictions, especially those caused by the terrible drought and economic hardships, and it needed a sign of hope from the palace.

Israi resented such advice. "The Imperial Mother does not choose a successor just to improve the morale of her citizens!" she declared. "We are not public entertainment, to be paid for and watched."

Temondahl, her aging, blue-skinned chancellor of state, bowed over his staff of office, but he did not relent. Through the years, he had served her competently and efficiently, putting up with her tantrums and willfulness. In exchange she had to endure a dry, stuffy chancellor who was tirelessly determined to persuade and cajole her into performing the countless mundane, boring bureaucratic chores required of the sovereign.

"The throne is never entirely secure," he told her. Now well into his lun-adult life cycle, he regarded her through half-lidded eyes that might have looked sleepy and stupid but never missed anything. "Rumors are beginning to circulate that the Imperial Mother's eggs are weak, making her unable to produce an imperial heir."

Outraged, Israi could only stare at him as her hands gripped the carved arms of her chair. Her rill flared out, stiff and dark blue, while she gasped for an answer to such a ridiculous charge.

"It is only a rumor, majesty," Temondahl said smoothly. "But rumors can sometimes do harm. This one should not be allowed to grow into general belief."

"Our eggs are strong and healthy," Israi declared, unable to get past the insult. "Always we have produced many."

"A solid, consistent number," Temondahl said.

It was flattery, but it was not agreement. Israi eyed him suspiciously. "What do you mean?"

"Surely the Imperial Mother realizes that while she produces excellent eggs each year during Festival, modern numbers cannot compare with those of earlier days when double or three times as many eggs were laid by—"

"History!" she said contemptuously with a sweep of her hand. "We are not interested in the past."

"Then let us focus on the future," Temondahl said. "A successor is imperative. Many citizens are losing hope. With the empire so shaken by a myriad of problems, there must be a firm sign from the palace that the future is secure."

Israi sighed. Why did he have to make a speech about it?

"Three years into your Imperial Majesty's reign, I urged you to choose a successor. You did not."

"We want a perfect heir," she said, flicking out her tongue in annoyance.

"A noble objective, but perhaps the standards should be lowered slightly."

Her eyes dilated in shock. She could not believe Temondahl had said such a thing. "What do you mean? A less than perfect sri-Kaa? Unthinkable! You cannot be serious."

"Perfection is difficult to find."

Her rill raised even higher behind her head. "Are you now saying our chunes are substandard?"

The dangerous edge in her silky tones made Temondahl pause before replying. The look he gave her was cautious indeed, but he did not retreat.

"Not substandard," he said. "The Kaa's progeny are lovely creatures. But few chunes today exhibit the health and vigor of previous generations."

Israi sighed impatiently. "All the old ones say that. It means nothing."

"It means that our scientists still cannot find a cure

for the Dancing Death. Nor can they bring back our—"

"We will *not* discuss plague," Israi said in dismissal. "You worry about things that are not happening. This is a waste of our time."

"Forgive me for straying too far from the subject," Temondahl apologized smoothly.

She flicked out her tongue. "Besides, you say that we should name our heir, yet in the same breath you say that our chunes are not as vigorous as they should be."

Temondahl puffed out his air sacs. "Majesty, let us not fall into semantics. I believe we agree that there is need for an heir. My other concern has to do with time. A sri-Kaa should have many years of training and education in order to be worthy of the position he or she will someday hold. Although certainly everyone at court hopes that the Imperial Mother will enjoy a very long life, we must . . ."

He droned on, but Israi stopped listening. Inwardly she fumed. He was right, curse him. Right as usual. But he did not understand the problem.

"We will consider your remarks," she said, just to silence him.

Temondahl's rill extended slightly. His tongue flicked out, and he said nothing.

His expression offended her, and her own rill stiffened. "What now? Would you have us choose this very moment? We have said we will consider the matter. Surely that is enough."

"For how long will the Imperial Mother consider it?"

She felt the heat of anger course through her veins, throb in her rill. Her tongue coiled in her mouth. "We will not be rushed," she said curtly. "We will not make an unconsidered choice."

"There are presently twenty-five chunen and three hatchlings living in the palace," Temondahl said. "All are exquisitely marked and colored. All show signs of intelligence and wit. Any would do, depending on temperament and—''

''Shall we close our eyes and point?'' she broke in icily. ''How dare you suggest this be done rashly! The succession is a matter of the greatest importance. Great care must be taken.''

''Yes, majesty. As long as the decision is made quickly.'' Temondahl spread out his hands. ''Fresh rebellion is breaking out among the rim worlds. Lord Commander Belz has already departed with the main flotilla of our warships to quell it, but a successor will make the throne look stronger.''

''Our throne is very strong,'' Israi said angrily.

Temondahl bowed his head. ''Your majesty knows what I mean.''

Israi felt driven into a corner, and she did not like the feeling. Yet she knew if she dismissed him, he would only return on the morrow and mention the subject again. If she continued to put him off, he might bring it up before a general meeting with all her chancellors and ministers. They would welcome a chance to meddle.

''I can question the attendants to learn more about the chunen's personalities,'' Temondahl suggested delicately.

Israi sighed and held up her hand. ''We fear making the wrong choice. We believe the sri-Kaa should be a true reflection of our glory, evident to everyone immediately. We were chosen as sri-Kaa straight from the egg, within a few hours of our hatching. Yet none of our progeny has stood out so clearly.'' She let her tongue flick out in momentary distress. ''We wait, Chancellor Temondahl, for the right one to hatch. We wait and we wait, but no one equal to us has yet hatched.''

There, it was said. Her deepest fear, her greatest insecurity about her maternity. Why could she not produce a glorious heir? Why?

Temondahl regarded her in silence until she could no

longer bear his scrutiny and rose from her chair. She walked to the window of her study and stared out it blindly. Her back felt prickly from his gaze. Seldom had she so openly exposed herself, yet there were very few of her secrets that Temondahl did not know.

"Majesty," the chancellor said at last, measuring his words. "This fear should be put to rest. How natural that the Imperial Mother should regret the absence of a hatchling as glorious in beauty and grace as she. Yet, consider the matter from a different angle. When your father reigned, you shone as a rival star to the sun of his greatness."

Despite her distress, Israi brightened. She turned and looked at the chancellor. "Really?"

His heavy-lidded gaze never wavered. "This your majesty knows to be true."

She did know it. She remembered how the people had always cheered her as much as they cheered her father. The memory pleased her intensely, but then her spirits crashed again. "This is what I want in my own chune."

"Ah, but consider. Does the Imperial Mother really want a rival for the people's affections?"

The point he made startled her. She had never considered it that way. Flicking out her tongue, she gave him her entire attention.

"Does the Imperial Mother really want a sri-Kaa so beautiful the people weep and clamor for sightings? Does the Imperial Mother really want a sri-Kaa her equal in grace and ability? Does the Imperial Mother really want a sri-Kaa who will grow up impatient to rule? One who is so certain of the people's favor, he or she constitutes a danger to the throne?"

His words soaked in. Israi recognized the oblique reference to her own days as an impatient vi-adult. She knew how often she had pushed her father, how often she had tried to reach for imperial privileges that were his alone. She knew also that had he not died young, she would have given him a great deal of trouble. For she had wanted the throne for her own. Wanted it with a desperate, burning, ambitious single-mindedness. Had he lived his full span of years, she could have become lun-adult while waiting to become Kaa. The wait would have driven her mad, or into committing treason. As it was, she had almost done the latter anyway.

Calculations ran through her mind. She saw the wisdom in what Temondahl advised, and she agreed to visit the imperial nursery to make a choice right away.

In the afternoon, she canceled her scheduled audiences and went to the nursery. Arriving with her entourage of Kelth heralds, richly dressed attendants, and favorite courtiers, Israi gazed at her hastily assembled chunen. How dazzled and wide-eyed they looked to see her. When permission was granted, they gathered tentatively about her, staring at her face, her complexion, the jewels sewn like stars across the full skirts of her brocade gown. She did not visit them often. In fact, as the tiny hatchlings drew back shyly from her, she realized with a guilty start that she had not visited since Festival that spring, when she'd inspected her newest offspring.

Her visits were too rare. The chunen barely knew her. She reached out to some of them, stroking tender rills and touching soft, perfumed skin. The chunen trembled beneath her caresses, some of them hardly able to breathe from awe.

Still, the sight of them pleased her. Temondahl was right about their making a handsome collection. She had chosen well the males that fertilized her eggs. But which chune should succeed her? Which was worthy of the throne? Instinctively she still wanted one like herself, as bright and ambitious and as ruthless as she. Someone strong enough to hold the throne no matter what befell the empire.

But she did not want a rival. How strange that it

should have been Temondahl who recognized that truth rather than Israi herself. She could not bear the thought of the people loving anyone more than her.

She swept her gaze across the upturned faces of her progeny. One female was strikingly pale, with just a hint of green in her skin. Her eyes were green as well, and arrestingly intelligent. She was the tallest, probably the oldest.

Israi stared at her a long while and finally beckoned. "Come to us."

Her daughter moved forward, walking tall and slender, with a graceful sway that Israi found very pleasing to the eye. An attendant murmured in Israi's ear canal: this was Nairei.

Israi smiled and allowed Nairei to take her hand. "We are pleased by how well you have grown, Nairei," she said. Her musical voice, always considered an instrument of beauty, had deepened in the past few years, producing a richness of tone that remained much admired.

Nairei lowered herself in perfect obeisance to her mother. "Thank you, majesty," she said with the correct amount of formality. Her voice was light and clear, with a purity that made Israi catch her breath. It was much like Israi's voice had once been, and suddenly Israi saw just how special this chune was, how delightful and intelligent she could prove to be. Only her coloring displeased Israi, because Israi had never liked green skin. But she knew that Nairei's paleness would make her exotic and therefore fashionable at court.

She was a splendid candidate for a successor, and in an instant Israi's heart flamed with jealousy.

One of the ladies in charge of the nursery came forward with a flyta in her hands. The instrument was fashioned of gold, silver, and ivory, carved into a fanciful shape of long-stemmed loba blossoms entwined together. "If it will please the Imperial Mother, Nairei will play a composition of her own in your majesty's honor."

Israi said nothing, but she lifted her finger in permission. Without a trace of shyness, Nairei took the flyta in her long-fingered hands, holding the instrument like a master. Her wrists were displayed at a graceful angle that showed off how slender and lovely they were.

She played a melody that was both simple and sophisticated. Every note was perfect. The whole formed a harmonious, pleasant composition that showed a great deal of musical talent.

Israi listened, and her eyes grew cold. This daughter indeed had all the right qualities, but Israi hated her. She examined Nairei's flawless, almost radiant complexion, and saw all the advantages of youth which were no longer her own. If Nairei were sri-Kaa, the two of them would have to appear at many official functions together. Each time, the disparity between the young, blossoming daughter and the aging, declining mother would become more obvious.

Israi knew she was still very beautiful, but she now had to work hard to keep herself that way. She could no longer eat platters of civa cakes and the tiny din sansans covered with hoh seeds. At night, she endured long rituals of having her skin oiled and tended. The sun now had to be avoided whenever possible so that she would not burn her complexion. Her rill had to be exercised to keep its underskin firm and taut.

The song ended, and Nairei lowered the flyta. She fastened her luminous eyes on her mother and waited for praise with her lips slightly parted.

"Well performed," Israi said flatly. "Well done. You have pleased us, and you shall be rewarded."

Hope flared in Nairei's face, and at that moment Israi understood that the chune had heard the rumors that a sri-Kaa might be chosen soon. Nairei believed she was the choice. It was all there in her expression.

Israi stripped one of the jeweled bracelets off her wrist

and held it out. An attendant hastened to take the bauble for Nairei, whose rill darkened in obvious disappointment.

Her lady in waiting hovered uncertainly. "Remember your courtesies, Nairei."

The chune bowed to Israi. "My mother honors me greatly," she said softly. Her eyes were downcast now.

Israi left the nursery without another word.

For the rest of the day and into the evening, the entire court was abuzz with rumor and speculation, driving Israi finally to take refuge here in her apartments, away from the stares and whispers.

She could not do it. She could not surrender even a sliver of her position to Nairei. Already she had heard the chune's name spoken too often. She was sick of it. How pretty was Nairei? How graceful? What color was her skin? Was she old enough to have started storing fat in her tail? How did her beauty compare with the Imperial Mother's? Did she resemble the Imperial Mother in wit and personality? Would the two of them look enchanting at functions together? Which designer would dress the chune? How many jewels would she be allowed to wear?

On and on it went, the gossip and speculation. The whole palace blazed with an excitement that Israi had not seen in years.

It infuriated her. She could not bear it that the court should discuss her daughter more than her. Now, in the privacy of the night, Israi once again began pacing back and forth across her balcony. She wished she had never listened to Temondahl. She wished she had never set foot in the nursery.

She wanted to banish Nairei from court, yet she knew it was unfair of her. The chune had done nothing wrong, other than exhibit altogether natural expectations.

One thing was certain, however. No daughter of Israi's would succeed her. There was too much danger in choosing female to succeed female. No doubt her father had understood this. Perhaps that was why he had not chosen a son as his heir.

Israi flicked out her tongue. She would look at her sons instead of her daughters.

Leaving the balcony, she crossed her sitting room, with its plush carpets and richly upholstered furniture. The hangings were soft. Muted lights gave off a dim glow. No attendants were present, but Israi summoned no one. With her own hand she activated her link and called up information on her sons, scrolling each individual likeness across the screen.

The people wanted a sri-Kaa, she thought with savage resentment, and they would get a sri-Kaa.

She scrolled up the likeness of the youngest male, a hatchling born only this year. Blue-skinned with bronze markings on his rill and around his eyes, he was a comely little one but inclined to be sickly. According to the information given, he was a poor eater and did not take the heat well. His name was Cheliharad.

Israi flicked out her tongue. If he died, she would name another male in his place. The youngest, the weakest of her sons. Never mind that tradition had decreed the sri-Kaa should be the strongest and the best. Her father had followed tradition slavishly. She would not. If the next chune died, she would name another, and another, until she grew very old and tired of the game. Then she would choose someone worthy of the throne. But only then.

Without further delay, she summoned Temondahl on the link, waiting impatiently until his sleep-bleared face appeared on the screen. He wore a richly patterned robe and had fastened on his rill collar. His eyes were blinking rapidly, as though he were trying to force himself fully awake.

"Majesty?" he said.

She gave him a cold stare. "Cheliharad will be sri-

Kaa. Draw up the proclamations at once. We wish the news to be broadcast to the people in the morning."

"Yes, of course, majesty. This Cheliharad—"

"Yes," she said, giving him no time to question her. "We shall set my seal on this first thing tomorrow."

"But, majesty, which one is—"

"Our decision is made," she snapped. "There will be no discussion."

"Of course," he said, bowing his head to her. "May I offer the Imperial Mother my congratulations on—"

"Thank you," she said and broke the connection.

The silence around her seemed to be saying something. She did not want to hear it, any more than she wanted to hear her own conscience.

The Kaa went back to bed.

CHAPTER SEVEN

Dawn in the forest. Coolness in the air like a blessing. The sleepy twittering of birds. The sigh of wind in the treetops swaying overhead. The first pearly glow to the sky in the far distance, a herald of life continuing yet a little longer.

Ampris stood over her sons, both of them snoring softly in their bedrolls atop a mat of narpine needles. It was good just to listen to their steady breathing; knowing both were alive and well.

She moved away in silence, creeping stealthily through the trees and climbing slowly up to a jutting finger of rock that overlooked the sleeping camp. Turning herself to face the sunrise, she sat, holding the Eye of Clarity cupped in her hands while she softly whispered the fragments of ancient Aaroun prayer songs in thanksgiving.

Despite the shrill accusations of the Kelths, Steegin's death had been ruled an accident. But Nashmarl was harshly reprimanded by each of the adults in turn for his part in that accident. Watching tensely, Ampris saw Nashmarl stand at first tall and defiant in the circle of his elders, but as each criticism and accusation was hurled at him, his shoulders hunched more and more. His head flushed pink, then red beneath its pale, downy fur. He was not allowed to speak once the ruling was made.

Yet, although he clearly suffered humiliation from the verbal reprimands, Nashmarl's punishment could have been far worse. Ampris was still weak with relief at the council's mercy.

Harthril rose at the end. His crooked shoulder threw a strange shadow behind him. Flicking out his tongue, he said, "Nashmarl be young. Foolish, too. Time he think of others before self. Time he not shame mother who is worth much to us. Nashmarl, speak now."

The cub never lifted his head, never looked up. Ampris watched him and held her breath. If he turned surly and said something unforgivable now, everything could still be ruined. But Nashmarl only drew in a ragged breath. "I'm sorry," he mumbled, keeping his gaze on the ground. "Steegin hurt my feelings, but I didn't make her fall. I didn't want her to die."

Harthril flicked out his tongue and waited, but Nashmarl said nothing more. "For three days, you will serve camp. You will build fires. You will fetch water. You will dig latrine area and cover it when we leave."

Nashmarl looked up then, but he said nothing.

"Anything told you to do, you will do," Harthril said sternly. "No protest. No whining."

Nashmarl's fists clenched at his sides, but he stayed silent.

"Council over," Harthril said. "Go to bed, young cub. In future, more careful you will be."

Nashmarl wheeled around and strode out of the circle. His face was still burning, and his green eyes were ablaze. With his fists clenched at his sides, he came stomping past Ampris.

She reached out to comfort him. "My son—"

He wrenched away from her. "Leave me alone," he muttered and went stumbling on toward their camp.

She watched him go, wanting to follow him and try

to help him get over his humiliation, but there were things she needed to say to the council, matters to be discussed that had nothing to do with Nashmarl's misbehavior. By the time she finished and returned to check on her sons, Foloth was sleeping soundly and muffled whimpers were coming from Nashmarl's bedroll.

Ampris grieved for him, yet she knew time would quickly heal his hurt. He was young and resilient. There were other lessons still to learn. The world was a harsh place, despite all her efforts to shield her sons as much as possible. She could not protect them forever.

Now she sat high above camp, chanting softly under her breath, and looked at the future. She had had ample time to think about her plan during the long walk across the mesa. As soon as Nashmarl's reprieve came, she'd made her decision to leave in the morning light. The council had accepted her proposal.

Now, all that remained was to tell her sons where she was going.

"Goldie?"

The soft voice belonged to Elrabin. She hadn't heard him, and he'd approached her from upwind, so she hadn't smelled him either.

She broke off her prayer and let him come to her. He was only a gray shadow, his fur blending in perfectly with the misty, predawn light. Settling himself on the ground near her, he grunted wearily.

"These bones ain't so good with the ground anymore. You get any sleep?"

"Not much," she admitted.

"This ain't a good idea, see? You going to Vir by yourself."

She already knew what he was going to say. "No," she said firmly. "You can't come with me."

"Come with you?" He yipped sarcastically. "I ain't about to stick my nose back in Vir unless I get dragged there by a patroller. You shouldn't go either."

"It's the only way," she said grimly.

"Doubt that."

She turned on him. "So what do you suggest that's better? You didn't have much to say in council last night."

"My head hurt too much," he said. "Enough people arguing already, see? Why should I join in?"

"Because Harthril is trying to lead us into terrible danger," she said with passion. "Because the more voices against his plan that are heard, the better."

"I ain't for his plan," Elrabin said. "Said so last night. Saying so now. Don't rip out my throat."

She squeezed his shoulder in apology. "We mustn't give up our freedom and go back to Vir."

Harthril was indeed taking them to the city. She'd suspected it as soon as she saw this mountain range and the Plains of Filea beyond it. Until their second council last night, however, she'd had no chance to question him openly about it. Harthril's plan was simple. They had almost no food; hunting was increasingly difficult; their options were running out; in Vir the Rejects were given food and clothing as charity. Harthril proposed that they enter Vir and live off that charity, at least for a while.

Ampris and Elrabin had been horrified by the suggestion. And only the general fear of what might befall them in Vir had kept the others from siding with Harthril.

But they were hungry and homeless and exhausted. Ampris believed that it wouldn't take much more adversity to drive the group into adopting Harthril's plan.

"I know I can do this," she said. "It's our best shot at surviving. All we need is knowledge and—"

"Yeah, yeah, I heard the speech last night," Elrabin said with a yawn. "But you be the last one who needs to go poking around Vir."

"Who else but me could get into the Archives?" Ampris replied. "I know Bish will remember me and let me in. Once I learn how my ancestors preserved food without the benefit of current technology, we can begin to stockpile our stores and gain some—''

''I said I heard the speech already,'' he said more sharply. ''It's crazy, Goldie. Crazy.''

''It's necessary.''

''No. We should turn around and head back to the old region. We did fine there.''

''We were starving there when we left,'' she reminded him. ''That's why we came to the fields.''

''Yeah, and our luck keeps going bad the closer we get to Vir.''

''We're not going any closer to the city,'' she told him. ''If I succeed, we'll never have to go there.''

''Except you.''

She nodded. ''Except me.''

He snarled and rubbed his narrow muzzle. ''I don't like it. Too risky, see?''

''Elrabin, this land is polluted and dying. You saw what Luax killed when we first made camp here.''

Elrabin snarled with distaste. ''Ain't eating no two-headed grassen.''

''Of course not. But if we find one deformity, there are bound to be others. This land is polluted. We could get sick here.''

''Then we just leave,'' Elrabin said.

She nodded. ''I agree. But we're so close to Vir right now, closer than we've been in years.''

''Yeah. Too close. Makes my fur stand up every time I think about it,'' Elrabin muttered.

''But when will I ever have this opportunity again?'' she persisted, repeating some of the arguments she'd used to persuade the others.

''Yeah, yeah, the great opportunities,'' he said without enthusiasm.

''We need information,'' she said. ''This drought is ruining what remains of good land and water. We have to find ways to live other than the old hunting and gathering system.''

''We can head for Lazmairehl and steal what we need from there.''

''That's a good way to get killed,'' she said sadly. ''We tried that before, remember?''

''Yeah, it's risky, but so what? We got—''

''And is my visiting the Archives any riskier?'' she broke in. ''Once we know how to preserve food, we can travel far from here and find land unpolluted by the Viis settlements.''

''Yeah, yeah, you made a big argument for that. But I'm looking at the practical, see? How you going to walk all the way to Vir from here by yourself? How's that leg of yours going to hold up?''

''I'll make it.''

''Oh, sure.''

She glared at him. ''I know my capabilities and limitations. I can make it.''

''Fine,'' he snapped in reply. ''But you got to hunt. That takes time, especially in unfamiliar territory. You don't got enough time. Harthril's crowding you on that deadline.''

''I'll manage,'' she said.

Elrabin snarled something beneath his breath. ''With those cubs to keep up with? They'll slow you down, and you need—''

''I'm not taking the cubs.''

His eyes widened, and he stuttered a moment before he forced anything out. ''Not taking them,'' he repeated. ''Where they be going, then?''

''I want them to stay with you,'' Ampris said.

By now the light was growing stronger. She could see the open dismay in his expression before he ducked his head.

''Can't do it, Goldie,'' he said. ''Can't do it.''

''You must,'' she said, suddenly worried that he

might truly refuse. "You're the only one I trust to take good care of them."

"Aw, that ain't it," he said. "You got to understand that I—"

"I know they're difficult—"

"Difficult!" he said with a yip. "That's saying it low."

"I'll talk to them before I go," she promised. "They can behave. And they've known you all their lives."

"That don't mean we like each other. We don't get along, Goldie. Sorry. But the cubs don't like me, never have."

He fell abruptly silent, but she could guess the rest of what he'd been about to say.

"And you don't like them," she said softly. "Is that it?"

He squirmed, but met her eyes. "Not much."

Disappointment sank through her. She couldn't argue with him, when he put it that bluntly. "I'm sorry," she said at last. "I've tried and tried, but they have so much against them. I feel so sorry for them, yet I can't make the world any easier, no matter what I do."

"Maybe that's what you're doing wrong."

"What? Making things too easy?"

"Feeling sorry for them."

"I—" Her protest died in her throat. She backed her ears, not liking what she was hearing. But he was talking truth, and she knew it. She sighed. "I guess you're right."

"You been trying to raise them like Aarouns, see?" Elrabin said. "They ain't Aaroun."

"What do I do, bring them up as Viis?" she retorted, stung.

"They ain't Viis either."

"Then what—"

"I don't know, Goldie. Wish I did. But I ain't no advice machine. Only, what you been doing up till now ain't working so good. They be trouble walking on legs. Lots of trouble.''

''But they can be good,'' she said, wanting it to be so. ''They're smart and clever. They learn more every day.''

''Ain't learned enough.''

''And what were you like at their age? Living on the streets? Thieving? Being sold at auction?''

He sucked air through his teeth, making a low whistling sound. ''That ain't a fair thing to say.''

''Truth can hurt,'' she said, then raised her hands. ''I'm sorry. I don't want to quarrel with you. I just want to know they're safe, and with someone who will protect them—from themselves as much as anything.''

He sat in silence a long while, then sighed. ''What can I say?'' he finally muttered. ''You going off to risk your neck for all of us, and I can't turn you down.''

''Then you'll do it?'' she asked, holding her breath.

After a long pause, Elrabin shrugged. ''Yeah, I guess I will,'' he said as though disgusted with himself.

Ampris grinned in relief. ''Thank you, Elrabin! I knew I could depend on you.''

''Just for twenty days,'' he said sharply. ''Ain't taking this job forever, see? If you don't come back—''

''Believe me,'' she said happily. ''Going to Vir is the last risk I want to take. But think of it . . . a chance to access the Archives.''

''If they still be there,'' he said. ''You always been a nut for knowledge, but from what I can tell, all that you learn just gives you more crazy ideas.''

''This is the source,'' she said in excitement. ''The largest information base in the entire empire. We can learn so much, discover—''

He reached out and put his hand over her muzzle to silence her. ''The Crimson Claw is back, I be thinking.''

She shoved his hand away in annoyance. ''No. That's over.''

"Ampris and her Freedom Network."

"No. That's over too. Long gone. There couldn't be anything left after all this time."

His eyes bored into hers, missing nothing. "You saying that now, Goldie, but in your heart you be hoping for otherwise."

"I am going straight to the Archives. I am going to get the information we need to survive, and I'm going to return," she said grimly, her ears back. "That's all. If I don't return in the amount of time we agreed on, then the group can move into Vir and live off the dole. That's the deal. I'll keep my end."

Elrabin shook his head, chuckling softly. "And you really think that's the way it will go down."

"I know it will," she said firmly. "I gave my word."

He leaned back against a boulder and rubbed his head as though it still hurt him. "Well, well. I climbed up here, thinking I would suggest we part company with the rest of the group. Let 'em march off to Vir and be shackled faster than they can blink. You, me, Velia, maybe Tantha, and Robuhl. Those cubs of yours. Plenty of folk to stick together. We head out on our own. We'd do fine."

She looked at him sadly, wondering how to refuse his offer. "Oh, Elrabin."

He held up his hand. "But as soon as I got up here and started hearing that old snap in your voice, I knew my idea be no good. Getting into Vir makes your blood pump like in the old days. You can shake your head at me, but you miss that old excitement. I know it. You know it."

"Off for adventure, eh?" she said lightly, not denying it.

"Yeah." He stared at her a moment longer, then leaned forward. "Okay, now listen close. If you be set on this craziness, then you be set. When you get to Vir, *providing* you get there, it ain't going to be no swim to get inside. The city is locked up under security fields, see?''

She nodded. ''The walls. I remember.''

''More than walls. Security fields *and* guards that be checking registrations.''

Ampris touched her arm. ''I'd been thinking about how I was going to get past that. I guess I was hoping the security would be lighter for those trying to enter—''

He yipped scornfully. ''Naive you still be sometimes, you know that? Look, the scanners will be calibrated pretty tight for the implants. That means they can be messed with easy. You got to wait by the gates for a transport or a cargo hauler.''

''And I hitch aboard?'' she asked eagerly.

''Yeah, hop on back and hide in that sweet spot where the cams can't pick you up. But pick one hauling metals, see? It messes up the scanners.''

''I understand.''

''Once you're in—''

''I can do that part,'' she broke in impatiently with a glance at the ruddy horizon. ''The sun's almost up. The cubs will be waking soon.''

Elrabin gripped her wrist hard. ''Listen,'' he said sharply. ''No one here knows the ghetto better than me. You ain't never been in it. There's territories you got to cross, going west, to get to the Archives, see? But you also got to get through the barrier before you can get to the palace district of the city.''

''Without an implant, I can go through.''

''But not with patrollers around. Not with sniffers hovering. You wait until dark, then you go through. Go with a crowd, so the scanners don't count you and notice there ain't no number. Got that?''

''Yes, Elrabin,'' she said impatiently.

''Then, you got to stay off public transit, if it still works. Stay away from vids. Stay away from—''

"Elrabin," she broke in. "I can do this. I really can. Stop worrying so much."

He swiveled his tall ears back. "Just want you to return in one piece, Goldie."

"I know," she said, grateful to have such a good friend. "Believe me, I intend to be. But now it's time to go."

He opened his mouth to say something else, but Ampris rose to her feet, cutting off the conversation. They were just hashing over matters that had already been discussed and settled, and she saw no need to cover it again, especially since dawn had arrived. It was time for her to bid farewell to her cubs and go.

She wanted a fast departure.

Climbing down the hill, she returned to camp. Both of her sons were awake. Their bedrolls lay in scattered disarray, and they were passing the water skin back and forth between them in a rare show of cooperation.

Pleased, Ampris smiled at them. "My sons," she said.

Both cubs looked up at her. Foloth rose to his feet, but Nashmarl stayed crouched on the ground with the water skin in his hands.

Ampris gazed at them, her heart a tangle of love and sadness. She did not want to leave them, but there was no easy way to break the news.

"I am leaving you for a time," she said.

Foloth yawned and stretched himself. "Are you going to hunt all day?" he asked. "I'll go with you."

"No," she said.

"Nashmarl here has to spend the day digging a latrine," Foloth said with a smirk. "But I'm free to—"

"I said no, Foloth," Ampris broke in. "Thank you for the offer, but I am not going hunting. I am going to Vir to visit the Imperial Archives. It will take me perhaps six or eight days of walking to get there and at least that long to get back. I—"

"Wait," Nashmarl said, rising to his feet. He stared

at her in consternation. "You're going to Vir? Why?"

"Yes, why?" Foloth echoed.

Side by side, her sons stared at her. She smiled at them, reaching out to caress Foloth's jaw, then tweaking the folds of Nashmarl's hood, which lay back on his shoulders.

"To help the group survive better," she said. "It was decided last night."

"Are you being shunned?" Nashmarl asked, his green eyes suddenly wide with fear. "Are you being driven out of the group?"

"Don't be stupid," Foloth said to him impatiently. "You're the problem, not her. They'd shun you, but never her."

"What do you know?" Nashmarl retorted. "She's leaving."

"Both of you, listen to me," Ampris said firmly. "I'm not being shunned or driven away. I will be back as quickly as I can, in about twenty days."

"You're going too far," Nashmarl said. "It's dangerous in Vir."

"Yes, there are risks," she agreed evenly. "But you must remember that I grew up in the city. As did Elrabin—"

"Is he going with you?" Foloth asked sharply.

"No," she said. "I am going alone."

"Why?" Nashmarl asked.

Foloth said, "I will go with you."

She smiled at her eldest son, who looked so fierce and protective. "Thank you, Foloth, but this journey I must make alone."

"But why just you?" Nashmarl persisted. "Why not everyone?"

"Elrabin will explain things to you," Ampris said. "I must get ready."

Leaving the cubs exchanging puzzled looks, she collected her neatly tied bedroll and filled a battered rucksack with a change of clothing, a small wooden box filled with salve made from tanbok fat and herbs, the side-arm with its half-depleted charge, and a packet of fat, bright yellow pumkana seeds that she'd saved for emergency rations. She had just finished packing these few items when Luax and Tantha came to her.

Luax stepped up first and handed her a small sack of chuffie roots, freshly dug that morning. "May your journey go swift and well, Ampris," she said formally. "May your return be swift."

Ampris was touched by her kindness. She took the roots with gratitude. "Thank you, Luax."

Tantha shouldered up beside the Reject female and bared her teeth at Ampris. She reached out and touched the Eye of Clarity hanging around Ampris's neck. "Come back to us, Golden One."

"I intend to," Ampris replied.

Tantha handed her a full water skin. As Ampris slung it over her shoulder by its leather cord, the weight of it felt reassuring. She did not know how much drinkable water she would be able to find on her journey. The Plains of Filea were so arid they were almost desert.

"Thank you, Tantha," Ampris said. "It is good to leave with the gift of fresh water."

"You come back to us safe," Tantha said fiercely.

"I will."

By then everyone had assembled in a circle around her. Ampris looked at their faces, some containing sorrow, others looking hopeful, and some, like Frenshala's, appearing indifferent. Clutching her Eye of Clarity, Ampris smiled at each of them, then turned back to her sons.

The cubs looked very grave and alarmed. She realized she should have taken more time to prepare them for what had to seem like an abrupt departure, but she knew they would be all right in Elrabin's care.

The Kelth stood behind the cubs now, with Velia beside him. He nudged his mate, and Velia scuttled forward with visible reluctance to press a small pouch of leather into Ampris's hand. Although the top was tightly closed with a drawstring, Ampris smelled the pungent aroma of herbs.

"To refresh you when you are weary," Velia said. Her tilted golden-brown eyes met Ampris's briefly, then she darted back to Elrabin's side.

Ampris thanked her, but it was Elrabin who smiled in return.

"I want to go with you, Mother," Foloth said. His voice sounded small, with none of its usual assurance.

She shook her head and then pulled him close and gave his forehead a lick of love. "You mind Elrabin and Velia," she said. "Do as they tell you. Stay out of trouble. Promise me this, Foloth."

He glowered, and she took his head between her hands, holding his gaze with her own. "Promise me," she repeated.

"All right," he said at last. "I promise."

She released him and reached for Nashmarl. But he ducked out of her grasp, refusing her caress. His green eyes were dark with emotions. "You might not come back."

"I will," she promised him, understanding his fears. "I promise I will."

"Can't promise something like that," he whispered.

Elrabin stepped closer to him and gripped his shoulders from behind. "Goldie always keeps her word," he said.

Ampris smiled at him. "Be well, my old friend."

He nodded, and she knew her good-byes were over. She turned abruptly and set her face toward Vir, lengthening her stride as the sun lifted above the horizon and spread its morning rays of gold through the trunks of the forest. She did not look back.

CHAPTER EIGHT

Eleven days later, Ampris came hobbling over the last dusty rise and saw the walls of Vir towering before her. For the past three days she'd been able to see the city, like a beacon before her, shimmering distantly through the heat waves, giving her hope despite the raw sores on her feet and the grinding pain in her crippled leg. Now she stumbled to a halt, breathing hard and feeling light-headed from heat exhaustion. It was mid-afternoon, she knew by the harsh slant of the sun, a time when she should have been resting under the sorry shade of a bush, but Ampris was too close now to rest. She forced herself to keep going, planting one foot in front of the other without looking up—until now . . . when the city stood across her path in all its immensity.

The walls ran as far as she could see on either side of the wide gates. To her right, a slum of decrepit hovels and lean-tos grew from the base of the wall like an unhealthy fungus. Even at this distance, she could smell the stink of the place. She knew immediately what it was, although she had never seen it except on occasional vidcasts when she was a cub. Reject Town, it was called by some.

Although many Rejects lived in abandoned buildings in the heart of Vir, they were periodically rounded up by patrollers and dumped outside the city gates. It seemed to be the official hope that they would leave the city and go elsewhere, but they never did. Instead, the slum grew in size every year, as more and more Viis hatchlings were rejected as unfit for normal society.

Although it had been many years indeed since Ampris left Vir, the imperial city looked unchanged—at least from out here. She recognized the distinctive tall buildings of the Zehava District, their outlines smudged in the polluted air. As a cub she had often stood at the windows of the palace, gazing at these same tall buildings and wondering what life was like in the rest of the city. Now her memories were a tangle in her mind. She had traveled across the empire and back, had seen amazing sights, yet she'd never expected to return to Vir.

As she stood there in the heat, staring, a skimmer roared past her, whipping up a cloud of dust with its air jets. Coated in the stuff, Ampris coughed and slapped dust from her fur, then forced herself to hobble forward.

Her heart began to beat faster with every step. At long last she was coming home.

For the first few days of her journey she had denied that, telling herself sternly that the city had never been her home, that she was and always had been an outcast. But somewhere on that difficult journey, as her small food supply ran out and she had scant luck in hunting more, she stopped pretending anything to herself. She was coming home, and her growing anticipation had eventually been all that kept her going.

This morning, when she rose to start the last few miles of her long journey, her leg had given under her, and she'd fallen hard, so hard the wind was knocked from her lungs. She lay on the ground a long while, aching and weak with hunger, her mouth withered with thirst. But finally she'd scratched together the remnants of her willpower and forced herself up once again. Slowly, with the city shimmering before her, she'd managed a small, excruciating step, then another, then another. After an hour of this painful progress, the knots in her muscles had loosened, bringing mercy from the worst of the pain, and she'd been able to walk without fear of falling again.

She had one mouthful of water left in her water skin. She could hear it sloshing with every step, tormenting her. But she had sworn to herself that she would not drink it until she stood inside the city walls. Then, she would celebrate.

In the distance, the Cuna Da'r River curled lazily toward the city from the opposite direction of Ampris's approach. She could smell its marshy, fishy scent despite the dust clogging her nostrils. It made a loop around one side of the city before meandering on. She could not see it from here, but many memories of playtime along its verdant banks kept lifting into her mind like bubbles.

She smiled to herself, hobbling along one step at a time.

Another skimmer zoomed past her, its Viis occupants only a blur. Then a transport rumbled by, coating her with dust again. Ahead, traffic jammed and hovered impatiently, horns blaring, while security scans cleared each vehicle in its turn.

Ampris picked her way carefully, angling away from the passenger traffic to the cargo area. More and more transports were lining up, at least a dozen now. Remembering Elrabin's advice, she looked them over in search of one carrying metals or energy-plasma canisters. None of them looked right.

She dodged another one pulling up and spied a cargo hauler parked on hover near a docking platform. Abiru workers, panting in the heat, were transferring a load of heavy crates to its bay.

Excitement leaped inside her. This was the only prospect in sight. She inched her way forward, aware from the corner of her eye that three transports were now flying through the gates, along with twice that many skimmers. No other vehicles pulled up behind them, however, and Ampris worried that she would be noticed if the traffic thinned any more.

Trying to be cautious and casual, Ampris skulked around the end of the docking platform. It was stacked with pods, crates, and cylinders awaiting transport. The cargo hauler itself looked almost full.

Crouched against a pillar, she kept her head level with the top of the platform and watched the workers. If any of them saw her, they gave no indication of it.

Her gaze moved to the hauler, gauging the distance. She would have to cross in the open. There seemed no way to climb aboard without being seen. She tipped back her head to look for any overhead scanners floating about. There was no supervision that she could see; that didn't mean it wasn't present.

Maybe the workers would ignore her. Maybe they wouldn't sound an alarm if she stowed aboard.

Those were big maybes, she told herself, panting worriedly.

A hand grabbed her from behind, yanking her off her feet and dragging her backward.

Snarling in surprise, Ampris tried to twist free, but another set of hands seized her by the ankles, and she was lifted bodily off her feet. She saw this one, a Toth. For a moment she was frozen with fear. He was huge, even for one of his kind, and flies swarmed his head of matted dark hair. Grunting to his companion, who had her by her shoulders, the Toth said, "Now," and together they slammed her hard against the ground.

The world spun around her and went momentarily black. Ampris could not hold in her grunt of pain. Fighting off unconsciousness, she glimpsed one of the dockworkers glancing down at her with complete indifference before resuming his job.

"Help me!" she shouted, but one of the Toths hit her

in the jaw with a fist like a hammer. Pain exploded through her head, and again the world spun.

Through a blur, she could feel hands patting her expertly, hands ripping impatiently at her jerkin and stripping off her water skin and pack. Her old fighting instincts awakened, and she was suddenly driven back to consciousness by a surge of fury.

Roaring, she reached up and gripped the wrist of one of the Toths, snapping it.

He bellowed and slung himself around, dropping her pack and clutching his arm. Ampris sat up and tried to scramble free, but the other Toth butted her in the side with his massive head.

All the wind whooshed from her lungs. She collapsed, struggled up, whooping for breath, and tried to crawl under the dock. The Toth grabbed her crippled leg and dragged her out.

The pain blazed up her leg, making her yelp. She twisted around and swiped blindly with her claws, but the Toth hit her again, knocking her flat.

She lay there, heaving for air, unable to make her body move. *Fool,* she thought in a dim corner of her brain. *Should have been more alert for trouble.* She'd been caught flat-footed, like an arena trainee, and she was ashamed of herself.

A tug at her neck brought her around. The tug came again, and she realized the Toth was trying to take her Eye of Clarity. His comrade with the broken wrist grunted encouragement and bent to pick up her pack. Holding it by its broken strap, he said, "Take the necklace now. Get good price for it."

"No!" she shouted, surging up and sinking her teeth into the arm of the Toth trying to take her necklace. He bellowed with pain and jerked back. Savagely, she didn't let go, but gnawed and worried flesh and muscle, her strong jaws crunching down on bone. The taste of Toth blood filled her mouth, and then she was slung bodily to the side and slammed into one of the docking platform's pillars.

The Toth pulled away from her, bellowing curses and gripping his bleeding arm. Ampris got to her knees, her eyes aflame, her mouth smeared with his blood. She roared, and the Toth ran off awkwardly, still holding his arm. Of his companion, there was now no sight.

She looked around, breathing so hard she thought she might pass out. She was coated with dirt and blood, and all her belongings were gone except her necklace. Desperately, she gripped it with shaking hands, and felt relief spread through her. She could bear losing everything but this.

Holding it calmed her. After a few seconds her spinning senses steadied, and she tucked it out of sight inside her jerkin. She drew in a deep breath, then another, and finally raised her head. The dockworkers were gone. The cargo hauler was just floating through the gates.

Dismay drove her to her feet. She swayed and nearly fell, but managed to catch herself against the side of the dock. Unable to believe it, she watched the cargo hauler pass from sight. The gates, sheathed in a glowing, sparking force field, slowly swung closed.

"No," she whispered and spat in disgust to clear the taste of Toth blood from her mouth.

She glanced at the area which had been jammed with transports and skimmers only minutes before. They were gone as well. Backing her ears, Ampris straightened despite a sharp ache in her ribs and limped along the edge of the dock while keeping a wary eye out for scanners. Her lack of registration would identify her immediately as a renegade, and the bounty hunters would come after her.

At the end of the dock, she found a female Kelth lit, about half-grown perhaps, busy sweeping the platform clean of metal shavings and other debris.

"Hello," Ampris said quietly. It hurt her ribs to talk.

She pressed her hand gingerly to her side, hoping nothing was broken. "When will the next transport come through?"

The lit appeared to ignore her as she continued sweeping, but she glanced at Ampris from a corner of her eye. She was a skinny little thing, with brindled gray and brown fur that was falling out in patches down her arms. "You fought them Toths good," she said in a voice even softer than Ampris's. "Ain't never seen Toths whipped before."

Ampris winced. The way she hurt all over, she wasn't sure she'd call it a victory.

"What about the transports?" Ampris asked. "How long do you think before another comes by?"

"Ain't the way to get in the city," the lit murmured and swept harder.

"How then?"

The lit said nothing.

Ampris glanced around swiftly, aware of the need to be cautious. No patrollers seemed to be in sight. No scanners were hovering. A sort of quiet had fallen over the area, broken only by the sound of sweeping and a distant quarrel deeper in the slum.

"How do I get in?" Ampris repeated.

The lit glanced at her unwillingly. "Catch you on a cargo hauler or a transport, they shoot you on sight. I seen it happen."

"Tell me another way," Ampris said, beginning to feel a little desperate. She'd come so far, and she was going to get inside, no matter what it took.

The lit giggled. "Ain't no other way," she said. Whirling around, she trotted out of sight.

"Wait!" Ampris called after her, forgetting caution. "When's the next transport due?"

But the lit was gone, and the platform stood deserted.

Ampris swore to herself, then trudged away, heading for the edge of the slum. It was a filthy-looking place, with crooked dark streets and the unmistakable look of being dangerous. In the distance she saw a light flashing, and heard the mechanized patter of a huckster trying to lure the unwary into a gambling den. As Ampris walked closer, the stink grew into a terrible effluvia of unwashed bodies, rotting garbage, and open sewage. It mingled with the dead-fish stench of the river. The smell seemed to pervade her fur and skin, clinging to her like the dreary despair of this place. Every breath she unwillingly inhaled coated her tongue with a sour, vile taste. Yet threaded through the fetid odors came the smells of food and cooking. Her mouth watered, and she panted with thirst.

Ahead of her, a gang of Reject males stood clustered together, chattering loudly.

She skirted them warily, keeping plenty of distance between herself and them.

Behind her, she heard the echoing thump of the city gates sliding open. She spun around, wincing as she moved too fast, and saw a battered, decrepit transport rumbling out of the city. It stopped as soon as it was through the gates, and disgorged a load of Rejects, all of them coated with plaster dust and looking weary from a hard day's work.

The gang scattered to meet the new arrivals, calling out a mixture of greetings and insults. "You get paid?" someone called.

"You get fed?"

"You bring any food?"

One of the workers powdered in white slapped at his ragged clothing and raised his rill. "None that I'm going to share with the likes of you."

The two of them went at it in a fight, while the others circled them and shouted encouragement.

Ampris slipped down a narrow street and saw an Aaroun female standing in the doorway of a shack constructed of crate and packing materials held together with pieces of rusting wire. It looked like it might fall down at any moment.

"Excuse me," Ampris said politely to her. "Will any more transports be going into the city soon?"

The Aaroun looked at her blankly for a long while. One of her eyes was blue with blindness. The other eye, brown and vacant, held only bleak despair. But she finally seemed to rouse herself.

"Ain't no more for th' night," she said. "Shift over. Din't you see?"

Ampris probed at her aching jaw. "No, I guess I didn't notice. When will they—"

But the Aaroun turned and stepped inside her shack, leaving Ampris in mid-sentence.

Backing her ears, Ampris glanced around and tried to figure out what to do next. She hurt. She was desperately hungry, and every scent of food made her stomach rumble painfully. The sun was going down, and she needed to find a place to spend the night.

She had the feeling of being watched, although she saw very few Rejects or abiru stirring. Behind her, she could still hear the sounds of the fight going on, louder even than the mechanized come-ons of the gambling den. A female Reject with hostile, cynical eyes brushed past her, and Ampris felt the quick fingerings of a pickpocket.

Growling, she slapped the thieving hand away, and the Reject hurried on without a backward glance. Ahead of Ampris, a yellow light glowed dimly in the gathering shadows, marking a brothel.

Ampris veered away from it too, wanting to avoid all trouble. She realized she was lost, and her poor physical condition was keeping her from thinking clearly. She shouldn't have ventured into Reject Town, she thought. She should have stayed near the city gates. Now it would be dark soon, and if she stayed here she would be easy prey for whatever hunted in these squalid streets.

Thirst made up her mind for her. She headed deeper into the slum, intending to find the river. The water was probably unsafe to drink, but Ampris was past caring. She would sleep on the bank somewhere, in the freshest air possible, away from this fetid place. Come morning, she would try again to slip inside the city. She might even look for sewer tunnels, although Elrabin had warned her against trying to enter the city that way. He'd told her tunnels were guarded by ruffians and thieves who used them for hideouts and storage of stolen goods. They were well-guarded, no place for an amateur.

She would decide in the morning; that is, if she survived that long.

Following her nose, she blundered down dim, twisting little streets, trying to find the river, and coming to dead ends far too often. There was no kind of order here. Shacks had been built anywhere their owners wanted, facing in haphazard directions, and sometimes planted right in the middle of the street itself.

Of course, "street" was too generous a word for these trails through filth. Skeks sorting through garbage squeaked and fled from Ampris's approach, only to follow at her heels. She tried several times to shoo the short, multilegged vermin away. They would scatter momentarily, waving their boneless hands stupidly over their heads, and come right back.

Then she heard the scrape of a footstep behind her. Instantly the fur bristled around Ampris's neck. She glanced back and saw a Reject in a stained coat following her. She tensed, wary and alert now. When she looked forward, she saw another Reject blocking her path.

He had emerged from nowhere, melting into sight like a shadow. From her left came two more; from her right, at least three or four.

Ampris's heart started pounding. She panted, her ears flicking back nervously. She was standing in one of the wider streets of the slum. On one side rose a section of the city wall, tall, smooth, and unassailable. On the other side, a pair of shacks that had fallen in some time ago had created a clearing of sorts. The rubble and debris, however, made the footing unstable. It would be easy to stumble and fall if she tried to run or fight.

As the Rejects closed in on her from all sides, they began to make a peculiar hissing, humming sound. Her lips skimmed back from her teeth instinctively, and she growled low in her throat as she turned slowly around to face as many of them as possible.

"I have nothing to steal," she said, aware of the Eye of Clarity tucked inside her torn jerkin. She hoped it hadn't slipped into sight to betray her. "The Toths already stole everything I had."

"You don't belong here," one of the Rejects said, while the others hummed and hissed with increasing menace. "Abiru *filth,* taking our space. Eating our food."

"I haven't—"

"This our place," the Reject said. As he came closer, she saw that he had red eyes. His square pupils were dilated and huge. Flicking out his tongue, he did something clever and quick with both hands, and two knives slid from inside his sleeves to appear, shiny and lethal, in the expert clutch of his fingers. "This our place!" he repeated. "Not for abiru. You get out!"

Ampris forgot that she was weak with hunger and thirst. She forgot that her crippled leg was aching and nearly useless. She forgot the blisters on her feet and the bruises on her body. She looked around to where the circle was the thinnest, and she ran for her life.

With less than three hours left before her scheduled departure, Israi was still seated in private audience with Lord Nalsk, head of the ominous Bureau of Security. He had brought her the latest dispatches of intelligence from the rim world rebellion.

Israi listened to the male in stony silence. She had not yet forgiven him for canceling her vacation to Mynchepop yesterday. For the past several years, she had made an annual summer visit to the exquisite pleasure planet to escape the heat of Vir. It was a trip that she looked forward to with great anticipation, but with war raging along the outermost edges of the empire, it had been deemed inadvisable for the Imperial Mother to leave the safety of Viisymel.

She was furious. She had never found disappointment easy to accept, and to be denied her wish was something rare and most difficult to swallow.

Now she sat on her red-cushioned throne in the audience hall, closed to all while she met with Lord Nalsk, and glared at him through half-slitted eyes. She had given Nalsk increasing power over the years, and his network of intelligence agents had proven invaluable to her, but she hated anyone who thought he could tell her no.

Had a passenger ship not been attacked in recent weeks, she would have ignored his order and departed for Mynchepop as planned. But Israi was no fool. She knew some risks were too costly. Therefore, as soon as her audience with Nalsk ended, she would close the court and go instead to her lodge in the mountains.

There was much optimism among her courtiers that the mountains would be cooler. They would not be as cool as Mynchepop, which had no adverse weather. But any respite was better than nothing.

She slumped lower in her chair, leaning her head on her hand, and flicked out her tongue.

Nalsk's droning voice stopped. "Do I bore the Imperial Mother?"

He had an icy way of speaking and a disdainful way of looking between his nostrils. His rill was held up by a tall collar of engraved silver, and he wore a coat of plainly woven blue silk. Not for Lord Nalsk the outrageous, extravagant fashions of the court. But although he might sometimes prove boring, Israi knew he should never be underestimated. She could ill afford to make an enemy of him.

She flicked out her tongue again. "Not bored, my lord," she replied smoothly. "Merely fatigued."

He bowed, displaying streaks of pink along his rill spines. "My report is perhaps too long?"

"No longer than any of the other reports we have received this day," she said. "Yours is the eighth or ninth. None bring us good news."

"The war goes poorly," he said.

She slammed her fist down on the arm of her throne. "Then when will it go well?"

Nalsk puffed out his air sacs. "Lord Belz has reached the area of greatest fighting. He reports the next battle will commence our time tomorrow. I will continue to send your majesty reports on that matter during your majesty's absence."

She barely concealed her grimace of disgust. "Thank you." Oh, yes, she thought bitterly, he would flood her with reports, as would every other official on her council. Going to the lodge was hardly getting away. And she was tired, so tired her head buzzed all the time and she could barely concentrate. It seemed of late that never a day passed without several new crises. The desk of her study was heaped with problems, and she could not cope with them all. Even Temondahl looked weary and worried.

And yet, she had to try to get away from Vir, even if her rest was interrupted. She knew she must take care of herself first.

Nalsk was staring at her, as though he had said something she'd not heard and now expected an answer.

Israi stared back at him, and he finally bowed.

"Very well, majesty," he said. "I shall give as many reports as is possible to the chancellor of state. But he is not cleared to see everything. Nor should he be."

"Do your best," she replied.

He seemed to be turning to leave, and Israi straightened in her chair in hope, but Nalsk was only pulling another document from a pocket inside his wide sleeve.

"There is one last thing," he said.

This time Israi could not conceal her sigh of impatience. "Yes?"

"It concerns your egg-brother Oviel."

At once he had her complete interest. A surge of hatred washed over Israi. Her brother had been in exile for years now, living far from court as punishment for his attempt to steal her throne. Israi refused to have his name mentioned in her presence, and no courtier dared defy her.

Except Nalsk, who feared no one, not even her.

"What about the creature?" Israi asked coldly.

"He has served his term," Nalsk said. "His exile officially ends tomorrow."

"No!"

"I'm afraid so, yes." Nalsk's eyes were the green hue of the ocean. They regarded Israi steadily. "He cannot live in exile indefinitely. The law does not allow for that."

"The law should have allowed for his neck to be broken," she said, fuming.

Nalsk permitted himself a small smile. "Even so, Chancellor Temondahl has approached me on the matter and—"

"Temondahl!" Israi said in surprise. "He has discussed Oviel with you?"

"Asking advice," Nalsk said. "Asking when the term would expire. Asking whether Oviel might return to Vir and the court in safety." Nalsk flicked out his tongue.

"The Bureau cannot offer him security without the Imperial Mother's permission."

"Never!" she said, outraged. "We find it difficult to believe that Temondahl is so interested in the welfare of our brother."

"Chancellor Temondahl concerns himself with many details," Nalsk said. "In many different areas."

Israi wasn't going to waste her time trying to figure out what he meant by that. "We do not want Oviel here," she said. "He betrayed us, and we are not yet ready to forgive him."

Nalsk bowed. "As the Imperial Mother commands. But I thought I would warn your majesty of the matter. Temondahl will bring it up, and in such delicate affairs it is best to be prepared."

"Why is it a delicate matter?" she asked. "Oviel is a traitor."

"Some," Nalsk said with care, "do not think so."

"Who?" she demanded with fresh anger. "We demand their names."

"That would entail submitting half the names at court."

Israi rocked back in her chair, too shocked to speak. For the first time in years, she felt disquiet. Had she no better hold on her subjects than this? It seemed inconceivable that a scrawny, overly ambitious upstart with no legal claim to the throne should be able to make so much trouble for her. Yet Oviel had always surprised her that way.

"You are saying that he is popular," she said slowly.

"According to my shadows, yes," Nalsk replied.

"But he has been gone all these years!"

"Perhaps that has helped with his popularity," Nalsk said.

"How great a threat to our throne is he?" she asked.

"Perhaps very little."

Surprised, Israi stared at him. That was not the answer

she had expected. "We fail to understand."

"The common citizens think of him seldom, yet he is of imperial blood and therefore of some interest. The aristocrats believe he has been punished enough for a youthful indiscretion—"

"He betrayed us!" Israi exclaimed.

Nalsk looked down at her from where he stood, and she forced herself to be silent.

"The term of exile was very long, majesty. During that time, Oviel has behaved himself. He has not attempted to leave his remote villa. He has not spoken against your majesty. He has not been in contact with certain subversive groups under our most serious suspicion. In short, he has conducted himself on model lines. This is generally known and greatly in his favor."

"And?" she prompted.

"It may mean that he no longer covets your majesty's throne."

Israi laughed harshly. "Oh, he wants it. He will always want it."

"But if the lesson has been learned, it is possible he will not reach for it."

"Is that your recommendation, Lord Nalsk? That we allow him to return to our side?"

Nalsk flicked out his tongue. "I make no recommendation. I merely bring a report to your majesty's attention. Others will make recommendations, but now your majesty is prepared for them."

Soon thereafter, he bowed and left her.

Israi sat scowling in the empty audience hall, making no attempt to leave it. She knew that Oviel would bring her nothing but trouble. She could not allow him to return. She dared not allow it. He would take every advantage of his presence at court. He would twist words, and tempt subversives, and start new intrigues. She had enough problems to deal with already. She did not need him to add to her difficulties.

A soft tapping on the door broke her concentration. Flicking out her tongue, Israi replied.

Temondahl entered, carrying his staff of office and bowing. "Your majesty's shuttle is almost ready for departure. Your majesty's luggage is being loaded, and the attendants—"

Israi waved these minor details aside. "Come here, chancellor, and speak with us."

Temondahl obeyed, halting just a few steps short of her throne. His rill was extended in surprise and expectation. His old, half-lidded eyes regarded her patiently.

"We hear," she said, unable to keep a rasp from her voice, "that Oviel will soon be released."

"Tomorrow," Temondahl said too promptly.

She felt a flare of suspicion and did her best to conceal it. "We hear that he wishes to return to court."

"Yes, majesty. He has written to me, requesting it."

"To you," she said coldly, her anger growing steadily. "But not to us."

"No, of course not," Temondahl replied. "The Imperial Mother has said she would not hear his name spoken, would not see his name written. How could he write to your majesty without violating this command?"

Some of Israi's anger deflated. She flicked out her tongue, turning over Temondahl's words in her mind, seeking any deceit.

"We dislike our brother," she said at last. "We are in no mood to forget old wrongs."

"But these wrongs are *very* old," Temondahl said. "Regret has been expressed. I think your majesty will find your brother much changed."

She said nothing. Her heart was stone.

"Majesty, I hesitate to say this, but Lord Oviel's popularity has grown in recent years. He has behaved himself flawlessly, and the people have heard of this. He has expressed contrition, and the people know of that. He has caused no trouble, made no attempt to flee from a villa in a most inhospitable part of Viisymel."

Yes, Israi thought. Oviel had been sent to live in an area called the Anvil of the Gods. Nothing grew on the land. Nothing lived on the land. The temperatures were hotter than anywhere else on the planet. Terrible sandstorms raged almost daily. Heat and dust and poisonous insects ruled the place. She had hoped he would die there. But it seemed he had thrived instead. Cursing him silently, she clenched her hands around the arms of her throne and told herself she could not relent.

"He has done nothing less than he was supposed to do," she said. "Why should he be rewarded?"

"Would the return to court be a reward?"

"Would it not?" she replied, astonished that Temondahl would make such a naive remark.

"Please, majesty, do not misunderstand what I am about to say, but as food becomes scarcer and more costly, the people—well, the people do not revere the Imperial Mother as they once did."

"We are aware of the polls," Israi said harshly. The hurt never went away. But she always told herself she did not care. The people could curse her if they dared, but she was Kaa and would remain so.

"I believe that the Imperial Mother's popularity would rise if she decided to show mercy to her egg-brother," Temondahl said cautiously. He looked at her as though he expected her to fly into a rage. "Politically, it would be wise to allow his return."

"Politically it would be a disaster," she said. "He will cause trouble."

"I don't believe he will. May I show your majesty his letter?"

Her rill flared to its fullest extension. "You may not," she snapped.

Temondahl retreated a step and bowed low.

Israi rose from her throne and began to pace back and forth. She was tired, and she wanted only to get aboard her shuttle and leave the palace as fast as she could. Yet the problems stayed with her, as though attached to the hem of her gown. Her mind turned the issue over and over, seeking a solution.

"And if we turn Oviel away?" she asked at last. "If we refuse his return? Will he go offworld?"

"That is doubtful."

No, she thought. He would never leave Viisymel while his presence could still bring her trouble.

Anger throbbed in her rill. She hesitated, battling inside herself. She hated being put into a corner, but she could see how Oviel had accomplished it. He had acquired a certain finesse over the years, and he had Temondahl's help now. She had a memory of her father's deathbed, when she had seen Temondahl deep in conversation with Oviel and their uncle, the very radical Telvrahd. Traitors both—and perhaps Temondahl was a traitor also.

The thought of no longer being able to trust her chancellor was a disquieting one. Fatigue burned through her, and she felt overwhelmed.

"Very well," she said. "Permission is granted, but Oviel will have no privileges of imperial rank. Do not expect us to welcome him as a long-lost brother."

"As the Imperial Mother commands," Temondahl said.

As he went out, Israi observed that his eyes were sparkling.

She stared after him with the hollow certainty that she had made a huge mistake. With her chancellor's loyalties belonging to Oviel instead of to her, and with Lord Belz on the other side of the empire, she had few strong allies indeed.

She flicked out her tongue, hesitating a few minutes longer.

An attendant entered cautiously. "Majesty, the shuttle

is ready for departure. When will it please the Imperial Mother to board?''

Ignoring the lady, Israi summoned a herald. ''Bring Lord Nalsk to us at once,'' she told him.

She had to wait a long time for the head of security to return. It seemed he had left the palace to attend a dinner party elsewhere in the city. Increasingly impatient, Israi went to her apartments to change her court gown for comfortable traveling attire. When she emerged at last, with a slave fastening the clasp of her jeweled bracelet for her, she found Nalsk waiting for her.

He bowed, and she dismissed her servants with a gesture.

''We shall be brief,'' she said and told him what had transpired between her and Temondahl.

''It is wise to allow Oviel's return,'' Nalsk said. ''He can be watched better if he is here.''

''He can meddle better if he is here,'' she said angrily.

Nalsk inclined his head in silence.

Israi paced back and forth. The hollow feeling was back, and she did not like it. ''We want him watched day and night,'' she said. ''Put your shadows on him. Let nothing go unreported.''

''As the Imperial Mother commands.''

''Watch Temondahl also,'' she said.

Nalsk flicked out his tongue as though surprised, but she had the momentary suspicion that he was pleased. ''It shall be done,'' he said.

Israi left her palace wondering if Nalsk had just intentionally driven a wedge of distrust between her and her chancellor that had not been there before. Perhaps it was Nalsk she should be worried about.

And that was the most disquieting thought of all.

CHAPTER NINE

Chased by the shouting Rejects, Ampris could not hope to outrun them. Grunting with pain, she dodged down a narrow, shadowy street with them hard on her heels. A hand gripped the back of her jerkin, and suddenly she was falling, knocked off her feet by a tackle.

But while she might be hurt, weary, weak, and out of practice, Ampris had not forgotten her old training. She hit the slimy ground and rolled with a kick that freed her from the pursuer who'd taken her down. Snarling, she leapt up to meet the attack of another, gripping his skinny shoulders and using his own impetus to launch him off his feet. He slammed into the side of a rickety shack, caving in a wall. The roof fell in on top of him, and with screams and shouts, a whole family of Rejects emerged in all directions.

Ampris seized the opportunity and fled again. In seconds, she was panting, and her leg hurt so bad she sobbed with every step, but she knew she had to keep going.

From behind, she heard curses and running footsteps. She darted down a cross street and ducked inside a windowless hut lit only by a sputtering lamp that was obviously losing its charge. The occupant was an extremely tall female Reject with mottled red and pink skin, a rill larger than any Ampris had ever seen before, and fierce white eyes that made her look blind. She turned on Ampris, however, and hissed. Her rill stood stiff behind her head, and her pupils dilated just before she came at Ampris with a stick.

Ampris could hear her pursuers coming. At the last second, she dodged the flailing stick and caught it in both hands. She wrenched it easily from the female, who shrieked at her.

Holding the stick like a club, Ampris pinned her against the wall behind her cooking fire and clamped her hand over the female's mouth.

"Be quiet," she said in Viis. "I won't hurt you."

The female's eyes widened. She tried to struggle, but Ampris held her fast. Viis muscles were never a match for Aaroun ones, and Ampris would not let her captive break free.

Outside, the thudding footsteps passed. Ampris waited a few seconds longer, listening, then stepped back and released the female.

The female's white eyes blazed at her. "Thief! You will not have my hut. You will not!"

Again she came at Ampris, flailing with her long thin arms. Ampris ducked her and exited the hut.

She looked in both directions, but did not see the gang of Rejects.

The female hit her in the back. "Get out! Get out!" she shouted. "You abiru have no right to be here. Get out!"

Ampris turned on her and snarled so fiercely the female's rill dropped.

She stepped back with her white eyes wide and frightened. "Do not hurt me. Do not rip out my throat. You can have my—"

"I am not a thief," Ampris said with a growl. "Or a savage. I do not want your home. Only your stick will I take, so you won't hit me."

The Reject stared at her uncomprehendingly. Ampris hobbled away, using the stick as a cane. She desperately needed to go to ground and nurse her hurts, but there was no place of refuge here. She followed her nose the rest of the way to the river.

The street ended right on its bank. A fallen shack lay in a heap of weed-covered debris and beyond it coursed a sluggish brown stream less than half its usual size. The reeds once growing along the water's edge were now yellow and dead. White scum edged the water, and a flock of black, molting birds were busy pecking at dead fish lying on the mud. When Ampris appeared, the birds winged upward with squawks of alarm.

She staggered across the dried curls of mud and knelt at the river's edge. Slapping away the white scum, she lifted a handful of water to her muzzle. The smell was awful, the taste even worse. Despite her thirst, she lapped only a little before she spat it out.

Weary and discouraged, she gazed around in hopes of finding a place where she might take shelter for the night. Maybe under an overhang of the bank would do, she thought.

The sun was going down in a blaze of color. Long shadows filled the fetid street behind her. She wanted only to lie down and nurse her aches and pains for a while.

"There she is!" came a shout.

Startled, Ampris looked up and saw the gang of Rejects heading her way. Many were armed now with stones and clubs.

Ampris's fist curled tighter around the stick in her hand. As a weapon it wasn't much.

"Wait!" she called, holding up her hand as they clustered above her on the bank. "I mean you no harm. I am not here to steal your food or your homes. I just want to—"

"Liar!" someone yelled. "Abiru thief!"

A stone thudded into her shoulder, and another hit her side where the Toth had kicked her earlier.

Crying out, Ampris clutched her side and doubled over. The Rejects swarmed down the bank toward her, yelling and throwing sticks, chunks of stone, pieces of garbage—anything they could use as a missile.

There was no reasoning with them. Ampris gritted her teeth and went stumbling across the dried riverbed to the water. While she splashed into it, more rocks thudded into her back. She dived into the shallow water. The murky brown water closed over her head, and she swiftly closed her nostrils while she struggled forward.

The current tugged at her, and she felt the bottom slope sharply under her feet. Suddenly she was in very deep water, in the main channel itself. She tried to paddle, but her crippled leg could not kick. Flailing about, she found her air running out. In desperation she struggled to the surface and thrust out her head with a gasp.

The shouting Rejects were running along the dry part of the riverbed, still throwing things. Little plops around her told her their aim was not very good at this distance. The current in the channel was stronger than it had looked from shore. It pulled Ampris out, and none of the Rejects entered the water to pursue her.

After a few minutes, they stopped running and watched her bobbing away from them.

Ampris grinned to herself, thrusting her muzzle high to keep her mouth out of the water. That was one way to escape them, she thought. But now that the excitement was over, she found new problems confronting her. The water was filthy, choked in places with trash and the bloated corpses of fish and animals. It stank terribly. The cuts and raw places on her feet were stinging from immersion. And every time she tried to do more than paddle, the pain in her side flared up sharply. It was all she could do to keep her head afloat.

The walls of the city ran parallel with the river. Occasionally she could hear city sounds over the rush and gurgle of the water. Skimmers and other traffic flew overhead occasionally, sunlight flashing off their bright sides, then Ampris found herself floating past a tiny settlement of tents and shacks clustered at the water's edge. Young Aaroun cubs with short legs and rounded tummies were poking among the reeds with sticks. Seeing her, they watched wide-eyed and solemn as she floated by.

Ampris waved at them, but while their heads turned to watch her, they made no other response.

Her muscles were tiring now. Her shoulders ached, and she felt leaden and heavy. While the river had saved her from that little Reject hospitality committee, Ampris knew if she didn't get out of the water soon, it would sweep her far from Vir. Eventually she would be one more corpse bobbing along with the others.

It was hard to pull free of the current, as sluggish as it was. Her muscles were very tired, and with her crippled leg all but useless in the water, she had to make her arms work twice as hard.

Desperately she struggled, calling on all her reserves, and finally angled her way to the shallows. Coughing and gasping for air, she came weaving and staggering up from the water, through the mud, where slimy reeds entwined about her, clinging to her fur like bands. She yanked and tugged to get free of them, lost her balance, and fell flat in the mud.

For a while she lay there, too spent to move, until a sharp peck on the back of her head brought her to.

She jerked up her head, and the bird squawked and flew off. Others wheeled above her, and with a shout she waved at them, driving the carrion eaters away. They would come back, though. She had to get out of here.

Somehow she found the strength to climb to her feet. She twisted and pulled free of the reeds, which left her smeared with loathsome green slime, and took two steps before she staggered to her knees again. Then she crawled across the ground, the dried curls of mud snapping to dust beneath her hands and knees, until she reached the eroded bank.

The base of the wall loomed above her as she collapsed near it. Sobbing, she cradled the Eye of Clarity in her filthy palms and gazed into its mysterious depths. "What do I do?" she asked it. "What do I do?"

No answer came, but after a while she grew calmer, comforted by the stone as always. Her eyelids grew heavy, until she could no longer lift them. She slept in the last blaze of sunset across the river, and the dying rays of light turned her muddy fur golden before twilight closed in and made her one more shadow among many.

The solemn tolling of a bell awakened her. With a start, she sat up and for a moment did not know where she was.

Then memory returned to her, and she lifted both hands to rub her face until she was fully awake. The rest had done her good. She still ached all over, and her fur was caked stiff with dried mud that stank, but the immersion in cool water had refreshed her by lowering her body temperature. Now an evening breeze blew, and it seemed to be cooler than usual from coming off the water.

Facing it, she sat there in the darkness, gazing at a sky that glowed with the reflection of city lights instead of stars.

She had been lucky, she decided. Despite her mistakes, she had survived. But she knew she had been too long away, too long isolated from the worst of the cruelty so typical of the empire. She'd forgotten how vicious life on the streets could be. Not that she'd ever been long in that environment. Elrabin had tried to warn her, but as usual she didn't listen.

She sighed, wishing he were here now, with his common sense and straightforward encouragement.

As for the others in their group, none of them had ever been to Vir. None of them could possibly imagine how it was in this city. She pictured Harthril's astonishment were he to come leading their little group into Reject Town and be met with such a welcome.

She smiled at the thought, but her amusement faded quickly. That might still happen, if she didn't accomplish what she'd come to do. Although she'd escaped trouble, she hadn't managed to get inside Vir. And if she didn't obtain her objective quickly and return, Harthril would bring the others to this city, to be sucked as victims into its evil.

The bell that had awakened her tolled again. Ampris cocked her head, thinking it sounded familiar. The faint perfumed scent of a blooming garden wafted to her nostrils.

Ampris looked up in sudden alertness and twisted around. For the first time she noticed that lamps atop the walls were shining down, reflected in the river. Only the new section of the palace had lamps on the walls.

Excitement burst inside her chest. She scrambled unsteadily to her feet. She was in the right part of the city, exactly where she needed to be.

The luck of it overwhelmed her. She thought about it for a moment and shivered. Too coincidental. No, it could not be luck. Whispering gratitude, she touched the Eye of Clarity hanging from her throat.

"You brought me here," she murmured. She straightened her shoulders, standing more erect. Fresh energy filled her, and she felt hopeful again.

If she was this close, there had to be a way. The Archives were located in the underground passages beneath the old part of the palace. They were agonizingly close, yet unreachable. For to climb the palace walls meant instant death.

She wanted to roar with frustration.

Not knowing what else to do, she began to walk along

the base of the walls. The darkness was shadowy, incomplete, sometimes lifted by lights shining from tall windows in ornamental towers. Yes, she recognized the palace now. She could hear the sounds of the changing of the guard from within. She could smell the gardens, their fragrance like paradise itself. Her heart was thumping hard, and she panted from excitement and a strange sense of fierce joy.

She was home.

Yet it was not home, she kept reminding herself, feeling anger too. The days when she'd been a carefree cub, pampered and privileged beyond all imagining, were long over. Too much had happened since then for her to go back. Nor did she want to be the naive young innocent again.

Still, to hear the sounds, to smell the gardens, to feel the heat of the day radiating from these old stone walls . . . it took her back to sweet memories of lazy days napping on sun cushions by the garden pools, to adventurous days prowling the reed marshes of a river that ran full, fast, and clean, to days of laughter, racing up and down the polished stone corridors of the palace, to days when civa cakes were fresh and warm.

Growling to herself, Ampris pushed away her memories just as she stumbled over an obstacle unseen in the darkness and nearly fell.

Breathless, she stepped back, wincing at the throbbing pain in her foot. When it faded, she explored cautiously and discovered that it was a mound of rubble where part of the wall had fallen.

Bending down, she felt of the stones and her fingers found chisel marks and grooves. The stones felt old, worn smooth with time and exposure. Ampris knew that the modern section of the palace wall was not built from stone like this. Her heartbeat quickened.

She was indeed outside the old part of the palace, the part deserted long ago. Weeds were growing over the rubble, which meant this section had fallen long ago and never been repaired. What was wrong with the palace, that it had grown so careless?

Behind her, she could see the modern section, its lamps shining in pale, iridescent orbs. The deadly force field that shielded the walls glowed white, but here by the older wall, no force field was on.

Ampris wondered why she had not realized it immediately. Perhaps weariness had slowed her wits.

Cautiously, knowing her hand could be blasted to bits, Ampris slowly placed it on the wall. She felt the stored heat of the day radiating from the stones, but no other power hummed there. The shield was not active.

Relief coursed through her. With renewed energy, she began climbing. The fallen stones shifted beneath her weight, and the poor footing threw considerable strain on her crippled leg. But she had hope now, hope and a chance. She kept climbing grimly until she was on top of the fallen stones. Before her, the wall rose several more feet, but Ampris gathered herself both mentally and physically.

Sliding her hand inside her jerkin, she clutched her Eye of Clarity tightly in her fist.

"Help me now," she murmured, closing her eyes in supplication. "Help me find the strength of my youth."

The clear stone in her hand seemed to grow warmer. Ampris focused on the sensation, letting her consciousness seep into it and become one with it. Over the years, she had gradually learned to stop hurling her desires and will at the stone. Instead, she had learned to calm herself inside and listen. When she did that, her mind always grew clearer. Usually the solution to her problem was then easily found.

The old voices of her gladiator trainers circled in her mind. Without realizing it, she nodded several times, remembering what to do. She imagined herself when she was young and powerful, at the peak of her physical prowess.

Her muscles rippled under her golden fur, and as she opened her eyes, she leapt upward. Her fingertips just hooked over the broken edge of the top. Gasping with the strain, she felt her arms shudder as she struggled to pull herself higher. She could not do it, could not make it. Yet Ampris gritted her teeth and kept on, despite the fiery burn in her arms and shoulders. With her right foot, she scrabbled for toeholds, pushing herself up, *pushing*.

Just when she thought she would burst a vessel from the strain, she hooked her elbow over the top, pulled, and rested her belly there. She lay on the wall a long time, panting hard, her eyes closed, arms and legs dangling over the sides. Gradually she grew aware of an intense, throbbing ache in her injured ribs, but Ampris did not care. She had made it. That was all that mattered.

It was a long time before she could straighten and sit up. She did so cautiously, grimacing with pain, and kept a lookout for scanners. But all the security measures seemed to be concentrated on the perimeter of the modern part of the palace compound.

As she perched there, she could see the imperial palace itself. Many lights shone from its oblong windows. Now and then a distinctive Viis silhouette appeared, then vanished. Faint laughter and the soft notes of music told Ampris that courtiers were strolling the grounds, probably savoring the delights of the gardens just before they went inside to dine.

The lazy, indolent life at court. How well she had once known it, she an Aaroun cub from nowhere, abducted at birth and sold on the black market to eventually become the beloved pet of a young and pampered sri-Kaa. What a fable it all seemed now. So long ago. So hard to believe any of it had ever happened.

The sound of a flying skimmer broke the quiet, and recalled Ampris to caution.

She looked over into the old palace compound and saw only darkness and the dim outlines of scattered buildings. Not daring to hesitate longer, she slid herself over the wall and let herself drop.

Landing with a jolt that shook her from her heels to the top of her head, Ampris bit back a yelp of pain and staggered several steps before falling to her knees and then sprawling full-length on the ground. Nothing was broken, but that drop had taken the final bits of her strength.

Wearily, she let her head sag to the ground, and lay where she'd fallen.

The kiss of sunrise woke her. Yawning, she stretched and sat up, wincing at how the hard ground had given her body new aches and sore places. Stiff and desperately hungry, she managed to get to her feet and looked around at an eerie, desolate ruin.

Restoration work, probably ordered by Israi's father, had obviously at one time begun to make progress in repairing the crumbling buildings, but the work had been abandoned for quite some time.

Ampris saw collapsed scaffolding beneath an exquisite plaster frieze half-repaired and left unfinished. Weeds covered neat stacks of stones that had been brought in and then never used. She found a hydraulic chisel lying abandoned where the worker had laid it down next to a halved cornerstone. The chisel had rusted and been ruined from years of exposure, never to be picked up again.

And it was silent here. She listened to the sound of the wind whispering among the ruins. In the distance she could hear muted sounds of the city, and the bells that rang over the new palace, but here nothing stirred save a few insects. Ampris focused on them, pounced, and ate, crunching through the sharp bitter taste. It wasn't enough to alleviate the terrible gnawing emptiness in her belly; forcing back desperation, she concentrated on finding the Archives.

Wandering about, she eventually came to a domed structure rising from the ground to about the height of her waist. Steps had been cut into the ground, leading down to a door. Perhaps it was an old workmen's entrance. It looked abandoned and partially fallen in.

Discouraged, Ampris sank down to rest. Her legs were trembling weakly from hunger. She had come so far, risked so much, and now she wondered if the Archives even existed anymore.

In a few minutes, she pushed herself upright and went to check the door. From a distance it looked decrepit, but when she climbed down the crumbling steps, she found the door stout and well-made. It did not budge when she pushed it, and a complicated lock secured it.

Drawing in a breath, she bent to examine the lock more closely. Elrabin could have picked it, but it was beyond her skills.

The sound of footsteps made her straighten with a jerk. She hurried up the steps as fast as she could and came face-to-face with an elderly Myal garbed in a brown linen robe.

Flinging up his head so fast his mane rippled back from his face, the Myal stared at her in wide-eyed alarm. His broad mouth hung open, and he dropped the small bundle of lunch he was carrying.

Her nose told her it was meat globes and spice cakes. Her stomach growled and her mouth watered, and for a second she could think of *nothing* except food. It took all her willpower not to grab the fallen bundle.

Instead she licked her mouth and lifted her gaze to his. "Please," she said hoarsely, her voice weak and unsteady. "Are you an—"

"Get away from here!" the Myal said angrily. He seemed to have recovered from his fright. His long, prehensile tail shot straight up into the air behind him while he flapped his hands at her. "Get away! You don't belong here."

Her mind was wavering. She was so hungry, so tired, so desperate. She knew he had to be an archivist, but his hostility was one more obstacle in a row of too many. He had to help her, but she couldn't find the words she needed.

"Please," she said, holding out her hands to him. "Help me."

"I don't have to help you. A dreadful ruffian you are, sent here to rob us," the Myal accused her. "Go away. It is forbidden for the likes of you to come here. Go back to the master you ran away from. Go!"

She had to make him understand. "Please. Are you an archivist? Is this the way in?"

He looked more alarmed than ever. "You can't get in. I won't let you in. I'll call the guards right now."

Turning away from her, he hurried off on his short, bowed legs.

Ampris tried to go after him, but after a few steps she was staggering and spent. Her breath came in short gasps, and her vision was blurring. She was furious that her body should fail her now, at this most critical time.

"Help me!" she called after him. "I am seeking—"

"I'll help you, yes!" he shouted, still waddling away. "I'll help the guards come and throw you back over the wall, or however you got in here."

"Wait!" she said, but her voice was failing her too. She tried again to pursue him, but her legs gave under her, and she sank to the ground. Lying there in the dust, she wanted to sob with despair and humiliation. "I am a friend of Bish," she said desperately. "I've come to see Bish. Tell him my . . . my name is . . . Ampris."

Several meters away, the Myal stopped in his tracks as though he'd been shot. He spun around, staring at her incredulously. ''Ampris!'' he said. ''The Golden One? Ampris?''

But she was falling into a heavy darkness, sinking deep into a place of bottomless oblivion, and could not answer him.

CHAPTER TEN

When she awakened, she found herself lying on a soft bunk with a blanket tucked around her. Six Myals sat in a semicircle at the foot of the bed, staring at her with varying degrees of anxiety and fascination.

She had been bathed, and instead of pain she felt a hazy sense of well-being. Looking under the blanket, she found various medication patches attached to her.

The room was small and without a window. A single lamp burned softly in one corner, casting clear, even illumination. The air felt cool and slightly damp. She realized she must be below ground, possibly in the warren that made up the Archives. It was evident that the Myals had decided to help her and not turn her in. With a sigh of relief she let her eyes close.

"Ampris."

Her eyes opened, and she found the Myal she'd talked to outside now standing beside her bed. He was old, with streaks of gray running through his mane of red hair. His brown eyes, however, were sharp and alert, bright with an emotion she could not identify.

"You are Ampris?" he asked again. "The one of legend? The Golden One?"

"Once I was called that, yes," she replied. Her voice

sounded strange to her, weak and far away. "But I am no legend."

"You wear an Eye of Clarity," he said. "Where did you get it?"

"From the hand of my enemy," she said.

The Myal stared at her. The other Myals stared at her. She looked at their faces for Bish, but he was not there.

"Is this the Archives?" she asked. "I need to see Bish. He was once kind to me. I have a favor to ask of him."

The Myals exchanged glances.

"She is the one," a thin, black-maned Myal said. "She is Nithlived, the warrior-priestess reincarnated."

"Can you be sure, Brother Prynan?" another asked fretfully. "We must be sure."

"Who else could she be?" asked a third. "She has appeared, as though the sky opened and dropped her here. She wears the Eye."

"She came here by climbing over the wall," said a fourth sourly. Plumper than the others, with a mane streaked red and brown, he glared at Ampris with deep suspicion. "Exactly the same as any other abiru thief can if repairs are not made soon."

"But her feet, Brother Non. She has walked so far."

"The legends say that so did Nithlived the First walk a long pilgrimage," Prynan intoned. His eyes were distant, gazing far into the past. "She walked across the vast grass plains of her world, to a mountain with shining waters at its foot. Kneeling on the shore, she prayed for wisdom, asking for help in leading her people. A voice did speak to her, calling her into the water. She walked into it, deeper and deeper, until the waters closed over her head. And when she came forth from the lake, purified and cleansed, some of the sacred water did remain in her hand, solidified into a stone as clear and transparent as the water which formed it. Thus did she acquire an Eye of Clarity, and thereafter she returned to her people to lead them in battle.''

Listening to Prynan recite this legend, which she had never heard before, Ampris felt a shiver pass through her. For an instant it was as though she stood on the verge of understanding great knowledge, and if she could make one last effort she would at last reach through the veils of confusion to see all that she had ever wanted to.

''Ask her more questions, Brother Quiesl,'' Non said, breaking the spell. ''Make certain of her identity.''

The red-maned Myal standing over Ampris sent her a glance of sympathy. ''She is weak still, my brothers. We must not tax her. Let her rest now. There will be time for more questions later.''

They rose to their feet to leave, mumbling among themselves.

Ampris held out her hand to Quiesl. He took it cautiously; his smooth, hairless fingers were warm and strong. ''Please,'' she whispered. ''I want to see Bish. I know he's important and probably busy, but if you told him it was me, he might—''

''I am sorry,'' Quiesl said in a gentle voice. ''But Brother Bish has been dead these past three years. No longer does he work among us, except in spirit.''

''Oh.'' She did not know what else to say. She'd been so certain she'd find him here, so certain he would remember her despite the long years since their last meeting, so certain he would forgive the carelessness of a cub who had not understood or valued what he tried to teach her. She'd counted on him to be a friend still, one who would give her the information she needed and send her on her way. Now, she did not know how to reach out to these strangers.

Quiesl brushed her face gently with his fingertips. ''You weep for him, Aaroun called Ampris. You mourn him?''

She nodded, her eyes blurring with tears. "He was a friend," she whispered. "He was kind to me."

The other Myals shuffled out, leaving her and Quiesl alone. "Except for Brother Prynan, they are afraid to believe," he said to her, his eyes shining once again. "But Brother Prynan is not, and I am not. While I have not yet embraced Brother Prynan's theory of reincarnation, for sometimes he does tend to become rather fanciful, still do I know that you are the one we have waited for. You are Ampris of the Freedom Network."

She blinked, her tears forgotten. "You heard those old messages?"

"Oh, yes. All of them I have recorded and saved. You tried very hard in those years, yes, you did."

She sighed, holding away memories of risks and intrigue, of the sedition she'd preached to any abiru she could contact during her travels as a gladiator. "I tried," she agreed. "Little was accomplished."

"The foundation was laid for the real work," Quiesl said. "Now we can begin anew."

Ampris tried to sit up, but found herself too weak.

At once he patted her shoulder. "Please, you must rest. I speak too soon of matters that can wait a little longer."

But Ampris couldn't wait. She felt sudden urgency. "How long have I been unconscious?"

"Two days only—"

"Two days!" She lifted her hand and rubbed her muzzle. Time was running out. "I must get up. Help me, please."

"You need rest. You are very weak."

But Ampris struggled, gasping and feeling a wave of gray weakness wash through her. She kept at it until at last she was sitting up with her legs dangling weakly over the side of the bed. The small, windowless room wavered and tilted in all directions.

"You are unwell, Ampris," Quiesl said in concern. "This is most unwise."

She reached out and gripped his arm to steady herself. "I have others depending on me. Friends . . . family . . . Somewhere in your records, there must be information of how the Aaroun people once gathered and preserved food. Without modern technology. Without—"

She found herself suddenly breathless. The room spun around her, and she sank down again.

Quiesl helped her. "Too soon, Golden One," he fussed. "You have been most unwell. You came to us from a long distance."

Frustration made her weep, and she hated her tears, hated her weakness. "I walked for eleven days. It took too long to cross the Plains of Filea. I don't have enough time to be ill."

Quiesl tucked the blanket more tightly around her. "The body works in its own time. Be at peace. Healing will go faster if the mind can rest."

"But they're waiting on me, depending on me—"

"Ampris," he said, placing his hand lightly over her mouth. "Be at peace. You are our guest. You shall have all that you need. Sleep now, and when you next awaken, I shall bring food to you."

His voice was low and soothing. Despite her sense of urgency and distress, Ampris found her eyes closing. She tried to resist, but she found her consciousness following the rise and fall of his voice, no longer aware of any words, only sound, only motion, only sleep.

Quiesl was as good as his word. When Ampris awakened, she was presented with both a tray of food and a small viewer with an array of sivo data crystals.

Overwhelmed and excited, she did not know whether to gobble the offerings of fruit and meat or to switch on the viewer. Filling her mouth and gulping food faster than she should have, she started the display of information.

Within several hours, she had played all the crystals. While her head was spinning with new knowledge, Quiesl made her sleep again, then brought her more.

"Everything within the Great Library of the Kaas is at your disposal, Ampris," he said to her. "Any history, any kind of record, any vidcast is yours. You have only to ask."

Lying there in bed while her battered body slowly healed, Ampris lost track of everything except this wealth of information, so long denied her eager mind, and now brought to her like treasure.

She forced herself to concentrate first on what she'd specifically come for and soon collected diagrams and methods for drying meat into jerky and how to dig certain roots and tubers at specific times of the year so that they would not rot. But she also took the chance to listen to public vidcasts and caught up on the news of the empire. For the past twelve years she had lived in an information vacuum, and the changes that had come during Israi's reign both fascinated and saddened her.

The empire lay in economic ruin. Right now a war was raging out in the rim worlds, and the mighty Viis flotilla of warships was there, fighting the rebels. The drought on Viisymel continued unchecked. The solutions offered by public officials and scientists seemed ridiculous to Ampris. She read sivo crystals on Viisymel's past and learned how pollution problems had wrecked its ecological and climate systems. She also came across files on Viis history, endless rambling accounts of how they rose to prominence with a flourishing, ruthless culture of conquerors and warriors. But the empire's strength collapsed during the long-past plague of the Dancing Death, called that because of the way dying victims spun around and thrashed in their death throes. Millions had died in one year. The survivors had been affected genetically, and fewer and fewer eggs were hatched with each successive generation.

"You are dying," Ampris murmured to the pictures of Viis citizens. "It is taking generations, but your race is dying out."

"Talking to yourself?" Quiesl asked, coming into her room with a cursory knock.

She looked up from the viewer and smiled. "More crystals?" she asked eagerly.

The Myal laughed and tickled her jaw with the tip of his tail. "Indeed, I believe your thirst for knowledge exceeds that of any archivist working here. Would you rather read than eat?"

She hesitated over that question as Quiesl stepped out for a moment, then returned with a tray of food. This time, only a single data crystal lay next to her plate.

She picked it up in disappointment. "Only one? I—"

"One is enough, this time," he said. His smile faded, and he looked very serious. "Eat first. Promise me."

"Of course."

Puzzled by his mood, she backed her ears slightly and watched him gather up the crystals she'd played. He carried them out as he closed the door quietly behind himself.

When she'd finished eating her dinner, she put the tray aside and plumped up her pillows. Then she fitted the crystal into the viewer and switched it on.

Within seconds she was sitting bolt upright, gripping the viewer with both hands. For this was apparently the true account—presented with still shots and reenactments while a Myal voice narrated—of how the Aarouns originally came to Viisymel.

Shaken, she froze the viewer for a moment and drew in several deep breaths. All her life she'd heard nothing but lies and half-truths. Now at last, it seemed she would be able to solve the mystery.

Finally, when she felt calm enough to proceed, she let

the viewer play, and the Myal narrator's voice filled the room:

"Many, many generations ago, the Aarouns lived free on their own world, Sargas III. They knew about the Viis empire far from their boundaries, but the empire scarcely touched their lives. Several times Viis agents came, requesting permission to establish agricultural colonies on their world. The Aaroun leaders refused these requests. They knew the Viis owned many worlds. They did not wish for the Viis empire to own theirs.

"The Viis requested that the Aarouns raise food commercially and sell it to the empire. Again the Aarouns refused. They did not wish to change their traditions, customs, and general way of life in order to work according to Viis rules.

"Every year for a decade the Viis came with these requests. Every year the requests became more insistent, until they were demands. Always the Aarouns refused.

"Then Viis armies arrived.

"The warrior-priestess Nithlived led Aaroun forces against the invaders. Although outgunned, the Aarouns proved to be fierce fighters and would not surrender.

"The Viis general was a male descended from the Fifth House, a general of proud lineage and great cunning. Having observed the Aarouns' bulky size and powerful muscles, having seen their culture and arts, having witnessed their fairness and honesty, the general realized that the Aarouns themselves would be a greater asset to the empire than their small, undeveloped planet.

"With the permission of his Kaa, the general released a bacterial contaminant into the Sargas III ecosystem. Within days, plant life began to die; water grew undrinkable. The problems spread rapidly. Not possessing the technology to combat such a biodisaster, the Aarouns found themselves facing mass starvation.

"The Aaroun scholar Osoa, valued among his people for his wisdom and honor, feared that the Aarouns faced

extinction. He sent forth an appeal to other planets, asking for help.

"But the Viis blocked outgoing communications from Sargas III, and only the Viis responded to Osoa's call for help. Withdrawing their armies, the Viis leaders pretended great concern over the plague and offered to help the Aarouns save their world. Viis scientists came and consulted with Aaroun leaders, warning them that it would take at least one generation to restore the damaged ecosystem. Aarouns could not live on their world for that length of time. The Aarouns were afraid, for they had nowhere else to go. Yet the Viis leaders gave them a solution. If the Aarouns agreed to be deported en masse, and if they agreed to work for the Viis empire until the debt they owed was repaid, the Viis would save their world.

"Despite Nithlived the Third's outspoken objections to this arrangement, a treaty was drawn up between Viis negotiators and Osoa. Fearful of Viis trickery, Osoa strove to create a document that would protect his people. Smooth-tongued and urbane, the Viis negotiators filled the clauses with vague wording. With people dying daily of hunger, Osoa simply ran out of time. The treaty that was forged stated the terms of the Aaroun obligation, specifying the Aarouns' skills as builders, architects, sociologists, healers, and musicians. The treaty said the Aarouns would be permitted to leave their Viis employment when Aaroun lands grew verdant and lush and when Aaroun water flowed clear and pure.

"With great reluctance, the people left their dying homeworld. Many wept during the exodus, knowing they would never see Sargas III again. Their only hope was that their cubs would be able to return.

"Once the Aarouns had been deported, however, Viis spaceships blasted Sargas III into an uninhabitable piece of rubble. Thus did they trick the honest Aarouns into slavery, using them for the most menial jobs that

often required great strength and physical endurance.

"A generation passed, and then another. Gradually the Aarouns forgot the great promise of the Osoa Treaty. They worked as slaves, downtrodden and without hope. It was forbidden to sing their prayer songs. It was forbidden to talk of their great leaders and warriors. Until at last, the Aarouns were truly a lost people, with no home and no memory of their own rights."

Exhausted, Ampris switched off the viewer and sat there, staring into space with burning eyes. The narration appalled her, and she wanted to weep for what had been lost, yet she couldn't. Her anger burned away her tears.

All her life she had seen evidence of how much deceit and trickery the Viis people were capable of, but this was appalling. The Viis had no honor at all. They never had.

And the Aarouns of today had no idea of what they'd had, or of what they once were. Ampris realized the prayer songs she had gradually learned in bits and pieces over the years were snippets of the forbidden history and vestigial memories of the promise of the great return. No one understood the old songs anymore. Those that had been preserved were garbled and misused. And they were all that was left.

Except for this.

Taking the crystal from the viewer, Ampris turned it over and over in her hand. The Myals knew the truth, yet they were forbidden to share it. Even the Viis no longer knew the difference between their lies and what had really happened, not just to the Aarouns but to many other races and cultures as well.

"You have much to answer for," Ampris said, growling in her throat.

A knock came on the door. Backing her ears, she glared at Quiesl as he came inside.

He saw the crystal in her hand, saw her flattened ears, and sighed. "You are finished, then."

"Yes."

"It is very late. Time for you to sleep."

She snarled. "No, Quiesl, it is time for me to think."

"Tomorrow."

"No, now."

He took the crystal from her hand and put the viewer aside. "Bish left this sealed for you. He believed you would return to learn more."

"And now I know the truth," she said bleakly. "It is worse than I imagined."

"It happened long, long ago," he replied. "Such a great wrong cannot be righted immediately. There is time enough—"

"No," she said sharply, striking the blanket with her fist. "For every whip laid across an abiru back, there is not enough time. For every ration of food withheld from a starving cub, there is not enough time. For every Viis injustice—"

"Perhaps I should be recording this speech as the first new message of the revived Freedom Network," Quiesl broke in gently.

Despite her outrage, she gave him a reluctant smile and sank back against her pillows. "Perhaps," she agreed. "You said you had them recorded. Can you persuade someone at the station to broadcast them?"

"Yes."

Ampris blinked in surprise. She hadn't expected him to answer so readily.

"Do I have your permission?" he asked.

She nodded. "Yes, of course. The Viis have no legal right to keep us enslaved, Quiesl."

"No, Ampris," he agreed. "No legal right at all. The Myals, however, sold themselves into bondage in their greed for knowledge. We have been better treated than your people, but we were fools just the same."

"They can't hold us if we resist," Ampris said. "We are stronger. There are more of us. Do you realize how foolish and lazy the Viis are? They can't fix anything, and yet I have seen manuals and technical diagrams here that would solve so many problems. Why do they—"

"Later," he said, smiling at her while his tail rose behind his head and waved gently back and forth. "You've had enough excitement. Time to sleep."

She lay down and let him change her medication patches. He turned off the lamp and went out, closing the door. But Ampris did not sleep. Her mind kept turning busily.

The Aaroun homeworld had been destroyed, but according to the account she'd read the treaty's wording had been vague and open. It didn't actually mention Sargas III by name. That meant the Aarouns could substitute another planet for their homeworld, and "return" to that planet, without violating the terms of the treaty.

But even as the thought crossed her mind, she was laughing grimly at herself. Oh, yes, honesty must be a genetic trait of the Aaroun blood, she thought. For centuries the Viis had oppressed and enslaved them, for centuries the terms of the Osoa Treaty had been broken, yet here she lay, trying to think of a way to meet its terms.

Snorting, she turned her thoughts instead to Ruu-113, a fabled planet that upon its discovery had been hailed as a promised land for the Viis. Ruu-113 was to said to be almost identical to what Viisymel itself once was, before its inhabitants exploited and ruined it. But Ruu-113 could not save the Viis from their poisoned, dying homeworld, for it was unreachable except through a failed jump gate. How ironic that the Viis had first poisoned the Aaroun homeworld, and had now poisoned their own.

Ampris felt no sympathy for the Viis plight. She remembered that the Zrheli engineers on the space station Shrazhak Ohr were rumored to have sabotaged the jump gate to Ruu-113. They guarded that secret still, and the

Viis could not repair the damage themselves.

Drawing her blanket up over her shoulders, Ampris smiled grimly to herself and felt a renewed sense of purpose. For too long she had let the cause of freedom slide, believing it to be hopeless.

Now she was ashamed of herself. The Aarouns had legality on their side. Freeing them from slavery was no longer about simple rebellion. It was about seeing justice done. It was time to get to work doing just that.

The imperial lodge in the Kreige mal-Hahfra Mountains was old and quaint and boring. Israi had loved it as a chune, but as an adult she saw its flaws and structural problems. The place was showing its age rather badly, more so with each successive year. It needed repair, and one wing was no longer usable. There was no money in the treasury to repair it, even if Israi had been interested in doing so. She knew from watching her father's efforts that restoration meant pouring vast amounts of money into a bottomless hole. Since she'd first come to rule a bankrupt empire and found even her personal fortune to be less than half of what she'd expected, she had refused to spend a ducat on fixing any building.

As a vacation, especially when she'd been looking forward to the very decadent delights of Mynchepop, her sojourn here in the old-fashioned lodge was less than satisfying. There was nothing to do. The season was wrong for hunting, and although the mountains were cooler than Vir, they were not cool enough. The courtiers were also bored and bickered among themselves in numerous petty feuds. She wished she'd banished each of them to their country estates.

The new sri-Kaa did not travel well. He cried almost incessantly and would not eat. Israi could not bear to have the hatchling near her.

Bad news from the war filtered in constantly with the arrival of every dispatch.

Israi was reclining on a low, gilded couch, her musicians plinking out a doleful tune, when the heralds stirred and the door was opened for the latest messenger from Vir.

He came striding in, a tall handsome male with a magnificent green rill and clear yellow eyes. The dispatch box, sealed behind a force shield, floated beside him on the security tether attached to his wrist.

"Majesty—"

Israi could stand no more of it. She stood up and gestured for silence. The murmuring of her courtiers stopped, and the musicians ceased to play. The messenger halted in his tracks, the dispatch box floating beside him.

"No," Israi said firmly. "No more."

Without another word, she turned and left the room, hearing the rising babble of consternation in her wake and taking no heed of it.

She strode through the corridors without benefit of her heralds or her guards. Startled servants sprang to open doors for her. Someone called out a question, but Israi did not pause.

Heedless of her afternoon gown of sky-blue silk embroidered with threads of real gold, she went outside and hurried around to the stables. There, she gestured impatiently and stamped her foot until startled servants shook themselves free of their lazy siestas or dice games and hurried to warm up the engines of a skimmer.

Across the courtyard, her guards were scurrying to her, their green cloaks billowing out behind them. "Majesty, wait!" one called.

Israi fumed. "Hurry," she snapped at a servant, who finished tinkering with the skimmer controls. He stepped out of her way and she jumped aboard the little craft, feeling it bob and adjust to her weight.

Before the guards could reach her, Israi gunned the skimmer across the courtyard and out through the open gates. While she was glancing behind her to see if they were going to bother coming in pursuit, she nearly hit a tree.

The automatic warning systems on the skimmer blared, and she wrenched the controls over, scraping the trunk so closely that her heart pounded in exhilaration. For the first time all day, she smiled. Then she extended her rill and laughed, loud and long, letting the wind whistle around her.

She had been cooped up too long. She would go out of her mind if she had to lounge around one more hour in that dreary lodge. What she wanted was to wait until late at night when the capital city of Mynchepop was alive and thrumming with energy, then dress herself incognito and go dancing in the zavda clubs, feel the savage beat of the drums fill her blood with recklessness. She wanted to drink and gamble and laugh, forgetting for a time that she was Kaa, held a prisoner by her own power, little more than a glorified clerk endlessly attending to the stupid details of the empire.

But there were no dancing clubs or gambling halls here in the mountains—only rocks and sky and soaring narpines. She rocketed as high as a treetop, then plunged toward the ground with such speed a crash would have killed her instantly. At the last moment, she lifted the controls, forcing up the shuddering nose of the small skimmer.

She made the engines cry in protest, and the frame shake, and still it was not enough to settle her.

Not knowing where else to go, she headed off toward her waterfall, a place where she had gone often as a chune to escape her lessons or Lady Lenith.

So far, her guards were not in sight. Laughing and pleased that they had not yet found her—although they had only to set a scanner on her craft to locate it—Israi gunned the skimmer even faster, darting in and out recklessly through the trees with such speed and abandon the slightest mistake would have crashed her to pulp.

She did not care. She was alive, and this at least was fun.

Several minutes later, she reached the clearing where as a chune she'd watched the waterfall go thundering down the mountain in a great cascade of water, throwing up rainbows of mist above a deep pool basined in natural stone. It was a magnificent place. Always it had had the power to awe her and make her appreciate the beauty of nature. She had not come here in several years now, feeling that the special places of chunenhal should be left alone. But today she wanted to feel young again. She needed renewal, desperately.

The clearing was still here; she had not forgotten the way to it. Sunlight slanted down through the trees, casting the place in a golden haze. But the waterfall did not seem as noisy as in years past.

Slowing the skimmer, Israi flew into the clearing slowly, wanting to feel that uplift in her soul at the beauty before her.

Instead, she found the waterfall diminished to a trickle, less than two-thirds its normal size. The lush plant life that had always grown on the rocky cliff beneath the fall, sending out long streamers of magenta blooms in summer, now lay dead and yellow. The vines dangled lifelessly, leafless and ugly. Below, the pool looked dark and stagnant. Large blooms of algae floated on its surface.

Appalled, Israi let her hand slip from the controls. The skimmer automatically went on hover and parked itself, humming there while she stared, aghast, at the place she had loved so much.

It seemed to be a symbol of her entire adult life. Every year, things grew worse and uglier. She remembered her chunenhal as a golden time, when courtiers laughed and gossiped, resplendent with jewels and showing not a care in the world. There had been food aplenty. The slaves were quiet and obedient. The palace seemed happy, full of life and music.

Was it her? Had she poisoned the land and ruined the aristocrats? Was her entire reign to be doomed by problems and trouble?

Israi stared at the dying waterfall and knew she could no longer deny what she saw daily on the vidcasts. The whole planet was in peril. The drought was strangling the life from everyone. Even the protected imperial lands were not exempt from the climate problems. She stared around her. The narpines, so tall and straight, looked yellow, with drooping needles and many dead branches. She knew the yellow was a sign of combined pollution and drought damage.

But how had it reached this far? How had it come here, to her own property? Why had her servants not stopped it somehow?

She had wanted only a few moments of peace and beauty. She had wanted to come here and find a haven, unchanged from what she had always known.

Instead . . .

Israi flicked out her tongue and buried her face in her hands.

The sound of stealthy rustling from nearby startled her. She looked up and saw a strange figure crouching near a cluster of wilted faizein lilies on the opposite side of the pool.

At first Israi thought he was one of her guards, but almost immediately she realized she was mistaken. She sat in her skimmer, too startled to move, and wondered why her guards had failed to catch up with her. Instantly fear stabbed through her heart. She'd been the target of an assassination attempt before, when she was a vi-adult. She'd never forgotten that terrifying experience. Now she was alone and unprotected.

When she remained motionless, the stranger slowly rose erect from his crouch. He was skinny and dressed in rags. Although he had the build of a Viis, he was not. His head was deformed, rounded on top and flat of face. His dark eyes held a piercing intelligence and expression remarkable even at a distance. Israi stared back, and for a moment the shape and color of his dark eyes tugged at her memory, as though to remind her of someone she had once known.

But she would have remembered meeting any creature as deformed and hideous as this. He was a monster, somehow neither Viis nor abiru nor beast, but some terrible combination of all three, far worse than any Reject.

Israi drew in a sharp breath. Her servants should have been here to shield her imperial eyes from such ugliness. Her guards should have been here to protect her. Her lands should have been free from such a trespasser.

Anger filled Israi. She might be alone, but she was far from vulnerable.

The creature was still staring at her with its mouth open, as though enraptured. "You are beautiful," he said in a clear, youthful voice. He spoke flawless Viis, with the inflections and accent of the aristocracy.

Israi grabbed the side-arm from its clip beneath the controls of the skimmer and accelerated her little craft across the pool, heading straight for the creature.

He stood there, frozen and stupid, as she came zooming right at him, but when she aimed the side-arm at him he shouted something she did not understand and broke into a run. By then Israi was right on top of him. She leaned out of the skimmer and fired, but the craft veered under her shifting weight, and she missed.

Smoke curled up from a blasted bush. The creature screamed again, and dodged away from her, diving headlong into a thicket that her skimmer could not penetrate.

She flew around it, firing again and again into the thicket until the charge on her weapon registered empty.

Exasperated, Israi tossed the useless side-arm away

and circled the thicket once more. Nothing emerged from it. Nothing moved. Perhaps she had killed him.

She did not think so.

Wheeling her skimmer about, she flew straight up to the level of the tall treetops, then hovered there, watching the thicket with narrowed, intent eyes. The skimmer's hand-link was flashing an urgent red.

Israi took it from its clip and switched it on. "Where are you?" she demanded in a whisper. "We are in need of you immediately."

"Majesty!" the static-filled voice responded, sounding both relieved and alarmed. "Our scanner shows shots have been fired."

"Of course shots have been fired. We are hunting," she said in exasperation. "Better game than the huntmaster has shown us thus far."

"Hunting, majesty?" the guard asked in puzzlement. "But without the huntmaster or weapons?"

"We need our long-range equipment," she said in hushed excitement. "Scopes and sniffers . . . everything. Bring this to us at once and summon the huntmaster."

"Perhaps the Imperial Mother should return to the lodge and allow us to outfit her properly," the guard suggested.

Her tongue flicked out, and she nearly threw the hand-link from the skimmer. "Fool!" she said louder than she meant to. "How can we keep this creature pinned if we fly away from it?"

"Majesty, you must wait for us to arrive," the guard said in alarm.

"We have waited too long already," she said impatiently. Below her, a bush in the thicket trembled ever so slightly. Israi drew in her breath with a hiss. So the monster was not dead. Her instincts were right.

"Please, majesty. Give us your location—"

"Have you no scanner?" she said furiously. "If you

know we have been shooting, then you should be able to find us.''

''Majesty, it's malfunctioning,'' the guard said, sounding acutely embarrassed. ''If you will keep the channel open on the hand-link we can follow the signal.''

Fuming, she tossed the hand-link to the floor and put both hands on the controls of her skimmer. Her heart quickened in anticipation. Now she waited, feeling her anticipation grow as the bush trembled again. She glimpsed coarse-woven cloth, a gleam of sunlight on pale skin.

Israi flicked out her tongue and tensed.

The moment the creature emerged from the thicket, Israi sent her skimmer plummeting straight at him.

The skimmer made next to no noise, but he heard it just the same and turned around in time to gasp and duck. Pulling up on the controls so that the skimmer's small engines whined in protest, Israi wheeled it around to block her quarry from darting back into the thicket.

He ran into the forest, slim and awkward, yet swifter than she'd have thought. Israi laughed and pursued him. She could have outdistanced him easily, but she kept behind him, dogging back and forth each time he looked over his shoulder at her. She wanted to play with him now, to exhaust him. He could not run forever.

Already his mouth was open, and he was breathing hard. His dark eyes widened as he glanced back again, and he veered toward the boundary line.

As though she cared where property lines lay. Israi flew past him and wheeled around to block his path.

The creature panted and stumbled, turning back. Israi passed him again, and once more blocked his path.

He twisted around and darted for a narrow gully strewn with rocks that cut into the hillside. Any normal individual would have broken his ankle immediately, but the creature scrambled over the rocks like a mud spider, crouching low and using all four limbs.

Looking ahead of him, Israi could see where the gully deepened gradually into a ravine choked with vines and undergrowth. Once he got inside that thicket there would be no flushing him out.

She cursed her lack of a weapon, and she cursed her incompetent guards, who still had not reached her. But Israi loved a chase, and she had no intentions of letting the creature get away.

When he was halfway down the gully, he paused atop a jutting finger of rock, gathering himself to jump. That's when Israi butted him from behind with her skimmer, knocking him off. He went sprawling in a tangle of thin arms and legs, his voice shrill with fright. It echoed along the forested slopes, carried away by the wind, and the creature himself rolled and tumbled down onto the rocks below, where he lay motionless.

Israi lowered the skimmer and hovered it as close to him as she could get without scraping her craft on the steep sides of the gully. He wasn't moving. A smear of blood stained the stone beneath his misshapen head.

Israi smiled to herself and reached automatically for the clip that should have held her weapon.

Empty.

She'd forgotten.

Furious, she hovered a few minutes longer, then lost patience. He looked dead. Perhaps this time he was.

Opening a tiny, streamlined bin, she withdrew a beacon. The device was slender and cylindrical. When she pressed a button on its side, both ends snapped open and barbed points locked into place. The directional signal it would broadcast could be located by the stupidest slave in the huntmaster's kennel. Israi hurled the beacon at her fallen quarry. It thunked into the ground next to his leg, its barbed end sinking deep, and quivered a moment. Then a green light began flashing steadily on its side.

Israi smiled to herself. She would return as soon as she collected the huntmaster. She would personally watch while they cut off this creature's vile head. It would be mounted and put in the trophy room. She, Israi Kaa, had slain a monster with no weapon. Even her illustrious father had not performed such a feat.

By the time she'd flown back to the waterfall, her wandering guards were approaching. A second skimmer followed with additional guards. Israi squinted past them to see if the huntmaster was coming, but she did not see him.

Her frustration flared immediately. "What were our orders?" she said as the skimmers pulled alongside her craft. "Did we not request the huntmaster's presence? Where is the weapon we asked for?"

"Is the Imperial Mother well?"

"Of course we are well, no thanks to you," she said. "We have killed it, or at least injured it. The beacon is flashing back that way." She pointed. "We want it brought in and beheaded for a trophy."

Lieutenant Moht blinked at her with his rill both red and extended. "What is it, majesty?"

"A monster, deformed and—and horrible." She turned her skimmer around, ready to lead them to it, but Lieutenant Moht positioned his skimmer quickly in front of hers.

"Forgive me," he said with a respectful bow, "but the Imperial Mother's presence is requested immediately back at the lodge."

"By whom?" she demanded in affront. "Who dares to interrupt us? Who dares to *summon* us?"

"A message on the uplink has come in from Lord Temondahl—"

"Oh, him." She flicked out her tongue indifferently. "You may return to the lodge, Moht, and relay our compliments to the chancellor. Tell him we are busy and cannot be disturbed.''

Moht's rill turned even redder. ''Forgive me if I seem to disobey the Imperial Mother. My orders are to escort your majesty back at once.''

Israi flicked out her tongue, so angry she wanted to hurl something at the officer. Would they never leave her in peace? Everything was always urgent, always in need of being addressed immediately. Her chancellors and ministers plagued her constantly. How dare Temondahl think he could summon her to the communications chamber like some flunky.

''Your orders are from the chancellor?'' she asked with false sweetness.

Moht's tongue flickered out from his mouth nervously. ''Yes, majesty.''

''And do the chancellor's orders supersede the Imperial Mother's?''

''Never, majesty.''

Israi lifted her head high with satisfaction. ''Then Lord Temondahl can wait. We have a trophy to collect.''

''But, majesty,'' Moht said in desperation. ''It has to do with the *war*.''

That got her attention as nothing else had. The war. Of course. She had forgotten it in the excitement of the chase. The war was far away, an abstraction. Here and now was a monster who had somehow broken the security field that should have been protecting her property. What was wrong with the security markers? The problem had to be dealt with immediately, or they might find more of the creatures wandering about as they pleased.

Sighing, she reached down and pulled the hand-link out from where she'd thrown it. ''If this message is indeed urgent, then we shall connect with—''

''No, majesty,'' Moht said.

Israi's rill flared out to its fullest extension and turned

indigo blue. "No!" she screamed. "How many times will you deny us, lieutenant? Do you wish your neck broken for impertinence?"

Moht flicked his tongue in and out rapidly. His rill now drooped over its engraved brass collar and had lost all color. "I beg the pardon of the Imperial Mother, but the message was coded red. It cannot be sent over an unsecured channel like your hand-link."

She felt cold then, her anger fading from her heart. "A code red message. Why did you not tell us this immediately?"

His gaze shifted uneasily to the other guards, and Israi gestured impatiently to stop him from answering. She knew the code red designation on an incoming message was supposed to be kept as secret as possible, for security purposes as well as to avert general panic. She had only her own impatience to blame for having forced him to reveal the situation's utter urgency.

"What has happened?" she asked in a quieter voice.

Moht looked at her, unable to answer, even if he knew. "Come, majesty," the officer said. "Please come."

"Yes, at once." But she took the time to point at the other guards. "You and you, go now to the beacon. Find the creature which we have hunted and make certain it is dead. We want its head brought to us as confirmation. If it has crawled away from where we took it down, then track it. Capture it. See that you kill it. Also, send a message to the huntmaster, and tell him that if he does not wish to lose his honorable position, he will make sure no other creatures such as this are wandering on imperial lands. Go!"

The guards bowed, but while they were assuring her they would obey, she wheeled her skimmer around and flew off in the direction of the lodge. Moht flew close behind her in grim silence.

Israi fumed to herself the whole distance. Temondahl

had no need to invoke code red status for his communications. Just because she had ignored his last two calls did not mean she wouldn't eventually talk to him. But, no, he could not be satisfied unless he ruined her entire vacation. No matter what difficulty had arisen in the battle, she knew she could rely on Lord Belz to solve it. She had no finer commander than him. Temondahl worried too much.

She took no pleasure now in flying at dangerous speeds. She flew swiftly, but not at maximum. The lodge would not see the Imperial Mother blasting home in a panic.

When she landed in the courtyard, more guards hastened out from the lodge to escort her inside. Gathering up the broad sweep of her skirts, she entered, with the guards falling in smartly behind her. Two of them walked ahead, and Moht followed close at Israi's heels as protocol dictated when she was under official military escort.

Israi did not like the air of tension running through the guards. Moht looked very stern, and the others were stiff-rilled. They must know something, Israi decided. The palace guards had their own system of communications that kept them well-informed.

Perhaps this was truly important. Perhaps they had lost a warship in the battle. Israi quickened her pace slightly, but she refused to surrender her imperial dignity. Holding her head high, she moved regally up the sweeping staircase and along the corridor. Her courtiers were knotted anxiously outside the door of the communications chamber. They parted hastily for her and her escort, allowing her to walk inside without pausing. The guards peeled off smartly to her right and left and stood at attention on either side of the doorway. Lieutenant Moht closed the door behind her, leaving her alone inside the communications chamber.

A low hum sounded as the security fields were activated in the walls, ceiling, and floor, making the chamber impenetrable to any scanning devices.

Israi coiled her tongue in her mouth, beginning to feel seriously worried, and looked at Chancellor Temondahl's likeness frozen on the large link screen.

"Activate," she said.

The screen faded, then came back to life. Combing filters and security measures fuzzed the image, but at last Temondahl's face was in clear focus once more. He was seated at his desk, writing something. But immediately he glanced up at her and rose to his feet to make a deep bow.

When he straightened, his rill was extended fully behind his head. His eyes looked very grave.

"Majesty," he said without preamble, "I regret to bring you bad news."

"What is it?" she asked impatiently. "Has the palace fallen down? Has the Cuna Da'r stopped flowing?"

Temondahl blinked at her as though thrown by her sharp-edged flippancy.

She gestured. "Are you relaying a message for us from Lord Belz? I wish to hear only about a victory."

"Majesty—"

"Oh, get on with it. Speak!"

Temondahl bowed again. "I regret to say that Lord Belz is dead, majesty."

She stared at him without comprehension and said nothing.

"Can your majesty hear me?" he asked. "Lord Belz is dead."

"Dead," she echoed stupidly. She still could not understand what he meant.

"The battle for the rim worlds is over," he was saying while her thoughts buzzed and tumbled. "Our losses were heavy. We sustained—"

"Our lord commander is dead?" she asked, breaking in.

"Yes, majesty. His ship was blown apart near the conclusion of the battle. There were no survivors."

Allowing her rill to drop, Israi turned away from the screen. How could this be? Crusty, gruff, battle-scarred Lord Belz was her most powerful ally. He saved her throne for her when her father died. He stood behind her when her actions to salvage the economy proved to be unpopular. He held the powerful Viis armies in her name, keeping them loyal to her, and protected her from her enemies. He'd recommended Lord Nalsk to run the Bureau of Security. No, there must be some mistake, she thought. Belz could not be dead. He was irreplaceable.

"No," she said. "We do not believe this report."

"Majesty, I grieve with you," Temondahl said, "but it is true."

"No!" she shouted. "There is a mistake. We know he has survived. His other ships will have picked up his escape pod. He will be found. You must have courage—"

"Majesty, I am sorry," Temondahl said firmly. "There is no mistake. The remnants of our flotilla are fleeing the area now, heading back to home base. We estimate they will arrive in—"

"Fleeing?" Again she echoed him. Why was he saying such stupid words? The flotilla of the Viis Empire did not *flee*. "Have them stop and look for survivors."

"There are no survivors, majesty," Temondahl said wearily. "None."

"How can you be sure?"

"Because the rebel forces are destroying every escape pod they encounter. Because the imperial forces destroyed every pod they came across when they left the battle area. There was not time to pick up survivors, and no Viis should bear the shame of capture and imprisonment. They barely escaped with—"

"What behavior is this?" she demanded. "Are they fleeing like craven cowards? We fail to understand."

"Majesty, we have been defeated," he said harshly. "We lost the battle. Most of the flotilla is destroyed. Less than a third survived, and many of those ships have sustained heavy damage. They may have to be abandoned and destroyed to keep them from falling into enemy hands. Right now the rebels are not pursuing, but the rim worlds—all our mining operations—are lost."

She felt cold and brittle. It could not be true. The empire never suffered defeat. The empire never lost worlds, not even rebellious ones. Her lord commander was not dead, his bones spinning forever in the grave of space. This must be a terrible dream, something unreal. She must awaken from it.

"Lord chancellor," she said at last, and her voice was small and unsteady. She stopped, unable to think of anything to say.

Temondahl looked at her with a combination of sorrow and pity. "Perhaps the Imperial Mother should return at once to the palace. An official statement must be prepared for the people."

She nodded, agreeing, grateful for something specific to do. Her hands were trembling, she realized. Her whole body was trembling. But she was Kaa, and a Kaa could not indulge in shock.

Israi lifted her head regally. "We shall return at once," she said. "Let preparations for mourning begin. Lord Belz was an able warrior, who served us well for many years. His officers likewise shall be honored for their valor."

Temondahl bowed. "As the Imperial Mother commands. I shall make sure all the war ministers are assembled for your majesty's return. A new lord commander of the armies must be named quickly. The officers may rebel if they are not given a voice in the decision, but their choice could prove difficult for the council to accept."

Israi gestured, unable to listen to such plans. The politics of the military had always bored her. Right now, it all seemed unimportant.

"Have we ever been defeated before?" she asked.

Temondahl puffed out his air sacs. "Not officially," he finally said.

She felt naive and unable to cope, the way she had often felt during the first year of her reign. The people would have to be told, but she did not want the writings of history to say that the worst defeat to the Viis happened during her reign.

Her head lifted and she faced Temondahl again. "Do nothing until our return. Perhaps this does not have to be officially known either."

"Oh, majesty, I fear it must. This is not something that can be concealed."

"Then it is worse than you have told us."

"I fear it is very bad indeed. By the Imperial Mother's return, I shall have the final reports ready," he said. "There are strategies to be developed. With this successful rebellion on the part of the rim worlds, I fear others will also attempt—"

"We will crush them!" she said in anger, clenching her fists. "We will crush them all without mercy. The Kaa acknowledges no defeat."

"I'm afraid the Kaa must, this time," Temondahl said.

She knew then that there was something he had not told her. She looked at his likeness on the screen and curled her tongue inside her mouth. A voice inside her head was screaming, *Don't ask,* but she had to.

"What else have you not told us?"

"It can wait until the Imperial Mother's return."

"No," she said coldly. "You will tell us now."

He sighed, and his rill sank low across its collar. "We cannot salvage it. It is a declared defeat. When Lord Belz died, his subcommander, Lord Ahftelzin, surrendered to the enemy forces."

She stared, unable to believe what he was saying. "Impossible."

"I fear not. Lord Ahftelzin's surrender offered our entire battle flotilla to the enemy in exchange for the lives of all survivors. Fortunately, Lord Kelhdar mutinied and rallied the other commanders around him. They fought their way free, killing the coward Ahftelzin in the process, and are returning."

Now she was shaking with rage rather than shock. "Lord Ahftelzin was of what house?" she asked, her voice strangled.

"Third House."

"Arrest all members—"

"Majesty, please wait," Temondahl broke in, daring to interrupt her. "The Bureau of Security is already investigating the matter."

"We want this treachery punished!" she shouted. "How far does such craven cowardice reach?"

"That will be determined by the Bureau," Temondahl said. "Please, majesty. Let us not be hasty. Return to Vir, and we will all gather to discuss the necessary strategies."

Strategies to cope with defeat. Israi nodded, feeling ashamed and numb and outraged and horrified. No matter what Temondahl advised, there would be executions for this. But she would receive the Bureau's report first.

Without a word of farewell, she left the screen activated and walked out of the communications chamber.

"Lieutenant Moht," she said coldly.

He snapped to attention before her.

"Prepare the imperial shuttle for immediate return to Vir."

"At once, majesty." Saluting her smartly, he passed the order to another guard and stayed close by her side. She knew that while they were under code red conditions, Moht would not let her out of his sight.

Israi gestured at one of her ladies in waiting. "See

that packing commences immediately. The servants will be left behind to finish the task. We shall depart as soon as our shuttle is fueled and ready.''

The lady bowed low. ''Your majesty's will is done. Will the Imperial Mother tell us what has happened?''

Israi lifted her gaze to the female's pretty face. The news could not be concealed, Temondahl had said. Very well. Let there be no secrets.

Israi glanced around at her silent courtiers, and her eyes were as hard as the jewels adorning her collar. ''It is defeat,'' she said baldly. ''Defeat with dishonor. We have lost the war.''

Someone gasped aloud. Before anyone could start asking more questions, Israi turned and walked away toward her apartments, leaving them staring stunned after her.

CHAPTER ELEVEN

Ampris walked along the musty, lamplit corridors of the Imperial Archives, passing endless rows of stored data crystals, ancient scrolls sealed in their original cases, and numerous alien artifacts that had been used long ago to record information and histories. The sheer amount of knowledge contained down here never failed to amaze Ampris. If she lived another hundred years and spent every waking hour in study, she still could not hope to absorb it all.

But tonight, she was not here to study.

She was rested and well again, her cuts and bruises healed. A steady diet of plain but nutritious food, plus being underground in the coolness, had given her new reserves of energy. She felt an old ease and springiness to her muscles. Earlier today, she had worked out, stretching and conditioning herself. It was good to be back in civilization, good to feel clean, good to have a food supply on hand, good to feel safe.

But safety, even in a place such as this, was always an illusion.

Ahead, the corridor curved to the left. Just past the curve stood a doorway. Ampris heard the buzz of voices, and saw Quiesl waiting for her. When she came into his sight, he smiled at her and his tail waved gently behind his head. He was the only Myal she'd ever met who did not habitually coil his tail nervously around one leg or the other. Even now, when Ampris's own heart was beating fast in nervousness, Quiesl's broad features seemed as calm and composed as ever.

She paused before him and gave him a quick smile. Her hands smoothed down her fur and patted the folds of the soft blue robe the archivists had given her. After having worn coarse-woven cloth for many years, this fine-spun, synthetic stuff felt wonderful. *I must not let myself be seduced by these luxuries,* she reminded herself. She had goals to keep, responsibilities that stretched far beyond the concerns of this night.

"Are you ready, Ampris?" Quiesl asked her.

Her ears went back. "Ready to commit treason?" she asked breathlessly.

His eyes remained steady and fearless. "Yes," he said without hesitation.

Ampris lifted her muzzle, drawing on his courage. "Yes," she echoed. "It's been a long time. Are you sure they remember me?"

"They remember," he said and slid the door open fully to let her in.

She walked into a circular conference room furnished with a long oval table and mismatched chairs. Perhaps a dozen abiru of various races were gathered there, some standing watchful and silent at the edges of the room, others arguing heatedly.

"Ampris is here," Quiesl said, walking in behind her. His clear, calm voice silenced the conversations abruptly.

A dozen pairs of eyes turned to stare at her. For a moment Ampris felt frozen, but long ago she'd known the stares of thousands of spectators. She drew in a deep breath and forced her ears to stand forward. If these abiru remembered a champion, then Ampris knew she must look and act like one.

"Thank you for coming," she said, making her voice clear and strong. "I understand from my friends here in the Archives that you are the leaders of various resistance groups in the city."

"Thugs and thieves, more like," growled a tattered, gray-furred Kelth with one eye and one ear. He glared balefully at the others. "Rather steal than work honest."

A big Aaroun in a striped vest, wearing a grimy brimless cap on his head, swaggered forward and glared at the Kelth. "You got nothing to say here, Luthien. You ain't no—"

"Please!" Ampris said sharply, regaining their attention. "We're here to discuss joining forces. I'm asking you to forget your feuds and disagreements, at least temporarily, so that we can work together for freedom."

Luthien backed his single ear and yipped. "And here I thought we'd hear a long speech. But you come right out with it first, eh?"

Ampris concealed her embarrassment. She was no politician. She possessed no diplomatic arts. Straightforward honesty had always been her strongest trait. So she looked Luthien in the eye and said, "Yes, I see no reason to waste time."

A dwarf-sized Reject waddled forward on his crooked legs. His rill was extended and his eyes held suspicion. "And you?" he asked, pointing at her. "You come out of nowhere and ask for meetings so you can talk treason. How do we know you're not a spy for the Bureau of Security?"

Ampris backed her ears. "I am no spy!"

"That's what *you* say," the dwarf Reject said, coming even closer. The others clustered behind him, silent and dangerous. "But how do you prove it?"

Dismayed, Ampris stared at him. She'd had such high hopes for this meeting, from the moment she'd learned there were scattered resistance groups in Vir, from the moment she'd heard that their leaders would come to listen to what she had to say. Now, she realized her hopes had been naive. How could she have expected to gain their trust right away? Already the meeting was falling apart.

"You came here tonight," she said. "To talk with each other, and to listen. You must want freedom."

The mutilated Kelth yipped scornfully. "You recording all this? You want us to give you our names and confess right now? What kind of *nolos* you think we be, eh?"

"I already have *your* name, Luthien," Ampris said.

Luthien turned away from her and lunged at the Aaroun in the striped vest, snapping at his throat. The Aaroun growled and shoved Luthien off. Snarling, the two circled each other.

The rest of the group cheered and howled, spreading out to let them fight.

Ampris looked at Quiesl, who raised his hands in dismay and said, "Please, please. You agreed there would be no fighting. Please."

But Luthien and the Aaroun paid him no heed. Still circling each other, they bared their teeth.

Ampris could see at once that they were all bluster and bravado. If they were really going to fight, the combat would have already been over. She lost her temper. "Enough of this nonsense."

She started toward them, but Quiesl gripped her arm. "No, Ampris," he said. "You will get hurt."

Gently she removed his hand and took a running skip that favored her crippled leg, yet was fast. She slammed into Luthien, and as he yipped in startlement and turned on her with a vicious snap of his teeth, she gripped him by the front of his grimy coat and slung him bodily into the Aaroun, knocking both of them down. As they went sprawling in a heap together, the Aaroun roared with anger and thrust himself upright.

Ampris kick-boxed him twice, rapid-fire, then

dropped back, masking a wince as her weight came down too hard on her bad leg. Staggering off balance, the Aaroun righted himself with a roar. He glared at her, and she glared right back.

"Want more?" she taunted him.

He snarled and rubbed his chest where she'd kicked him. He did not move to accept her challenge. The others jeered loudly.

By now Luthien was back on his feet. Cursing vividly, the one-eyed Kelth rushed at her, but Ampris caught him expertly, spun, and used his impetus to toss him over the top of the table. He slid down its polished length, yelping with fright, his arms flailing uselessly, and crashed among the chairs on the other side.

Someone started laughing, and another Aaroun cheered.

"The Crimson Claw!" he yelled enthusiastically, stamping his feet. "Money I used to win on her."

Luthien floundered about, still tangled with the overturned chairs, and shot her a look of hatred from over the edge of the table. "You—you—"

"If you are going to fight, then fight the Viis," Ampris said tartly.

That got their attention. The hoots, jeers, and laughter stopped abruptly. They turned toward her once again.

"Please," Quiesl said worriedly. Now his tail was coiled tightly around his leg. "Please, you must make less noise. This room is not scanned, but too much noise can be registered and might trigger an investigation by Security."

"You swore this room be safe," the Aaroun in the striped vest said.

"Yes, it is, provided you do not brawl."

"She started it!" Luthien said, gaining his feet at last. He was panting and furious. "She attacked me. You all saw her."

"We saw you whipped by a crippled female older

than you,'' said the dwarf Reject. ''Be quiet, Luthien. You are a fool.''

''Yes, a fool you be!'' someone else echoed.

The Kelth slammed his fist down on the table, snarling, and headed for the door. ''Then this fool be leaving.''

Exasperated with him, Ampris moved to block his path.

Luthien stopped, looking at her warily. ''You let me out of here,'' he said in a fierce voice.

''Or what?'' she asked. ''You'll turn us in?''

''Maybe you going now to turn us in anyway,'' the Aaroun in the striped vest said.

Luthien glared at him with his single eye. ''So now you think I be a traitor, eh? Harval, you been known to sell your own mother.''

Growling, Harval started toward Luthien once more, and again Ampris stepped between them.

Both of the males backed away from her. She glared at first one, then the other. ''You're wasting time,'' she said. ''And I can see why all of you are still slaves.''

None of them liked that, but at least they were listening . . . for the moment. ''You're slaves because you won't work together,'' she said to them all. ''Look at you, feuding over petty—''

''Luthien betrayed my group,'' Harval said hotly. ''Gave us to the patrollers last week for—''

''It doesn't matter!'' she shouted.

''It does!'' Harval said. ''He don't belong here, not with us. He'll turn us in as soon as he goes out of here.''

''Liar!'' Luthien said, yipping. ''You Aarouns think you be better than everyone else. It ain't so. You got no right to come in on my territory.''

''It's the Viis who should be our enemies, not each other,'' Ampris said. ''As long as we're divided, the Viis can keep us in chains.''

''The Viis got too much firepower,'' said the Aaroun

in the back. "Got patrollers, got Security. We can't fight them, even if we do join together."

"How many abiru live in Vir?" Ampris asked them.

They looked at each other. Many shrugged.

"How many Viis live here?" she asked.

"The official registry lists two point five million Viis citizens," Quiesl said quietly. "Slave registrations number approximately five million, although probably neither number is accurate. There has not been a census taken in—"

"Twice as many of us, in this city alone," Ampris said, breaking in before Quiesl could start a lecture. "We outnumber them."

"But they have weapons," Harval said, tugging at his striped vest. "They control the food supply. They have—"

"Who operates the machinery that makes this city work?" she broke in. "Who does the maintenance, the repairs? Who unloads the food supplies shipped here?"

They were silent again, but she could see her words sinking in. She said, "The Viis citizens can't even dress themselves without someone to hand their clothing to them."

"But they own everything," a female Kelth piped up.

"What of it?" Ampris retorted. "It's the abiru folk who have the knowledge and skills necessary to run the Viis civilization. A Viis household cannot cook for itself. It will not do the marketing, or the cleaning. Viis citizens possess few practical skills. Strip a lord of his guards, his servants, and how long could he survive?"

Many were nodding.

Ampris's spirits rose. "We can accomplish more than you think."

"Abiru folk have rebelled before," the dwarf Reject said. "Always they have failed. You sneer at the Viis, but they are not as helpless as you say."

Ampris looked at him and realized she must take care

not to offend the Rejects. They might live in the ghettos of Vir, hidden away from public view, but they were still Viis. Quickly she said, "The Viis are an intelligent race. In the past they achieved great things. How could they have created such a vast empire if they were not clever, resourceful, courageous, and brave?"

Harval growled suspiciously, and his ears flattened to his skull. "What talk is this?"

"Listen to me!" she said. "The Viis were a valiant people once, but so were our ancestors. Just because our people were conquered and tricked does not make them inferior or worthy only of being slaves. But now, the Viis have become a cruel and lazy people. They rely on their slaves for everything. Their cities, their space stations, their ships, their jump gates, their equipment—all of it is falling apart, and why?"

"Because that is the way things are," replied the dwarf.

"No!" Ampris said. "Because no Viis will come down here to the Archives to look at repair manuals. Everything wrong with the empire could be fixed, if they would just bother to come and learn how. Everything! Do you know that once the Viis could control the weather? They never knew what drought and famine were. They designed technological marvels. They reached the stars. But now they rely on us *completely,* and they have forgotten almost all that they ever knew. Things keep breaking down. Often they do not even realize that we—resistance groups working in secret—are sabotaging them. Don't you think jump gates were engineered to last forever? Yet they keep failing across the empire. Why? Because someone makes them fail."

Ampris raised her clenched fists. "We can overthrow our masters, because they have buried themselves in denial and self-seeking pleasure. The only reason they have held us this long is because the abiru folk will not trust each other."

"Can't trust when we get betrayed all the time," Luthien said fiercely.

"That's good," Harval said with contempt. "And you with your middle name being Informer."

"That's a dirty lie!" Luthien shouted.

"Shut up!" the Aaroun in the back of the room shouted. "I want to hear the Crimson Claw speak, not the two of you."

"If we work together we can succeed," Ampris continued. "Our common enemy is the Viis oppressors. They have lied to us, deceived us, and tormented us for generations. As for the Rejects," she said, turning to the dwarf again, "your people have been treated the most cruelly of all."

"Them? Hah!" Luthien snarled. "They get free food, all they want, while we—"

"There won't be free food much longer," Ampris said. "Not if the drought continues. I have seen the stelf fields, the stelf that feeds you all, yes, even the Quixlix that you buy with your wages. Or steal," she added.

A few chuckled.

"The fields are blighted with a disease that makes the grain poisonous to any who eat it. I have seen the patrollers burning those fields."

"Not all. Grain still coming into city," said a brown-furred Kelth. He had a shrill, nervous voice. His eyes darted back and forth constantly, unable to meet anyone's gaze squarely. "Seen it on black market. Seen a tenement house over in the Red Quarter, and all in it found dead only this morning. Seen the patrollers going in there with condemned laborers to pull the corpses out. Me, I been eating meat globes and fruit. Ain't no Quixlix going down my gullet."

"That be a story you done made up," Harval said. "It ain't been on the vidcast."

The dwarf Reject raised his rill and flicked out his tongue contemptuously. "Do you think the government would broadcast news about something like *that*?"

"Yeah, and if they poisoned all the Rejects in the city, there'd be enough food for us abiru," Harval shot back.

The dwarf hissed, and again Ampris had to intervene. "The point is, we don't want anyone, Reject or abiru, to be poisoned," she said. "I brought it up only to make you understand that we're all in this together. The Viis have betrayed even their own kind, folk like you." She gestured at the dwarf. "And why? Because you look different? What reason is that? We are all different, individuals in our own way."

"Do not patronize us," the dwarf said furiously.

"I'm not," Ampris said. "I understand you better than you think."

"Why?" he asked, flicking out his tongue. "Because you once lived in the palace?"

She was startled. How did he know that? "No," she replied quietly, "because for a while, before I escaped and won my freedom, I was incarcerated at Vess Vaas."

Some of them looked blank, but behind her Quiesl drew in a sharp breath. Luthien actually blinked, and his mouth fell open. Harval stared at her with the dawning of sympathy.

"With Ehssk the Butcher," Luthien said.

"Yes." She looked at them all. "I carry scars from that place of horrors. Some of those scars will forever mar my fur. Others I carry inside me, where they cannot be seen."

"Vess Vaas was destroyed. Blew up and burned," Harval said.

She lifted her head proudly. "I did that. Had Ehssk been there, I would have ripped out his throat with my teeth."

Murmurs of approval passed among them. She saw those who knew what kind of chamber of horrors the laboratory had been busy whispering to the others.

"And while I was a prisoner there," she said, "I was

forced to bear cubs which were neither Aaroun nor Viis, but a combination of both. It was one of Ehssk's experiments.'' She faced them in the complete silence, seeking no pity. Her gaze locked on the dwarf's. ''My sons are rejected by Aarouns and Viis alike, yet they are mine and I love them. I did not set them aside at birth. But as they have grown up in a world that will not accept them for who and what they are, I have witnessed their pain. In this way, I understand some of yours.''

The dwarf stared at her. His tongue flicked out, but he said nothing. Anger, repugnance, and a measure of deep unhappiness swam in his eyes. After a moment, he ducked his head and looked away from her.

No one else spoke. Ampris waited a few seconds, then drew in a deep breath. ''I have read old treaties while staying here as the guest of the archivists. The Viis had no legal right to enslave the Aarouns. Originally we were supposed to work for them for one generation only. And even those terms were arranged through trickery. They have taken our cultures, our languages, our religions, and our histories from us. They have stolen our music and our accomplishments, claiming them as their own. They have been cruel and indecent masters. Will you consider my words tonight? Will you join together? Long ago, the Viis divided us and taught us to forget that our peoples were once allies. When they divided us, they defeated us. But if we unite, we can win.''

Breathless from her passionate plea, Ampris stopped speaking and stepped back. She stood there, her heart pounding, wondering if she had reached them at all. They were a motley group, all right, clearly a ragtag collection of beggars, cutthroats, dust dealers, laborers, and troublemakers. But they were here, and every individual who decided he or she should work toward achieving freedom created one more chance for them all.

A buzz of conversation broke out, with everyone talking at once.

Ampris turned to Quiesl, whose black eyes were shining, and held out her hands. ''Good enough?'' she asked.

He nodded so vigorously his mane fell across his eyes. ''More than good enough. Well done, Ampris. Well spoken. I feel honored to have heard such eloquence.''

She looked at their guests, all clustered in small groups as though they had completely forgotten her existence. They did not seem to be any more united now than they had been at the first.

''Well,'' she said with a sigh. ''I tried.''

''Have patience, Ampris,'' Quiesl said. ''This is a vast thing which we attempt, something Myals have been working toward for many years. It cannot be accomplished in an hour, a few days, several years, or perhaps many generations.''

She nodded, knowing he spoke the truth, yet she yearned to see some relief for her people. ''I want my sons to live free,'' she whispered.

Quiesl folded his hands together on his plump belly and watched the arguments and discussions. ''At least they are talking to each other. At least they came. It is a start, Ampris. A good beginning.''

''Yes,'' she agreed. ''I wish I could stay here and see it finished, but my time has run out.''

Quiesl looked dismayed. ''We will not discuss your departure now. Later, when they have gone.''

She stepped outside into the corridor, forcing him to follow. ''Quiesl, you know I must go back to my family.''

He shook his head. ''When you are stronger.''

''Stronger?'' She laughed. ''I am fully recovered.''

''It is a difficult journey. Brother Prynan has promised to figure out a way for you to go back without having to walk through such—''

''If I don't return within the allotted time,'' she said firmly, ''they will come here.''

"That is perhaps a good thing. Then you can continue the work begun here tonight."

She sighed. They'd had this discussion before. Quiesl seemed unable, or unwilling, to understand why she did not want to bring her sons to Vir. They were at an impressionable age, still trying to find themselves. She wanted them to be more mature, more centered within themselves, before they were exposed to the evils and brutality of this city.

"Let the Crimson Claw return!" called a voice.

Ampris went back inside and faced the rebels. "Did you agree that my suggestion has merit? Will you join forces and become allies instead of enemies?"

There was some jostling and nudging. Harval stepped forward and opened his mouth, but Luthien, who was standing with one hip slouched while he chewed on a stick of some kind of illegal substance, beat him to the reply.

"Yeah," he said. "We be willing. But we got one condition, eh?"

Ampris blinked in surprise. "Only one?"

"You understand there is much to be worked out," the dwarf said.

"Of course."

"We got to make agreements, signed in blood," Harval announced, glaring at everyone.

"But we'll do it all, if you meet our condition," Luthien said.

Ampris couldn't imagine what they wanted, but she was beginning to feel wary. Luthien looked like the sort to hold grudges, and she'd embarrassed him thoroughly in front of everyone.

"What is your condition?" she asked.

They all stared at her fiercely.

Harval pointed at her. "You," he said gruffly. "You the Crimson Claw. We want you to be our leader."

A cheer rose from their throats, and Ampris took a

step back in startlement. "No," she said, trying to make herself heard. "You're very kind, but I can't—"

Quiesl gripped her arm and gave it a yank. "Ampris, please be sensible. Accept."

She stared at him with her ears back, not at all pleased, and wondered if the Myals had set this up ahead of time. "You know I can't stay right now. Perhaps later, but—"

"You'll lose them, if you throw this away now," he said to her urgently.

"What's wrong?" the dwarf demanded, watching her closely. "You don't want to back up those big words you been spouting to us? It's fine for us to risk death as traitors, while you finish your speeches and just go home?"

"No," Ampris said. "Of course I will do all I can to—"

"Without Crimson Claw, count me out," said the Aaroun who had spoken up for her earlier in the back of the room.

She saw them going sullen and disheartened again. They were fickle and unstable. They couldn't be left on their own, not right now.

"You can count me out too, eh?" Luthien said with a snarl of disgust. "Figured you to be all words and no guts."

"Do I have to throw you across the room again?" she demanded hotly.

His one eye glared right back at her. "That be a gladiator trick, but what about treason, eh? You got the stomach for that?"

"Yes," she replied without hesitation.

"Then you prove it," Luthien said.

"Prove it," Harval echoed.

"Prove it," said the dwarf Reject.

"Prove it! Prove it!" shouted the others.

She backed her ears, but she had no choice. Shooting

Quiesl an exasperated look, she raised her hands to quiet them, and said, "Very well. But—"

They surged around her, laughing and clapping her on the back on their way out.

In fresh amazement, Ampris tried to keep them in the room. "Wait," she said. "We have to discuss—"

But they were gone, hastening along the corridor without heeding her. Ampris stared at Quiesl. "Where are they going?"

He shook back his gray-streaked mane in obvious relief. "Brother Non will see them safely out. There's little time. They stayed longer than the hour we specified. But they have to disperse before the next scan from Security."

Ampris felt a little internal catch of alarm. "You said this room was safe."

"Much of the Archives are," he assured her. "Our warren of storage rooms and corridors are simply too old and too vast for sufficient monitoring. But even so, there are areas that are watched. If too many pass through such an area at the wrong time of day or night, it looks suspicious. Our precautions are best."

She helped him right the chairs which had been knocked over. "What am I going to do? I must leave—"

"Ampris, your work is here," he said firmly. "You must realize by now that destiny has called you to a higher purpose."

"I am also a mother," she said.

"Then let your sons come to you here. They are welcome to stay with us, as you are."

"No," she said, knowing what havoc Nashmarl and Foloth were likely to wreak in this orderly little world. "Thank you, but I must refuse that offer."

"Would you keep them in the wild forever?" Quiesl asked her gently.

She sighed, feeling torn. "No, I know that's not feasible. Soon they will be old enough to start making their own way. It's just—I gave my word, and I must keep it."

"You gave your word tonight as well," he reminded her. "What will you do?"

She saw only one solution. "I shall leave at once, tonight. I've got to take the information I've learned to my friends. It will help them so much."

"And then?"

She could not bear to see the disappointment lurking in his eyes. In the past few days Quiesl had become a close friend to her. She valued him for his gentle manners, his intelligent mind, his refined scholarly method of approaching problems.

"My friends may do as they wish. If they still want to come to Vir, they can. I and my sons will return at once. This I promise, Quiesl." She gripped his hand, looking deep into his eyes so that he could read the truth in her words. "Make the others understand that I'll be gone only for a few days. Delay the next meeting if possible. I will travel as quickly as I can, and with rations I will not have to take time to hunt, but I must finish my obligations. I cannot abandon them."

"No, of course you cannot. We would not honor you if you did." Quiesl smiled at her and bowed. "Come. I will inform the brothers of all that has been decided tonight. Then we shall help you prepare for your journey."

The Kaa's shuttle landed inside the palace compound shortly after sunset. In the gloom of twilight, lights were set up in the ceremonial courtyard. Courtiers assembled in their finery. The imperial carpet was rolled down the steps of the palace.

Israi emerged from the shuttle to the usual fanfare and flourishing of trumpets. Priestesses in sleeveless robes lifted their arms and sang. Young female chunen, daughters of some of her most favored aristocrats, came running forward to hand her fragrant bouquets of exquisite flowers.

Israi forced herself to pause. She gestured for one of her ladies in waiting to take the bouquets. The disappointment, however, on the young faces turned up to hers made her reconsider. She reached out and took one of the bouquets into her hand.

"Who gives us these white flowers?" she asked. Although her heart was lead and she felt weary to the root of her tail, she forced herself to smile at a petite, bronze-skinned chune. "What is your name, little one?"

"I am Sheveil, majesty," the chune answered in a piping voice. She bowed low, then peeped up at Israi shyly and with a twinkling eye. "I selected them my very own self from my mother's garden."

"They are exquisite," the Kaa said. She placed her hand momentarily on the chune's head, then walked on.

Some of the courtiers applauded as they waited for her on the steps. She started her ascent, her heavy gown dragging at her tired body, and glanced back irritably when one of her attendants was too slow in picking up her train.

"Welcome home, my sister," said an all-too-familiar voice, a voice she had hoped never to hear again as long as she lived. Oviel stepped forward from the crowd and bowed low to her. "If I may be bold enough to offer a welcome."

Full adulthood had brought the beginnings of a slight sag to his jawline. His rill was flushed above its plain gold collar, and he looked nervous, as he should have. She noticed, in one sweeping glance of contempt, that his tailor was neither skilled nor knowledgeable as to the latest fashions.

But Israi was in no mood to cope with the unpleasant shock of coming face-to-face with Oviel the very moment she returned home. She still resented having to pardon him. She'd never expected him to be this bold.

As she gazed now into his bright, ambitious eyes, she knew nothing had changed for him. He had simply waited out the term of his exile, but now that he was back it would be as though the intervening years never happened.

He smiled at her, tilting his head to one side when she made no reply, and she hated him to her very core.

"The Kaa is displeased that I have presented myself so forwardly?" he asked, as though daring her to reprimand him.

Everyone was watching openly. The gossip and chatter fell silent. Israi pretended she did not notice their stares. They would soon have far weightier matters to worry them. As for Oviel, he was not worth her time.

Her gaze grew cold indeed, and still she said nothing.

One of the stewards crept forward through the throng, then lightly touched Oviel's arm and whispered in his ear canal. Oviel's rill flushed a dark red. Bowing low, he stepped out of Israi's way and said nothing else.

Israi swept on, climbing the steps as though nothing had happened. Behind her, the silence continued a second longer, then conversations buzzed anew.

Gossiping fools, she thought bitterly.

Temondahl was waiting to greet her just inside the massive doors of hammered gold. Holding his staff of office, he bowed very low.

"Lord chancellor," she said formally.

When he straightened, his heavy-lidded eyes met hers with an expression of great sorrow. She could not bear to gaze upon his grief, so unexpectedly revealed. For a moment she wondered if he had sons or nephews serving in the military. But then she forgot to inquire as her young Kelth heralds came running up to take their place in front of her.

"Reports?" she asked the chancellor wearily.

"In the morning perhaps," he said, surprising her

again. ''The Imperial Mother looks fatigued.''

She nodded her thanks to him, and went on to her private apartments. As soon as it was possible, she dismissed all her ladies in waiting, all the attendants and slaves. She did not want assistance in changing her gown. She was not ready to have her bath filled.

''We want no one at this time. Leave us now,'' she said sharply.

Staring at her with concern, everyone tiptoed out, jingling with bells and dragging scarves, their perfumes a cloud in the air.

As soon as the doors finally shut on the last one, Israi whirled around and smashed a priceless vase against the wall. It shattered with a crash that brought her guards immediately.

''Get out!'' she shouted at them, and they withdrew.

She broke another vase, one that had been her favorite, then felt new fury at its destruction. Raging to herself, she paced back and forth, her silk slippers making no sound on the polished floors.

But releasing her pent-up emotions brought her no ease. She knew she could smash everything in her chambers and still fix nothing.

They had been defeated, and there was nothing she could do about it. Probably at this moment other colony worlds were plotting rebellions of their own. Her world was dying, and her brother was back to scheme against her. And she, the Kaa of the Viis Empire, the Imperial Mother of all creatures, she could not change any of it.

She paced back and forth until she grew weary. Then she flung herself onto the silk cushions atop her bed and switched on the newscast.

There was no news of the defeat. The blackout still held, but she doubted that would last much longer. Somewhere in the palace, her speechwriters were busy preparing her statement. She switched channels, seeking anything to distract herself.

A report came on about the latest weather-related tragedy. Israi flicked out her tongue and started to turn it off, but the reporter's voice started droning on about how in previous centuries the Viis had the technology to control their weather.

Israi sat bolt upright on her bed and curled her plump tail against her legs. "What technology?" she asked the screen.

The report ended, and she switched off the vid. Suddenly her mind was whirling with renewed energy. If they had once possessed such technology, then there was no reason why they could not do so again. That would put an end to the drought. The people would have food again. The general unrest would die down.

Leaving her bed, she summoned her slaves. "Activate the uplink," she commanded. "We wish to speak to the scientist Ehssk."

He could not be immediately located. The longer she waited, the more Israi fumed. Here she had discovered the perfect solution, and she was kept waiting. It was intolerable. By the time Ehssk's oiled countenance appeared on the link screen, Israi's temper was short indeed.

"Majesty, what a pleasant surprise," he said, sounding a bit flustered and breathless.

He was dressed in a very fine coat of lavender brocade, with jewels winking on the cuffs and a great deal of lace beneath his rill collar. Israi's eyes narrowed. Perhaps he was dressed too finely. Over the years, she had continued her father's practice of funding Ehssk's research with generous grants. Perhaps he was spending that grant money on his own tailor instead of on finding a cure for the Dancing Death. Certainly his results, published annually in a report bound in leather and silk which she never read, were less than productive.

"Your majesty honors me greatly," Ehssk said. "Forgive me for keeping the Imperial Mother waiting. I was giving a speech at a dinner for the—"

"We wish to know about weather-control technology," Israi said, breaking in on his flustered apology. "Inform us of all you know."

Ehssk's eyes held bewilderment. His rill drooped on his shoulders, and he gestured vaguely. "Weather control, majesty? Um, I don't . . . that is, I believe it was once . . . Forgive me, majesty, but my field is biogenetics."

She stared at his likeness on the screen as impatience filled her. "You will not answer our question?"

"I'm afraid I cannot, majesty. It is not my field."

She turned her back on him and gestured for the channel to be cut. The screen popped as it went blank. Then a low beep told her the operator had returned.

"May I direct another call for the Imperial Mother?"

"Yes," Israi said. "Find another scientist, one whose field has to do with weather."

The hold delay seemed to go on forever. Israi went back to pacing, gulping down the wine her slaves brought to her in jeweled cups, a fresh cup for each refill.

Finally another scientist whose name she could not remember came on. He was plump with pale yellow skin and large wings of blue spreading out from the corner of each eye. He bowed to her, and would not look at her thereafter.

"Majesty?" he said nervously.

"Tell us all you know about weather-control technology."

"Weather?" he repeated. "Ah, yes, the weather has not been cooperative lately."

"We could once control it. Why don't we now? Has the technology been lost?"

He seemed daunted by her bluntness. "No, majesty.

Not lost. Certainly not lost. Adjustments have been made to the . . . well, we have studied the problem for quite some time now. . . . The drought is a considerable distraction, and we—''

''Can you end the drought?'' she broke in.

''Of course, majesty, given time and, of course, official funding. We are a small division of the—''

''Fool,'' she muttered beneath her breath and gestured for the channel to be cut once again.

Furiously, she circled her apartments. It seemed no one would, or could, supply her with an answer. She knew she could make an official request for information, but several weeks would pass before a report was issued. Israi wanted action *now.*

For years she had been vaguely aware of problems with failing technology in the empire, but now the problems had begun to impact on *her.* Her hunting lands were dying. Her guards could not find her because their scanners malfunctioned. Within the imperial palace, some of the mirrors no longer activated. The automatic doors had not worked since before she was born, necessitating that servants be stationed everywhere to open them on command. She had grown up thinking her father was old-fashioned and preferred antiquated traditions, when in reality he had just been concealing the many breakdowns in the general operating systems of the palace.

There was only one other place she could think of that could provide her with an immediate answer.

Israi summoned her servants. ''Bring our costume of incognito,'' she commanded them. ''At once!''

Down in the Archives, Ampris hefted her pack and found it far too heavy. Smiling to herself, she opened it and lifted out three carefully wrapped bundles that she had not placed there.

''Mystery gifts?'' she asked, holding them up.

The Myals ringed around her looked disconcerted.

"Ampris," Quiesl said chidingly. "Those were to be a surprise."

"Thank you," she said, her smile widening. "But you have given me far too much already. I can never repay your kindness and hospitality."

"You are our hope," Prynan said. "Our only hope."

"No," Ampris said firmly, wanting to squelch that idea once and for all. "I am not. You—the brotherhood of archivists—have done the most to keep the idea of freedom alive."

Quiesl stepped forward and gestured at the bundles she held. "Please, take our small tokens. They are to help you with your journey."

"Thank you, but I cannot carry so much," she said. "If I am to travel swiftly, I must travel light."

Ignoring their murmurs of protest, she went through her pack again, removing about half of its load. They had provided her with a tent that folded to a square hardly bigger than her two hands, blankets, extra clothing, credit vouchers, a folding shovel, fuel for cooking fires, ration packets with military seals on them, charge packs, sacks of fruit, a medicine kit, a small torch, and an illegal hand-link. Ampris kept one blanket, the food, the medicine, and the hand-link.

"Ampris, that is not enough to sustain you," Quiesl protested while the others looked shocked.

She added a water carrier, closed the pack, and strapped it over her shoulder. "More than enough," she said. "I can live on very little, and I must travel fast."

"But, Ampris."

"Please," she said. "Thank you for the rest of it. Please keep it for me until I return."

They looked both hurt and disappointed. She was sorry she had injured their feelings, but none of them could really imagine what lay ahead of her. She didn't want to think of the grueling journey either, but it had to be done. The quicker she left, the quicker it would be over.

"Good-bye, my dear friends," she said. She placed her hand on each archivist's shoulder in turn. "Thank you."

When she reached Quiesl, it was he who clasped her shoulders. "Come back to us quickly and safely," he said.

She smiled brightly to deflect the worry in his eyes. "I will."

Turning away, she went down the corridor and up two levels to the exhibition floor. At this late hour, they had decided she could safely risk exiting the Archives by an easier route than she'd come in.

Quiesl had prepared a crate of instructional materials to be shipped to Malraaket's small auxiliary library. Ampris was to exit the city inside it, then break out and be on her way.

"Wait!" Quiesl called, hurrying to catch up with her. "Not so fast. I am old, Ampris. I cannot walk so quickly."

She slowed down as she came to the exhibition rooms, giving him a chance to catch up. Then her nostrils caught a whiff of perfume, costly and rare. Beneath it ran the fragrance of scented skin oil and Viis.

The fur bristled around her neck. She stopped dead in her tracks and Quiesl bumped into her.

"I beg your pardon," he said.

She lifted a hand to silence him, and gazed around with all senses on alert. The exhibition rooms were unlit except for the dimmed lights in the display cases. Ampris studied the shadows, knowing that an intruder was with them.

"What is it?" Quiesl asked. "What's wrong?"

A shadow at the far end of the room moved, turning around and walking toward them. Ampris stiffened, but she knew she'd been seen. There was no point in hiding now.

Beside her, Quiesl uttered a low moan of despair. She gripped his arm in reassurance. One Viis could be dealt with.

As the figure drew closer, Ampris saw that it was female, very tall and swathed in heavy purple robes patterned with a strange design she had never seen before. The female was masked with a hood drawn over her head. Ampris knew from her old days at court that sometimes great ladies would go forth dressed incognito to secret assignations. If this one was escorted by guards, they weren't in evidence.

Ampris kept sniffing the air, however, to make sure.

Quiesl gulped in air several times and coiled his tail tightly against his leg. Casting Ampris a look of worry, he walked forward to meet the visitor and bowed low.

"Great lady, how may I serve you?"

The female halted and stared at them through the slits in her mask. "We come seeking information on weather."

"Weather? Ah," Quiesl said as though this were an everyday request. "Perhaps during normal hours of—"

"Fool!" The Viis female's voice cut him off viciously. "Do not toy with our patience. We are here now. Serve us at once!"

Ampris's head snapped up and she stared very hard at the masked figure. She knew that voice, that temper, that imperial arrogance. But most of all, she knew that scent masked beneath the perfume.

She stared, stepping forward without being able to stop herself. "Israi," she said in astonishment.

The masked lady drew back, flicking out her tongue in affront. "Who dares—"

"I do," Ampris said. She crossed the distance between them, gently shoving an agitated Quiesl out of the way, and plucked off the lady's mask.

Israi's aristocratic, golden-skinned face was revealed, still as chiseled and lovely as ever, but now looking frozen with outrage.

"Lights, brighter," Ampris said, and the overhead lights came on.

Israi was very tall, her regal posture making her seem even taller. Her skin had darkened over the years to a deep golden hue, with a tint of bronze. Too much wine had puffed Israi's jawline and carved little lines around her eyes. As a consequence of egg-laying her body had thickened, a look considered extremely beautiful among the Viis. Ampris supposed she herself must look very changed too, with her scars and crippled leg and tough muscles. In all her dreams and imaginings, she had never believed she would ever again stand face-to-face with Israi.

It seemed like a dream. Their worlds had grown too far apart for such a meeting to happen, yet here they stood.

She faced Israi, still holding the mask, and tilted her head to one side. "Don't you recognize me?"

Israi's eyes widened. Her mouth opened, and her tongue flicked out. She lifted her hands to push back her hood, and her rill rose to its full extension behind her head. "Ampris," she whispered.

CHAPTER TWELVE

The sunset arched over another hot, hungry day. Crouched on a jutting finger of rock that gave him a vantage point above the road winding across the Plains of Filea, Elrabin wiped the sweat that matted his fur and stung his eyes.

For the past two hours, he had been sitting here, watching the road for Ampris. There was no sign of her. Nothing moved at all out there on that broad, brown flat. It was as though all living creatures had died, and only the land remained.

He sighed and allowed himself one small sip of water. Now he was growing fanciful. It was time to return to camp.

But still he lingered, until the sun finally went down in an angry blaze of red that made the horizon itself look on fire. Ampris was now three days overdue. Elrabin felt bleak with worry. She would have been here unless something had happened to her. Ampris *kept* her word. Always.

He never should have let her go alone.

When the shadows lay thick among the trees, Elrabin pushed himself to his feet and trudged back to camp. He felt tired and dispirited. It was his and Tantha's job today to hunt. The pair of tunals he'd brought down were thin, stringy birds. They were hard to pluck, and at best they made poor eating. He hoped Tantha had had better luck.

The camp itself was new and not very comfortable. They had wedged it into the bottom of a canyon, to help hide their cooking fires from Viis surveillance, which had increased on the imperial lands ever since Foloth almost led a party of hunters and guards straight home. The cub was recovering now from a gash on his head and the serious fright he'd taken from nearly getting himself killed.

If he hadn't come home already hurt, Elrabin would have beaten him. Even now, two days later, Elrabin was still fuming. Foloth usually had more sense than to wander off on his own, strictly against orders, and put them all at risk. This had been something that Nashmarl was more likely to do, but Nashmarl had been subdued since Steegin's death and was keeping himself out of trouble. The other adults seemed satisfied that he'd finally learned his lesson, but Elrabin wasn't so sure. It was hard to tell what went on in that odd-shaped head of Nashmarl's, but the cub acted moodier than ever. Elrabin wished he could shake some sense into them both.

Tonight, the camp had only one cooking fire burning, and it was a small, cautious one. Wedged in the bottom of the canyon, their shelters received no cooling breeze. As a result, nights were hot and miserable.

They would have to leave soon. They were too far from water, and Velia had been complaining about the inconvenience of carrying it. Game grew scarcer every day. Poaching on the imperial lands was now too risky, thanks to Foloth, who'd frightened the Kaa herself and stirred up the Viis.

But if they left, how would Ampris catch up with them? How cold a trail could she track?

"See her?" Velia called out to him when he entered the camp. She was leaning over a steaming cooking pot, boiling something—roots, he supposed. "I know you've been back to the old campsite, watching."

"Yes, I was there," he said wearily and laid the tunals on a stone next to her. She glared at them, swiveling back her ears, and he met her look with a sigh and shake of his head. "All I could find. The world is empty of food."

"Not in Vir," she said, picking up one of the birds and starting to pluck it without much enthusiasm. "Harthril wants to call a council meeting tonight."

Elrabin bowed his head, feeling cornered and stubborn.

"Did you hear me?" Velia asked shrilly. "There is to be a meeting."

"I heard," he said. "Where are the cubs?"

"I don't know," she snapped. "I can't watch them, and do most of the cooking, and keep an eye on old Robuhl. He tried to climb the canyon wall today, and nearly fell off. He is becoming a problem, Elrabin."

"Yes," Elrabin said, barely listening to her. He nuzzled her throat a moment, then trudged off to find the cubs.

They were crouched under the ribs of Ampris's old tent, now stripped of its cloth to make them both cloaks. They had taken apart the viewer, and parts and pieces of it lay scattered on the ground between them.

Elrabin knew it would never be put back together. Anger stirred inside him, but he quelled it. Ampris had valued that viewer greatly, even if its charge was exhausted. But perhaps Ampris was never coming back, and if not, what good was the viewer to anyone else?

"Cubs," he said, interrupting them, "come and eat."

"Is she back?" Nashmarl asked.

"No." He knew of no way to soften the bad news. "Harthril wants to meet tonight. I know we can't wait here much longer."

Nashmarl jumped to his feet. "But we have to. She can't find us if we—"

"Mother isn't coming back," Foloth said, picking through the tiny pieces of wire and circuitry. "I knew that when she left."

Nashmarl whirled on him and kicked at his hands, knocking pieces of viewer in all directions. "Liar! You don't—"

"Stop it!" Elrabin gripped Nashmarl by the back of his new cloak and pulled him away from Foloth. "Both of you, slack off." He released Nashmarl, who eyed him sullenly. "Clean up this mess and come eat."

Leaving them, he returned to the fire.

They fell into another squabble while the pitiful supper was being ladled into each person's bowl. Tantha's luck in hunting was even worse than Elrabin's. So it was another night of berry soup, flavored with stringy bits of tunal, and a few chunks of root. Less than appetizing. Horrible. Elrabin accepted his, trying to keep from showing his revulsion. Velia moved around ladling a ration into each bowl and sniffing to herself.

Elrabin realized she was crying and trying not to show it. His heart squeezed painfully in his chest, and suddenly he was angry. It was no good, living like this. They were slowly starving. And no matter where they went next, it was going to be more of the same.

"I can't eat this slop," Foloth declared, tossing his bowl on the ground. The soup splashed out, and Velia yelped in outrage.

"We haven't enough to go round, and you throw yours away?" She hurled the ladle at him, making him duck.

Nashmarl jumped up and pushed her, toppling her over and spilling the whole pot.

Then they were all on their feet, shouting and quarreling. Elrabin forced his way through, snapping at someone's ear to clear a path for himself.

By the time he reached Velia, she was back on her feet, sobbing now. "I hate them. I hate them!" she wept on his chest as he pulled her into his arms. "You have to do something."

"Yes," Harthril said. He was holding Nashmarl by one arm as the cub attempted to twist free. "They are your responsibility, Elrabin. Yours."

"Yeah, yeah," Elrabin muttered. He released Velia and went over to pull Nashmarl free of Harthril's grip.

"He hurt me," Nashmarl said, ducking behind Elrabin and glaring at Harthril. "He hit me and he has bruised my arm."

"So what?" Elrabin said without sympathy. "Where's your brother?"

"He ran," Nashmarl said contemptuously. "Didn't want to get in trouble."

"He was born in trouble, and so were you."

"Foloth started it," Nashmarl began.

"I ain't going to listen to no whining about this. March," Elrabin ordered and shoved the cub off to the edge of camp.

By this time, Nashmarl was shooting him uneasy looks. "I'm sorry," he said. "I want to go back and eat. I didn't—"

"You made sure no one gets to eat tonight," Elrabin said.

"It wasn't my fault."

"What is?" Elrabin demanded, exasperated. "What is ever your fault, cub? You so sure the rest of the world is out to get you that you set up extra trouble for yourself."

"I don't have to listen to you," Nashmarl said sullenly. "You hate me, just like all the others."

"I don't hate you," Elrabin tried to explain to him. "I hate what you *do*. Why can't you behave? Just for one day. You think maybe you could try sometime?"

"I was just defending Foloth," Nashmarl said. "She

had no business throwing that ladle at him."

Now Elrabin was really starting to lose his temper. "Oh, so now it's all Velia's fault?"

"She threw it at Foloth."

"You try cooking all day, working on something that ain't fit to eat in the first place. You try doing half of what Velia does, and see where your temper goes by sundown. Anyway, it don't matter if she throws something or bites your head—she's an adult, see? You ain't."

"Just because she's grown doesn't mean she's better."

"No, but you got to respect her."

"Why?"

"Because she's grown and you ain't."

"That's no reason."

Elrabin growled to himself, feeling as though he were chasing circles. "Just you shut up about it, see? You go and find Foloth. Tell him to come back and apologize to Velia."

Nashmarl's green eyes widened in outrage. "No!"

"Why not?"

"Because she's not—"

Elrabin's growl grew louder. "Not what?"

Nashmarl's face turned red and he wouldn't meet Elrabin's eyes.

Elrabin gripped Nashmarl by the front of his cloak and twisted hard, backing the cub up against a tree. "Now you listen good. She's my mate, and she ain't going to be insulted or knocked down by a pair of *nolos* like you. I been real easy on the two of you so far, but you're pushing my temper, see?"

Nashmarl looked back at him with open insolence. "You won't do anything," he said. "You never do."

"How come Foloth ran?"

Nashmarl said nothing.

Elrabin wanted to bite him, but instead he pulled the

cub along to his shelter and pushed him inside.

Nashmarl tried to come out, but Elrabin blocked the way.

Nashmarl scowled. "I don't want to be in here! What are you doing?"

"You going to stay in there until you be ready to apologize, yeah, and to see that your brother apologizes too."

"Go mate with a Toth," Nashmarl retorted.

Elrabin slammed shut the rickety door constructed of slim branches lashed together, and latched it with a stick slid crossways through the tough vine loops. Nashmarl kicked the door, but it held.

Growling to himself, Elrabin went off to find Foloth.

He had no luck in his search—not that he tried very hard—and finally he came tramping back into camp, with twigs and leaves caught in his fur, his stomach gnawing a hole out his back, and his temper in shreds.

The others had finished eating whatever was left of the ruined supper, and had gathered for the meeting. Velia slid a half-empty bowl of cold soup into Elrabin's hand and he drank it in three angry gulps.

Giving her a quick lick on one ear, he handed back the bowl and saw Harthril beckoning him.

The tall skinny Reject looked very stern tonight in the flickering illumination of their small fire. Everyone else sat on the ground in a circle around the fire, but Harthril remained standing. Elrabin stood before him, feeling like he was on trial.

"You punished them?" Harthril asked.

"One of 'em," Elrabin replied. "Ain't found the other one yet."

"I hope you beat them," Frenshala said.

Elrabin glared at her. "No one asked you."

She jumped up in outrage. "I have a right to speak," she said shrilly. "We are part of this group now. I can say what I wish to say."

"Just keep your muzzle out of my business, see?" he said.

Harthril held up his hand before Frenshala could reply. She snarled an insult and sat down. The other Kelths murmured to her, yipping and growling among themselves.

"We have bigger decision to make tonight," Harthril said, raising his voice slightly to be heard. "Is time to break camp. Already we stay here too long."

"Now wait," Elrabin said. "Don't get so hasty, Harthril. We promised to wait for Ampris."

"Yes, but three days past her time to come," he said harshly, flicking out his tongue.

"Three days?" Elrabin tilted his head to one side and scoffed. "When you're walking across the Plains of Filea with your feet on fire and your brain melting inside your skull, maybe you find it takes a little longer than you meant for it to. Get it?"

"We give her extra time," Harthril said. "She not come. Now we go."

"Where?" Elrabin asked him. "Going someplace special or you intending to roll a dice bone in the morning and strike out the way it points?"

"Elrabin," Velia said from across the circle. He glanced at her, and she shook her head in reproof.

Elrabin shrugged his shoulders under his tattered coat. Things used to be pretty good, but he was tired of the way the camp ran now. Everyone at each other's throats all the time. No leadership worth spitting at. Too many fool decisions, like this one.

"I ain't going to Vir," he announced, baring his teeth.

"There is food in Vir," Luax said quietly as she leaned forward. "We must eat."

"Sure, I like to eat, but I ain't going back to that stinkhole just to get dinner," Elrabin told her. "Listen to me, all of you. Ampris had a plan to keep us out of there. When she gets back—"

"We listened to her and we agreed with her," Harthril broke in. "But Ampris did not come back."

"Give her time."

"We have no time," Harthril said. "The game is gone. Foloth scared the Kaa, and now the guards want our hides. They hunt us, every day, and they will catch us soon. We must go."

"Give Ampris a chance to come through," Elrabin said. He faced them in the firelight, pleading with them. "Have faith in her, folks. When's she ever failed you?"

"Ampris does not fail," Harthril said fairly. "But maybe Ampris is hurt or dead. Is long way to Vir."

"Yeah, and a long way back. We can hold out another couple of days," Elrabin said. "Give her a chance. Come on."

Robuhl rose to his feet, tottery and white-maned and frail. "We shall wait for Ampris!" he declared, his voice quavering.

Tantha lifted her hand. "I vote we wait."

Elrabin stared hard at Velia, who backed her ears and snarled at him. But obediently she rose to her feet. "We wait," she said in a soft voice.

"But how long do we wait?" Frenshala asked. "Till we starve? Harthril be speaking right, and we know it."

"She'll come," Elrabin insisted.

"But she has not come yet," Frenshala said fiercely. "Do we wait forever?"

"If we have to," Elrabin said stubbornly.

An outcry rose at that, and he lifted his hands. "Hey, slack yourselves. I know we can't do that. So we compromise, see? We wait a little longer."

"How long?" Luax asked.

"Five more days."

Frenshala howled, and Harthril's rill turned red. He shook his head. "One day, Elrabin. Only one more day."

"Four," Elrabin said.

Harthril flicked out his tongue. "Two."

"All right, all right," Elrabin said, giving in. "Three days."

"Two."

"Come on! Three days is fair. She's probably almost here—"

"Three days already we have given her," Harthril said, lowering his rill. "Two more is all we can spare. Then we must go."

Elrabin stared at their faces, shadowed by the uneven firelight. They looked tired and gaunt. He knew none of them could hold out much longer, no matter how much they might want to. Worry gnawed at him, and he wondered what would happen if Ampris couldn't make it back? With that crippled leg of hers, she was an inviting target. She could be lying out there, fevered with thirst, with carrion eaters circling her.

Desperately he closed off his imagination. He could tell Harthril wasn't going to budge. The Reject had been pushed all he would go. Elrabin sighed and bowed his head.

"Okay," he said, knowing he'd accomplished more than he expected. "We wait two more days, and then we strike camp."

In the airless dark of Elrabin's shelter, Nashmarl crouched with his back against the wall and panted for a while. He hated Elrabin. He was tired of the old Kelth's lectures, tired of being told what to do. Like Elrabin was anybody in the first place. He was just an old thief and a slave, street filth, as Foloth called him behind his back. He couldn't even hunt as well as the others, but he thought he should always be telling Nashmarl and his brother what to do.

From a distance, Nashmarl could hear what was being said at the council. He had extremely keen hearing. Sometimes he considered it a curse, especially when he overheard someone making fun of him. But tonight the adults were talking about Mother. They wanted to leave without her, and Elrabin didn't want them to.

Nashmarl sighed. He guessed the old Kelth had a few uses, after all. But not many.

From outside the shelter, he heard a stealthy sound like someone walking on the grass.

Nashmarl turned around and listened. He picked up Foloth's scent, and relaxed.

"What do you want?" he asked. "You got me in trouble tonight, so I don't—"

"Shut up," Foloth's voice came to him. "Start digging."

"Why?"

"Because I'm going to help you escape."

Nashmarl rolled his eyes in the darkness. Sometimes Foloth was very clever. But ever since he saw the Kaa, he'd been daft. "You're crazy," Nashmarl said. "All you have to do is unlock the door."

"Dig!" Foloth said. There came the sound of dirt being scratched away from the bottom of the shelter.

"I'm not crawling out through a hole," Nashmarl said. "Not when I can leave by the door. Quit fooling around and unlock it."

"No," Foloth told him. "I'm going to dig you out. That way when Elrabin comes by to check, he'll think you're still trapped inside."

Nashmarl sighed. Tonight his brother really was stupid. "So if you pull out the stick and let me out, you can't put the stick back?"

Silence fell outside the shelter. After a few seconds the door opened and moonlight shone in over Foloth's shoulder.

Nashmarl hurried outside, giving his brother a shove of scorn.

Foloth shut the door behind him and fastened it again

before hurrying around behind the shelter to scoop the dirt he'd dug back into place.

Nashmarl followed him, feeling superior. "Seeing the Kaa really broke your wits. You ain't been right in the head since then. Got us wearing cloaks like courtiers and pretending we're Viis—"

"We *are,*" Foloth insisted. "Half, anyway, which makes us better than everyone else in camp. They can't tell us what to do anymore."

"Listen," Nashmarl said to him. "I overheard the council—"

"So did I. They aren't leaving."

"No. They're going to wait for Mother like they promised," Nashmarl said in relief. "I was worried that they'd—"

"The agreement ended three days ago," Foloth broke in. "They're fools to wait."

"But—"

"Listen to me," Foloth said. "Mother isn't coming back."

Furiously Nashmarl glared at him. "That isn't so! That isn't—"

Foloth shoved him down and sat on him, mashing his face into the dirt. "She isn't coming back. Why would anyone come back to this once they're in the city?"

Nashmarl felt the old sense of abandonment twisting his stomach into a knot. There were always other things more important to her than her cubs. She was always leaving them with Robuhl or Harthril or Elrabin while she went on her adventures. He scraped his face on the ground and wanted to weep, but he couldn't while Foloth was sitting on top of him. He didn't want Foloth to know he still cried.

"Besides," Foloth said eagerly. "I'm tired of living out here like an animal. If we go to Vir, we can live as Viis. We can—"

"We'll be going soon enough," Nashmarl said dully.

His voice was choked behind a knot in his throat.

"I don't want to go to Vir with the others," Foloth said. "Look at how they treat us. We can't even sit at the council as their equals."

Nashmarl lifted his head. "That's because we're cubs."

Foloth thumped the back of his head, hard enough to hurt. "Don't be stupid. It's because we're different."

Bitterness filled Nashmarl's heart. "Yeah, we're freaks."

"No, we're half-Viis. I want to live like the Viis do," Foloth said, letting him up at last. "They have all the privileges. They get—"

"We don't look like Viis either," Nashmarl said bleakly. The world seemed like a pit to him, and he was at the bottom of it.

"It doesn't matter. In a city like Vir, everyone is sophisticated. I'm sure they're used to seeing exotic creatures from everywhere in the empire. We'll blend in," Foloth said with confidence. "Anyway, you can do what you like, but I'm going."

"How?"

"Like Mother did. I'm going to walk there."

"By yourself?" Nashmarl snorted. "You won't last a day."

"I will if I take supplies."

"What kind?"

"The kind that Harthril has hidden in his shelter."

Nashmarl caught his breath, intrigued in spite of his doubts. "What?"

"Want to come see?" Foloth asked him. But then he slapped his palm against Nashmarl's chest. "Only if you agree to go with me."

"I don't want to run away," Nashmarl said. "It's too far."

"Fine," Foloth said coldly. "Then stay here and let Elrabin keep you locked up."

"I'm not going back inside that shelter," Nashmarl said fiercely.

"You will if he puts you in there. He'll have you scrubbing cooking pots and digging latrines again."

Nashmarl clenched his fists, hating the humiliation he'd gone through recently. It had been unfair to punish him for Steegin's fall. He hadn't pushed her, but everyone treated him like he had.

Suddenly he was tired of all of them, tired of being criticized, tired of the angry looks he got just for hanging around and breathing. Nothing he and Foloth did ever measured up. Without Mother here, it was worse.

He thought of the large, special, golden presence of his mother. He missed her with a deep, intense ache of loneliness he dared not reveal because Foloth would only make fun of him. But if he went to Vir with his brother, then he could find Mother. Of course, she wouldn't really want him with her. She never did. The thought of her rejection made him both angry and sad. Oh, she'd promised she would come back, but this time she hadn't. This time she'd gone farther away than she ever had before. And if Foloth was right, if she wasn't ever coming back, then Nashmarl knew he had to find her. He couldn't let her get away. He would *make* her keep him this time. And maybe, if Foloth was right about Vir being a place where people of all kinds lived, maybe his looks would no longer shame Mother. Maybe in Vir she would stop giving him that sad, pitying smile while she stroked his head and sang softly in the evenings. She thought she was giving him comfort when she did that, but she only made him unhappy.

"If Mother is staying in Vir, then I want to go there," he said, making up his mind.

Foloth clapped him on the shoulder. "That's more like it. Come on. Let's go get Harthril's food stash before the meeting breaks up."

CHAPTER THIRTEEN

Ampris and Israi stared at each other for what seemed like an eternity, then Israi regained her wits and drew back with a hiss. It seemed impossible that this large, gaunt creature could be Ampris, her once adorable, golden Ampris, whom she'd romped with so happily as a chune. Although Israi was taller than Ampris, the Aaroun was still quite large, with heavy shoulders and muscular arms. She looked dreadful, however, all scarred and battered. A cheap, ridiculous-looking bauble hung from her neck on a leather cord, and her clothing was the tawdry, synthetic stuff slaves and common laborers wore. She still had her distinctive dark brown mask of fur across her eyes, but her golden pelt was dull, and there were multiple scars in her ear, showing where she'd worn ownership rings.

As once she wore my cartouche, Israi thought. She shuddered and coiled her tongue inside her mouth. Clearly Ampris was now some kind of renegade. She had a feral, dangerous look in her dark eyes, a look that bored into Israi in a way the Kaa found offensive as well as uncomfortable. No abiru slave had the right to look at the Imperial Mother in such a way, as though judging her, as though finding her somehow lacking.

Israi pulled her wide skirts close to herself and turned

around to leave, but quicker than comprehension, Ampris jumped ahead of her and blocked her path.

"No," Ampris said in the impeccable, aristocratic Viis that Israi had once, so innocently, insisted she learn. "We will talk, you and I."

Israi hissed again. "There is nothing to say."

Again she tried to push past Ampris, but the Aaroun stepped in close and gripped Israi's arm. Astonished that she would dare risk death in this fashion, Israi opened her mouth to call her guards, only to remember that she had slipped away without them. Quickly she pressed the inside of her wrist, only to remember that she had deliberately taken off her miniature hand-link so that no one, especially the Bureau of Security, would be able to trace her movements. Even a Kaa needed some secrets.

But twice now, in recent days, she had gone off impetuously without her guards, and twice she had needed them. Israi drew in deep breaths, holding her alarm under tight control. In these troubled times, it seemed she could no longer get away with such recklessness. Well, she had learned her lesson. Never again would she leave her guards behind.

Still gripping her arm, Ampris shoved Israi deeper into the Archives. "Quiesl," she said to the Myal archivist who was gawking at them both, "a room where we can be private. Quickly."

"Yes. Yes." Wringing his hands, he shook back his mane and hurried away on his short legs, preceding them down a short corridor and into a dusty room where artifacts that looked like brown daubs of dried mud lay scattered on a table in need of cleaning.

Ampris pushed Israi inside, making her stumble. Catching her balance, Israi turned around to command the Myal to summon her guards at once.

But the short archivist had disappeared, and Ampris was shutting the door. Israi heard locks engage, and a hollow feeling opened within her at the root of her tail.

Yet she knew better than to show any fear, for that was to hand the first advantage to an enemy.

Yes, she thought, studying Ampris through slitted eyes, *an enemy*. Even as a cub, Israi recalled, Ampris was always rebellious and full of improper questions. She frequently forgot her place, and she required endless reprimands. With a chune's innocence, Israi had thought her pet quite spirited. She realized later, of course, that Ampris was all the trouble the courtiers had always expected her to become. Ampris the traitor. Ampris who tore Israi's young heart in two, without a care for how she wounded her mistress. Ampris had been the first betrayer of many. But Israi knew how to deal with betrayers—ruthlessly and without mercy.

But that would have to wait. For the moment Israi was Ampris's captive. Israi raged inside. Ampris would pay dearly for this insult, Israi promised herself; she would have her skinned alive and her hide tacked to the wall. Outwardly, however, she remained poised and regal, staring haughtily with her rill extended, prepared to let Ampris remember Israi's behavior as a sign of trouble, if she could.

Ampris seemed unconcerned. She let the silence stretch between them, her intelligent brown eyes calm and watchful.

"You are insane, Ampris," Israi said, unable to let the silence continue. "You have lost your wits. This goes too far."

"In what way too far?" Ampris replied coolly. To Israi's fury, she had not bowed once. She now spoke in a crisp tone, without deference. No respect shone in her eyes. "Too far for me? Officially I was killed in the destruction of Vess Vaas. I do not exist."

"That status will change immediately!" Israi promised her. "Let us go!"

"Not until we have talked." Ampris looked her up

and down. "The years have been kind to you, Israi. I hope you have laid many healthy eggs."

"Do not address us in such a fashion!" Israi said, shocked yet again. "We are not intimates."

"We were once," Ampris said, and her voice held the yearning of old memories.

Israi flicked out her tongue. "The past is past."

"Yes, it is," Ampris said, lifting her hand to clutch the cheap glass bauble which hung from her throat. "And since you bring up the past, let us discuss—"

"We have nothing to say," Israi snapped. "The old tie between us was broken long ago, by you."

"No, let us discuss a past far distant from our own," Ampris said. "Let us go back to the days of the Osoa Treaty."

Bewilderment filled Israi. She had no idea of what Ampris was talking about.

"The agreement between the Viis government and the Aaroun government."

Israi laughed, but even to her own ears the sound was shrill. "What Aaroun government? You have lost your senses."

"Before the Viis Empire tricked my people, took them from their homeworld, and then blasted it into a barren rock," Ampris said, baring her teeth. "*That* Aaroun government."

"Absurd," Israi said with indifference. "Antiquity is dust. Your world is dust. Live in the present, Ampris. Realize that you should have stayed hidden and left well enough alone."

"I will see justice done," Ampris said. "My people deserve—"

"Nothing!" Israi retorted.

"The treaty still stands, violated by the Viis. Which means the Aarouns have the right to leave."

"And go where?" Israi replied. "You have invented this fable. No such treaty ever existed."

"Oh, but it did," Ampris said with a peculiar light of passion in her dark eyes. "I'll prove it to you."

"We care nothing for your proof," Israi said sharply.

Ampris went over to a console and activated a screen. "I'll call up the file here and now. You'll be able to read it and—"

"You will release us this moment," Israi said in a low, furious voice. "If you do not obey immediately, you will die. The penalty for holding the Imperial Mother against her will is—"

"—death, yes, I know," Ampris broke in. "Come and read this, Israi. You will see I do not lie."

Israi saw a screen filled with words, and her rill stiffened in affront. "We shall look at nothing."

"But, Israi—"

"We are the Kaa!" Israi shouted, stamping her foot. "You will address us with proper respect, or your tongue will be cut from your head."

Ampris stared at her, then began to smile. "All right, majesty. Forgive me for offending you."

She said the correct words, but there was still no respect in her tone. Israi seethed, but as long as she was locked in this room there was nothing she could do.

"Please listen to me, just for a moment," Ampris said. "The Aarouns were to work for the Viis for one generation only. That debt has been repaid a thousand times over. Let us go."

"Never," Israi said. Her rill was so stiff it throbbed. She understood now. Ampris was just another part of the rabble, the freedom fighters, the troublemakers and traitors who spread through the city like Skeks, causing problems wherever they went. Well, Ampris's heart had always been in the wrong place.

"Slavery is morally and ethically wrong," Ampris was saying. "Your empire has technological capabilities that make the need for slaves superfluous."

"Such big words," Israi said, mocking her. "Perhaps

it was a mistake to educate you after all. You have made poor use of all that we gave you."

Anger flashed in Ampris's eyes. "You gave me everything, then you took it away."

Israi smiled and flicked out her tongue. "Such was our right. You were our possession. When a toy is outgrown, or it breaks, that toy is thrown away."

Ampris growled, and Israi's rill stiffened. They glared at each other. Ampris was the first to drop her gaze, and Israi sighed in smug satisfaction. This interview was tiresome, but she knew that Ampris would bend to her will as she always had. The early years of training would tell.

"We need not go into what happened between us," Ampris said after a moment. "What's important now is the fate of the abiru—"

"Which concerns us not at all," Israi said dismissively. "Enough of this chatter, Ampris. You will release us at once."

Suddenly there was a pounding on the door. Israi's spirits leaped. At last her guards had come. She lifted her head very high as Ampris opened the door.

But no guards in distinctive cloaks of green stood there. Instead, it was only a clutch of Myals, blinking and staring in at her.

"It's true," one of them said. "The Imperial Mother."

A second one started to kneel, but the others jabbed him with their elbows, and he sprang upright with a look of confusion in his eyes.

Enraged, Israi hissed and started toward the open door. "Out of our way!" she commanded.

Two of the Myals stepped back, but the others blocked the doorway, and Ampris moved to stand between it and Israi.

"Let us go!" Israi commanded.

"Not until you listen to all I have to say."

"We have heard your pathetic petition. The answer is no."

"But, Israi—"

"No!" she shouted, her rill so stiff it ached. "Never, Ampris. Never! You would have used your time better in asking for a pardon for yourself. The rest of this is too absurd to consider."

"But the people are going hungry," Ampris said quietly, her expressive eyes pleading with Israi the way they used to when she would beg for one civa cake too many. "The empire is crumbling. We know you lost the war with the mining worlds—"

"How could you know that?" Israi blurted out in astonishment before she could stop herself.

The Myals and Ampris exchanged grim looks. "That confirms it," said Quiesl, the chief archivist. "The rumors are true."

Israi could not believe she had been tricked so easily by these lackeys. She fought to control her temper, telling herself that they were more clever than they appeared. She would have to take care. Somehow, she had to win her freedom.

"My point is made," Ampris said to her. "Why hold on to the abiru, when you can no longer feed or control them? Why not shrink and consolidate only the best of the empire until it can recover financially? We are a burden on your economy and—"

"Ah," Israi broke in with a sneer. "And now you are a minister of finance and economics, Ampris. We are amazed at your many skills. How kind of you to advise us on matters that are none of your concern."

"Israi—"

"We are Kaa!" Israi shouted, losing control of her temper. "We are the sun and the stars to you! We are as the heavens above you, while you crawl on your bellies like the basest insects. Get on your knees to us and give us the respect that is our due!"

No one moved. They only stared at her as though she had gone mad. Breathless and astonished by their lack of reaction, Israi stared back. Her sense of unease grew, coiling and twisting inside her.

She flicked out her tongue and asked, "Are you going to kill the Imperial Mother?"

Ampris's eyes widened with pity that only infuriated Israi more. "No, your life is in no danger here," Ampris said.

By now Israi was almost too angry to care. "Then get out of our way and let us go."

"Will you at least consider my request?" Ampris asked.

"Do you think we are bargaining here?" Israi replied in amazement. "A slave does not bargain with the Imperial Mother."

"I am not your slave," Ampris said in a low voice of menace. Her eyes were suddenly flat and hostile, all their wide-eyed charm gone as though it had never existed. "I do not bow to you. I do not acknowledge you as my owner. You sold me. You cannot have me back."

Israi met her glare with equal anger. Neither of them spoke.

"What are we to do?" Quiesl asked, breaking into the tense silence. He was wringing his hands and his tail was coiled tightly around his leg. The other Myals had begun to look frightened and alarmed. "Ampris, she does not relent. Must we keep her here as a prisoner?"

"Yes!" said another Myal, one with a black mane and the burning eyes of a fanatic. "She is our hostage. We can force the Viis government to release the abiru in exchange for her."

Israi laughed. It was scornful, contemptuous laughter. She could not hold it back. "You poor fools," she said. "Our egg-brother has been released from exile and is back at court. If we are kept a prisoner, our throne will be taken in a coup, and Lord Oviel will be named Kaa in our place. You have nothing with us as your hostage, nothing except a death sentence.''

They blinked, their momentary bravado punctured.

Ampris backed her ears and nodded. ''It's true,'' she said. ''Viis politics provide no allowances for the ransoming of kaas. We cannot hold her.''

Dismay flashed in their faces. ''But, Ampris,'' Quiesl said, ''is there nothing that can be done?''

''Israi has given us her answer,'' Ampris said, casting Israi a glance of disappointment. She stepped aside and gestured at the Myals. ''Let the Imperial Mother go.''

Reluctantly they parted, moving away from the doorway. Israi did not hesitate. With her head high and her rill stiff, she swept through the room and up the corridor and out of the Archives. She did not look back even once, but her heart was swollen with venom.

Ampris watched the Kaa stride away, wide skirts sweeping the floor, jewels flashing, rill turned a dark indigo blue. Every line in Israi's body betrayed her fury. But as vain and as headstrong as she still was, as impossibly stubborn, as ruthless, and as cruel as Israi was, she had undeniable courage. For a second, Ampris let a trace of her old admiration leak through her, then she shut it away once more. Israi made a formidable adversary, and Ampris knew her too well to even hope she would forgive this incident.

The moment she was gone, Ampris drew in a sharp breath and turned on her friends. ''Hurry!'' she said with an urgency that startled them. ''Whatever is most valuable, get it now.''

Quiesl blinked at her. The others simply stared in bewilderment. ''What?'' he asked. ''What's wrong?''

''We have only a few minutes. The moment Israi reaches her guards, she will send them here. There will be no mercy. Save what you can, and hurry! We have to get out of here!''

They jostled each other, milling in confusion. Ampris looked at them in despair, realizing she'd panicked them. Swiftly she gripped Quiesl by his arms and nearly lifted him off his feet.

"Listen to me!" she ordered. "Don't panic. Think, Quiesl. What is your procedure for an emergency evacuation?"

He gulped, his broad mouth working. "The crown jewels. No, I cannot remove them from the vault without authority. Let me think. Oh, yes, I am responsible for the Scrolls of Antwar."

"And I the Histories," said Prynan.

"The shoes of Nithlived," said Non.

"The sword of Zimbarl," said Hoptwith.

"The Revelations of the Dreamer and all the collected works of—"

"Don't stand there," Ampris told them. She gave Quiesl a shove. "Each of you, get whatever you're assigned, and head for the workmen's entrance on the north side. Don't deviate from the plan. I'll collect your belongings from your quarters. Hurry!"

They scattered, short and purposeful, creatures of preservation in action.

Ampris limped downstairs to a lower level, wondering if she would ever see any of them again. She hoped she was wrong, but she knew how swiftly an arrest force could strike. They had only minutes to get out of here. Even if she took the time to lock the place, Security could override their locking systems. Instead, she swept through the small, spare cells, gathering up blankets, clothing, holo-cubes with images of loved ones, anything that looked precious and portable. Loading the stuff on a blanket, she dragged it with her, stopping only in the galley to clean out cupboards of food.

That was all she dared do. At the last minute, on impulse, she picked up a slim wooden box, clearly ancient and blackened with age, and tossed it into the blanket also.

Her burden was heavy and awkward to drag, but Ampris did not slow her pace. Inside her head, time was ticking. She wondered which of the archivists would wander off too far into the vast holdings of this treasure trove, seeking some additional item to save.

To her surprise, however, all of them but Prynan were waiting at the exit she'd specified by the time she reached it.

Non ran to help her. "Ampris, that is too heavy for you. Careful, careful. You are not well enough to handle such a load."

She waved him back. "Open the door. Let's go!"

"But Prynan has not come—"

"He knows the way. Just *move*!" she ordered.

Her impetus carried them forward. Clutching bundles and artifacts, they trotted through the door that Quiesl unlocked. Then it was up the crumbling stone steps and into the darkness of night, with the ruins of the old palace surrounding them.

"Go!" Ampris said. "Keep moving. Head for where the wall is broken."

"But, Ampris," Quiesl asked. "Do you expect us to throw ourselves in the river?"

"Yes," she said, panting hard as she struggled with her heavy bundle. "Do you want to be executed on the next vidcast? Go!"

"We must wait for Prynan," Non protested.

"We can't," she said ruthlessly, shoving them forward. Sweat poured into her eyes, stinging them. She grunted and heaved the bundle up onto the rubble next to the wall. "Hoptwith, you're the strongest. Get on top of the wall. Everyone, throw your loot to him, and he'll drop it on the other side."

"Drop it!" Non exclaimed in horror. "But—"

"It will survive, or it won't," Ampris said. "Go!"

Hoptwith scrambled onto the wall, with Ampris boosting him from behind. With Quiesl's help, she lifted her heavy bundle to Hoptwith, who groaned as he wrestled it over the top of the wall. Ampris heard the thud on the other side, the sound of something breaking, and a splash.

The Myals stood there in horrified silence. Ampris grabbed Non's precious artifact, unable to see it well in the darkness, and tossed it up to Hoptwith, who barely caught it.

"Careful!" Non said in agony.

By then the others were complying, handing up their armfuls one at a time.

Quiesl paced back and forth, wringing his hands. "We'll never get things straightened out. All those crystals mixed up, and, oh, *gods*!" he swore. "I forgot a viewer—"

"I got one," Ampris assured him. "If it didn't break. Start climbing."

She helped him reach the top of the wall, then boosted each of the others.

Non perched awkwardly up there, looking like he might fall off at any moment. "Look!" he shouted, pointing. "It's Prynan!"

Ampris felt a spurt of relief, but at the same time she grabbed Non's foot in warning. "Be quiet! You'll lead them straight to us."

"Sorry," he said, sounding abashed. "Come on, Prynan! Hurry!"

Since he would not stop shouting, Ampris grasped his foot and shoved upward, toppling him off the wall and onto the other side. He went tumbling, his arms flailing, and she heard a series of muffled thuds and a groan. Ignoring the protests of the others, she gestured furiously.

"Jump!" she commanded, her voice low and fierce. "Scatter. Hide."

"But, Ampris," Quiesl said. "What about—"

Ignoring him, she turned back to Prynan, who was stumbling through the darkness, after having left the door open behind him, allowing light to shine up the well of steps. She could have throttled him for being so careless. He was hunched over; obviously his arms were filled with more than he could really carry. She hurried to him and grabbed his elbow, jostling him so that some of the items tumbled from his arms.

"Oh, no!" he said. "Get them. Get them!"

"No time," she said. "Go to the wall."

"But—"

"Hurry!"

She grabbed some of the items from him as others scattered across the ground. He was yelling at her in protest, stumbling over his own feet, and she had to shove him hard to keep him moving.

At the wall, she dropped what she was carrying onto the ground and stripped off her travel jerkin. Scooping up the data crystals and miniature volumes, she piled them on top of the garment.

"Do the same with yours," she said. "Hurry! The guards will be sweeping through here at any minute."

"But I saw none. The security screens were on, and there wasn't anyone coming in when I left," Prynan said while he piled his treasures onto his robe. He picked up some that she'd dropped. "You're being far too careless. Have you any idea—"

"We'll get the rest later," she said. Something was wrong. She couldn't hear anything, couldn't smell anything, yet the fur was standing up on her neck. An instinctive growl rumbled in her throat.

She rolled up her jerkin and tossed it over the wall, then did the same with Prynan's robe.

He climbed awkwardly, and she boosted him too hard, jamming his face into the stone and making him grunt with pain. On top of the wall, Hoptwith grabbed Prynan's arm and pulled him the rest of the way. Ampris jumped, and they both caught her arm and pulled while she scrambled, panting desperately, to the top.

Just as she reached it, she heard a low, ominous noise that swelled rapidly. Then an explosion rumbled through the ground, shaking the wall and toppling more of the ruins. A great orange belch of fire burst through the open doorway they had exited, blazing up the stairwell into the night sky and filling the darkness with noise and heat and terrible light.

The force of it knocked Ampris off the wall, along with Hoptwith and Prynan. She fell hard, her ears ringing, her eyes blinded. The wall shook, and for a dazed second she thought it might collapse on top of her.

The ground was still quaking. Ampris knew she needed to move. There was something important she had to do, but she could not seem to shake off the ringing and the darkness. Her body felt heavy and liquid, not under her control.

She felt a sensation of wet, and slowly realized she was being dragged into the water. The smell of the river came to her, filthy and strong. Her head went under. She struggled, and came to the surface, gasping and floundering.

Rubbing her eyes, she managed to focus blurrily. Giant flames blazed skyward above the wall. Debris was raining down steadily, hitting her. She sank lower in the water, and a hand gripped her arm and tugged her along, towing her to safety.

A long while later, when dawn was slowly breaking over the city and the fire still raged in the old section of the palace, Ampris knelt on the riverbank under the drooping branches of a dying tree. Its roots, exposed by the erosion of the bank, were knotted and hard. Her hearing was coming back, although her ears still rang, and she had painful flash burns on her arms and one side of her head.

Those would heal.

Prynan had a broken wrist. Quiesl had sprained his ankle and was hobbling about painfully. They had made a little inventory of what they'd saved, and when the black wooden box that Ampris had picked up at the last moment off a table in the galley was revealed, Prynan had cried out and flung himself at her, weeping against her neck.

"You saved it," he cried. "You saved it."

The box contained a book, a strange artifact she had never seen before. It was a slim volume with pages of fine vellum bound on one edge and wrapped in leather. It was the journal of Nithlived the mother, and Nithlived the daughter, and Nithlived the granddaughter, all warrior-priestesses, all members of the great Heva clan. It contained their writings, much of which could no longer be deciphered, as most of the Aaroun alphabet and ancient languages had been lost in time, but it was the only record of their thoughts and wisdom now in existence.

"I couldn't find it with the Histories," Prynan explained, still sobbing. "I looked and looked for it, thinking it was misshelved. I'd forgotten about taking it upstairs to be cleaned."

He went on weeping, and gently Ampris held him. They all looked ready to cry with him. The sadness and bleak horror in their faces was not for themselves or for the home they'd lost, but for the fact that Israi, in her need for retaliation, had destroyed the Imperial Archives just to punish them. All the history, all the knowledge and information stored there, was now gone forever.

Ampris stared across the river at the city of Vir, its spires and rooftops gilded with the rising sun, and her heart felt cold and small with amazement. Israi embodied the supreme ignorance of her race. For not just the records of the abiru people had been wiped out, but also all that was Viis. Israi could have saved her empire had she accessed the information stored beneath her own palace floors. Instead, she had destroyed it.

Truly, the empire was now doomed.

CHAPTER FOURTEEN

By the time Nashmarl reached the gates of Vir, he didn't much care anymore.

Coated with dust, footsore, and wishing he'd never tagged along with Foloth on this adventure, Nashmarl had been excited the first time he saw what looked like the city rising up through the shimmering waves of heat.

But it turned out to be nothing but a fueling station.

The next day, Foloth jabbed him in the ribs and pointed excitedly. "Look!" he shouted. "There it is! There it is!"

But that turned out to be Port Filea, the spaceport servicing Vir. Oh, it was wondrous enough, with its tall communications towers, the revolving solar chargers, the glass-encased terminal curved like a comet's tail. The port was like a hive of insects, with workers in orange coveralls going in all directions. Ground-space shuttles—amazing craft shaped like needles—landed and took off almost constantly. The tremendous, ground-shaking booms as they entered or exited the sound barrier frightened Nashmarl at first, but Foloth stood at the perimeter fence with his face tilted up to the sky, eyes squinted against the sun as he followed the trajectory of a takeoff.

"Beautiful," he said.

Yes, Nashmarl agreed it was beautiful, but the place

was also loud, deafening him not just with the sonic booms but also with blaring sirens, and voices channeled through loudspeakers, and screaming brakes, and roaring engines, and the clackety rhythm of the cargo haulers and the passenger trams. Everything went too fast. It was too much to see, all at once.

Then the sniffer found them, and suddenly it was blaring right over their heads: "Warning! You are too close to the security boundary. Step back six paces. Warning! You are too close to the security boundary."

Nashmarl turned and ran, certain that the authorities would be coming to pick them up at any moment. Foloth, who had almost touched the fence, turned and strolled away in a big show of bravado that didn't impress Nashmarl at all.

It took three more days of walking to reach Vir, three days of choking on the dust tossed up by transports and other freight traffic. The cargo haulers were the worst. They were slow-moving and almost skimmed the ground with a full load. The exhaust they belched choked Nashmarl and made him long to be back in the mountains, breathing the clean, narpine-scented air. Sometimes they had to abandon the road and hide themselves when patrollers went by. That slowed them down, and the rations they'd stolen from Harthril's shelter the night they left were starting to run out.

There was nothing to hunt; all the vegetation looked burned up by the sun and dead. Panting in the heat, feeling his head throbbing beneath his hood, which was almost smothering him, Nashmarl wanted to go home.

Foloth glared at him. "Don't be stupid. We've come too far to turn back. Besides, we're almost there."

"And what're we going to eat when we get there?" Nashmarl asked. "There's no hunting in a city."

"You have the brains of a *worm,*" Foloth told him. "We're Viis. We'll be fed just like everyone else."

Nashmarl gritted his teeth and forced himself to keep

up with Foloth's pace. "We're half-Viis," he said. "Who's going to give us food?"

"The same people who give away food to the Rejects. It's a law or something. They have to take care of us."

Nashmarl couldn't believe the confidence he heard in Foloth's voice. "No one *has* to take care of us," he said. "We ain't even Rejects."

"Aren't," Foloth corrected him. "Say 'aren't.' "

"Why?"

"Because you're Viis. You mustn't talk like the abiru folk."

"I *am* abiru!" Nashmarl shouted. "Mother is abiru, and that makes us both—"

"Viis blood is stronger than Aaroun," Foloth said. He pointed. "Look, Nashmarl. There is Vir."

Nashmarl was looking at his feet, at the puffs of dust fogging around his ankles with every step. "Vir is a fable," he said stubbornly. "Made up. It doesn't exist."

Foloth shoved him, nearly knocking him off his feet. "There! Look at it."

Nashmarl looked, and there before him was a vast, sprawling metropolis shimmering as though a mirage. Mother had told them Vir was a large place, but nothing had prepared him for the immense size of it. It stretched on and on across the horizon, bordered on one side by a brown muddy river. He had seen towns before, but even if they were all placed together, they would not be this big. He stared, his mouth hanging open, and felt suddenly small and insignificant in the scheme of life. He was frightened as well, but Foloth was hurrying on. Slowly, Nashmarl followed.

They walked all day, camped in a dry ditch off the road far away from some other travelers who looked like dangerous cutthroats, and walked another half-day before they reached the city gates.

The walls, built of pale stone, towered tall and straight. Beyond the walls, Nashmarl could see buildings of fabulous shapes looming up even taller. Airborne traffic swarmed in all directions, glinting in the sunlight. Patrollers wearing black body armor and carrying sidearms had a checkpoint station at the gates themselves. More patrollers stood atop the walls, which were also fitted with scanners and other surveillance devices. Sniffers floated here and there.

Nashmarl and Foloth ducked off the road to avoid getting run down by the heavy traffic going in and out. Nashmarl tried to follow his brother, but he kept finding himself standing still and simply staring. Nothing had prepared him for this. The size, the noise, the congestion all overwhelmed his senses. He realized he and Foloth should have never come here. They had no chance at all of finding Mother in a place like this, no matter what Foloth said.

"What's the matter with you?" Foloth asked, jolting him from his thoughts. "Come on!"

Nashmarl shook his head. "I have a bad feeling. We'll get lost in there."

Foloth's dark eyes narrowed. "Do you think I'm going to turn back now? After we've walked all this way? We're here, Nashmarl!"

"I don't care," Nashmarl said. "I don't think we should go in there."

"I am going," Foloth said in a cold, tight voice. "And you are going."

Nashmarl took warning from his tone and whirled to run, but Foloth tackled him from behind and knocked him flat. Sitting on Nashmarl's back, he mashed his face into the hot dirt.

"Enough of this," he said. "I never expected my brother to be a coward."

Anger made Nashmarl lift his head despite Foloth's efforts to hold it down. "Not a coward!" he said, spitting out a mouthful of dirt.

"Afraid of the big city," Foloth taunted him.

"Not—"

"Afraid. *Afraid!*"

Nashmarl flailed and struggled, finally managing to dislodge Foloth from on top of him. Squirming around, he caught Foloth and hit him, but Foloth shoved him back and kicked him.

The kick caught Nashmarl in his thigh muscle and hurt enough to make him yell.

"Baby," Foloth said.

Nashmarl's pride was hurt now. He scrambled to his feet, coated in dirt, and glared at his brother. "I am not a baby, and I am not afraid," he said breathlessly. "I just don't think we can find Mother in a place this big."

"The baby wants his mother," Foloth taunted him.

Rage flared in Nashmarl. Yelling, he ran at Foloth and butted him with his head, knocking his brother flat on his back and flailing away at him until Foloth managed to shove him off.

"Stop it!" Foloth shouted at him. "If you felt like this, why did you wait until now to mention it? Why did you come at all? Eating my rations. Wasting my time. I'm better off without you."

Giving Nashmarl a look of disgust, Foloth turned his back and marched away.

Nashmarl got to his feet and realized Foloth was heading for the gates without him. He couldn't walk back to camp by himself. And he knew that if Foloth ever vanished into the city without him, he would never see his brother again.

Alarmed, Nashmarl muttered a curse and hurried after Foloth. "Wait!"

Foloth never slowed down. But when Nashmarl caught up with him, he said, "Thought you weren't coming."

Nashmarl glared at him and didn't answer. Foloth always had to rub it in.

They joined the end of a line of other people on foot,

mostly Gorlican traders who had to hand over their cargo manifests personally in order to get through. A Viis male garbed in dirt-colored clothing and towing a line of half-grown abiru in chains gave the cubs a hard look.

Nashmarl pulled his hood farther over his face, and felt suddenly nervous. "Is he a slaver?" he whispered to Foloth.

Foloth started to stare at the Viis, but Nashmarl gripped his arm. "Don't stare at him. Don't attract his attention."

"He's already looking at us," Foloth whispered.

"Cleared," the patroller checking papers said in a bored voice, and the slaver gathered his property together, whipping them forward with short, quick slashes.

Someone behind the cubs growled and gave them a shove. Nashmarl stumbled forward, tugging his hood even farther forward. A fresh worry occurred to him. "We don't have any papers," he whispered. "No—"

"Abiru?" the patroller said to them without glancing up. He reached behind him and picked up a handheld scanner. "Hold out your arms."

They didn't have registration implants. Nashmarl's mind suddenly remembered all the warnings their mother had given them, again and again, through the years. Now, here they were, bold as anything, making the worst mistake of their lives.

Foloth had his hood up too, but he held his head high. Arrogantly he said, "We don't have arm registrations. Your scanner will register nothing."

He spoke in Viis, and Nashmarl's alarm grew. He wanted to hit Foloth, and make him stop this, but it was too late.

The patroller lifted his gaze slowly to them and his red eyes narrowed suspiciously. "Abiru, talking Viis?" he said in disbelief. "What is this?"

"We are not abiru," Foloth said and threw back his hood before Nashmarl could stop him.

The patroller swore and jumped from his stool as though shot. He stared at Foloth in horror, and his rill extended behind his head. "Lieutenant!" he shouted.

Nashmarl gripped Foloth's arm. "Let's run for it."

"No," Foloth said curtly, shaking him off.

An officer, who along with two other patrollers was examining the bottom hull of a low-slung cargo-hauler as if they suspected it of having hidden compartments, straightened when called and turned around.

He was carrying his helmet under his elbow as though it were too hot to wear it, but when he saw Foloth his rill stiffened, and he came hurrying over at once, with the other two patrollers right on his heels.

"What is this?" he asked.

The patroller who'd summoned him stiffened to attention and saluted crisply. "I do not know, sir. This creature appeared and says it has no registration."

"I should think not," the lieutenant said. "Look under the owner's registration or—"

"Excuse me," Foloth broke in, still speaking Viis with an arrogance that made Nashmarl flinch, "but we have no owners. We are free, like all Viis, and we wish directions to the imperial palace."

"Foloth, no!" Nashmarl exclaimed, too shocked to remain silent.

Everyone ignored him. The lieutenant flicked out his tongue and glanced away from Foloth.

"Clear this horror away," he said. "And the other one, too. It's probably worse, that it hides its face with such shame."

"Wait," Foloth said. "You don't understand—"

Nashmarl gripped his arm. "Let's go!"

He tried to pull Foloth away, but the three patrollers were on them by then. One of them clubbed Nashmarl across the back of his head with a stun-stick, and the world suddenly looked a sick yellow, then gray, then black.

He dropped to his knees before the world came back into focus around him. Foloth was tugging at him, and Nashmarl thought his brother was trying to help him up. But as he staggered to his feet, he found himself shoved by Foloth. He realized his hand was still gripping Foloth's arm and Foloth was trying to pull free of him.

A patroller, faceless inside his black-visored helmet, hit Foloth across the back of his shoulders, knocking him sprawling.

Another blow crashed into Nashmarl's shoulder. He half-fell across his brother, crying from the pain and fear. Someone kicked him, hard enough to make him yell.

"Get out of here, freaks," a patroller said.

"They aren't even Rejects. Look at them."

Nashmarl found himself yanked upright. His hood was torn back, exposing his head and face to the merciless sunlight. He squinted and held up his hands for mercy.

"I don't want to look at them," another said. "They sicken my eyes."

The one holding Nashmarl shook him so hard the cub thought his neck might snap, then shoved him away. He tripped over Foloth, and fell down again.

"They are too stupid to run."

"They don't understand the drill, which means they aren't from Reject Town."

"They aren't Rejects."

"No, something far worse." The patroller who spoke unclipped his side-arm from his belt and aimed it right at Nashmarl's head.

Nashmarl couldn't breathe. He could see nothing except the business end of that weapon, glowing red as it charged. He opened his mouth, but no plea for mercy came out. It was as though whatever had paralyzed his lungs had frozen his throat as well. He no longer had a voice. He no longer had any reason, except one single certainty.

Flinging himself around, he somehow gained his feet and dodged to one side. The shot scorched the air between him and his brother, and the plasma slug hit the ground, turning a rock into a little puddle of slag.

Foloth screamed and scrambled in the opposite direction.

Laughing, a second patroller fired on them, first at Foloth, who was running full tilt now, then at Nashmarl. The shot hit Nashmarl's heel, and pain flared up his leg. He was thrown off his feet and went tumbling. His fear was like something wet and clammy coiled about his throat. It was pulling him down, keeping him down despite his efforts to get up and go on running.

"Foloth!" he called desperately. He dragged himself on the ground. His leg was numb now, useless. He couldn't even pull it up beneath him to get back on his feet. "Foloth, wait for me!"

Foloth glanced over his shoulder, calling something that Nashmarl did not understand. Foloth didn't stop, and he didn't come back to help. He just went on running toward the shacks clustered a short distance away.

Nashmarl was weeping and screaming in fear. He dragged himself desperately, flopping facedown and floundering as he tried to get on his feet again. Behind him he could hear the patrollers laughing.

"Run, freak!" one of them called out.

Somehow Nashmarl got on his feet. His injured one wouldn't support his weight. He hobbled, nearly fell, and kept hopping forward. For the first time in his young life, he realized how his mother's crippled leg must hinder her.

Another shot kicked up the dirt at his heels.

Nashmarl screamed, certain the next shot would plug him through the back and melt his spinal column, but it didn't come. He heard the cultured tones of the lieutenant now, berating the patrollers for wasting ammunition when a beating would have sufficed.

"Didn't want to touch the freaks, sir," someone answered.

By then Nashmarl had reached the shacks and the narrow, dark streets leading into Reject Town. He was still hopping, still desperate to get himself away and out of sight. His facial fur was wet with tears and streaked with mud. His injured foot came down to the ground as he tried to go faster, and a fresh jolt of pain shot up his leg like fire.

Foloth wasn't even in sight.

Hating him, Nashmarl staggered behind a shack and dropped into the shadows, gasping and shuddering, certain he was going to be sick. He never should have come here, he told himself, moaning as he gingerly ran his hand down his leg to his foot. He never should have listened to Foloth, with his crazy ideas. He never should have left the camp while Mother was gone.

And he wouldn't have, if she hadn't deserted him. It was all her fault for going away and staying away.

And now he was here in this awful place, and Foloth had abandoned him too. Foloth had the pack with the last of their rations and the water skin in it. Nashmarl figured he could starve to death here in Reject Town before anyone would help him. This wasn't like their camp, where folks might squabble but everyone knew they had to help each other. Here, there was no one to help.

And now he was alone, and hurt.

"What are you doing?" Foloth's voice demanded. "Crying? We haven't time for that."

Nashmarl looked up, relieved to see his brother and furious at being caught crying. He slapped his hands across his face, smearing the tears and grime even worse.

"You left me," he said in a bitter voice. "They shot me and you just ran away."

"How could I help you if I got shot too?" Foloth asked him reasonably.

Nashmarl glared. His brother always had a logical answer.

Foloth nudged him with his toe. "Come on. Stop feeling sorry for yourself. Let's go."

"I can't," Nashmarl said. "I'm wounded."

Foloth crouched beside him and grabbed his foot.

"Ow!" Nashmarl yelped. "Take it easy."

Foloth dropped his foot, letting it thud against the ground. Pain jolted all the way up into Nashmarl's throat. He gasped, rigid with agony, until it eased off.

Blood pounded in his head, making him almost dizzy. He tried to kick Foloth, but his brother dodged and stood up.

"You aren't hurt," Foloth said without sympathy. "You aren't even bleeding."

Slowly Nashmarl unclenched the clods of dirt he'd gripped during the worst of the pain. With a mutter, he hurled one of them at Foloth, who didn't duck fast enough. Dirt splattered across the front of his jerkin.

Foloth brushed it off and glared at Nashmarl. "Get up now, or I really will leave you."

He turned and started away. Nashmarl glared at him, seething with resentment. He wished he could just sit here forever, letting Foloth disappear and never be seen again.

But finally he levered himself to his feet. His foot wasn't bleeding, just as Foloth had said. It should have been, but Nashmarl could find no visible wound. His heel, however, was bruised and extremely sore to the touch. Maybe the patrollers hadn't all been using lethal plasma force. Maybe he'd been shot with a stun bullet instead.

It still hurt.

Limping and cursing Foloth under his breath, he followed his brother deeper into Reject Town.

It took but a few minutes before Nashmarl was regretting ever coming into this slum too. Even Foloth had slowed down and was looking around with a grimace of disgust on his face.

Nashmarl had never been anyplace so squalid. He'd never imagined such filth could exist or that anyone would be willing to live in it.

Reject hatchlings, smeared with grime and wearing rags or nothing at all, ran from them, screaming.

A female trudging along with a water yoke across her shoulders saw them and stumbled to a halt so abrupt she sloshed water from both her pots. She turned around and trotted away from them as fast as she could carry her heavy burden.

Nashmarl stopped in his tracks. "Foloth, wait!" he called.

Reluctantly Foloth looked back. "What now?"

"Where are we going?" Nashmarl asked him. "What are we going to do here?"

Foloth looked at him impatiently. "We're going to find someone who can get us inside the city. I want to see the imperial palace."

"Well, you're a long way from it right now," Nashmarl said.

"Over that wall," Foloth said, pointing at the pale stone rising above the roofs of the rickety shacks around them. "Mother said it's on the side where the river runs."

"You're crazy," Nashmarl said. "We can't even get through the city gates, much less close to the palace. What would you do if you got there, anyway?"

"I want to see it," Foloth said.

"No, you're hoping to see the Kaa again," Nashmarl said. "Ever since you saw her, you've been unable to think of anyone else."

"She was beautiful," Foloth said, his eyes lighting up. "Like a vision, all in gold. Her skin was the color of the sun, and her eyes were like fire. She was wearing a gown like the sky itself. The cloth shimmered with colors. There were jewels sewn on it, and—"

"You've said all this a thousand times already. I don't want to hear it again."

"It was a sign," Foloth said gravely. "A sign of destiny."

"Whose destiny?" Nashmarl asked scornfully, pulling his feet from the mud. The stench made him feel sick. He wanted out of here. He wanted to go home.

Foloth was staring around them at the squalor and poverty with grave interest. "I think Mother was born in a place such as this. And then she was taken to live in the palace. I think my seeing the Kaa means that we'll also go to the palace."

Nashmarl stared at him, unable to believe what he was hearing. "Is that why we've come all this way? Is that why we've been beaten and shot at?" he demanded, his voice rising to a shout. "You really have gone crazy. And I shouldn't have come with you."

"Then leave," Foloth said coldly. "I don't need you."

That hurt, like a stab over the heart. Nashmarl glared at Foloth to hide how wounded he felt. "I don't need you either," he said angrily. "And I don't want to be a Viis. They're cruel and vicious, just like Mother always warned us."

"Mother doesn't know everything," Foloth said. "And she doesn't tell us everything."

"What do you mean?"

"I mean she's a hypocrite," Foloth said, stepping closer. "Warning us about the Viis, always criticizing the Viis, when her real opinion is very different."

"I don't understand. What are you talking about?"

"Where is she?" Foloth asked.

"I don't know!" Nashmarl replied in frustration. "Maybe she got hurt, or maybe she's been arrested."

"Or maybe she's gone back to her Viis lover and abandoned us," Foloth said.

His voice was very hard and cold when he said those words, words that shocked Nashmarl into silence.

Foloth glared at him, and his dark eyes were almost black with resentment. "Don't look so surprised," he said to Nashmarl. "You fool, how do you think we came into being?"

Nashmarl turned away from him, not wanting to talk about it, not wanting to think about it. He was crying again, and he didn't want Foloth to see.

"Oh, yes, cry about it," Foloth said with scorn. "I wish I hadn't brought you. Especially now that you're causing me this much trouble."

"Trouble bigger than you think," said a voice neither of them recognized.

Startled, Nashmarl spun around and found himself looking at the hostile faces of four Reject adult males. Each one was carrying a mesh-sided sack full of stones.

"Lots of trouble, you coming here," the Reject said. Blue-skinned with lavender shading at his throat, he had no rill at all. "Abiru thieves, coming here all the time, stealing our food, taking what is ours. Get out!"

Foloth backed up, pressing against Nashmarl, who had to step aside. Together, both cubs retreated from the advancing Rejects.

"Please," Nashmarl said, his voice quavering enough to shame him. "Don't hurt us. We'll go."

But the Rejects were already reaching into their sacks. When they threw the first barrage of stones, Nashmarl knew what the sacks were for.

The stones thudded into him and Foloth with painful accuracy. He cried out, and heard Foloth grunt.

"Run for it!" Foloth shouted.

Together they spun around to go back the way they'd

come, but their path was blocked by two more Rejects, who also threw stones at them.

Surrounded, Nashmarl and Foloth huddled together, while the Rejects closed in and the stoning began in earnest.

CHAPTER FIFTEEN

A call on Quiesl's hand-link to Luthien got Ampris and the archivists smuggled into the city. Harval, the Aaroun, stashed them in the dank basement of an abandoned tenement. Although they were grateful for the hideout, within a day they were all growing restless.

"We must find a way to check on the Archives," Quiesl said. "Perhaps if even a small part of it survived, we will be able to salvage something of—"

"No," Ampris said. "It's too dangerous. Right now they think all of you are dead. You're safe as long as they go on believing that."

Non sat in a corner, rocking himself from side to side the way many Myals did when seriously stressed. "I forgot the Poetics," he said, not for the first time. He twisted his tail in his hands. "How could I overlook them? They were sublime, written in an age when the Viis could—"

"They were stored in a fireproof case," Prynan assured him. "They will survive. All the storage on Level Two was fireproofed. Those items will be fine."

"Not if the explosion destroyed the structure," Quiesl fretted. He clasped his hands behind his back and wrapped his tail around his wrists. Back and forth he paced. "At tonight's resistance meeting, I shall ask for assistance in visiting the site. We must start sifting through the ashes before more is lost."

Ampris gave up trying to convince them that it would be futile to return to the Archives. They had spent their adult lives taking care of the place. They would need time to adjust to the fact that the Archives no longer existed.

"I'm going out," she said.

At once, their discussion stopped. Quiesl and Non looked at her with expressions of worry. "Ampris, this is unwise," Quiesl said. "You know what you encountered yesterday."

She backed her ears, growling softly with frustration. She had tried to leave them on the river before Luthien's cohorts picked them up. But Quiesl had protested, claiming that without her presence as leader the resistance groups might fail to help them as promised. Yesterday, while the archivists were getting settled here in this crumbling old building, Ampris had tried to leave the city, but she found her likeness—dredged up from old gladiator publicity records—being broadcast on every public vid. Warrants had been issued for her arrest, and citizens and abiru alike were urged to report any sighting of her.

Being trapped like this left her nerves frayed and her sense of worry stronger than ever. If she couldn't get out of the city, how was she going to return to her family? She couldn't just abandon them.

She had broken her promise to her cubs and to her friends. She had let them down. Although it had not been her fault, she felt ashamed. Ampris hated to fail at anything she did. If Harthril led them here to Vir, they wouldn't last two days without coming to some kind of harm. How would she ever find them?

Now, she met Quiesl's gaze with determination. "I have to check the city's eastern gates. In case they've come through."

"No one will tell you," Quiesl said. "If any patroller sees you loitering there, you'll be arrested."

"Or shot," Non added.

"I cannot abandon my family!" she cried. "If they come here, I'll never know it. I have to do something."

Quiesl put his hand on her arm. "At the meeting tonight, perhaps you can ask the abiru to watch for your friends. That is safer than you risking capture."

She sighed, not liking the idea, and yet it made sense. Reluctantly she nodded. "Very well."

The sun had dropped midway in the afternoon sky, the hottest part of the day. Elrabin trotted steadily along the road, ignoring the heat that made his skin feel like it was melting beneath his fur. He was panting, but not in distress. Beside him, Harthril strode along tirelessly on his long, thin legs. The Reject's eyes were slitted against the glare of the sun, and his rill lay flaccid on his shoulders. Their shared water skin bounced on his hip, half-empty.

Elrabin kept an eye on it, and licked a rim of salt off his mouth. He wanted a drink with every pore of his body, but neither of them would stop for water until the sun started to go down.

Ahead, the walls of Vir loomed high. The cubs were only a half hour in front of them, and Elrabin was toying with the idea of stopping and waiting out the rest of the afternoon before going on to pick them up at the gates. There was no way Foloth and Nashmarl could get into the city. There was nowhere for them to go, now that they'd reached the end of this ill-planned journey.

Elrabin cast a sideways glance up at Harthril. "Nearly there," he said, panting.

Harthril blinked but otherwise did not waste his breath on talking. His pebbled skin was wrinkling and growing darker from sun exposure. Otherwise he just seemed to absorb the heat, no matter how intense it became.

"Want to stop for a while?" Elrabin asked. "We can let 'em prowl around the gates and get turned back in our direction, see?"

Harthril's stride never faltered. He said nothing.

Elrabin groaned to himself and kept trotting. "Guess we don't quit now. Guess we don't let the guards shake 'em up like they deserve."

Harthril glanced at him stonily. "Thieves," he said.

Elrabin rolled his eyes. After the first few days, he'd figured the Reject would get over the theft of his food, but Harthril had a one-track mind. Forget that Elrabin had questions as to what the Reject was doing with food hoarded from the rest of the group in the first place, or where he got it from. Harthril answered only what suited him, and so far he'd said about three words since they'd set out on the cubs' trail several days ago.

They'd caught up with the runaways in a matter of hours. Whatever head start Foloth and Nashmarl had, they'd squandered it like the irresponsible cubs they were. They stopped to rest too often. They wasted time hunting for water when they still had a supply. With the food rations they'd taken, they did not have to stop to hunt. As a result, they could have made excellent time across the Plains if they'd been diligent about it.

Elrabin thought about Ampris, who had limped along in the burning heat with inadequate supplies, who had stopped and hunted when she must have been exhausted. Every night, he and Harthril camped fireless and silent near the cubs, guarding them in the darkness while they chattered and laughed heedlessly. Elrabin thought of their mother camping out here alone and friendless. Every day he expected to stumble across her bones bleaching in the sun. So far, that hadn't happened, but it didn't stop him from worrying about her.

Or from wanting to blister the backsides of both her cubs.

As soon as he and Harthril first caught up with the

cubs, Elrabin had wanted to grab them by the scruff of their necks and work them over. But Harthril had stopped him, suggesting they let the cubs make the entire journey to Vir on their own. Hoping the cubs would learn a few lessons along the way, Elrabin agreed.

But now, as they drew near the city and skirted the outlying clusters of fueling stations, roadside black marketeers, and straggling traffic, Elrabin told himself the cubs would have learned a lot more without those food rations. Every time he stepped over an empty packet that had been tossed down, he growled to himself and promised them a kick for it.

Now, he shot Harthril another glance. "You sure you don't want to take a break here? We can wait for the others to catch up."

Luax and Tantha were shepherding the rest of their group, coming very slowly and with great caution, perhaps a day or two behind.

Harthril did not even blink this time. He just kept striding along.

Ahead, Elrabin heard shouting and the sound of shots being fired. Instinctively he stopped in his tracks, but Harthril began to jog. Growling and muttering to himself, Elrabin hurried to catch up.

He saw the gates, closed right now with a line of traffic waiting for clearance. He saw patrollers clustered at the checkpoint, shouting and opening fire on the pair of lanky cubs, who were scrambling for safety.

Elrabin's heart nearly stopped. "Hey!"

Harthril gripped his arm, holding him back when he would have dashed straight to the trouble. "Wait," the Reject said.

"That was a plasma slug," Elrabin said, horrified by the danger the cubs were in. He might not like either of them, but he owed it to Ampris to keep them safe. "We got to get them out of there."

"How?" Harthril asked, still holding him back despite his struggles. "Look, they are running. They are safe."

Elrabin watched the cubs streaking across open ground, but they headed into the slum area like Skeks scuttling for the sewer. His heart sank. "The little fools. How we going to get them out of there?"

Harthril stood watching until the cubs were out of sight before he dropped his blue-eyed gaze to meet Elrabin's. "Maybe we don't get them out. Let them stay there."

"That's Reject Town," Elrabin said. "You'll fit right in, but they never will."

Harthril's rill extended behind his head. "Rejects will take care of them. Then there is no more trouble they can cause us."

Elrabin backed his ears angrily. "Quit talking like that."

"You really want to save them?"

"No," Elrabin said, deciding to be honest. "But I have to. I gave Ampris my word."

"What does word mean to a Kelth?"

Elrabin bared his teeth, deciding that sometimes he didn't like this Reject very much. "Hey, don't take it out on me."

He pulled free of Harthril's grip and smoothed out the wrinkles in his dirty coat. "You coming?" he asked.

Harthril flicked out his tongue, but when Elrabin trotted toward the slum, Harthril followed.

The slums were bad, all right. It took Elrabin one glance, and one whiff, to know that this part of town was a lot worse than the stinkhole where he'd grown up. He took in the front-edge businesses, gambling dens, dust drops, and brothels, and his instincts went on alert. He quickened his pace.

In minutes, he heard the sound of commotion—angry shouts and yells of pain. He jabbed Harthril in the ribs. "That's Nashmarl's voice. Come on!"

Together they ran down one of the narrow, twisting streets and came upon the cubs, surrounded by Rejects who were stoning them and shouting insults.

Elrabin didn't have to count heads to see how seriously he and Harthril were outnumbered. But if Elrabin had never learned how to fight well during his time as a servant for gladiators, at least he had learned how to fight dirty.

Baring his teeth, he rushed forward, fast and furious, giving no warning, and bowled over one of the Rejects from behind. Grabbing the sack of rocks from the startled Reject's hand, Elrabin rolled and came up lightly on his feet. Already he was reaching into the sack, and as Harthril clubbed another Reject down from behind with his walking staff, Elrabin started pelting the Rejects with stones.

Startled, they turned and ran in all directions, disappearing quicker than he'd have thought possible.

Elrabin glared around, expecting them to come back with reinforcements, and dropped his sack of stones on the head of the Reject he'd knocked down. With a moan, the Reject slumped in the mud and did not move.

Harthril was already bending over the cubs, who were lying on the ground curled around each other.

Elrabin hurried over to them and saw that both were still conscious. Foloth was bleeding from a gash on his forehead. Nashmarl was whimpering and clutching his stomach.

The cubs stared at him and Harthril as though they couldn't believe their eyes.

"How did you get here?" Foloth whispered.

Elrabin's ears were working back and forth, straining to listen in all directions. "Never mind," he said gruffly. The cubs were alive; he'd worry about details later. "Get up, both of you. Time to clear out of this place before trouble comes back."

Harthril grabbed Nashmarl under his arms and set him

on his feet. Elrabin tugged Foloth upright.

"Quick now, and no talking," he said.

Elrabin listened, heard someone coming, and took off in the opposite direction. The fact that it happened to be deeper into the slum instead of out of it made Harthril hiss a warning.

"Yeah, yeah, I know," Elrabin said, shooting him a glance. "Trust me on this one. This happens to be my area of expertise."

With that boast, he led them on a winding progress through the slum, directing them with a confidence that was mostly for show. All the time he continued to hear sounds of pursuit. His shoulders stayed tensed for an attack that didn't come.

Several minutes later, they reached the banks of the river. Elrabin stared at the stinking mud, with its mounds of dead fish. Garbage was being dumped in the riverbed, and trash lay scattered in all directions. The water itself was seriously polluted. Elrabin stopped short and started to revise his plan until he glanced over his shoulder and saw a gang of angry Rejects behind them, cutting off the way back.

"Now what will you do?" Harthril asked him in disgust.

Elrabin bared his teeth. "Just keep your tongue in your mouth, and you'll see. Come on!"

"I can't. It hurts too much," Nashmarl whimpered, but Harthril shoved him along when Elrabin started down the bank.

Foloth followed on Elrabin's heels in silence. He was still bleeding, but his gash didn't look too bad. Elrabin wasn't going to take the time to wrap him up now.

They squelched across the mud, which was slick and soft beneath scrim puddles of water and foam. Where the city wall curved to fit the bend of the river, the water grew deeper until it came up to Elrabin's knees. He splashed along steadily, keeping his gaze on the base of the wall.

"Hey!"

Harthril's warning came just as a stun bullet plopped into the water only a few centimeters away from Elrabin. Yelling, he jumped sideways and ran for the base of the wall. No more bullets came at him, yet he didn't stop until he was huddled a hand's breadth away from the stone. That close, he could feel the whining friction of the security field. He panted and swiveled back his ears as the others joined him. Tilting his head, he tried to look up at the top of the wall where the patroller who'd shot at him was standing, but couldn't see him at this angle. That was fine with Elrabin. He figured the patroller could no longer see *him* either.

Viis laughter rolled down to him. Snarling, Elrabin made the rudest gesture he knew.

Foloth was staring at him, wide-eyed. "Do they shoot at everyone here?"

"Sure," Elrabin said. "It's what they do for fun."

Nashmarl looked up. He was still shaking. "They nearly killed us."

"Who?" Harthril asked without sympathy. "Patrollers or Rejects?"

The cubs exchanged glances. "You saw the patrollers too?" Nashmarl asked, sounding humiliated. Misery welled up in his green eyes.

Foloth, however, looked angry. "You watched, and you didn't help us?"

Nashmarl heaved for air. "They said . . . they called us—"

"I heard what they called you," Elrabin said gently. He hugged the cub, and Nashmarl clung to him, sobbing.

Foloth, however, was made of sterner stuff. Wiping blood from his face, he went on glaring at Elrabin. "Why didn't you help us immediately? If you saw that we were in trouble with the patrollers, why did you—"

"What?" Elrabin broke in, still holding Nashmarl. "We supposed to take on patrollers and get ourselves shot along with you?"

"Mother made us your responsibility," Foloth said sternly. "You're supposed to take care of us—"

"Hey, cub," Elrabin said sharply, tired of this ingratitude. "*You* were supposed to stay in the camp where she left you."

"If you hadn't been so mean to us, we wouldn't have run away," Foloth said. "It's all your fault we got into this, Elrabin. You made us leave."

"Made you?" Elrabin glared at him. "Did I make you steal Harthril's food?"

"You are thief," Harthril said harshly.

Nashmarl stopped crying, but his face was flushed a deep red beneath his pale fur. Foloth glared at Elrabin and Harthril defiantly. "What about you, hoarding it like that?" he demanded of the Reject. "You're supposed to share what you have with the camp. That's the rule."

"No explain myself to you," Harthril said. His rill had stiffened and was beginning to turn pink at the edges.

"It's the rule, isn't it, Elrabin?" Foloth insisted.

Elrabin knew the brat was trying to deflect the heat off himself and onto the Reject, but he'd decided that nobody was going to get away with anything around here. Not this time.

"It's the rule," Elrabin agreed.

Harthril flicked out his tongue. "Food for emergency, when all hunting useless," he said. "Saved for camp, but you stole it. Now camp has nothing if trouble comes."

"Why didn't you say something about it before?"

"People have more courage, if think they must," Harthril said. "If know about rations, they cry for them too fast."

Elrabin met the Reject's stony eyes and didn't relent.

"You could have given some to Ampris," he said.

Harthril flicked out his tongue, and didn't reply.

When Elrabin went on glaring at him, the Reject lowered his blue eyes and shrugged with his crippled shoulder. "I made offer," he said. "She refused. She said to save it for Robuhl and Tantha's cubs. They weakest ones in camp."

Elrabin felt ashamed of himself for his suspicions. Harthril might be a Viis, but he was one of them. "Good enough," Elrabin said.

Foloth shrugged. "Easy enough to say now—"

Harthril slapped the cub, who howled and backed into the security field. The sizzle of burning cloth filled the air, and Foloth jumped away from it, twisting and trying to slap at his smoking cloak. "I'm on fire!" he shouted.

"Then go jump in the river," Elrabin said without sympathy.

Swearing, Foloth ran toward the water.

Nashmarl tried to follow him, but Elrabin kept a restraining hand on the younger cub's shoulder.

"The patroller will shoot at him if he goes into the water," Nashmarl whispered.

"Probably," Elrabin agreed.

A stun bullet plopped into the water right in front of Foloth. He stopped in his tracks, looking up at the top of the wall, and scuttled back to the others. "You burned me on purpose," he said, glaring at Harthril. "You will be—"

"Shut up," Elrabin said, tired of intervening, tired of listening to him.

Foloth's dark eyes grew black with anger. "I will say what I want."

"No, you will listen," Elrabin snapped. "You're a fool, Foloth. This was your idea, running off to the city. You got Nashmarl into this."

"No," Foloth said.

"Yes," Nashmarl said.

Foloth glared at his brother, but Elrabin refused to let them start bickering.

"You wanted to see the Kaa again," Elrabin said, repeating the boasting he'd overheard in the darkness while guarding the cubs on the trail. "You think the city is made out of gold, with jeweled windows and streets of pearl. Well, it ain't." He gestured. "You've seen it now. It stinks, cub. It's got buildings falling down, and cutthroats that don't like your looks."

"That's the slum," Foloth said in protest. "For the Rejects. We haven't seen inside Vir yet, where the real Viis live."

Harthril hissed, and his rill stiffened.

Elrabin shook his head, unable to believe the cub was really this arrogant and stupid.

Harthril advanced on him, flicking out his tongue. "You think I not real Viis? You think I not have Viis skin, Viis eyes, Viis blood?"

Foloth looked scared as he backed up a step. "Stay away from me! Don't crowd me against that force field again. Elrabin!"

"Your big mouth said the insult," Elrabin said quietly, letting Harthril loom over Foloth. "You take the consequences."

"I hope the next patroller does shoot you!" Foloth said, taking another unwilling step back toward the wall. "You're hateful and mean. You don't care anything about us. You don't even—"

Elrabin released his hold on Nashmarl and turned on Foloth. He was through being patient with the cub, through holding himself back for Ampris's sake. "Seems like I told you to shut up."

"I won't!" Foloth told him. "I don't have to do anything you say."

"So where do we stand?" Elrabin asked him. "I don't like you, I'm mean to you, and I should have saved you sooner? What am I, cub? Your slave?"

"You're abiru," Foloth said. "You were my mother's servant, and that makes you mine."

"And what do you be, cub?" Elrabin asked, his tone low and silky, his temper raging hot.

Foloth lifted his head very high. "I am half-Viis, which makes me better than you."

Elrabin's ears went flat, and he snarled.

"Foloth," Nashmarl said nervously. "Be quiet like he told you."

"And your mother, cub?" Elrabin asked Foloth. "She be abiru too. That make you better than her?"

Confusion flared in Foloth's eyes. He said nothing.

Elrabin bared his teeth. It wasn't a smile. "You fool," he said, his voice cutting. "You never learn when you make mistakes. You just blame everything on someone else and keep yourself clean and smelling sweet. Only it don't work that way with us, cub. We see what you really are. We know what you really are. Selfish little arrogant piece of work, that's you. Useless."

Foloth clenched his fists but said nothing. His eyes grew darker.

"Your mother be special, see?" Elrabin continued. "But she also gets blind when it comes to you. She thinks you two happen to be the center of the universe. But you ain't. You ain't even close. What happened today should have taught you that."

"She shouldn't have left us," Nashmarl said raggedly. "She didn't have to go, but she wanted to. She wanted to leave and not come back."

"She's in the city, enjoying all its luxuries," Foloth said coldly.

"Your mother is either hurt or arrested or dead," Elrabin said.

Nashmarl whimpered, but Foloth shook his head.

"No," he said with confidence. "We know the truth about her, Elrabin. We know she has a Viis lover. She's probably—"

Elrabin elbowed Harthril out of his way and hit Foloth across the mouth. The cub went reeling sideways and fell. Sprawled on the ground, he pressed the back of his hand to his bleeding mouth, and glared at Elrabin with hatred.

"It's true!" he shouted. "How else could we—"

Elrabin kicked him, and Foloth choked out a cry of pain.

"Ain't no one finer than your mother!" Elrabin shouted at him. "She's given everything she has to keep you two free, and you ain't worth it. You ain't worth one mouthful of food she's gone without to see you fed."

Foloth set his mouth in a stubborn line and glared at Elrabin.

Elrabin glared back. "You want the truth? I'll give it to you. You ain't got no da at all, cub. How's that for news? You were created in a laboratory experiment. While she was a prisoner, she had to carry you to term and give birth to you against her will. They tortured her, starved her, took your sister and cut her into little pieces to see what made her tick. Yeah, cubs, that's where you come from."

Nashmarl turned bright red. "It isn't true!" he said. "It isn't true! Mother never lies and she hasn't told us—"

"Your mother don't want you to know where you come from," Elrabin said fiercely. "She don't want you to carry that scar, see? No, she's been carrying all the scars herself. Scars in her soul, cubs. Scars that give her bad dreams at night. You've heard her scream in her sleep."

"She said the bad dreams come from when she was a gladiator and had to kill a lot," Nashmarl said.

Elrabin glanced at Foloth, who sat frozen on the ground, not moving, not speaking. "Yeah, but those dreams ain't so bad as the ones from Vess Vaas."

"She must hate us," Nashmarl whispered. His green eyes looked anguished.

Elrabin's anger faded, and he felt a small amount of remorse for having been so cruel. But not much. It was time the cubs learned what they needed to know. "No, she don't hate you," he said. "I would have, had I been in her place. But she's loved you since you were born, and if you don't know that then 'stupid' don't begin to describe you. She's sacrificed everything for you two. She even gave up her old dreams of saving the abiru from slavery. Yeah," he said as both cubs looked at him in astonishment. "She used to risk arrest every day, trying to spread the idea of freedom."

"That old stuff," Foloth said scornfully.

"Yeah, that old stuff," Elrabin snapped. "You try living with a restraint collar around your neck, cub, and see how you like it. You put an ownership ring in your ear, whether you want one or not, and you kneel when your master comes in. If your master kicks you"—he gave Foloth a light kick, knocking him over—"then you scramble up and you lick your master's foot. Property, that's you. And your master can do anything with you he wants. Ain't nothing you can say or do. Because if you make trouble or disobey an order or sulk, he can have you flogged. Or he can have your tongue torn out. Or he can sell you to someone else."

Elrabin let silence hang between them for a moment. Neither cub was looking at him now. "The only bad mistake I've ever seen your mother make is raising you two to be lazy, conceited, and stupid. Just because she thinks the sun rises and sets on you don't mean squat. Today you trotted into the big, cruel world all by yourself and you found out what it thinks of you."

Nashmarl was crying again, silently now, his shoulders shaking. Foloth glared at the river with his mouth pressed in a tight line. Elrabin and Harthril looked at each other as the silence lengthened.

Elrabin slapped his arms against his sides. He felt spent, like he'd talked too much. "Enough speech-making," he said finally.

Harthril nodded. "We going to camp in river to-night?" he asked. "Or we going to get inside city?"

"I'll take choice number two," Elrabin replied.

"How?"

"I'd kind of hoped the Rejects would help us get in," Elrabin said. "But these cubs have ruined that idea."

Nashmarl made a low, pained sound in his throat that Elrabin ignored.

"It is hard to gain Reject trust," Harthril said. "I know no one in Vir."

Elrabin tapped the side of his narrow muzzle and let mischief twinkle in his eyes. "So we go to another plan."

"Which is?"

"We're going to get in the same way the Skeks and the dust runners do. Through the sewers."

"The sewers!" Nashmarl said with repugnance. "Not the—"

"Oh, yes," Elrabin told him. The expression puckering Nashmarl's face cheered him greatly. "Come on. Let's start looking for a hole."

CHAPTER SIXTEEN

Noise awakened Ampris. The slam of a door, the rapid clomping of booted feet. She sat up in the basement hideout, her heart pounding, and a blinding light pinned her. Unable to see, her eyes streaming with tears, she held up her hands in an effort to shield herself from the light. Around her, the Myals were crying out in confusion and jumping off their cots.

"Freeze!" shouted a Viis voice, speaking the abiru patois. "All of you, stand where you are. Put your hands on your heads. If you move, you will be shot."

Bitterness flooded Ampris's mouth. She obeyed the order, standing still until she was shoved along with the others over against one wall.

"What is happening?" Non kept asking over and over. "What will they do to us?"

Ampris knew the answer to those questions all too well. The query spinning through her mind was, *Who had betrayed them?* Someone in Luthien's group? A resident on the street who had perhaps seen them or spotted a suspicious glimmer of light from the slitted basement windows? Or maybe she had been followed that one time she went out. Any answer could be correct.

"Are we under arrest?" Prynan asked.

The spotlight still shone on them, making them squint

and duck their heads. A patroller, only a dark shadow in his black armor and helmet, walked along in front of them and stopped when he came to Ampris.

He pointed at her. "She's the one."

Ampris's heart jerked in her chest. She snarled, and two patrollers closed in on her. She tried to spring free, intending to make a run for freedom. One of them hit her with a stun-stick, and immediately her muscles spasmed and locked up on her. She crashed heavily to the floor on her side and could not move, could not speak, while the nauseating effects of the stun spread through her body and held her captive.

As she struggled and raged internally, fighting her limp body, which could not seem to respond, she hoped it was only her the patrollers wanted. Maybe they would let the Myals go.

"Where are you taking her?" Quiesl asked as Ampris was picked up and shackled. "What are you going to do to her?"

"None of your business!" the officer replied. "Sergeant, get these Myals cleared out of here at once. Check their records and make sure they get full penalties for violating the regulation against squatters."

"Yes, sir," came the reply.

Grunting under her weight, the two patrollers carried Ampris up the steps and outside into the dark street. The skimmers were hovering without their flashing lights. Wanting to howl in rage and fear, Ampris closed her eyes a moment. Who had betrayed them? More important, how quickly would the patrollers execute her? Israi, she reflected bitterly, would have her revenge after all.

The patrollers tossed Ampris in the hold of one of the skimmers and secured her with restraint straps. "In for questioning, sergeant?" one of the patrollers asked as he walked around to get in the driver's seat.

"No, special orders for this one," the sergeant replied. "She's meat for the Bureau. Deliver her nice and fast."

The skimmer zoomed into the air, heading down the street on a whoosh of near-silent exhaust. Ampris tried again to force herself upright, knowing that if she could move she could break the straps and throw herself out of the hold—the sides weren't that high. And whether the fall to the street below killed her or not, at least she would be free.

But the stun held her immobile. She lay there, raging and afraid, knowing that interrogation at the hands of the Bureau of Security meant a slow and horrible death.

In the morning, the relentless heat collected beneath the shaded porticoes of the garden courtyard, and no matter how hard the slaves worked their fans, no hint of coolness reached the couch of Israi Kaa.

She reclined there, swathed in silk gauze and exquisite linen, savoring the soft, cold fruits that were her breakfast. Their delicate lavender skins were sweating with condensation. She crushed one between her teeth, letting the chilled juice squirt into her mouth. It was a delicious sensation. But the sun's strong rays were shining on her, and her skin was starting to burn.

She looked around, gesturing for her attendants to shade her. Strong Aaroun slaves were summoned, and they picked up Israi's couch with her on it and carried her deeper into the shade.

Without stopping their play, the musicians also moved away from the reach of the climbing sun. One of them hit a wrong note, and its discordancy irritated Israi.

She flicked her fingers together. "Remove them from our hearing."

"At once, majesty." Her chief attendant clapped her hands together sharply, and the musicians were hustled away.

In the sudden quiet, Israi heard the approaching *tap,*

tap, tap of a staff of office. She sighed, knowing Chancellor Temondahl's footsteps all too well.

He came up to her while she reached for another fruit, and bowed low. He looked fine this morning in a green coat of excellent cloth, embroidered with gold silk thread, and showing deep cuffs. His appearance—he was far better tailored than usual—pleased her, and so she gave him a smile.

"Chancellor," she said in greeting.

"A fine morning, majesty," he observed.

She raised her rill inquiringly. "You're in a pleasant mood today, Temondahl."

"The Imperial Mother is too kind. I bring good news."

Israi sat up and wiped her hands on a silk towel held out for her by a slave. "The arrest is made?" she asked.

"Yes, majesty."

Israi flicked out her tongue and laughed. "Aha! Then we have her!"

"Yes. She was handed over to the Bureau of Security at dawn."

"Excellent," Israi said in great satisfaction and waved at a nearby chair. "Please be seated, Temondahl. Tell us more."

The chancellor seated himself with a smile and even accepted a plate of the chilled plumots, something he rarely did. In mutual good humor, they ate together.

When Israi learned that Ampris and her coconspirators had escaped the Archives ahead of the explosion, she'd been furious. The investigators had found no evidence of charred bones. And the scattered trail of data crystals and assorted items left behind by the Myals led straight to the crumbling old wall and down to the river.

Tracks were found there, and the whole story was easily pieced together. Then it was just a matter of time, broadcasting Ampris's likeness on public vids and offering a generous reward. There was always a desperate abiru out there who would betray anyone for money.

"The information provided was accurate," Temondahl said. "The patrollers were able to make a surprise arrest. No resistance was possible."

"Excellent," Israi said, waving away a platter of spiced candies. She had plenty of fat stored in her tail these days; she needed no more. "Take her face off the vidcasts. We want no more public mention of the traitor's existence."

"At once, majesty. The Bureau has taken no action as yet. They wish your majesty's personal instructions."

Israi flicked out her tongue. "She is to be interrogated fully, and a copy of the report will be shown to our eyes only when the work is done."

Temondahl inclined his head. "Will your majesty wish to see the prisoner?"

"No," Israi said curtly. "There will be no trial. She dared lay hands on the person of the Imperial Mother. The penalty for that is death."

"And will the execution be public or private?"

"Private," Israi snapped.

Temondahl puffed out his air sacs.

"What?" she demanded, annoyed by this sign of disagreement. "What purpose would a public execution serve?"

"It would calm the sentiments of the people," he replied.

Israi stared at him blankly. "We fail to understand. The people have no say in this matter."

Temondahl sighed. "It seems the public circulation of Ampris's likeness may have been a mistake. The unrest is pronounced among the slaves."

"Unrest?" Israi said. "Nonsense. Put an end to it."

"Normally a simple matter, majesty," he said. "But there are problems."

Displeased, she drew back from him. "More problems? And so early in the day?"

"Increasingly large numbers of abiru are coming to the city gates," he said. "We believe the drought is forcing them here. Reports from the rural areas indicate that more and more landowners are releasing their slaves rather than feed them. Or they simply abandon the creatures, leaving them chained in their quarters. If they get free, they come here to Vir."

"Why?" she asked without much interest. "Drive them away."

"They have some resentment toward the Rejects, majesty. The Rejects receive charity—"

"Of course," she said impatiently. "It is the moral obligation of the Viis population to take care of the unseen ones."

"But the abiru want food also, majesty."

"The slaves?" she asked. "Demanding food from us? How dare they!"

"Hunger is driving them to desperation. The patrollers assigned to the city walls report they have never seen slaves so disorderly or disobedient."

"Deal with them," Israi commanded. "Have our prisoner executed and the rebellion squashed at once. Do not allow it to linger, or it *will* become a problem."

"Majesty, I don't think any solution to this will be quick or simple. The city's food reserves are growing low. We cannot spare anything for these hungry slaves."

"Of course not. Send out the army. Have them round up any abiru slaves gathered unlawfully outside the gates and deport them." She gestured, making the jeweled bracelets on her arms clink together. "Go farther. Any abiru dissident in the city, anyone known to be linked with Ampris or this resistance movement of hers, is to be arrested and deported. We want these troublemakers out of our city."

Temondahl inclined his head. "And where shall the army take them?"

She flicked out her tongue. "Anywhere. Someplace

private and remote, where they can be shot and disposed of without causing more unrest.''

''Ah. Now I understand the Imperial Mother perfectly.'' Temondahl sat quietly for several moments, until Israi glanced at him sharply, wondering if he was going to protest her command. Finally he roused himself and lifted his head. ''There are some labor camps on the other side of the planet, unused at present, now that so many building projects have been, er, postponed.''

She smiled. ''They would make ideal locations to execute prisoners, discreetly and efficiently.''

''Yes, majesty.''

''Yes. We will solve this problem of not having enough food to give the abiru.'' Israi reached out and popped a spiced candy into her mouth after all. ''They cannot eat if they are dead.''

Ampris was dragged into her cell and dropped on the floor. Panting hard, and trying to stifle a moan of pain, she lay there on the damp stones until the worst of the agony eased off. Screaming nerve endings finally calmed down. Spasmed muscles stopped cramping so tightly. She tried sitting up.

She failed the first time, rested a long while, moaning against the floor, and tried again. This time she made it and propped her shoulders wearily against the edge of her bunk slab. Not even a blanket softened its hard surface, and someone had died on it in the past—she could still smell the lingering scent of the fluids that had leaked from her predecessor.

Closing her eyes, she clutched her Eye of Clarity in her right hand and sank deep inside herself. It was the only way to escape the pain of her broken ribs and wrist. She thought something might be broken in one of her legs too, but she could not be sure. Yesterday they had clipped electrodes to her crippled leg and burned the ligaments that were still intact.

In that unbelievable agony, she would have screamed out the answers to anything they wanted, but her silent tormenters asked no questions. She wondered when the real interrogation would come.

A little shudder passed through her, and she felt her spirits crumble. She'd lost track of how many days she'd been in this place. Days and nights were lost in the gloom of her unlit cell. There were only times of agonizing pain and times of rest. Sometimes she heard other prisoners screaming. The one in the cell next to hers had coughed up blood for an hour, making terrible strangling noises. She thought he must be dead now, for no more sounds had come from his cell. No one had checked on him yet.

From down the corridor, she heard some of the patrollers laughing. A vidcast came on. They played it loud, as they always did, no doubt knowing that news of the outside world brought its own brand of torment to the minds of their prisoners.

And then she heard Israi's voice, prim and official, making a statement:

"Because of the terrible drought conditions, many abiru workers have been abandoned by their owners to starve. We hear the cries for help from these unfortunates, and we are taking steps to give them assistance."

Intrigued by this unusual sign of mercy, Ampris turned her head and listened harder.

"Rather than strain the resources of Vir unduly, we have ordered these abiru to be dispersed by transport to all the major cities of Viisymel. There is plenty of food for everyone. The people have the pledge of the Imperial Mother that no one will starve."

The announcement ended, and Ampris sighed. Perhaps, she thought, rubbing the smooth surface of her Eye of Clarity with her fingers, perhaps Israi was mellowing. Perhaps something Ampris had said to her that night in the Archives had gotten through. Israi was capable of great generosity when she chose. Surely this was a sign that things might yet improve.

Laughter erupted among the patrollers again, drowning out the rest of the vidcast. "No one will starve," someone said in a very good imitation of Israi's voice.

The others hooted and clapped their hands. "Can't starve if you're dead," someone else said.

"Welcome to your new city—Death Camp Central."

Listening to those callous Viis voices, Ampris felt herself growing cold to the bone. Israi had lied. The abiru would be going to extermination camps, not other Viis cities.

Ampris bared her teeth, wishing she could sink them into Israi's throat. Was there no end to the atrocities? Was there not a single Viis with a conscience?

Then another, even more horrifying thought occurred to her. Harthril had told her he would bring the group to Vir if she did not return. No doubt by now they were out there at the city gates, trying to gain admittance. The patrollers would be rounding up her friends, her sons, for death.

A feeble roar came from her jaws, ending in a racking cough that made her wince and clutch her side. She wanted to jump to her feet and rattle the door to her cell. She wanted to roar and scream and fight.

But she had no strength to do any of those things. She had only the pain and her own horror.

What a fool she had been to ever think there could be a peaceful solution to the abiru enslavement.

How naive she was still—after all these years, after all she'd gone through—to hope that any Viis would remember the meaning of honor and decency.

Ampris lifted her Eye of Clarity and pressed it against her muzzle. She closed her eyes.

"I vow," she whispered to it, "that from now on, it is war. Give my people strength to fight on. Give them hearts of defiance."

The stone's smooth surface grew warm against her fur. Surprised, Ampris lifted her head and looked at it glowing strangely on her palm, as though with a life of its own.

There had been times in the past when she thought she saw a spark of fire in its depths, but those instances had always been too brief for her to be sure. Now, however, the stone glowed with an eerie, lambent light that spread across her hand and dimly illuminated her cell. Ampris held her breath, unable to tear her gaze away. In that moment she forgot everything except the power radiating from this mysterious stone. Something, some kind of force that felt gentle and pure, crawled up her arm. She tried to hold herself still, tried to reach out to whatever was extending itself to her. She could almost feel herself falling into the center of that light, so white, so soft, so comforting.

Then someone in the distance screamed a piercing death cry. Startled, Ampris jumped. A fresh stab of pain pierced her side, and the light vanished as though it had never been.

"No!" she cried and cupped the stone with both hands, trying with all her might to bring the light back.

But except for the faintest vestige of warmth against her skin, it might have all been her imagination.

Several hours later, she was awakened from a fevered doze by the sound of her cell door slamming open. Armed patrollers surrounded her, and one of them kicked her hard.

Pain flashed through her like searing heat. She groaned, choked, and struggled to sit up. She was still on the floor, having never found the strength to crawl onto her bunk.

"Get up!" the patroller commanded harshly. "Prisoner one-four-zero, you are condemned to death. Get on your feet."

Ampris heard his voice as though from far away. Her

head was light, as though floating above her body. She pushed the pain from her mind, ignoring it as she had been taught during her years in the arena. She still had a few reserves of strength, and a great deal of pride. She drew on both now.

Swallowing another groan, she climbed slowly and stiffly to her feet and stood facing the three patrollers. Uniformed in black, they wore the distinctive insignia of a bloody dagger, the badge of the Bureau of Security. Helmeted, with their visors already down, their faces could not be seen.

Ampris did not want to see their faces. She drew her shoulders back and lifted her head. There had been a period in her life when she faced death every day. She had learned to channel her fear into aggression and not let it shackle her. Down the corridor, Ampris could hear other prisoners screaming and pleading for their lives, but she kept her dignity, letting no expression cross her face for the patrollers to enjoy.

All she felt at that moment was regret—regret that she would never see her sons again, regret that she would never see the abiru go free. She felt as though her life was incomplete and unfinished, but she supposed everyone facing death experienced the same emotion.

The sergeant pointed at the door. "To the transport."

"Why not here?" Ampris asked him defiantly. "Why not kill me here in this cell, or in one of the torture chambers? Why waste fuel transporting me to an extermination camp on the other side of the world?"

The sergeant gestured, and the other patrollers hit her, hard and expertly, leaving her gasping and doubled over. They took her arms and forced her outside.

Ampris had been beaten before. She had been thrown onto transports before. She had known despair and futility before. But this time was different. The other prisoners being herded outside across a paved courtyard to a waiting transport were moaning and yelping in distress. Most were Kelths, Ampris noticed. Several were missing hands, showing they had been punished for thievery. It was dark outside, as though the Viis were ashamed of this evil they did and wanted to hide it from the world. Ampris's fear faded and she found herself strangely calm. She felt almost safe, which surprised her. But she did not fight this new emotion, thinking it was merciful to feel this way.

She could barely walk because of her injuries. Her crippled leg would not support her, and she had to drag it. The patrollers shoved her into line and moved on. Ampris was not shackled or wearing restraints this time, but like the others she was too crippled and injured to be able to cause trouble.

Yet she found herself glancing around, counting the number of patrollers present, studying their placement. A few were clustered next to the door of the utilitarian building. More were talking at the front of the transport.

A clang and the grating of metal over pavement caught her attention. The gates were being rolled open manually by two sweating slaves. Amusement tickled the back of Ampris's throat. So even the Bureau, with all the dread and fear it inspired, had breakdown problems. But the open gate drew her gaze again. She found herself calculating whether she could get to it.

Someone prodded her in the back to make her move forward, and she nearly fell. Cold certainty flowed through her at that moment, and she knew she could not escape. All her strength, all her skills, all her courage were not enough this time. Her body was simply too broken.

She wanted to weep and rage, but those emotions were futile. Ampris had never been one to give up, and her tough spirit did not want to surrender now. But she could not do this herself.

Again she felt regret like a sharp stab and longed to see the faces of her sons once more.

But, she knew, it was not to be.

Sighing, she bowed her head and simply opened herself to acceptance.

As though a flower had burst open, the Eye of Clarity began to glow with that same lambent light it had displayed earlier in her cell. The light spread across Ampris's body, bathing her from head to foot. In wonder she raised her hand and stared at the aura of pure white light that encompassed each of her fingers. It looked so hot and fiery, and yet the feel of it was cool.

She felt filled with renewed strength. When she looked across the courtyard, the buildings, the transport, the condemned prisoners, and the gates had all vanished. Even the darkness was gone.

Instead, it was as though several moons shone in the sky, creating a clear, silvery light that was otherworldly and serene. Before her, she saw a vista of verdant hills and natural meadows, tall grasses waving in a breeze that smelled alien and yet sweetly inviting. She closed her eyes and inhaled, filling her senses with the new scents of greenery, blossoms, living creatures, and rushing water. There was no color in this moonlit landscape, but she did not care. It was as though she had reached a fabled place, a haven, after a long and difficult journey.

She had only to step forward to enter it. She had only to believe.

Ampris hesitated no longer. Although a corner of her mind was certain that if she walked toward this vision she would be shot by the patrollers, she stepped forward anyway.

In her vision, her body was no longer hunched and twisted by injury. Her leg no longer dragged with every step. She felt young and strong again. She walked slowly and steadily toward the meadow stretching before her.

Now she could hear sounds, faint at first, but growing steadily louder: the sigh of wind through the swaying treetops, the sleepy chirp of birds, the rustle of a small night predator stalking its rodent prey in the grass, the rushing gurgle of a stream of water.

She wanted to bathe in that water and be clean again. She wanted to drink that water.

Ampris closed her mind to all fear and thoughts of reality, and kept walking.

If she bumped into anyone she did not feel it. The illusion grew more real with every passing second. She could feel the grass now beneath her feet, soft and pliant, not stiff and crackling from drought. The breeze ruffled her fur, and she raised her nostrils to it, inhaling with pleasure. She had forgotten how pure and clean air could be.

She walked all the way across the long, long meadow. No one came after her. No one shouted at her. No one shot her.

When she reached the stream and knelt at its edge, Ampris dipped her glowing hands into the freezing water. "This is real," she said in wonder, then drank.

The first swallow was pure and delicious, sliding icy cold down her throat.

Then, without warning, the meadow and stream vanished. Jolted by the abrupt transition back to reality, Ampris found herself lying in a street gutter in some deserted quarter of Vir that she did not recognize. The white aura surrounding her was gone, and her Eye of Clarity hung around her neck as lifeless as usual. The gutter beneath her was dry. The air was thick with pollution, and the street smelled of uncollected garbage, dust, Skek droppings, and transport exhaust. It was still dark, but she sensed that it must be close to dawn. The sky had begun to show streaks of gray that told her the sun would soon be rising.

For now, the street was silent and deserted, but when traffic commenced, she knew, she must not be found here.

Ampris pushed herself to her knees. She was weak

and flushed with fever that made her pant. Dizziness made her hold on to the curb to steady herself. The vision had all seemed so real, as though she had actually journeyed to another place. Yet she was here, in Vir, she told herself. She had to be hallucinating.

But what kind of hallucination had gotten her out of the prison? She was far from the patrollers. What force had possessed her and protected her? Did she really just walk out of there, unseen and unnoticed? It seemed impossible to believe, and yet something had happened.

Ampris clutched the Eye of Clarity with a shaking hand. She knew she was on the edge of a great discovery, but she found herself unwilling to believe that it could be so simple. After all these years of trying to unlock the mystery of the Eye of Clarity, perhaps she had been going at it all wrong.

Perhaps all she had to do was listen, believe, and accept.

She leaned forward to grasp the curb with both hands, but she could not pull herself to her feet. She tried once more, and found herself racked with pain. Dizziness assaulted her again, and she whimpered softly. She knew she had to find a hiding place or she would be picked up by a sniffer programmed to find vagrants. You were allowed to starve to death in Vir, but you weren't allowed to lie in its gutters.

But another effort to move brought collapse instead. She felt herself falling, but the jolt of impact with the pavement seemed far away and not very painful. Ampris sank deep into darkness.

CHAPTER SEVENTEEN

Ampris dreamed that she was in a skimmer, flying high over Vir. The great city lay deserted and empty—except in the vast plaza at the end of the Avenue of Triumph. There, surrounded by bronze statues of great kaas, lay piles of Viis corpses, twisted in rigor, their skin frosted an eerie white.

"The Dancing Death," she whispered. "The Dancing Death."

"Ampris," a voice said to her. "Ampris, wake up. You must come back to us now. You have slept long enough."

The voice continued, pulling her attention away from the sight before her. After a while, the city faded and she could no longer see anything. She floated in her skimmer, flying blind, and then she lost the skimmer too and was only floating, like a leaf in a pond, floating to the surface, to light and the blur of anxious faces hanging over her.

She blinked slowly, hazily, and wondered who they were.

"Mother?" A strong hand gripped hers, crushing her fingers too hard. "Mother, do you know me?"

The face that went with the voice would not come

into focus. But Ampris inhaled his scent, and knew him. "Foloth," she whispered.

Her hand was released, and suddenly there was much noise and movement.

"She knows me!" Foloth said in jubilation. "She knows *me*!"

"Let me try," said someone else. Again her hand was gripped, this time not so tightly. "Mother, do you know who I am?"

It was a game, she realized. A guessing game, but she felt too tired to play it.

"Mother, please!"

She found herself being shaken and opened her eyes again. She knew Nashmarl's voice and tried to smile at him. But another shadow came and took Nashmarl away.

"Don't bother her," the new voice said to her son. "She's very weak. She must rest."

"She didn't know you," Foloth said, boasting and mocking at the same time. "She knew me, but not you."

"Shut up!"

"Hush, both of you," said the third voice. "Give her time. She has to rest now."

Of course I know Nashmarl, Ampris thought drowsily, sinking back into the eddies of darkness.

When she awakened next, it was very quiet except for the sound of low humming. Ampris opened her eyes and turned her head toward the sound.

At once it stopped, and a shadow came to hover above her. "How you feeling?"

She sniffed for scent and recognized this individual. A rush of affection swept through her, making her smile, while her mind groped for a name.

"Come on, Goldie," the voice said pleadingly. "Stay awake a little while this time. You need to come back to us, see?"

"Elrabin," she murmured.

"That's right." He rubbed her gently between her ears. "How you feeling?"

"Soft," she answered.

"Oh? Uh, sure. You feel soft. I guess that's good. No pain?"

"No."

He patted her hand. "That's the way we want it. You going to heal up just fine, see? Jobul's a medic, or at least an orderly, but he knows what to do. For a Myal, he's not bad."

She blinked, and found that things were slowly coming into focus. It was as though she had been looking at white light for so long, seeing things no one should, and had somehow ruined her vision. But it was coming back now.

Relieved, she gazed up at Elrabin's face and saw his quirky, sly smile and the mischief that always lurked in his eyes. "Hello, old friend," she said.

He bent over her and gave her face a quick lick. "Hello, yourself. You want some broth?"

"No."

"Sure you do. Got to get your strength back, Goldie. Can't lie there forever."

She smiled and let her eyes fall shut. "You don't eat in dreams."

"Maybe not." He came back with a small chipped bowl and a spoon that he let clatter against the rim. "But this be real life, and you got to eat something, even if it's just one swallow."

She smiled at him. "You're a dream."

His tall ears swiveled back and he grunted a little as he lifted her gently and propped something behind her. "That hurt you any?"

"No."

He sighed in relief and picked up the bowl. "Now open wide. Just one swallow, and I'll leave you alone."

"I'm tired."

"Come on. Open the gnashers for me. Just once, okay?"

She had to smile at him, and when she did he pressed the bowl of the spoon to her mouth. Some of the broth trickled across her tongue. It was tepid, but tasted surprisingly good. She swallowed and watched him scoop another spoonful. This time she took it willingly.

"Hey, you be hungrier than you thought, see?" he said with satisfaction, feeding her as fast as she would take it.

"It's good," she said.

Her gaze wandered about the modest surroundings in curiosity. They seemed to be in a one-room structure constructed of mud bricks with a low ceiling assembled from an assortment of scavenged building materials. Besides her cot, there were two others lining the wall, plus a mismatched collection of crudely made stools, a sleek chair of Viis design, and a rickety table. A burner supported by bricks and a pail of water in another corner seemed to make up the kitchen.

"What is this place?" she asked in wonder. "Where are the archivists, the brothers? And what are you doing here? If I am not dreaming you, then how did you get here? How did I get here? How did all this come about?"

"Hey, slow down," he said, putting away the emptied bowl. "Guess you be feeling better if you can fire off questions."

"I was in prison," she said, trying to remember. "I was being loaded into a transport for execution."

Elrabin suddenly looked very grim. "Heading off for the death camps."

"Yes."

"When we got into the city," he said, "it took us a while to get our bearings. My old contacts be mostly long gone, see? But I finally dug up some folk that knew what was what. That's when we found out you'd been arrested by the Bureau.''

She shivered, feeling a wave of weakness pass through her.

''Hey,'' he said softly, putting his hand on her shoulder. ''Maybe I better let you lie back again.''

''No,'' she said. ''Go on. My friends, the archivists. Did the Bureau get them too?''

''No, they got shook up good by the patrollers. Some of 'em got sold somewhere for hard labor. Supposed to be executed, but you know how corrupt the patrollers are—they'll sell anyone they can get their hands on and take a juicy kickback from the slavers to boot. A dry old stick named Quiesl's still around though. And someone named, uh, Non?''

She closed her eyes, grateful for Quiesl and Non's survival, already grieving for the fate of the others.

''I didn't know what to do when I found out you'd been arrested,'' Elrabin admitted, swiveling back his ears. ''Been worried sick about you, knowing what you were going through at the hands of those—''

He stopped, and stood silent, his eyes dark and murderous.

''My sons,'' she prompted him. ''I dreamed I saw my sons.''

''Yeah, they be here,'' he said with a blink. ''We all came.''

''I was afraid you would.''

''Couldn't be helped, Goldie. Course now that they're here, they ain't so happy about it. Velia's afraid of her own shadow. Tantha hates the place. Luax would howl if she knew how. She says the Rejects here live worse than the abiru workers.'' He grinned. ''Even sour old Frenshala's done lost her zeal for seeing the big city. Some folk just got to learn the hard way.''

''I wish they had not come. I wish Foloth and Nashmarl were safe.''

"Goldie, you could tie those two cubs to a tree and they still wouldn't be safe."

"Have they been much trouble?" she asked, knowing from his expression that they had. "I am sorry."

He squeezed her hand. "You ain't sorry for nothing. In a few days you'll be up and around, putting me in charge of them again. I know you."

She smiled, feeling very tired now. "But what is this place?"

"This be Jobul's home," Elrabin said. "Nice, ain't it?"

"Yes."

"He does all right for a Myal. Gets paid a better wage than usual, and he grows a garden on his roof, so he ain't spending all his credits on Quixlix—not that it's safe to eat that stuff these days. He found you, Goldie. You were unconscious in the street. He recognized you from some vidcast being spread around and brought you here. Then he notified the underground, and by then we'd linked up with them and we all ended up here."

Backing her ears, she thought over what he said, trying to remember.

"You know how you got away?" he asked softly. "You must have put up one heroic fight."

"No," she said and reached for her Eye of Clarity. Her hands were still unsteady, and he helped fit the stone into the curl of her palm. "The Eye saved me."

His ears pricked forward and skepticism filled his eyes. "Don't go softheaded on me now. Ain't no—"

"It did. I had a vision. I saw Ruu-one-one-three," she said. "Oh, Elrabin, it is so beautiful and unspoiled. That is where we must take the abiru people when we are free. It is perfect for us. We can start over. We can make a wonderful place for—"

"Sure," he said softly but without a gram of belief in his voice. "Sure we can. Someday. You better rest now."

"No, I have to tell you this. We have to get busy."

"No busy for you," he said firmly, tucking the blanket tight around her. "You got to rest."

"Elrabin," she said, and her tone made him stop fussing with the tattered blanket and look at her. "The Eye took me there. When I walked into its vision, I left the Bureau of Security. I don't know how it worked, but it did. Maybe the patrollers couldn't see me while I was in the light of the Eye, but I believe that what I saw was real. I smelled the air and grass. I drank the water. It's not as though I imagined it. I was really there, as though somehow the Eye transported me through time and space. I was in the prison courtyard, and then I wasn't. I can't explain it."

His eyes were troubled. He patted her hand. "Okay, Goldie. You got out of there somehow, even if no one ever gets away from the Bureau. They weren't much to talk about when I was a lit running around these streets, but things be different now. The folk say the Bureau has grown as powerful as the Kaa. I figured you were gone for good."

She curled her fingers around his. "I know how we can defeat the Viis."

"Hey, now. Wait right there," he said in alarm. "Don't you start working yourself into nothing like that. We can't fight the Viis, Goldie. When you get to feeling better, you going to remember that. We got no weapons, and we ain't likely to get any."

"Elrabin," she said, "we don't need weapons. We have knowledge, and that is more dangerous than any side-arm."

"Goldie, don't get into this," he said, making it a plea.

"We are already in it," she said. "I was spared so I could finish what I have to do. When will the others come back?"

"Tonight. I don't know where the cubs are. Tantha's

in charge of them today. They been pretty good lately."

"Can you get a message to Luthien or Harval?"

His eyes widened. "Harval the dust runner?"

"Yes."

"Goldie, you don't want that kind of riffraff around."

"Someone in their groups betrayed the archivists. That's how I was arrested, but they're still important contacts," Ampris said. "I was named the leader of the resistance. I need to meet with everyone. As soon as it can be arranged."

"Why? So they can betray you again?" he asked fiercely. "I'll take out Harval's throat if he sold you to the Bureau!"

"Is he who you worked for when you were a lit?" she asked.

"No. Rival gang, but they all be bad, Goldie. You can't trust any of them."

"And who *do* I trust?" she asked. "The Viis? No, Elrabin. Spread the word. We will meet tonight."

She fell asleep for the rest of the day, but by evening she felt stronger and more alert.

Foloth and Nashmarl joined her, coming to stand awkwardly beside her bed. She smiled up at them. As always, it delighted her to see their faces, to inhale their scent, to stretch out her hands and clasp theirs.

"My sons," she said happily, pleased to see them looking well. "I have missed you so much."

Nashmarl stared at her with a mixture of longing and confusion in his eyes.

Foloth squeezed her hand. "Elrabin says you will get well, Mother. I'm glad. I've been worried."

Ampris smiled at him. "Do not worry about me."

"Why did you stay away so long?" Nashmarl burst out as though he couldn't hold back his questions. "Weren't you ever coming back for us?"

"Hush, you fool!" Foloth snapped at him, and Nashmarl drew back with a scowl.

"Do not quarrel," Ampris pleaded. "Please. Not now."

"I'm sorry, Mother," Foloth said and glared at his brother. "Keep quiet, Nashmarl. We're not supposed to upset her."

Nashmarl glowered at the floor, saying nothing. Ampris tugged gently at his hand until finally he glanced at her.

Tears of apology were blurring her vision. "I could never abandon you, Nashmarl. Never. I was coming back for you when injury and arrest prevented me—"

"You're tiring her and making her cry," Foloth interrupted, still glaring at Nashmarl. His gaze shifted to Ampris. "Don't apologize, Mother. We understand what kept you here."

Hearing a trace of judgment in his tone, Ampris sighed. "Do you really?" she asked him. "I hope so. My thoughts have been with you every day we were apart. You've grown taller, both of you. Did you realize that?"

"We're nearly adults now," Foloth said, squaring his shoulders. "Not cubs. We should have a vote in the meetings."

"Elrabin already said no," Nashmarl told him spitefully. "He said not to pester her about it."

Closing her eyes a moment, Ampris let her grip slacken on their hands. Abruptly their bickering ceased.

Nashmarl touched her face. "Mother?" he asked, his voice shrill. "You aren't going to die, are you?"

She forced open her eyes, blinking away her tears and summoning a smile. "No, I promise you that I am much better. It just makes me sad when you two quarrel. You are brothers. You must learn to help each other in this cruel world."

Nashmarl's mouth quivered. "I'm sorry."

She looked at her elder son. "Foloth?"

"I'm sorry also, Mother."

Satisfied, she took their hands again, lifting one then the other to her muzzle in a brief caress. Silence fell over them as they shared this moment of togetherness. Ampris's heart filled with gratitude for peace among her family, however brief it might prove to be. Later, she told herself, she would try to talk longer with them about their recent experiences. She understood that more must have happened to them than she'd been told about thus far.

"Hey, uh, Goldie?" Elrabin said, coming up to them. "Hate to interrupt, but it's time to go."

Ampris lifted her head, eager to embrace the future. "I am ready."

The abiru conspirators met in the basement of an abandoned building, to avoid compromising Jobul's home. The Myal medic was young and very kind. He changed her medication patches and mixed up a potion for her to swallow that left her feeling clearheaded and able to endure being carried to the meeting place. With her cubs flanking her, quiet and subdued for once, both pressed close, Ampris sat in a chair, propped up with cushions, and faced the assembly.

She'd been filled in on events and knew that warnings had been leaked to the abiru folk outside the city walls. Yet more were arriving from the countryside every day. Patrollers had started sweeping the streets of Vir regularly, picking up anyone not on a work detail. It was safer to stay home and hide.

But Ampris knew they were past the point of playing it safe.

Luthien came to her first, in front of everyone, and confessed that one of his nephews had betrayed her. "I be ashamed of him," the one-eyed Kelth declared. "I had no part in that, Ampris. I swear it on my own blood."

Angry mutters filled the room, but Ampris raised her hand and they quieted. She met Luthien's fierce glare and believed him. "There will be other betrayals as long as people are forced to live in fear," she said. "I do not blame you."

Again voices were raised in anger, but Ampris ignored them. Luthien glanced around, then ducked his head in awkward thanks. "The nephew done been found in the sewers with his throat cut, Ampris. He won't betray anyone ever again."

She backed her ears, hoping Luthien himself had not murdered the nephew but knowing he probably had. "We are here to *save* the abiru folk, not kill each other," she said at last.

Luthien went back to his place, and the people next to him shifted away as though his presence was a contaminant.

"We have a place to go," she said to them all. Her voice was weak but clear. They stayed silent and respectful, listening to every word. The atmosphere of this meeting was very different from that of the last one. Ampris supposed it had something to do with the fact that she'd been tortured by the Bureau and survived. It was a hard way to gain respect.

"Ruu-one-one-three will be our new home. It's clean, unpolluted, unspoiled."

"Ain't no such place," someone said.

Elrabin glared at the speaker. "Hey, shut up. She ain't done talking."

"It does exist," Ampris said. "The Viis thought it would be their promised land, but it never will. The Zrheli believe this planet is sacred. They have guarded it from Viis spoilage and exploitation by closing the jump gate on Shrazhak Ohr. But this planet can be our new home."

"How?" Harval asked her, unable to keep quiet any longer. He rose to his feet, looking big and bulky in his striped vest and strange, brimless cap. "Another planet?

How do we get to it? You give us visions, Ampris, but we got to deal with the practical."

"Hear me!" Ampris called out. She leaned back against her cushions for a moment, letting a wave of weakness pass.

Looking worried, Nashmarl put his hand on her wrist. She smiled at him and continued, "My plan is no fable, no wish that cannot be achieved, Harval. There are hundreds of cargo ships orbiting Viisymel right now, empty and unused because the economy of this world is bankrupt. Israi Kaa cannot afford to send the ships out to collect the colony exports. If she could, the people of Viisymel would not now be going hungry. Those empty ships are our way off this dying world."

Commotion broke out, with several people talking at once. Ampris leaned back and let the hubbub go as long as it wanted. She was growing tired, and she had to conserve her strength.

"You're feeling worse," Nashmarl whispered to her worriedly. He stroked the fur on her head. "We'd better take you back now."

She smiled up at him, grateful for the concern in his green eyes. Nashmarl looked so quiet, so troubled. She reminded herself to find time to talk to him about all that was bothering him.

She sighed. "I mustn't leave yet. I have them listening. Now I must make them agree."

"You're losing their respect," Foloth said, his voice sharp with a far different kind of concern. "I thought they would follow you anywhere, but already you've lost them."

She looked at him, struck anew by how tall he'd grown during their separation. He appeared to be healthy and well, despite the gash now healing to a pink scar on his forehead, but he remained far too impatient. He had yet to learn so many things. "Wait and see," she said to him.

Elrabin and Harval shouted for silence until at last the uproar died down. Slowly the crowd resumed their seats, but Harval remained standing.

"No one can say you ain't got bold ideas, Ampris," he told her. "But we got no transportation and no weapons. How we going to get to those ships? The Viis ain't going to let us leave. They need us too much, even if right now they'd rather kill us than give us food."

"That's right!" a slim Kelth shouted from the back of the room.

"You're talking *everyone,* Ampris," Harval went on. "I know we outnumber the Viis, at least here in this city, and that's a lot of folk."

"There are enough ships," she said. "The cargo ships won't be comfortable, but they're big."

"But—"

She raised her hand. "My plan is very bold. It is risky. But if we stick together we can do it."

"Even if we could break into the armories, we couldn't—"

"Harval," she said, "stop thinking like a Viis. We cannot go to war with them. That is not our way. Anytime the abiru folk have tried to fight their way to freedom, they have failed. We must use guile and cunning. We are going to let the Viis defeat themselves."

Harval backed his ears, looking baffled. "That don't make sense."

"We are going to keep them off balance, play to their worst fears, and distract them until they do not care what we do." Ampris lifted her head and let her gaze sweep the room. "We are going to deceive the Viis, as once they deceived us. We are going to strike where they are most vulnerable. When we are finished, they will *make* us go."

Another Aaroun, as equally skeptical as Harval, rose to her feet. "And how do we do this?"

"We are going to ask the Rejects to come out of hiding," Ampris said.

She saw ears going back; the murmurs rose again.

"Hear me!" she called over the noise, and they quieted reluctantly. Foloth stirred beside her, but Ampris ignored him. "No more will the Rejects stay out of sight in order to avoid bringing offense to the Viis citizens," Ampris said. "No more will the Rejects be content to accept charity. I'm going to ask them to assert their rights and demand equality with their more fortunate brethren."

"What good will that do?" demanded Luthien, his one eye blinking rapidly. "That ain't no kind of plan."

"The Rejects are a reminder of the Dancing Death!" Ampris said, raising her voice again to be heard. She felt breathless and pain began to stir beneath her medication, but she never let her gaze waver. "That disease crippled the Viis Empire. It drove them into becoming the venal, lazy, inefficient creatures they are today. They pretend they do not worry about their dwindling population, but they worry all the time. The Viis live in fear, fear that the plague will come back. Every time they see a Reject, they relive a time in their past when they were defeated by a biological enemy unseen and unstoppable."

"This will torment them," Harval said. "But it will not do more than that."

"They must be prepared psychologically," Ampris said. "The recent defeat of the mighty Viis flotilla has them unsettled. Now the Rejects will continue to upset them. Because, my friends, we are going to bring back the Dancing Death."

Cheers went up from half the room. The others remained seated in skepticism. "How?" Harval asked.

"How?" Luthien asked.

"How?" someone else asked.

Ampris smiled, and it was a cold, grim smile. "I am

acquainted with a Viis scientist named Ehssk."

"Ehssk the Butcher!" came a shout.

"Yes," she said. "Ehssk the Butcher. He has been trying for many years to create an antidote for the virus, but he has failed."

"So?" Luthien said.

"He keeps vials of the virus sealed in his laboratory," Ampris said. "You are thieves, many of you. How hard is it to break in and take what we need?"

Luthien rose to his feet, his eye staring in astonishment. Harval's mouth hung open. One by one the rest stood up.

"The Crimson Claw!" came a shout from the back.

It was echoed around the room until the roar was thunderous. "The Crimson Claw! The Crimson Claw!"

"Freedom!" Foloth shouted back.

They took up the chant immediately. "Freedom! Freedom! Freedom!"

Elrabin came over to Ampris's chair and bent over her. "You look tired, Goldie, but you got a mind as devious and twisted as the Kaa's."

She smiled back, letting the cheers wash over her. "Thank you."

"They're yours now. They'll do it," he said in admiration. "It be a bold plan, though."

Her smile faded. "It is a very dangerous plan, Elrabin. For us, the real risks are just beginning."

His ears drooped. "No other way?"

"No other way." She gripped his hand, wanting him to have faith too. "But worth it, Elrabin. Worth it!"

The next day Ampris set to work. Still too weak to get about, she met with Luax, Harthril, and four other Rejects from her bed in Jobul's house.

One of the Rejects from Vir was the dwarf who'd been at her first resistance meeting in the Archives. Today she learned that his name was Mahradin. It was immediately clear that he was the chosen voice of the Reject population in the city.

"We hear," he said as soon as the perfunctory greetings were over, "that you want us to offend the citizens."

"Yes," Ampris replied. "To show yourselves in public, to cause disturbances—"

"Why should we?" he asked. Although she was lying propped on cushions and he was standing, he still had to look up at her. With his full-sized head, large rill, and shrunken body, he looked top-heavy. "We have rules, Ampris. We stay out of sight. We cause no trouble. We do nothing to remind the citizens that we exist. In exchange, each Viis household donates food and clothing to our distribution centers. Why should we risk what we have? We are not slaves. We have our freedom."

"Are you free?" she asked. "Free to do as you please? Free to go where you please? Have you ever been to a public concert, Mahradin? Have you ever been to the arena to watch fighting? Can you stroll down the famous floating walkways of the Zehava shopping district? No, you are not free. You live bound by the rules of those who will not accept you. You are chained by your dependency on their charity."

"At least we don't starve," he muttered.

She looked him right in the eye. "Is the charity as generous as it used to be?"

The dwarf's rill stiffened. He glared at her, but did not answer. They both knew there were shortages. As Viis citizens had come to feel the economic squeeze, their pockets had grown more shallow.

"We struggle," Mahradin admitted finally. "But you would see us cut off."

"You're going to be cut off anyway," Ampris told him. "I know there are only five distribution centers in Vir now; there used to be twenty. When they can no longer feed the slaves, why should they feed you?"

"Because we are still Viis," Mahradin said proudly.

Ampris sighed. That opinion was exactly what she had to change. "Yes, you are Viis," she said in agreement. "Every bit as Viis as the citizens. Yet you are shunned. Even your own families will have nothing to do with you. Why? Because you look different from them. What reason is that?"

His rill was turning red. "Why do you pretend such ignorance? You lived with the Viis once. You were pet of the sri-Kaa."

"Yes, I know that the Viis abhor anything ugly," she said, choosing to be blunt. "But beauty should be judged by many standards, not just one. Tell me, Mahradin: What do *you* consider beautiful?"

He flicked out his tongue, his eyes darting around the room. No one else said anything to help him out, however.

Finally he brought his gaze back to Ampris. "I see beauty in someone whole," he admitted. "In long, straight legs. A body that fits together proportionately."

"Yes, that is natural," she said gently, aware that he had hurt his pride in order to admit so much. "Look at Luax. Her limbs are straight. Do you consider her beautiful?"

Harthril stiffened his rill and started to speak, but Ampris gestured for him to be quiet. She watched Mahradin closely, observing the struggles in his face.

"She has a straight body," Mahradin said finally. "Yes, she has beauty."

"Yet Luax is a Reject," Ampris said.

Luax's eyes filled with hurt. She bowed her head, and Harthril put his arm around her.

Mahradin raised his clenched fists. "You have no right to preach to us about our own beliefs."

"No, but I think you bind yourself too hard to something that has no foundation," she answered. "In all honesty, when you are as intelligent and as capable as a citizen, how do you make yourself accept second-class standing?''

''We are not even second-class,'' muttered another Reject, a thin blue-skinned female with two rills layered on top of each other. ''We are no class.''

''I know you don't want to trust me,'' Ampris said softly. ''I am abiru and you're Viis.''

''Not Viis!'' the blue-skinned female said fiercely. ''Reject.''

''You are Viis,'' Ampris said firmly. ''The term 'Reject' is an insult. They do not want you, no matter whether they supply you with food or not. They do not want you. That must hurt.''

Harthril muttered angrily to himself and moved away. Luax watched him pace about and would not look at Ampris.

''I know I am saying things that upset all of you,'' Ampris admitted. ''I'm sorry. You have seen my own sons. You know that I can sympathize with your situation. Perhaps I'm wrong. Perhaps the Viis government won't turn against you. But I have personally seen the blighted stelf crops. I have seen patrollers burning the fields. I know the food stores are running low, and that the cargo ships have not gone to the colonies to bring back more. The food will run out. And when it comes down to a choice between the accepted Viis families and you, well—''

''Yes, yes, yes.'' Mahradin flicked out his tongue. ''We see the threat. Or we would not be here at all.''

Ampris held back her own impatience, wishing they could have reached this point sooner.

''You ask much of us,'' Mahradin said. ''But what do we get for risking our food? When the Viis drive you away, will they not remember the trouble we caused them and punish us?''

''You'll come with us,'' Ampris said. ''To Ruu-one-one-three. How ironic that your people should inherit those beautiful lands instead of your flawless Viis counterparts.''

Mahradin swung around and exchanged glances with the other Rejects. ''And we would have our own ship?''

''Yes,'' Ampris said. It was so easy to promise what she did not as yet have.

''You would accept us? Not torment us?''

''Yes.''

''You would give us our own land, not make slaves of us?''

''We are putting an end to slavery!'' Ampris said heatedly. ''Not taking it with us.''

Mahradin fell silent.

After a moment, Ampris backed her ears. ''I don't know what else to say to convince you. Only that we need your help. Without you, we cannot succeed.''

''Flattery is an evil thing.''

''Truth is truth,'' she said shortly.

At last he flicked out his tongue and nodded. ''Very well. We will cooperate. But do not forget your promise, Ampris. We make bad enemies.''

''I want no enemies,'' Ampris replied. ''I will not forget. When can you begin?''

He blinked at her eagerness. The others looked disconcerted.

''It is not easy to change the habits of a lifetime,'' Mahradin began.

''You must start tomorrow,'' she said. ''Today if possible. Not just in Vir. Can you persuade Rejects in the other cities to go along? The more widespread the trouble is, the better.''

''We will see what can be done,'' Mahradin said reluctantly. ''But take care, Ampris. You are setting something very frightening in motion.''

She no longer allowed herself second thoughts. Clutching her Eye of Clarity, she said, ''I know.''

That night it began, the first phase of Ampris's plan.

The Rejects might have been wary and suspicious, but they did not delay. On the evening vidcast, a report showed up about Rejects forcing their way into a fashionable restaurant and showing their features. Patrons had been upset. Many had departed immediately, in the middle of their meals. The proprietor had gotten the Rejects to leave, but he was distraught at the loss of the evening's usual revenues.

Elrabin laughed and tapped Ampris on the arm. "Get 'em in their pockets, see?" he said with glee while Velia sat curled up against him. "That's brilliant."

At first the Rejects were peaceful, as Ampris had requested. They simply turned up at any and every public event, making their heretofore-invisible presence known. Viis citizens apparently had no idea just how large the Reject population had grown in recent years. Now they never knew when they were going to be accosted by a Reject claiming to be a relative and asking to move in.

Soon, an incident of violence was reported. Then another and another.

"No!" Ampris said angrily. "No bloodshed!"

But the Viis grew more violent in repudiating the Rejects. And despite Ampris's advice, the Rejects retaliated in kind. Suddenly there were riots, break-ins, and looting.

"Mahradin," Ampris said during another hastily called meeting. "You must put some kind of control on this. Rejects are getting hurt. If the riots don't stop, the government will do something terrible to your people."

Mahradin looked up at her fearlessly. In the past few weeks, something had changed in his eyes. She saw it in other Reject eyes as well—a new pride, a new fierceness. "The government has done nothing," he said with confidence. "Oh, sometimes the patrollers come in and break things up. There have been some looters arrested. But no one wants to look at us long enough to put restraints on us."

"Take care," Ampris warned him. "If you push too far, the Kaa will order—"

"What?" he replied. "Many of us carry aristocratic, even imperial blood, you know. We may live in poverty, but our lineages are proud."

"I see," she said, understanding at last why the government was being so patient. "But take care. The Viis have never been very good at coping with moral dilemmas."

Mahradin smiled and flicked out his tongue. "That is exactly what we count on. Have you seen the latest vidcasts? Debates over the Reject problem on almost every channel. The patrollers can't be everywhere at once."

"And deportation of the abiru has all but stopped," Ampris added. "Yes, that is good news for us all."

"We're doing our end of your plan," Mahradin said. "Now it's time for you to do your part."

She nodded. "The second phase of my plan is already going into effect."

"And what is that?"

She had learned to value these varied leaders and co-conspirators, but she was wise enough not to trust any of them too completely.

She smiled at Mahradin and tapped her finger against her muzzle the way Elrabin did. "Elrabin the Kelth is in charge of phase two. When it is successful, you will learn all about it."

CHAPTER EIGHTEEN

As soon as Mahradin finally left, Ampris limped over to their linkup. Someone whose name she could not remember had stolen it and brought it here to their little headquarters. Velia sat hunched by it now, carefully trying to feed a surreptitious message into the link by piggybacking it onto a legitimate signal.

"Any luck?" Ampris asked.

Velia shot her a look of frustration. "I said I'll let you know."

Ampris veered away, not wanting to irritate her more. They had never gotten along, and there was nothing Ampris could do about it except leave Velia alone as much as possible.

Restless, she roamed about the one-room structure. So far they had been safe living here in Jobul's tiny house, although it could not accommodate everyone in the group. The others were scattered, and coming and going was risky, although less so while the patrollers were busy dealing with the unruly Rejects.

Ampris told herself, however, that they should not risk Jobul's home much longer. He had been kind and generous, surrendering his private space to a bunch of strangers. Thanks to his care, she was much stronger now, almost her old self, although she now wore a brace to support her leg. She peered out a narrow security slit at the street outside, wishing she could have gone with Elrabin and the cubs today. But she was not allowed outside. The risk that someone would recognize her was too great. Velia was here both to operate the linkup and to act as an unofficial guard.

"I have something!" Velia said sharply.

Startled, Ampris swung around, then hurried to her. "What is it? A voice signal?"

"Yes. Someone's gotten our message and is calling back. I've routed and cross-routed it so we probably can't be traced by any monitors, but don't talk too long. If I say cut it off, do it right then. Agreed?"

"Yes," Ampris said eagerly.

They had no picture capabilities, but she reached for the mike. "Shrazhak Ohr, this is the Freedom Network calling. Shrazhak Ohr, come in."

Static crackled over the speakers. Then a thin, hostile voice replied, "What do you want?"

"I'm calling the engineers of Shrazhak Ohr. This is Ampris of the Freedom Network."

"What do you want?"

Ampris explained in a few well-chosen sentences, keeping it as brief as she could.

Silence came back to her, a silence so long she wondered if the signal had been lost. Velia scowled, looking worried.

"Shrazhak Ohr, are you there?" Ampris asked.

"We cannot help you," the engineer replied.

Ampris backed her ears. Zrheli were always difficult. Their stubbornness, she figured, must be a genetic trait. "Please," she said. "If we can get the abiru population on the cargo ships, will you let them through the gate to Ruu-one-one-three?"

More silence. Velia fidgeted and began to pant.

"No," came the answer finally.

"Can't or won't?" Ampris asked.

"No."

"Look, I know the planet is somehow sacred to your people. I know you've closed it off to protect it from the Viis. I honor and respect that. But for most of us our homeworlds are either destroyed or still under Viis rule. We need somewhere to go, somewhere to live as free, self-governed citizens with our own way of—"

"No."

"What do you fear?" Ampris asked in rising irritation. To get so close and find herself blocked frustrated her. Trying to control her temper, she said, "We would live on that world with gratitude. We would honor it and take care of it. We intend no exploitation. We would not ruin it the way the Viis have ruined Viisymel."

The engineer said nothing.

"Please," she said. "Won't you help us? Have you no wish to live free yourselves? Think of your families. Think of what life could be like for them if they were free of Viis domination."

Nothing.

"Do you love your Viis masters so much?" she asked in desperation, not knowing how to reach these fierce, feathered scientists. They were rude, isolated, brilliant, and difficult to understand. But once, when she was trapped in Vess Vaas, she had succeeded in getting the Zrheli there to help her. She was praying now that she could do it again, but so far nothing was working. "I guess you do love them. I guess perhaps they have stopped killing you in the arena baitings as punishment for keeping the gate closed. If you are happy under Viis domination, then I shouldn't ask—"

"Who is happy in this box of death?" asked the Zrhel fiercely. "And you have killed some of us, Ampris. We know your name. We abhor it!"

She sighed. They would never forgive her for what she'd been forced to do. They would never trust her. And yet it had been a Zrhel, frightened out of his mind, who had savaged her in the arena, crippling her leg and ending her career as a gladiator.

"My apologies can never be strong enough for those I was forced to slaughter," she said quietly. "We all have our regrets, engineer. I am trying to pay my debts by seeing that all the abiru races go free—at least all who live on Viisymel. I can't help others in the empire now, not directly, anyway. But the mining worlds have broken free of the Viis. If we can break free too, then others will manage. Will you help us?"

"Can't."

Her ears pricked forward. This was an improvement from the bald no of earlier. "Can't? Why not?"

"Surveillance. We can't open gate. Masters would know at once."

Ampris's heart started beating faster with excitement and hope. "So it can be done," she breathed. "I knew it."

"What? Transmission unclear."

"If we can send a distraction for your station managers, something that will break up their surveillance, will you help?"

"In exchange for what?"

"Freedom to come with us."

"You have too many ifs in your plan, Ampris. How can you stop the surveillance on us—"

"Leave that to me," she said with confidence.

"And how will you get abiru slaves released and on ships? Who will fly those ships?"

"They can run on automatics all the way to the station," she answered. "But there are abiru pilots and equipment handlers. We'll figure it out."

"You cannot do this."

Velia was signaling her. Ampris backed her ears. "I'm out of time. I'm being traced. Promise me that if I deliver my end you will deliver on yours."

"Get off now!" Velia said.

Ampris leaned closer to the mike. "Promise!" she said urgently.

Static crackled, but his reply was cut off.

Roaring in frustration, Ampris swung around, but Velia glared right back.

"I told you I'd cut the signal to keep us from being traced," she said defiantly. "You had plenty of time."

"But now I don't know what his answer was," Ampris said, pacing back and forth. She wanted to smash something. She wanted to bite something. "How soon until we can call back?"

Velia bared her teeth. "No way. It was too risky the first time. We stay off this now. One activation could be enough to let a tracer finish coming right to us."

Ampris growled.

"Look," Velia said. "I know you think I'm useless. Maybe I don't have much courage, but I know about tracers. I know about patrollers raiding in the dark and dragging off people you love, never to be seen again. It ain't going to happen here, okay? We stay off this thing, until I think it's safe. Or I'll smash it. You understand?"

Velia's voice was shaking. Her tilted eyes held memories of things no one should have to remember.

Ampris's anger faded. In its place came sympathy and a certain measure of pity. "Yes, I understand perfectly," she said quietly. "We'll just have to proceed as though the engineer said yes."

Velia snapped back her ears. "But that's a lie! You don't know for sure."

"We're not stopping now."

"But if you get everyone all the way into space and we get stopped . . . No, Ampris, you can't do it! You can't take such a big risk."

"I can," Ampris said in a voice like iron. "And I will. Say nothing about this, Velia."

"I have to. Lives are at stake. I can't—"

Ampris advanced on her. "Velia, we're all in this too

deep now to back out. We have two choices now: We keep going with the plan and get off Viisymel, or we'll eventually find ourselves arrested and in the death camps. Make up your mind, but keep your mouth shut."

Velia panted, a mixture of resentment and fear on her face. "You don't talk to Elrabin like this. You ain't hateful to him."

"I don't have to be," Ampris said. "He knows which way to jump. It looks like you're still learning."

"Everything has to be your way."

"We agreed on the plan, Velia."

"You don't give folks much choice," Velia said in resentment. "You get folks in trouble so that they have to keep helping you in order to get out of it. That's the way you operate."

Ampris's gaze never wavered. "Freedom has to be earned. It's never a gift."

Velia lifted her muzzle proudly. "I won't betray my mate, if that's what you're thinking. You'd like me to, wouldn't you? So you could—"

"No, I don't want you to betray Elrabin," Ampris said wearily. "It would break his heart. He loves you deeply."

Velia blinked as though she hadn't expected Ampris to admit that. "No. He feels sorry for me. That's different. It's you he loves."

"Elrabin and I have been friends a long time," Ampris said, wishing Velia would grow up. "But I will never take a mate outside my own species. Nor will he. He adores you, Velia, or he wouldn't have taken you as mate. If you haven't figured that out by now, then it's him you should be having this conversation with, not me."

Velia looked confused. She rubbed her muzzle with both hands. "But he never says anything. He never shows me—"

"He comes home to you," Ampris broke in. "Elrabin

grew up on the streets. He had a dust addict for a father and a mother who worked two or three shifts a day trying to feed her family. Elrabin has always been able to walk out of any situation he didn't like. As I said, he comes home to you. If he can't show you any better than that, then talk to him. I'm not the problem in your relationship."

Velia sniffed and stared at the floor. "Sorry," she said after a moment. "Maybe I've been wrong."

"Maybe you have."

Velia nodded. "I won't tell the others about what happened today, not even Elrabin."

Ampris sighed in relief. "Especially not Elrabin."

But even as they smiled at each other perfunctorily and moved apart, Ampris wasn't sure she could rely on Velia to keep any promise at all. If only Velia hadn't cut the signal right at that second. It was almost as though she didn't want Ampris to get an answer.

Or maybe Ampris was just growing paranoid and too suspicious of everyone.

Maybe.

Elrabin lay on a rooftop, feeling baked to a crisp by the sun, and squinted at the oblong-shaped building. Constructed of ugly, utilitarian block units designed for temporary structures, it was only one story and much smaller than he'd expected. It stood on a vacant lot where a much larger building had been taken down. Discarded steps and broken glass lay scattered about. A tall wire fence surrounded the building, and a pair of Toths stood guard, looking half-asleep and bored at their posts. One was chewing his cud. The other one yawned and flicked his floppy ears at the flies buzzing around his head.

About fifty meters or so behind the building, a structure under construction had begun to take shape above its foundations. No one was working today, which suited Elrabin fine.

He nudged the hooded cub lying next to him. "Tell me what you see."

"It's a gray building. It has a fence around it and some guards posted," Nashmarl said. His voice was bored and as he answered he didn't look at the building once.

Elrabin sighed, wondering why he bothered with them. "Foloth?"

"Is this an exam?" the older cub asked coolly. "The building is drab and cheaply constructed. Obviously it is temporary and they are building something larger to house the laboratory."

"Never mind what it looks like," Elrabin said, trying to keep his patience. "It has—"

A quiet buzz on his hand-link interrupted him. He fished it out of his pocket and snapped it on. "Yeah?"

"Any luck?"

He recognized Ampris's voice and grinned. They were being cautious with the links and not using names that might get picked up by surveillance nets.

"Some. We've done been looking things over for an hour, and no patrols have been flown in that time. Guards ain't nothing. The locks will be the hardest part, just like I thought. Can't get closer to check them out. May have to risk going in and taking what comes."

"Fine," she replied.

"Or," he said, glancing at Nashmarl and Foloth, "we may just pry a hole in the wall. It all be built of temporary block. If a security field can even be rigged around this piece of junk, I want to see it."

"No problems, then?"

"Nope."

"Good. We need a diversion for the sky," she said.

Elrabin understood she was referring to the Zrheli on Shrazhak Ohr. "Got to talk to 'em first, see?"

"Did that. We have a go, but they're under constant surveillance and can't act unless we do something to break that up."

His mouth fell open and he swiveled back his ears. "You talked to 'em? *You?*"

"I did," she replied, and her voice was smug.

He couldn't believe it. He figured nobody could get through to the station—especially not Ampris. The last time she and Elrabin had been on the station, she'd been honing her glevritar blade on the guts of little nasty Zrheli, or at least she had been until one of them clipped the tendons in her leg with his beak and nearly killed her. Elrabin figured the Zrheli wouldn't want anything to do with Ampris.

"They agreed?" he asked, still not believing it.

She hesitated a moment on the channel. "Yes."

Elrabin rubbed his muzzle and glanced at the listening cubs with a wink. "You could talk the Kaa off her throne," he said in admiration.

"I doubt that," Ampris replied dryly. "So what kind of diversion can we deliver?"

"What you got in mind?"

"I'm giving the job to you."

"No," he said in protest, his admiration vanishing. "Hey, I don't want to be coming up with no clever ideas. You be the one—"

"I can't do everything," she said, cutting him off. "Get busy and think up something."

"But what about this case job?" he asked.

"Sounds like that's finished," she said crisply. "Turn it over to whoever can do it, and start on this new project. We need something fast. Going out."

"But—"

She was gone before he could finish his protest. Elrabin snapped off the hand-link and thrust it back into his pocket with a growl.

From the corner of his eye he glimpsed stealthy movement. He whirled around just as a Skek came creeping across the roof tiles and grabbed the water skin Nashmarl had laid down.

"Hey!" Elrabin shouted.

The Skek, small and covered with fur so dirty and matted it was hard to see the creature underneath, shrieked and ran in reverse. With its many legs it could go forward or backward with equal agility. It scuttled away, gibbering wildly and dragging the water skin by its strap.

Elrabin made a wild grab and missed.

Nashmarl jumped up and ran after it. "That's mine, you dirty thief! Give it back!"

The Skek eluded him, scuttling here and there over roof tiles and around chimneys. Nashmarl slipped and skidded, his arms flailing wildly for a moment before he regained his balance.

Elrabin rose to a half-crouch, whining without realizing it, certain the cub was going to fall off the roof to his death. By the time Nashmarl caught himself, the Skek was long gone and out of sight.

Nashmarl picked up a loose tile and hurled it as hard as he could. It went skidding across the roof, flew off the edge, and smashed into pieces on the pavement far below.

The Toths guarding the laboratory glanced up in their direction.

Gulping down a yelp, Elrabin dropped behind the cover of a chimney. Foloth did the same, holding out his hand to help Nashmarl come scrambling back.

They crouched there, barely breathing, and listened for any sounds of investigation. Finally Elrabin ventured a peek down at the guards.

They had resumed their places and were now chatting and grunting at each other.

Elrabin let out his pent-up breath in a long whoosh. "Close," he muttered.

"That filthy Skek," Nashmarl said. "They've pestered us all day. First they stole Foloth's lunch, and now my water skin. The only one they haven't bothered is you, Elrabin."

"That's 'cause I keep my pretties hidden and not lying about for them to pick up."

Under his hood, Nashmarl glared at Elrabin and his face began to redden. "That's not fair. It's just an old water skin. Who'd want it?"

"The Skeks steal because they like to," Foloth said. "I should have brought my sling. I could have practiced my marksmanship on them."

"Waste of time, trying to hunt Skeks," Elrabin told him, then he stopped a moment with his head cocked to one side. A feeling of glee made him chuckle. "That's it," he said. "That's it!"

"What?" Nashmarl asked him, looking baffled. "What are you talking about?"

"Skeks!" Elrabin said. "Come, let's go."

"Where are we going?" Foloth asked. "What about the lab?"

"You heard what your mother said," Elrabin replied. "We're going on a Skek hunt."

"You just said it was a waste of time to hunt them," Nashmarl argued.

Elrabin was already moving across the roof to the point where they'd climbed up. "It will be," he said and laughed.

"You're not making any sense," Foloth said. "What's gotten into you?"

"Inspiration, cub!" Elrabin said. "Sheer, brilliant inspiration. Come on!"

Three hours later, he managed to corner one in an alley that dead-ended. The Skek jabbered and rolled its eyes. Holding its thin arms high above its head, it scuttled this way and that, trying to dart past them as Elrabin and the cubs closed in. This one was fatter than most, but no less agile.

"All right," Elrabin said with determination. He took off his coat and held it in front of him with both hands. "The two of you look sharp. Don't let it get past you."

"We won't," Foloth said.

"Maybe I should try to grab it," Nashmarl offered. "You're kind of old, and I can move faster than you."

Elrabin backed his ears, but he wasn't going to make the mistake of taking his eyes off the Skek, no matter how insulted he felt. "You stay behind me," he said grimly. "If I miss, you catch it."

"I still think I should do it," Nashmarl said.

"Fine," Elrabin said shortly. "You think that all you want. Now stay sharp."

He advanced on the Skek, which darted this way and that, then backed away from him. Just as Elrabin reached the thing, it shrieked and skittered between his legs.

Cursing it, Elrabin spun around, trying not to let himself be knocked off balance. The Skek was getting away from him. He flung his coat over the Skek's head and made a clumsy tackle of the creature. It shrilled and tried to run backward, bumping into him.

Elrabin grabbed it around the middle, and the thing kicked and shrieked wildly.

"Help me!" he shouted.

Foloth and Nashmarl raced to join him.

The Skek rolled in Elrabin's arms, kicking him in the stomach. The pain made him curse, but although his grip loosened, Elrabin was angry now and he wasn't letting go.

He twisted the coat harder around the thing, and Foloth was suddenly hanging on to a leg for dear life. Nashmarl ran around them both as though he didn't know what to do.

"Nashmarl!" Elrabin said breathlessly. "Get hold of a—"

The Skek exploded in his arms. One moment Elrabin had been in possession of a solid mass of kicking, leggy fur; the next he seemed to be juggling pieces of Skek in all directions.

For a second Elrabin actually thought the creature had blown up, then a piece of fur no bigger than his fist went bouncing onto the pavement and skittered away from him as fast as it could go.

"Babies!" he said in astonishment as another piece of fur landed on the ground. The rest were squirming inside his coat, crawling up his arms, escaping him despite his every effort. He still had hold of the adult, although it was much smaller than it had been at first.

"Get them!" Elrabin said. "All you can catch!"

Nashmarl went running after the tiny creatures, pouncing on them and stuffing them in his pockets. Foloth let go of the adult's legs and ran to help his brother.

Still clutching the squirming adult firmly around the middle, its shrieking muffled inside the folds of his coat, Elrabin hoisted it higher and started carrying it home.

"How many you got?" he called to the cubs, who had run ahead of him almost to the mouth of the alley.

Foloth turned back at once with his arms full of squirming, wriggling balls of fluff. "I have eight—" One of them jumped free and darted through a hole in the sewer grille. "Seven," he said.

Nashmarl was still picking up tiny Skeks. With his arms and pockets full, he came back, skipping along, herding three or four along in front of him with his feet. "Get 'em!" he yelled at Foloth, who complied. "I got maybe a dozen," Nashmarl said triumphantly.

"You do not," Foloth said. "There couldn't possibly be that many."

"Hey, no arguing about it," Elrabin said. "We'll count when we get them home. *If* we get them home."

It wasn't easy. The walk seemed to take forever. Now and then the adult Skek fell silent and quiet in Elrabin's arms, but then it would struggle and kick until he wanted to throttle it. Baring his teeth and panting from exertion, he kept a tight hold on it. When he'd first captured it, it didn't seem to weigh much, but the farther he walked the heavier it grew.

As for the cubs, they kept juggling and grabbing and chasing down the babies that escaped them. Elrabin figured the pair of them wouldn't have any of the babies by the time they got back to Jobul's, but to his surprise both cubs proved more diligent at the job than he expected. Nashmarl seemed to have a flair with the creatures; by the time he banged his way through the door and went hurrying inside, his captives were fairly quiet and tame. Foloth's were still struggling, and Elrabin wished he could drop his own catch down the nearest sewer access.

When they burst in, Ampris was talking with Jobul, Quiesl, and Harthril while Velia paced back and forth restlessly. All of them jumped up in astonishment at the invasion.

"What have you got?" Ampris asked.

Nashmarl went bounding over to her. "Look, Mother! Skeks! Lots of them!"

"Skeks!" Velia said shrilly. "Those filthy things. Get them out of here at once."

"Um, yes," Jobul said, looking less than pleased at what had been brought into his house. "I don't think they should be in here."

"Yeah, well, think of somewhere quick," Elrabin said, panting heavily. He dropped onto a chair and wrestled with his squirming captive yet again. "Now that I got this mama and her brood, we ain't letting 'em go."

"I'm tired of holding them," Foloth said. "I'm going to let them go."

"No!" all the adults shouted in unison.

Startled, he stared wide-eyed at them, and Ampris came hurrying forward. "Wait just a minute," she said.

"We don't want them to get loose in here. They'll carry everything off."

"Dirty things!" Velia said in disgust, staying well back. "What did you bring them here for? Elrabin, have you lost your mind?"

"I have an idea," Jobul said. He headed outside at a run.

Quiesl came forward. "I have never seen an immature Skek of this small size," he said, waving his tail from side to side. "Are they as agile as the older ones?"

"Pretty fast," Nashmarl said. "You can hold one if you want. They don't bite."

The Myal smiled and poked his finger gently at one of the furballs. It responded by scuttling up Nashmarl's arm and climbing on top of his head. Nashmarl squealed with laughter.

Ampris smiled at him and turned to Elrabin. "What are you doing?" she asked.

"You wanted a diversion," he said breathlessly. "This is it. Course we need more, but these things ain't easy to catch."

"A diversion?" Ampris backed her ears while an unholy gleam entered her eyes. She drew in her breath sharply and laughed. "Elrabin, that's brilliant. Oh, it's perfect! Yes, yes, we must have more. As many as we can capture."

"Now *you* have the madness," Harthril said while Quiesl just gaped at her.

Jobul came running back inside with a large cage. Simply made of a wooden frame with fine gauge wire netting tacked to it, the cage was perfect for their purpose.

He opened the lid, and Elrabin dropped his captive inside with a grunt of relief. The adult Skek landed with a thud, lay there stunned a moment, then jumped to its multiple feet. Jobul closed the lid hurriedly. When he opened it again to allow Foloth to dump the babies inside, the adult tried to jump out.

Jobul banged its head with the lid, driving it to the bottom of the cage. The baby Skeks swarmed about the adult's feet. Many of them climbed their parent and clung to its sides, their fur blending perfectly in color and texture with its matted covering. Nashmarl released his captives into the cage more gently, dropping many of them onto the adult's back. They clung in place as though stuck there. In moments, the adult Skek seemed to be the single inhabitant of the cage, only bigger and woollier than before.

Jobul tied the lid shut securely, then placed a brick on top of it for added reinforcement.

Ampris was still laughing, and Elrabin grinned back at her like a fool. He enjoyed seeing her so happy; she hadn't laughed like this in a long, long time. She flung her arms around her cubs and gave them each a lick.

"My wonderful Skek hunters!" she said and went off into another peal of laughter.

"What's so funny, Mother?" Foloth asked her. "Why are you and Elrabin so thrilled about these creatures?"

"Yes, indeed," Quiesl said. "Please explain."

Ampris shook her head and pointed at Elrabin. The look in her eyes made him start chuckling too. But he managed to sober himself enough to answer.

"Skeks are big trouble," he explained. "Always getting into things, always stealing."

"If not stealing, then reproducing," Harthril said in disapproval, glaring at the occupants of the cage.

"Right," Elrabin said. He grinned and forced himself to stop looking at Ampris. "That's right. No matter how many we catch and send up there, there'll be more, see? By the time they get there."

"Many more," Ampris said unsteadily. "The Viis won't know what hit them."

"You were giving an explanation," Quiesl said politely.

"Right." Elrabin rubbed his muzzle. "See, the Skeks can tear Shrazhak Ohr apart in a few days."

"Yes," Ampris joined in, calmer now. "All stations have strict rules about vermin. But ships always have a few Skeks in them, no matter how diligent the ship's crew is. So the stations put ships through tough decon procedures. Now, if we conceal Skeks in, say, a cargo shipment, it will go straight into the cargo receiving dock and into the station. As soon as it's opened, the Skeks will run in all directions. They'll go into the ductwork first thing."

"From there," Elrabin said, "they can spread in all directions. As fast as personnel can get rid of some, the others will be reproducing more. They'll mess up the food supplies for sure. They'll tear off panels, and break circuitry. Ain't nothing they won't steal."

He pointed at the cage, where the adult Skek was now busily tugging at the wire netting.

Jobul looked at it nervously. "Are you sure it can't gnaw its way out?"

"No teeth," Nashmarl said. "I looked."

"Adults have teeth, surely," Quiesl said.

"Not important," Harthril announced. The Reject gave Elrabin a nod of respect. "Good plan," he said in approval. "Come. We go catch more."

Elrabin stood up, started to put his coat back on, then wrinkled his nostrils and handed it to Velia.

She looked at him defiantly and made no move to take it. "I ain't touching that. I'll burn it before I'll wash it."

Embarrassed, Elrabin backed his ears. Maybe she was right, though. The coat did smell like Skek now. Pretty soon, Jobul's little house would smell like Skek.

"Yeah, okay," he said, hating to see the loss of a perfectly good coat. Just because it was missing both sleeves and had some rips in the back didn't mean he couldn't still use the pockets. He fished out the hand-link and some other useful items and rolled the coat into a ball. ''Guess I'm out of a coat, but it makes a good Skek net.''

Harthril almost smiled. ''Maybe we make a real net and hunt Skek easier.''

Elrabin brightened at that. ''Yeah. That sounds good to me.''

''Can I come with you?'' Nashmarl asked. His green eyes were bright with eagerness.

Elrabin hesitated and looked at Ampris.

She nodded and licked Nashmarl's cheek. ''You have done well today. I am proud of you. When you come back, I will put you in charge of the Skeks, feeding them and so on, until it is time to ship them to Shrazhak Ohr. That is a very important job, and you will do it well.''

Nashmarl glowed under the praise. Watching him, Elrabin thought it was a shame the cub seldom deserved any. Still, since getting stoned by the Rejects Nashmarl had improved. He was quieter now, less boastful. If Foloth didn't provoke him, Elrabin mused, Nashmarl might even stay out of trouble.

But Harthril had not forgiven the cubs for stealing his food rations. He was looking stern and hostile now as though he didn't want Nashmarl along.

''Right!'' Nashmarl said in excitement. ''Then I'm going.''

Ampris put her hand on his shoulder. ''Harthril must give you his permission first.''

Red flushed Nashmarl's face. He looked at his mother, all his excitement crashing in his eyes. He did not look at Harthril. ''You're in charge, Mother,'' he said softly. ''You can tell him to—''

''No,'' Ampris said in a clear, level voice. ''I cannot.''

''Ask him then. Ask him! I want to go.''

All the adults sighed, and Elrabin looked away. He

hated to see Ampris have to deal with this. Although she was up and around, she did not have her old strength back. She looked thin, and even Velia's cooking could not always tempt her appetite.

"Nashmarl," Ampris said in quiet reproof. "If you want to go you must ask Harthril's permission."

"It is not given," the Reject said firmly, ending the discussion abruptly. He shot the cub a cold look, then glanced at Elrabin. "We go now."

"Sure," Elrabin said.

The Reject strode outside without another word. Elrabin stopped next to Nashmarl, who looked crushed.

"Hey, cub," he said quietly, feeling sorry for the brat. "You and your brother sure helped me today. If Harthril had seen how you can handle 'em, he would have let you go."

"No he wouldn't," Nashmarl said miserably. "He hates me."

"He doesn't hate you," Ampris said, drawing him under her arm. "But he is still very angry with you. It is hard for Harthril to forgive."

Elrabin left her to comfort her son and gave Velia a quick lick on her muzzle. "Be back for supper, I hope," he said. "Harthril on the hunting trail can be hard to stop."

Velia sent him a look from her tilted, golden-brown eyes that made him smile. "You find another place to keep them before you come home," she said sternly. "This one stinks enough."

She had a point. Elrabin nuzzled her throat, then hurried out. He had some Skek hunting to do.

CHAPTER NINETEEN

In the end, with other abiru pitching in, Elrabin and Harthril rounded up about three dozen Skeks, caged them, and loaded them into crates. A Kelth named Fashier worked in shipping at Vir Station Four. He processed the crates and slipped them into a shipment of supplies bound for the space station.

Ampris and the others hovered over the vidcasts, waiting to hear about the station's newest problem. Nothing appeared on any channel.

"It didn't work," Velia declared. "I told you it wouldn't."

"Maybe the Skeks died in transit," Nashmarl said sadly. Now that he no longer had the creatures to care for, he seemed lost and restless again.

Disappointed, Ampris rubbed her son's head and turned away from the vid. They had left Jobul's house and taken up residence in a tenement building condemned for demolition. It stood practically under a guidance sling for Vir Station Four, and the noisy landings and takeoffs of the shuttles went on constantly overhead. But the noise and commotion from the station provided a useful cover for their equipment use. With so many linkup signals clustered around the station, monitoring by Security was ineffectual, which gave them a great deal of freedom to get on with their work. Ampris now broadcast daily messages of hope and encouragement to the abiru population over a vacant channel. Every time Security managed to block the channel, they simply switched to another one. Ghosting, it was called. From all reports, her messages were getting through. The slaves were united as they had never been before. Many of them clustered in vacant lots and city parks, singing about freedom or chanting Ampris's name until patrollers chased them away. Rewards had been posted for information on Ampris's whereabouts, but no one betrayed her this time. Still, Ampris was staying off the streets. As Elrabin said, no point in taking unnecessary chances.

The building they had taken over also had a basement with access to a dry service tunnel, long abandoned and with empty conduits that had once held wiring. Members of the Freedom Network came and went that way, with Luthien's gang guarding access. There was no outside activity to arouse the suspicions of the neighbors. Externally, the building was just a sagging, condemned structure with boarded-up windows and broken steps. Kelth lits and Aaroun cubs from the next tenement played golloobail in the street except when patrollers swept the area. But inside, the place hummed with activity and purpose.

Besides the recording equipment for Ampris's messages, a machine that duplicated data crystals ran night and day, producing cheap copies of Ampris reciting the terms of the broken treaty between the Viis and Aarouns. Quiesl boiled the history of the Myals into a thirty-minute encapsulation and recorded it as a reminder to his people of their highly accomplished past. Even Elrabin, protesting and stiff with nervousness, was persuaded to mumble three Kelth poems of war, peace, and family life that Non taught him. The Imperial Archives were gone forever, but Non and Quiesl both had perfect recall and could recite for hours material that they had read and translated. These crystals were smuggled across the city, given free to anyone who would take them. The word was spreading.

Although no message came from Shrazhak Ohr, Ampris continued to proceed as though everything was on schedule. She was afraid to do anything else, afraid to admit how worried she was inside. The planned raid on Ehssk's laboratory was successful, a clean, quick break-in. The professional thieves of Luthien's gang brought Ampris fourteen vials of clear liquid, which now rested upright in a case labeled with dire warnings. Her staff and group leaders gathered around the case in awe, staring at the sealed tops of the vials.

''We could kill all the Viis,'' Luthien said. ''Just break these on the streets, and let the Dancing Death out.''

Ampris closed the case with a feeling of shutting the door on temptation. ''Put it in the cooler,'' she said to Elrabin. ''Lock it.''

Harval growled. ''You don't trust us now?''

She met his gaze fearlessly. ''I want no accidents. Nor do I intend to commit mass murder.''

''Ampris, we have the solution in our hands,'' Harval said fiercely. ''We can wipe them out, take Viisymel for our own.''

''And then what do we have?'' she retorted. ''A poisoned, polluted planet, stripped of its natural resources? I want Ruu-one-one-three, where we have a chance and a future.''

''Ain't getting Ruu-one-one-three,'' Luthien said sourly. His one eye glared at her. ''Zrheli ain't going to help us. Been over a week now since the Skeks should have been up there. We ain't heard nothing. They don't care 'bout nobody but themselves, the nasty—''

''Ampris!'' called out Quiesl's voice. He came pushing through the crowd, his gray-streaked mane wild and tangled, his eyes burning with excitement. "Ampris!"

"Let him through," she said in concern.

The old Myal came pushing and struggling until he reached her at the front of the room. He was breathing hard, and his tail was coiled up rightly.

Ampris's heart sank. "What has happened, my dear friend?" she asked, fearing the worst. Things had been going well for a time, but today the patrollers had swept through the ghetto, netting many abiru in unexpected arrests. Frenshala had been taken. Velia was almost captured. She hadn't even come to tonight's meeting. Instead, she was huddled upstairs in a blanket, with Tantha keeping her company. "Catch your breath, Quiesl, and tell us."

"More arrests?" Luax asked. Harthril had gone out tonight to join a Reject raid on Zehava. Luax had been tense and silent all evening. "Are the patrollers coming here?"

Quiesl puffed and shook his head. "No, no, my good friends. Do not be alarmed. I bring good news."

Murmurs rippled through the crowd. Ampris looked at him in surprise. "What is it?"

"This message came through," Quiesl said, handing her a docking ticket. "On the back."

Ampris turned it over in her hands and read the message that had been printed on the bright green card: SHIPMENT RECEIVED. WORKING. WILL ASSIST.

Her heart soared. There was only one place this could have come from. "Quiesl!" she said in excitement.

He was beaming, his broad mouth stretched in a smile. "Yes, yes. The message came through on the abiru shift. An abiru operator took it."

"When did it come in?"

"Yesterday. The operator had to wait until her shift was over, and at the last moment she was assigned double shifts. She didn't dare entrust it to anyone, and brought it to me.'' He hesitated, then said with pride, ''My daughter.''

Ampris clutched the ticket with both hands and turned to the others. Her heart was pounding too fast, but she didn't care. ''The Zrheli are going to help! The Skeks are on the station, and our plan is working.''

Elrabin yipped loudly, and then everyone was cheering.

Ampris stood there amid the noise, smiling foolishly, so happy and relieved she thought she would burst. A moment ago, they had seemed close to failure, with everything on the verge of falling apart, and now they had taken yet another important step toward their goal. She wanted to dance and sing with relief, but her mind leaped ahead and she felt suddenly shaky and cold. Quickly she clutched her Eye of Clarity and fought to keep her composure. Now they could go on, and that's what frightened her.

''My friends,'' she said at last, when she felt strong enough to speak. ''My friends.''

''Quiet!'' Elrabin shouted. He gestured and shouted until everyone fell silent and gave her their attention.

Feeling thankful and very serious now, Ampris faced them. ''My friends,'' she said, still clutching her Eye of Clarity, ''it is time to begin phase three of our plan. This is the most difficult part of what we hope to achieve. It is the most dangerous. It will ask much of us. Not all of us will survive it.''

The room was deathly silent now. No one stirred or coughed or interrupted.

''Some of us will have to sacrifice our lives,'' she said. ''I will ask for volunteers only. I cannot choose any of you. I will not choose any of you. You must make the choice for yourself.'' She paused, praying for strength, knowing she was asking innocent people to die, knowing she would have to live with that the rest of her life. ''We will begin tomorrow. I ask that the volunteers come to me then. It is time to bring the Dancing Death to the Viis people and make them fear us."

Fresh cheers broke out, making further speech impossible. Elrabin tried to quiet them, but Ampris gripped his wrist and shook her head.

"Let them celebrate for now," she said. "The dying will begin soon enough."

Israi was attending a party given by the patriarch of the Twelfth House. The villa stood right on the bank of the river, its architecture as old as the abandoned part of the imperial palace, but in much better repair. Magnificent gardens still in bloom despite the drought had the guests exclaiming in pleasure and delight. A near-invisible grid overhead spewed forth scented mist that lowered the temperature in the gardens enough to make walking in them pleasant. Israi sat on a dais beneath a canopy of pleated silk, nibbling chilled fruit soaked in wine and listening to a concert being performed in her honor.

Israi was in a very bad mood.

The sri-Kaa was ill tonight from some trifling chunenhal fever, and everyone who had made obeisance to Israi this evening had inquired about him. Not about her, but him. As though Cheliharad were more important than she. Israi's replies had grown increasingly curt. She sat now, listening to the concert without enjoyment, and promised herself that if one more person inquired after the sri-Kaa's health, she would order removal of the offending tongue.

A short female Myal was conducting the music with such enthusiasm that Israi surmised she must be the composer as well. Israi found it far too elaborate and intricate for her taste. The melody swelled in a great crescendo, and Israi toyed with her new bracelet of carved Gaza stones. The green jewels were now very precious indeed. The empire no longer owned the world which produced such exquisite stones.

She sighed. By now, most of her anger had faded, leaving her feeling petulant and bored. She was tired of these social appearances, scheduled to support morale among her subjects. Last night she had attended the symphony. Many seats in the concert hall were empty, which had displeased her. This morning she had listened to a report naming the owners of those empty seats and providing explanations for their absence. Almost half of them had allowed ownership to lapse because of financial difficulties.

Israi hated getting such reports. They depressed her.

Tonight, at least, in this magnificent home, there was no evidence of financial hardship. Lord Rakiel was in his otal cycle of life—quite ancient, in fact—but his mental powers had not yet failed him. He had been minister of finance before Israi's father was Kaa. Some whispered that during his term of office, Rakiel had dipped deep into the public treasury to line his private coffers. Certainly he had not allowed his personal fortunes to fall with the imperial ones. Israi studied her host tonight, wishing she could persuade him to return to public duty. But no one in the otal stage of life could be asked to serve, not even by the Kaa.

She sighed again. It was a pity.

Oviel leaned over her. "Is the Imperial Mother unwell?" he asked softly.

She looked up at her egg-brother without affection. He had been well-behaved and quiet enough since his return to court. At Chancellor Temondahl's urging, Israi had been persuaded to let Oviel join her entourage this evening. But she remained cool toward him, for she would never trust him or forgive him for his past treacheries. "We are well," she said curtly.

Oviel bowed and backed away from her. His manners were perfect and gracious. He acted as though he only wanted to serve her as the others did, but just as he bowed his head, she caught a flash of resentment in his eyes.

At once she felt vindicated. No, Oviel was not the mealymouthed courtier he was pretending to be. She had been right to distrust him. In the morning, she would remind the Bureau to continue its surveillance on his activities.

The music swelled and soared in a complex, intricate passage. Israi wondered how long until it would end and stifled a yawn.

From his chair at the foot of the dais, Lord Rakiel immediately gestured to the conductor. The Myal shrank within herself but had the musicians cut abruptly to an abbreviated flourish. The music ended.

Slaves raced about to light lanterns hanging from tree limbs. The surprised audience broke into polite applause. Israi rose to her feet, grateful this ordeal was over at last. Had she liked the composition, it would have been customary to speak briefly to the composer and perhaps award her a small token of appreciation. Israi did not even look in the dejected Myal's direction.

Lord Rakiel stood up with assistance from one of his house slaves. All of them wore broad collars of real gold and sleeveless livery with the crest of the Twelfth House embroidered across the back. Lord Rakiel found his balance and came toward Israi with a very slow but extremely graceful stride.

In otal cycle, most Viis were considered too ancient and ugly to be seen and hid themselves away from the public gaze. But Lord Rakiel had managed to preserve his fine looks despite his advancing age. He was still unstooped and lean, with the stored fat in his tail concealed by the skirt of his long coat. His rill—the skin still firm and elastic—lay arranged in attractive folds across a very tall collar. His jewels winked in the lights.

He bowed to her. "May I escort the Imperial Mother through my sabellia garden? I imported new varieties this year from Rantoon. They are exquisite, quite at the peak of their bloom."

Israi was ready to go home, but to depart so early would be an insult to a powerful family. Lord Rakiel had donated many expensive sabellia blossoms to the memorial funeral rites conducted for Lord Commander Belz earlier in the week. It was a generous gift, indicative of the tremendous wealth he still possessed.

She needed to find a way to persuade Rakiel to share some of that wealth with the imperial treasury. More important, she wanted to find out which cosmetic surgeon he employed. Rakiel looked so natural that she couldn't tell whether or not he had been augmented and lifted. Which meant he had surely had it done.

She smiled and allowed him to take her hand. "We would be honored to see your gardens."

They set out at a slow, stately pace along the white paths of crushed shells. Other guests parted to make way for them, bowing low to Israi. She was not used to walking quite so slowly, but Lord Rakiel was tall and very handsome. He had the grand, antiquated manners of Israi's grandfather, and his great air of dignity and refinement pleased her. She found herself relaxing in his company. He told her charming little anecdotes, revealing a wit as sharp as it was wicked.

Israi laughed aloud, enjoying herself for the first time all evening.

The sabellia garden proved to be a tiny enclosed area filled with large, sword-leaved plants. In the light of lanterns bobbing in the cool, artificially created breeze, stalks of scarlet blooms as large as Israi's head stood in stately formation. Their fragrance filled the air with heady perfume that made her feel slightly intoxicated. Oh, indeed, this was an exquisite garden, the perfect spot for a tryst with a lover. In the distance, more informal music now played, traditional rhythms throbbing through the warm summer night.

Israi leaned over to inhale the fragrance of a magnificent bloom just as one of her attendants came hurrying up.

Rakiel raised his head and his rill stiffened. He thrust out his gold-banded staff, planting the tip in the attendant's chest and holding him back.

"What do you want?" he asked sternly.

Israi had closed her eyes, letting her senses swim in this perfume like no other. She moved her face closer to the giant flower, but the attendant said, "I bring the compliments of the Lady Lorea. She says the imperial litter is waiting to conduct the Imperial Mother to the palace at once."

Lord Rakiel never lowered his staff. "Who is this Lady Lorea? Does she have the power to summon the Imperial Mother? Begone with you! I'll have your tongue for this interruption."

Pretending to be totally absorbed by the flower, Israi buried her face in its petals again and smiled to herself. Oh, if only the messenger could have been Oviel, she thought. She would have loved to see his chest poked by Rakiel's staff.

But the attendant did not withdraw as ordered. "I beg your lordship's pardon, but Lady Lorea told me to insist that the Imperial Mother return. A message has come from the palace. It is terrible news, I think."

Now Israi did straighten. She turned to face the nervous attendant—a Viis male vi-adult of excellent family, sent to her service so that he might acquire court polish. Flicking out her tongue, Israi asked, "Are we to run home in a panic? This emergency can be dealt with by Lord Temondahl."

The attendant bowed, looking as though he did not know what to do. Rakiel poked him hard with his staff. "Go!" he ordered.

"I beg the pardon of the Imperial Mother and of you, Lord Rakiel," said Oviel, walking up through the darkness. A lantern bobbing overhead from a tree cast an uneven glow across his face. "It was thought best to give the Imperial Mother this news in the privacy of her litter, but if she will not come I must convey the news here."

Israi glared at him. "Then say it," she said impatiently.

Oviel bowed very low. "I regret that Lord Temondahl has called from the palace. The sri-Kaa is dead."

Rakiel dropped his staff and turned to Israi with an expression of shock and profound dismay. "Oh, no," he said.

Israi stood there, her hand suddenly crushing the stem of the sabellia bloom. For a moment she felt nothing at all and wondered why these three males should be staring at her with such expressions. Even Oviel showed no satisfaction, no triumph, but only regret.

"It was just a fever, a trifling affliction," she said.

Oviel stepped forward. "Majesty—"

"No!" She whirled away from him, standing with her back to them all. She thought of Cheliharad, with his narrow, serious face and big eyes. His frail blue-skinned fingers had clung to her hand tightly only a few days ago when they'd stood in the processional for Lord Belz's funeral. He had been so little, so fresh from the egg, so somber in his tiny coat of indigo blue and his jeweled sash of rank. Now there would be another funeral.

Regret touched her. She felt guilty for having chosen him as her successor so callously, knowing he might die, knowing she might have to choose another of her progeny. She had calculated it all so coldly, and now too soon it had come to pass. As though . . . as though she had wished it upon him. As though she had cursed her own son.

Her shock, however, lasted only for those few moments. Lifting her rill as she regained her composure, Israi turned to face Lord Rakiel.

"Forgive me," she said, her voice cold and toneless. "We must depart at once."

Rakiel bowed low. "Of course, majesty. May I offer my most sincere condolences—"

"Thank you." With a gesture, she cut him off, in no mood to receive sympathy. She hated funerals and all their attendant mourning ceremonies. The public rituals of grief were a dreary business, and she was tired of conducting them. Turning to her egg-brother, Israi flicked her fingers impatiently. "Oviel, conduct us to our litter now."

It was late at night and the warehouse stood deserted. Inhaling the powerful scents of kafalva beans emanating from the sacks piled nearly to the ceiling, Ampris pushed back the hood of her robe and tried to wait patiently while Elrabin finished rubbing finger oils off the container which had held the stolen viruses. He dropped it, eyed it a moment, picked it up, rubbed it carefully, and dropped it again. This time it landed on its side, and he seemed to approve. He unstoppered a vial bearing the distinctive yellow label of the Dancing Death and dropped it beside the container. The vial shattered, and liquid seeped onto the floor.

Elrabin glanced up, his eyes very serious in the dim torchlight, and met Ampris's gaze.

She nodded back and thumbed on the hand-link. She used the correct codes to call straight into the palace, on Israi's direct line.

Years ago, when she'd first been sold to another owner by Israi and Ampris had still been naive enough to believe it was all a mistake, she had called Israi directly. That time, she had not gotten through. This time, she believed she would. The hand-link had been programmed—at great expense—to connect with a coded, inner-palace channel not normally accessible to outside calls.

The hand-link beeped softly and a Viis voice said sleepily, "Who is calling, please?"

"Tell the Kaa that it is Ampris."

There was silence, as though whoever had answered was too stunned to speak. Ampris waited, mentally counting off the passing seconds. She only had so much time before the trace would be made. Standing a short distance away, Elrabin did not move. He seemed to be frozen with tension. All the strain of this attempt could be seen in his eyes.

"The Kaa is unavailable right now," said the voice at last.

"Awaken her," Ampris said harshly. "Quickly!"

"How did you get this coded line?" asked the voice.

"You're delaying me so a trace can go through, but it takes a long time to route the trace out of the in-palace loop and out into the city, which is where I am. Meanwhile, Israi is missing the opportunity to speak with me."

"The Imperial Mother is in mourning and cannot be disturbed by—"

"Who is this?" a female voice said sharply. "I am Lady Lorea, chief lady in waiting to her majesty. You are—"

Muffled noises came over the line. Ampris lowered the hand-link and took some deep breaths. She was still counting in her head, feeling the time flashing by.

A faint series of little beeps sounded on the line. She knew then the tracer had left the in-palace loop and was now searching city channels. Only a few seconds were left.

"I have a message for the Kaa," Ampris said clearly into the link. "Tell her the current troubles are just the beginning. She must let the abiru folk go free. If she does not—"

"Ampris!" Israi's regal voice came on, cutting her off. "How dare you call us this way? How dare you threaten us? You—"

"I don't want to threaten you," Ampris replied. "I just want freedom for my people."

"*Your* people!" Israi said angrily. "They are *our* people."

"Not anymore. You've abused them, and that has cost you the right to be their mistress."

"Ampris, you are a fool," Israi said. "We know you are behind the current unrest and riots. We blame you. And we warn you that your location is being traced at this very moment. In seconds you will be arrested and shot on the spot for treason."

"You've already condemned me to death," Ampris said calmly. "The Bureau let me go."

"You escaped," Israi said, her voice sounding furious now. "But you can't elude arrest forever. If you think the abiru have been oppressed, you are wrong. But now, you have condemned them along with yourself. We warn you of this. All the blame shall be on you."

Elrabin stirred, running to the door of the warehouse and gesturing urgently. Ampris could hear the sound of a patroller shuttle approaching fast.

"No, Israi," she broke in on what the Kaa was saying. "I'm afraid it's your people who are doomed. I'm sorry it has come to this."

She broke off and dropped the hand-link on the floor next to the torch and the broken vial. Elrabin was already running across the warehouse, gesturing for her to hurry. Ampris limped after him, struggling with her brace, and together they vanished through a trapdoor just as the main doors of the warehouse burst open and patrollers came running in.

An entire squad of patrollers entered the warehouse ahead of their officers, shouting for Ampris to come out of hiding. Two sniffers were activated and released into the air. Clicking and whirring, they went floating through the large building in opposite directions.

By then, however, one of the patrollers was already kneeling to pick up the abandoned hand-link. "She was here, all right," he called back to his sergeant. Then his gaze fell on the broken vial and the empty container with its biohazard warning labels.

The patroller jumped to his feet, running backward with a curse that brought others to him.

Too horrified to speak, he pointed at the vial. "The Dancing Death."

The rest of the squad also backed away, breathing hard.

"What is it?" the sergeant called to them. "What is wrong with you?"

The patroller who had found the broken vial turned around to face him. "Sir, Dancing Death has been released in here. We have found the stolen—"

The sergeant shot him in mid-sentence, blasting a lethal hole in his chest.

Shouting in fear, the rest of the squad tried to scatter, but the sergeant shot them all in quick succession.

Behind him, a lieutenant came running in. "Sergeant, what is the meaning of this? Who ordered shots fired?"

"Sir, it's the Dancing Death. The abiru have set a trap for us. I—"

The lieutenant shot him down, leaving the sergeant sprawled in the doorway of the warehouse. Stumbling back along the loading dock, the lieutenant found his heart beating frantically and his air sacs booming within the confines of his helmet. He snapped his visor shut in reflex, even as a corner of his mind told him that was no protection against the plague.

I didn't go in, he told himself, trying to believe he had a chance. *I didn't get too close. I didn't go in.*

"Sir?" said another sergeant from the second squad which had just flown up. "We heard shots fired."

The lieutenant stopped running, but his heart went on racing. "Report in to headquarters," he said breathlessly. "The plague has been released. I have killed the others to stop it from spreading. The Bureau must be informed at once—"

The officer in charge of the second squad shot the lieutenant where he stood. "Back away!" he shouted, gesturing frantically. The shuttle reversed directions at once.

As it flew off, siren blaring, the officer called in a report, giving instructions for the street to be sealed off immediately. His tongue was a knotted coil in his mouth, and his air sacs seemed unable to inflate. Inside he was thinking, *I didn't get too close. I'll be safe. My squad is safe. We didn't get too close.*

By mid-morning the next day, the street in question had been barricaded and the warehouse was burning down. A shuttle had flown overhead shortly before dawn and bombed it. Now scientists in bulky environmental suits were laboriously scanning the area, checking for contamination.

Israi's council had convened, and the chancellors and ministers were all but in a panic. Temondahl was trying to calm them with his usual platitudes and assurances, but his voice had no effect.

Israi herself was in a rage. Pacing up and down, ragged after having had no sleep, she cursed Ampris from the bottom of her soul. "There is no plague," she said furiously, silencing them at last. She glared at their frightened faces. "It is a trick, a cheap abiru trick."

"The Dancing Death has been released," Oviel said from where he was standing with the silent attendants. He was not supposed to speak at this meeting, but it seemed he had forgotten that. "And now the sri-Kaa is dead. Perhaps his fever was—"

"No!" Israi said, appalled that he would suggest a

connection. "Be silent, Oviel. You know nothing about this matter. Your imaginings only make things worse."

"Perhaps Lord Oviel is correct," quavered Lord Brax. Normally puffed up with assurance and self-conceit, this morning he looked seriously shaken. "Perhaps it is spreading through us all—"

"You forget that we know the mind of this traitor Ampris," Israi said icily, interrupting him before he could panic the whole room. "She would never dare—"

The door opened and Lord Nalsk entered. Garbed in black, his throat encircled by a plain brass collar, the head of the dreaded Bureau of Security came striding in unchallenged.

Israi faced him with relief. "Lord Nalsk, good," she said. "We know you will put an end to the council's fears."

"The problem has been contained," Nalsk said. His eyes, piercing and always suspicious, swept the room. "The warehouse is destroyed. No contaminants have been detected in the surrounding area."

A sigh of relief passed through the room.

Israi shoved her own relief aside. She'd known Ampris wouldn't carry out her threat. Ampris had always been softhearted. Oh, she might growl and show her claws, but she did not have a ruthless bone in her body. As a bluff, it had almost worked, but now the Aaroun would find out how costly her ploy had been.

"But, Lord Nalsk," Brax said worriedly, "there seems to be a possibility that the sri-Kaa's fever was this—"

"No," Nalsk said firmly. "Forgive me for interrupting you, Lord Brax, but such a rumor is unfounded. The physicians examined the sri-Kaa carefully." As he spoke, his gaze drifted momentarily to Israi's stony face. "His heart had been weak since birth. It could not sustain him. The plague did not cause an imperial death."

Murmurs swept the room, while Israi stood there with her hands clenched on the back of her throne. As soon as she could command her legs, she moved around the throne and sat down. Holding her head high, she glared at them all.

"Lord Nalsk," Israi said, regaining his attention. "Although the scare has proved to be only a bluff, such a threat to the empire cannot pass unpunished. Have you arrested Ampris?"

"We have not yet found her, your majesty," Nalsk replied. He made no excuses for his continued failure to smoke her out. It was not his way.

Israi's rill stiffened, but she dared not berate him. "If you cannot find her, then turn your attention to the ghetto. All abiru there are to be deported immediately. Not just the troublemakers—anyone you find. If anyone resists or tries to flee, shoot them."

"Very well, majesty."

"But—but—" Lord Temondahl sputtered.

Israi glared at him. He always tried to meddle when she needed to be strong. "Yes, chancellor?"

"Does this edict apply to our servants as well?"

"The Imperial Majesty specified the abiru living in the ghetto," Lord Nalsk replied for her. "Do your personal slaves habitually go there?"

"No!" Temondahl replied in affront, his normal composure slipping. "Of course not."

"Then do not fear on their behalf. Have I the Imperial Mother's leave to go?" Nalsk asked.

She nodded, grateful for his ruthless efficiency. She had already asked him in private to become the lord commander of the Viis army. He had refused, saying he had more power in his current position. She did not feel entirely easy about that, but for now he was her ally and she was satisfied.

As Nalsk left she faced her council. "There is nothing to fear," she said. "Make sure the rest of our court does not panic.'' Her gaze went to Oviel's face and grew hard. ''We need no more false rumors besetting us during our time of tragedy.''

Oviel dropped his gaze. His rill had turned pink, giving him away. Israi loathed him and wondered how hard she would have to negotiate with Lord Nalsk to arrange for Oviel's permanent disappearance. As much as she wanted to demand the elimination of her despised egg-brother, she was leery of putting herself too deep into Nalsk's debt.

The council rose to its feet at her dismissal. She let them bow to her, then walked out through their midst, heading back to where the mourning silks hung in her chambers and were draped across the door leading to the nursery wing. Lady Lorea was waiting for her to make a choice on the funeral arrangements, and Israi wished she could flee into her gardens and be lost for the rest of the day. No parent should ever have to arrange a funeral for a little chune, she thought; it made the world seem as though all order had been turned upside down and nothing would ever be right again.

Israi was napping that afternoon, exhaustion having claimed her at last, when Chancellor Temondahl came and awakened her.

Confused and groggy, Israi sat up among her cushions, waving away the slaves who had been fanning her. Another came with a tray of wine and chilled fruit, but Israi did not want it.

''What is it now, chancellor?'' she asked wearily, yawning and stretching her arms.

Temondahl did not look well. His rill was stiff behind his head, and his eyes held shock. ''Terrible news,'' he whispered as though his voice had failed him. ''I regret to bring more terrible news to your majesty.''

Her head was aching. The room was too hot. Why had the slaves allowed the air to grow so stuffy? But even as the impatient thought ran through her mind, she knew the answer. Lady Lorea, still distraught over the death of little Cheliharad, had forgotten her normal duties and had not remembered to remind the slaves to keep this room cool.

"We are tired of receiving bad news, chancellor," Israi said irritably.

"Forgive me." He paused a moment, filling his air sacs. "Patrollers have come across three corpses in the abiru ghetto. A Kelth, an Aaroun, and a Myal."

"Abiru die all the time there," Israi said impatiently. She yawned again and beckoned to the slave who held the tray of wine. Sipping from her jewel-encrusted cup, she wished Temondahl would get on with it. "Just say what you have to say."

"Their bodies were twisted and stiff. Clearly they died in terrible agony. Their eyes were frosted white." His voice was unsteady and he paused to swallow. "The signs of plague are unmistakable, majesty. The Dancing Death has indeed been released in Vir by your former pet."

CHAPTER TWENTY

''Chaos has erupted across the Viis districts of the city,'' the reporter's voice said, tight and crisp. On the vidscreen, only the flushed color of his rill gave his emotions away. ''Shops and businesses are closing. Please be aware that aristocrats have first right of way in all traffic situations. You must yield to their shuttles and litters. All citizens are reminded to remain orderly and to obey all traffic and transportation rules. Further information will be forthcoming in the following public announcement from Lord—''

Israi gestured and a slave hurried to switch off the vid. Around her, slaves and attendants were rushing to pack her belongings. The palace was in chaos. Most of the courtiers had already fled, only to find themselves caught in the massive traffic jams at all city gates, or to be stranded, unable to hire shuttles to transport them safely out of the city.

Lady Lorea came hurrying up to Israi and bowed. ''Majesty, the ladies in waiting for the imperial nursery report that all chunen are packed and ready for immediate departure.''

''Do not let them board yet,'' Israi said.

''But, majesty, they are—''

"Not yet." Israi flicked out her tongue, and Lady Lorea bowed and backed away from her.

A tap must have sounded at the door, for slaves opened it. Israi was not sure how anyone could hear anything in the commotion.

Lord Nalsk strode in, his black clothing a sharp contrast to the vivid colors worn by the ladies in waiting. They shrank back in surprise at his entrance, and the room fell abruptly silent.

Israi turned and watched him approach her. Normally no male except her chancellor of state could enter her private apartments uninvited and live, but normalcy seemed to have left them forever.

"Lord Nalsk," she said.

He stopped and made his obeisance. "Majesty, I have been in discussion with a delegation of scientists. Ehssk and his colleagues, to be precise. They wish an audience with your majesty."

Israi flicked out her tongue. "They are too late. We are on the verge of our departure."

"If your majesty will wait and see them," Nalsk said, his tone insistent. His piercing eyes never left hers. "This is important."

"More important than escaping the plague?" she asked sharply.

"Far more important," he replied.

Though extremely annoyed, she went to her study and received the scientists. Ehssk bowed low to her and stepped forward as the delegated speaker.

"Majesty," he said in greeting.

She looked at his embroidered coat, with its cuffs turned back almost to the elbows. His pewter rill collar was studded with pale, semiprecious stones too large for good taste. She wondered if he thought he was dressed in accordance with court fashion. Next to the other scientists, in their plain coats and unadorned rill collars, he looked absurd. Given the circumstances, his finery seemed in even worst taste than usual.

"Speak quickly, Ehssk," she said. "We have little time."

"Thank you, majesty, for giving us this audience," he said, and the others bowed again behind him. "We have come to assure the Imperial Mother that there is no plague. At least, it is not the Dancing Death."

Astonished, Israi leaned forward in her chair. "What?" Her gaze shot to Nalsk. "But the report of the dead abiru—"

"Perhaps a bit premature," he replied smoothly. "Chancellor Temondahl has been shaken from his usual composure by the combination of recent events. It was unwise of him to alarm the palace so thoroughly."

"Indeed." Israi folded her hands in her lap and flicked out her tongue. Her gaze, cold and hard, returned to Ehssk. "Go on."

"You see, majesty, the victims were of assorted abiru species. A Kelth, an Aaroun, and a Myal. Not one Viis death has been reported—not one. I personally have examined the corpses, and while their symptoms are similar to those associated with the Dancing Death, the fever which killed them is something else entirely."

"Are you sure?" Israi asked him.

"Oh, yes. You see, majesty, abiru cannot contract the Dancing Death. Nor can they transmit it to us. Whatever has struck the slave population, it cannot pose any danger to the Viis citizens."

Her gaze moved to the faces of the other scientists. One of them she recognized, although she did not remember his name. The others were strangers to her. They looked respectable and knowledgeable. Ehssk, of course, had been the preeminent expert and authority on the Dancing Death for decades. She had no reason to doubt his findings.

A shiver passed through her, and she unfolded her

hands. They were clammy and cold from nerves, she realized. For the first time it became clear to her just how frightened she had been.

Frightened over a false scare. A slow, simmering anger began to build inside her. She had come within half an hour of abandoning her palace and her capital city to the abiru. Their trickery was vile indeed. And Ampris was far more clever than she had realized.

"Thank you, Ehssk," Israi said graciously. "Your warning has come in time to save us great embarrassment. We shall not forget your service."

"The Imperial Mother is very kind," he said with too much eagerness. "About my—"

Nalsk stepped forward, signaling the guards at the door. "If you will show these delegates out," he said.

They had no choice but to leave. Alone with Nalsk, Israi rose to her feet and began to pace back and forth behind her desk. "This was insidious," she said angrily. "To panic an entire city, to make us run like fools. Oh, Ampris has more tricks in her than we expected."

"She is clever, this Aaroun," Nalsk said coolly. "She knows exactly how much we all fear the plague. She's playing on that."

"Yes, and she will regret it," Israi vowed. "The abiru will never be released. *Never!* Have you attacked the ghetto as we commanded?"

"Not yet, majesty," Nalsk replied. "The patrollers have been too busy trying to keep order. The traffic is—"

"Get things straightened out quickly," Israi ordered.

He bowed to her. "As soon as order is restored, we will see that the abiru get the punishment you commanded."

"Well, be quick about it! We want her caught," Israi said. "Increase the rewards. Persuade someone to betray her."

• • •

Within a few days the initial panic faded. The gates remained closed, refusing to allow citizens to exit. Patrollers escorted nervous aristocrats back to their villas. Because the Kaa's flag continued to fly over the palace, and Israi was even seen in public, riding in her litter to the temple to pray for her dead sri-Kaa, people began to believe the public announcements about the abiru fever. With great pomp and ceremony, the sri-Kaa's funeral went on as planned, the processional passing through nearly empty streets. Cams floated alongside Israi, sitting veiled and alone in her litter. They broadcast images of her, riding in the open air through the city and along the Avenue of Triumph, to all of Viisymel and across the entire empire. The Imperial Mother was clearly not afraid of contracting the plague. The ancient musical instruments wailed songs of mourning, and the priestesses sang and threw flower petals into the air as a symbol of the passage of Cheliharad's small soul. The patriarchs of all Twelve Houses marched in solemn lines behind the litter that carried Cheliharad's tiny body. Clearly these aristocrats did not fear the plague either.

In the ghetto, afflicted abiru of all races staggered with fever. Some of them fell in the streets, convulsing to death. But on the whole, these victims were scattered and few in proportion to the size of the general population.

Israi herself recorded a rare vidcast to her subjects, stating that there was no epidemic. She blamed the abiru fever on poor hygiene and overcrowding.

Then a call came over the link from Ampris. This time, the operators in the palace had all been carefully instructed by Nalsk's agents. Ampris's call was put through immediately to the Kaa, and tracers started running fast.

Israi had no desire to talk to the traitor. She wanted to scream at her, to see her marched into prison and tortured until she sobbed for mercy. But Nalsk had had long discussions with her. Israi took the call.

"Ampris, you are a fool to think we would believe such tricks," she said without preamble. "Better that you turn yourself in before you cause more damage to your fellow slaves. They are dying because of you."

Ampris faced her, clear-eyed and unremorseful. The screen was focused tightly on the Aaroun's face, showing nothing of her surroundings.

"I ask the Kaa to release the abiru," she said.

"Already we have given you our answer," Israi replied, tired of dealing with her. "Never."

"There are empty spaceships in orbit around Viisymel, unused ships," Ampris said. Her dark, expressive eyes, so intelligent and compelling, stared at Israi from the screen. "We could take them and leave your planet. We would cause you no more trouble."

"You, Ampris, *you* cause us trouble," Israi muttered. She was finding it harder than she expected to hold her temper. "You will be arrested soon. You will be—"

"I have already been arrested once and tortured," Ampris said coldly, showing no fear. "I escaped."

"You won't escape a second time."

"Let us discuss the plague in my remaining seconds of airtime," Ampris said. "The disease is spreading with greater rapidity."

"It kills only abiru," Israi said, flicking out her tongue. "We say good riddance to you all."

"Would you rather see us die than be free?" Ampris asked sadly.

Her naivete amazed Israi. "Yes!" she shouted. "A thousand times, yes! You belong to us, Ampris. Freedom for the abiru will never happen. Never!"

"The infection will soon reach the household servants of even the best Viis families," Ampris said. "It is transmitted through the sharing of bodily fluids. A sneeze, a cough . . . the contagion spreads. We can't stop it."

"Are you asking for medical assistance?" Israi asked coldly. "The less of you, the better."

"If you value us so little, why not let us go?"

"Principle," Israi said.

Ampris backed her ears. "You mean stubbornness and pride. Is that all? Because we want our freedom, you will not give it?"

"Death will apparently be your freedom," Israi said.

"But this fever can reach the Viis," Ampris said. "Why not work together and save us all?"

"It cannot reach us," Israi said with a laugh. "The abiru fever cannot cross species to harm any Viis. Ehssk, our authority on the Dancing Death, has assured us—"

"I know Ehssk very well," Ampris said, growling. Her eyes were suddenly hostile and ferocious. "He is lying to you."

"He has no reason to lie."

"Doesn't he? I lived in Vess Vaas before it was destroyed," Ampris said. "I was part of his experiments. In all the years he has been working to find a cure, what has he actually accomplished? What are his results?"

Israi opened her mouth to reply, then closed it. An icy finger of doubt slid into her heart. It was true: Ehssk had never found a cure.

"This is how he has been spending your government's money," Ampris said. She reached offscreen and pulled someone next to her.

Israi stared at the hideous, misshapen face now looking back at her. It was the same creature she had seen and tried to kill in the forest, or if not the same, then one almost identical. That odd, flattened face. The eyes, intelligent and dark, so much like Ampris's; the rounded forehead and those vestigial nubs for ears.

"My son Foloth," Ampris said from the screen. "He and my other son, Nashmarl"—she pulled a second hideous creature over to stand next to her—"are half Aaroun and half Viis. Ehssk created them, plus a female, my daughter, whom he dissected at birth.'' She growled, while Israi stared at her in horror. ''My cubs are genetic impossibilities, yet they live,'' Ampris said harshly. As she spoke, she caressed the back of the creatures' heads. The dark-eyed one smiled at Israi, and she gasped in affront. The green-eyed one never moved. Rigid and expressionless, he stared at Israi with eyes that seemed to bore right through her.

''Ehssk told you only part of the truth,'' Ampris said. ''His secret experiments have succeeded in creating strains of the virus that *can* cross species. Or did he admit that to you?''

Stunned and repulsed, Israi still could not speak. She found herself unable to tear her gaze away from the creatures' faces, so ugly, so horrible.

Backing away, she cut off the link and stood there, staring at nothing, shuddering violently.

A Bureau agent came running into her study. ''Majesty, what happened to the transmission? I almost had her in—''

''We could not look at those—those *things*,'' Israi said, still shuddering.

''But, majesty—''

''Leave us!'' she cried, burying her face in her hands.

The agent backed out and closed the door. Israi hurried to it and locked it. Only then was she free to give way to her shock. The sight of those two monsters spawned by Ampris . . . How could she admit having them? How could she stand to touch them, to keep them with her?

As for Ehssk, had he created more of these creatures? She knew him too well to suppose Foloth and Nashmarl were the only living results of his work. What other hideous surprises had crept from his laboratory? For years there had been rumors and whispers about Ehssk and his work, but Israi and the government had turned a blind eye to such stories. Officially he was supported, and she had not bothered to change that status.

Another of her father's wretched mistakes, she thought bitterly.

As for Ehssk, she could no longer believe anything he said. His entire field of study was nothing but a sham, she told herself with horror; he probably knew no more about how to stop the Dancing Death than she did. And if Ampris was telling the truth about genetic engineering and species combination, then no doubt the plague *could* cross from abiru to Viis.

Israi unlocked her door. To the guards standing on the other side, she said, "Notify your commander that I want my personal slaves thrown out of the palace immediately. All abiru are to be removed at once."

The guards stared at her in astonishment. "It shall be done, majesty, but—"

She withdrew, slamming the door on their questions.

That evening, Israi reclined on her banquet couch, fingering food which looked terrible and tasted worse. The courtiers eating with her grumbled and picked at their food.

Her impetuous order had deprived them all of anyone to cook, anyone to serve, and anyone to clean up. The attendants, bumbling and ineffectual, many of them looking insulted, were trying to serve. Nothing was edible, except the cheese—cut raggedly—and the fruit—unchilled. Israi finally took a tray of what was supposed to be kaloups, delicacies of tiny pastries filled with minced vegetables and seeds simmered in a fine sauce, and hurled it onto the floor. The tray crashed, echoing through the banqueting hall.

Israi left her couch, and everyone else had to rise. "The meal is over," she declared and marched out.

When she returned to her quarters, her ladies in waiting were distraught. There was no one to draw the bathwater for the Imperial Mother, no one to press the sleeping robe, no one to turn down the coverlet and arrange the sleeping cushions the way the Imperial Mother liked them. As for the nursery, Lady Lorea informed her, word had come that the chunen were in chaos. They had not been bathed. They would not eat their food. They had thrown toys everywhere, and one of their attendants had slipped and fallen, spraining her ankle.

"Do we wish to hear this?" Israi shouted. "Go! Leave us now!"

"But how will the Imperial Mother retire without—"

"Go!"

Fearing her temper, they went out. Israi was left alone in the disorder. Her ladies had pulled out a selection of sleeping robes and tossed several of them on the floor. No slave was here to pick them up. No slave was here to pour her wine. Israi looked about, but she had no idea of where the wine and her jeweled cups were kept.

She understood, for the first time in her life, how dependent she was. It frightened and angered her. "Damn Ampris!" she said aloud. The abiru had no business wanting their freedom. They belonged here, serving their Viis masters as they had done for centuries. It was the only way to live an ordered and civilized life.

Fuming a moment, she activated her linkup and called Nalsk. Within seconds he answered. "Ah, majesty, I was just about to call you."

"We want this stopped," she said coldly. "Bring us the head of Ampris, without more delay."

"When she is found, I'll be happy to obey."

"Then find her!" Israi screamed. "She is destroying us! Eliminate her and the others will crumble. There is no resistance movement without her."

"She's well-hidden and well-guarded," Nalsk said.

"It's all a lie, tricks and lies," Israi muttered. "She frightens us, panics us, convinces us to throw out our own servants. We need our slaves. Who will work if they are gone?"

"That problem has occurred to many in your majesty's government," Nalsk said.

Israi fumed. "Find our slaves and return them," she said.

His expression grew guarded and he flicked out his tongue. "That is perhaps unwise, majesty. I have someone running background checks on several common Viis citizens who will be put to work in your majesty's service until more skilled and uninfected abiru can be imported from offworld."

"But it's just another of her tricks," Israi said. "The plague cannot infect us."

Nalsk looked grave. "I believed not, majesty, until an hour ago. But another report has come to me, one so disturbing that I had to examine the situation personally."

Israi closed her eyes. More bad news. She was ready to scream. "What now?"

"A Reject corpse has been found in the street."

Israi opened her eyes and stared at him. Her blood froze in her veins and she felt fear shoot to the tip of her tail. "No," she whispered.

"I am afraid so. Dead of the plague. There is no mistake. I saw the corpse myself. I have a recording of it if your majesty wishes to see—"

"No," she said hastily, stepping back from the screen as though the contamination could reach through it to her. She was starting to shake, starting to absorb the true impact of this shattering news. The end had come at last to her people. They could not escape the Dancing Death. Ehssk was a fool. He had no cure for them. They would die, and for what?

It was time to run as she had intended to earlier. Or else to give in and release the abiru from Vir. She hoped they all died of their accursed fever. She wanted no more to do with them, ever.

Opening her mouth to give the order for their release,

Israi was interrupted by Nalsk, who turned away from the screen momentarily to accept something handed to him.

"What is that?" she asked.

He frowned at the message as though he had not heard her question, then at last looked up. "Forgive me, majesty. Another call by link just came in from Ampris, wanting to know if your majesty had seen the Reject corpse yet. We did not channel this call to you. It was very short and came in over a scrambled line. Her equipment is getting more sophisticated. That means she has gained help from—"

"Never mind who she's gained help from!" Israi screamed. "Did she ask that we release the slaves?"

"Yes." He flicked out his tongue. "Actually she demanded it. She is a bold Aaroun. I find it a pleasant challenge to—"

"Silence!" Israi snapped, losing her temper with him. "This is not a game, Lord Nalsk! She is playing with our lives."

His eyes turned cold and flat. "I'm well aware of it, majesty."

"Then do something!" Israi ordered. "Find her. Kill her!"

"Will you meet her terms, majesty?"

"Her terms?" Israi laughed a bit too shrilly. "She is not our equal, to demand and order us. We are Kaa, and we will not be beaten by an Aaroun nobody."

"What are your majesty's orders?" he asked.

Israi did not hesitate. "Shoot all infected abiru on sight and burn their bodies."

This time the attack from the patrollers came through the ghetto swiftly and without warning. With the abiru slaves removed from the palace, the rebellion's best informants were gone. Ampris had no idea people were being gunned down until Foloth came running inside with blood on his jerkin and his eyes wild.

"Foloth!" she said in alarm. "What's happened?"

"Shooting!" he said, out of breath. "Shooting everyone. Barely got away."

"You're hurt," she said, going to him.

But he pulled free of her grasp. "No, someone fell on me, knocked me down. I didn't get shot. Mother, they're shooting from shuttles. Just flying over people and mowing them down."

Her eyes widened with horror, and for once she wished they had broken into the armories and stolen weapons. Then they could shoot back, defend themselves from this wholesale butchery.

Another fear occurred to her. "Where is your brother?"

"I don't know," Foloth said. He dropped onto a stool and gasped for breath. "I haven't seen him all afternoon."

She wanted to run outside and search for Nashmarl, but she knew that would be foolish. She did not have the least idea of where to start.

Picking up the hand-link, she called Elrabin and got him, over terrible static.

"Can't hear good," he said. "Got sniffers and scanners all over us. They . . . channels blocked and . . ." Static covered his voice, fading it out.

"Can you come back?" she asked.

"Not now. Pinned down while they're shooting."

She thought of him concealed somewhere on a street, at the mercy of anyone flying overhead. "Are they shooting at you from shuttles?"

"No."

"Then be careful. That's going on too."

". . . right. Will try . . ." More static obscured what he was saying.

Ampris shook her hand-link in frustration. "Is Nashmarl with you?"

"Mother," Foloth whispered, touching her arm. "No names over the link."

She ignored his warning, straining to decipher what Elrabin was saying. "I didn't get that. Is he with you?"

". . . get back soon. Tell . . ."

"Can you warn the others?" she asked, her heart sinking.

Static fuzzed the rest of the transmission. They must be right over him, she thought. She stood there, frozen with worry, until Foloth took the hand-link and turned it off.

"They had to be right there, or the static wouldn't be so bad," he said. "I'm sorry, Mother. I hope he gets back all right."

She barely listened. She kept thinking of the worst, kept asking herself what had gone wrong. She'd been so sure the Reject corpse would tip the scales in their favor. But Israi wasn't going to relent. This, clearly, was her answer.

"She's mad," Ampris muttered. "She must be."

"Mother, you should sit down," Foloth said to her.

At last she registered what he was saying, and turned on him with a growl. "Sit down?" she echoed. "And do what? Look at my thumbs while people are dying? This was my idea, Foloth. I got them all into it. I have to go help."

He jumped in her path, blocking her way. "No, you can't go outside. You'll only get hurt."

Gently but powerfully, she swept him aside with her arm and limped toward the stairs leading down to the access tunnel.

"Tantha!" Foloth yelled. "Help me stop Mother from going out!"

The spotted Aaroun came running, with two of her small cubs bouncing in her wake. She looked back and snarled at them, and they sat down abruptly in surprise.

One of them started to wail, but Tantha ignored them to plant her bulk in Ampris's way.

Ampris glared at her. "Move aside."

"No," Tantha said. "Foloth is right. I can hear shooting outside. Not good for you to go."

"I can't just stay in here!" Ampris said in frustration. "You don't understand!"

"Yes I do," Tantha said harshly. "You be leader. This hard work—waiting, being safe, while others die."

Ampris growled, but Tantha didn't back down.

"No, Ampris," she said, baring her teeth. "You need to fight, you fight me, right here, right now."

"Tantha, no," Foloth said anxiously, but both adults ignored him.

"Get out of my way," Ampris said. She tried to push past Tantha, but the spotted Aaroun shoved her back.

Growling, Ampris gripped Tantha's arm and spun her off balance. She shoved the spotted Aaroun down and hopped over her awkwardly, moving as fast as the brace would permit.

But Tantha sprang up with a roar and caught her from behind. Tackling Ampris, she knocked her to the ground, then landed on top of her and pinned her there.

"Tantha!" Foloth said in shock. "Be careful!"

With the air smashed from her lungs, Ampris began to wheeze. Fury drummed in her ears, but a cold part of her brain knew how little formal combat training Tantha had, and was busy calculating.

Ampris waited until she felt Tantha's weight shift. Clearly Tantha thought the fight over and was relaxing. At that instant, Ampris heaved herself to her hands and knees, sending the Aaroun sprawling. She kicked out hard and expertly, and Tantha screamed as something popped in her knee.

With Tantha writhing on the floor, Ampris scrambled out of reach and went limping down the stairs into the tunnel.

"Stop her!" Foloth yelled, his voice echoing ahead of her. "Mother, come back!"

Grimly Ampris kept going until she reached the Kelth-guarded checkpoint. These two members of Luthien's gang looked ratty and disreputable, but they had proved to be capable guards.

Ampris eyed their illegal stickers and side-arms. "There's shooting outside. I want weapons," she said.

The Kelths looked up at her. They must have seen the controlled rage in her eyes, for one of them handed over his side-arm without hesitation.

"You know how to work that?" he asked.

She nodded. "I'm better with a blade, but I know which end shoots plasma."

"Yeah, well, don't get too cocky. It ain't got much charge left."

She nodded and strode on, pausing only to glance back once. "Don't let Foloth leave."

The Kelths gave her a sloppy salute. "Whatever you say, boss."

Exiting the building, Ampris climbed out into the bright sunshine, to find a scene of carnage. The Kelth lits that usually played in the street in the afternoons now lay sprawled in blood. An adult female Kelth, who must have run outside to save them, lay on the steps where she'd fallen.

At the corner there was more of the same. The patrollers had struck during a shift change when workers were either going in or coming home. Ampris stepped over bodies, twisted and heaped together.

Across the street, a bloodstained Kelth female was crouched next to a dead loved one, howling her grief. A few frightened faces peered out through the shattered windows of a shop.

In the distance, Ampris heard the blare of a siren and the sound of gunfire. Rage rumbled in her throat, and she hobbled in that direction, cursing her leg brace with every step.

Before she reached the next intersection, she saw a transport lumbering along a cross street. It was swaying from side to side. Patrollers stood on top of it with a flamethrower mounted on the roof.

While Ampris paused in her tracks, staring in disbelief, the patrollers opened up the device, and flames shot along the street, igniting the corpses. The air filled with smoke and the stench of burning fur and flesh.

Gagging and coughing, Ampris retreated and took cover in a recessed doorway. The transport rumbled past her, flying slowly as the flames swept from side to side in front of it. Holding her breath, Ampris watched it go past. A patroller looked in her direction, but his gaze moved on. Apparently he had failed to see her inside the doorway's shadow.

As the transport moved on, she emerged and aimed her side-arm. Plasma shot out, straight and true, and hit the back of the patroller operating the flamethrower.

Flames suddenly went sideways and raked up the side of a building as the patroller screamed and fell against his companion. Both of them went rolling off the top of the transport, falling to the street below. The third patroller whirled around and fired at Ampris.

She ducked and the shot missed, but the plasma slug melted brick, dripping hot slag onto her arm.

The pain was like fire, smoking her fur and branding her hide. She grimaced, holding back a cry, and fired again.

She missed him, but her shot crossed his and spoiled it. Instead of hitting her, his shot hit the top of the doorway. It collapsed in a shower of bricks, cascading down on top of her. She fell back, throwing herself against the door with all her might. At the last second its weak lock gave beneath her strength. The door opened, and she tumbled backward while the front of the building collapsed in on top of where she'd been only moments before.

CHAPTER TWENTY-ONE

Eventually Ampris worked her way free of the rubble, which had nearly crushed her to death, but by then the attack was over.

She went limping home, feeling wrenched and empty with the futility of it all. Charred corpses lay where the patrollers had left them, males, females, and little ones alike. It was ruthless carnage, merciless, and the sight of it left her stunned.

In the darkness, it was Elrabin who found her wandering along their street like someone lost, smeared with soot and grime, tears running down her muzzle, the emptied side-arm still clutched in her hand.

He brought her inside, wrapped her in a blanket, and forced her to drink a mug of thick soup. Her teeth chattered on the rim. Everything she swallowed threatened to come up again.

Finally, however, she began to recover. She looked at him, standing sadly over her, and gripped his wrist. "You're alive," she said, relieved.

He nodded wearily. The fur was singed on one side of his face, but he looked unharmed otherwise.

"Nashmarl," she said, gazing dully around the meeting room. Members of their organization were slowly arriving, the survivors of the bloodbath. Reeking of smoke, bloodstained, dull-eyed, they came inside. Some accepted the soup. Others stared at it as though they did not know what it was. She saw Foloth, staying apart from everyone in a corner by the recording equipment, his dark eyes wide with alarm. She didn't see Nashmarl.

Fear flooded her heart. She began to weep and would have dropped her mug of soup if Elrabin hadn't caught it.

"Hey," he said softly. "Slack the tears, Goldie. You be fine, see? There's more folk coming in all the time."

"Not Nashmarl," she whispered.

"He's fine," Elrabin said. "He was down in the sewers, trying to catch himself a baby Skek to play with, when this all went down."

She gasped, still caught somewhere between tears and relief. "He's not hurt?"

"No. I saw him around here someplace," Elrabin said, glancing to his right and left. "Hey! Over there. See?"

He pointed across the room, and Ampris looked in that direction. She saw Nashmarl talking to one of the Kelths, safe and sound.

Ampris made a tiny noise in the back of her throat. Closing her eyes a moment, she offered up a quick, intense prayer of gratitude for his safety.

Elrabin tapped her shoulder. "Stop that worrying now. He's fine. They both are."

"Yes," she said, drawing in several deep breaths, and trying to smile.

Elrabin frowned at her. "Is that why you were out there, looking for him?"

"I—I went out to help," she said, still feeling shaken. "To fight back. But I only killed one patroller."

His fingers tightened on her shoulders. "That's one less than before."

She growled, backing her ears. "Not enough. I should have—"

Suddenly Harval showed up, his striped jerkin hanging in black strips on his back. Luthien was missing. So was Harthril. Quiesl was dragged inside unconscious, covered in blood.

Slowly, as the evening wore on, things were sorted out. People were fed and counted. The missing were totaled up. Half their organization was missing, presumed dead. They tried listening to the vidcast for statistics on how bad the total strike had been, but no news was running tonight on any channel.

"Big mistake," Harval muttered, picking at his singed fur. "Big mistake, listening to her."

Heads lifted and conversations stopped.

"We done risked our necks, and for what?" he asked, agony clear in his voice.

Elrabin rose to his feet, baring his teeth. "You shut up, Harval."

Velia reached for her mate. "No, Elrabin, don't speak up for her," she said, casting a dirty look at Ampris.

"The big plan for freedom's done backfired," Harval said. "Right on us. Right on those lits lying out there in little bits of black bone. All 'cause we listened to *her*!" He pointed at Ampris, who sat huddled on her stool.

"What was that big speech, Ampris?" he asked. "That big speech about no violence, eh? What was that about volunteers? You wouldn't choose who would die? You'd let people make their own choice? Well, what about this? Which of us chose this? You tell me that, Ampris. You explain that to me."

A Kelth farther back stood up. "We're all in danger now. Our families. Innocents who don't even know about us. They struck at everyone they could."

Nashmarl stepped forward, his green eyes shocked and angry. "The Kaa won't let us go. After all this, she'll never let us go, Mother. You've risked our lives for nothing."

Foloth joined him. "You showed us to her like we were *things*. You said you knew her. You said you could persuade her to give folks their freedom. You were wrong."

Velia rose to her feet, her eyes filled with anger. "You've stayed here, safe, while everyone else takes terrible risks. Are you planning to be the Kaa of the abiru?"

"Velia, hush," Elrabin said sharply.

"I won't hush," Velia retorted. "I have the right to speak too. What kind of crazy idea was this, talking folks into poisoning themselves, into dying of the fever, just so she could scare the Viis."

"She scared them, all right," Harval rumbled. "Right into a massacre."

"They been slaughtering abiru anyway," Elrabin said fiercely. "Only you ain't been seeing it. What about the deportations to the death camps? Only difference today is they let us see the killings."

Harval snarled at him and started to answer, but Ampris rose to her feet and faced the angry assembly.

The room slowly quieted to let her speak. She looked at their angry, resentful faces, and her heart ached for them.

"You have every right to be angry and afraid," she said. "This has been a horrible retaliation, something I hoped would not happen."

"She hoped it wouldn't happen," someone muttered. "Now I feel much better."

Nashmarl scowled at Ampris and turned away sharply.

Ampris tried to ignore the criticism. "It doesn't surprise me, though," she said, making her voice carry clearly to every corner of the large room. "We all know what the Viis are capable of doing. We went into this knowing there would be risks, terrible risks. I warned you that freedom is not easy to achieve."

"Looks like it's impossible!" yelled the Kelth in the back.

Ampris looked right at him. "You swore to die if necessary."

Nashmarl glared at her. "And what about you, Mother? You must be a coward, because you haven't risked anything. You haven't been out there, fighting. You haven't—"

Elrabin gripped his arm and pulled him away from her. "Shut up, cub!" he said while everyone else stared at Nashmarl in shocked silence. "Your mother was a champion. Don't you talk to her like that."

Wounded by Nashmarl's accusation, Ampris closed her eyes a moment. She had thought her relationship with Nashmarl was improving lately, but now she realized their apparent progress was just illusion.

"The Crimson Claw ain't never been no coward," someone said.

Ampris stood there, trying to remember what else she'd been about to say to these people. But her words of encouragement and solace had dried up in her throat. She found herself unable to continue.

"I'm sorry," she said at last, her voice filled with emotion. "I never quit in the arena until it was over. I can only tell you now that for me, this fight is not over. I will not quit until I have done all that I can."

Turning away, she limped from the room, leaving them quarreling and shouting behind her. As her eyes blurred with tears, she dragged herself wearily upstairs to her room and locked herself inside.

It was a small space, containing only a cot, a tiny table with a lamp cube, and a stool. The window was boarded up, allowing no light to escape outside.

She stood there a moment, then sank onto the stool and wept.

A soft tapping sounded on her door. "Goldie?" asked Elrabin. "You okay in there?"

Ampris lifted her head. "Please leave me alone," she said.

"You been doing your best," he said through the door. "Better than anyone else. Don't you lose hope on us now."

"Thank you," she said flatly. "Please go."

He waited, but she only sat there, locked away, with tears running silently down her muzzle. Finally she heard the soft patter of his departing footsteps. She sighed and rubbed her face.

All along she'd had doubts. She'd managed to hide them because she needed to look strong in order to keep the others encouraged. But now there was no more reason to hide. Even her own sons thought her wrong, a coward.

Perhaps her vision was a false one, she thought, her mind crowded with doubts. Perhaps she'd been deluding herself for years, believing in something that could never be. After all, who was she to think herself a leader?

And what kind of genetic demon had Ehssk bred into Nashmarl, that he could be so cruel?

She clutched her Eye of Clarity, so tired and disheartened she wanted to give up everything. Perhaps, she thought bitterly, it would have been better if she'd just let the patrollers kill her in the street this afternoon.

But the Eye began to glow inside her hands. She turned out the lamp cube and cupped the Eye on her palm, watching its white, eerie light grow brighter until it illuminated the small room.

The pain in her heart felt heavy, and she was so very tired. Yet as she watched the light, she began to see a city before her, as though the boards on her window had been taken away.

It wasn't Vir that she saw, however, but a foreign city. One she had never seen before.

She saw Foloth, grown tall and adult, with broad shoulders and lines of strength in his face. His dark eyes looked ambitious and empty, as though he had never learned compassion. He was standing on the steps leading into a building, gazing out at the distance.

A short distance from Foloth, she saw another figure walking slowly, looking up at him. It was Nashmarl, also grown tall and broad-shouldered. There were shadows in Nashmarl's face. He looked haunted and unhappy, as though facing a decision he did not want to make.

She wanted to reach out to both of them, yet she seemed to be frozen in place. And a ring of certainty opened in her mind. She saw her sons staring at each other, with Foloth on the steps and Nashmarl at the foot of them. They were divided on some issue, probably on opposite sides of it. It was an issue they both cared passionately about, and eventually they would work it through. Both her sons would live long and achieve much in their lives. Foloth would experience many triumphs, although he would never be kind and he would never know lasting joy. Nashmarl would experience great tragedy, and it would change his life forever, perhaps for the better.

The vision faded as though a mist had filled the room, then the light within the Eye was gone, and Ampris sat there on her hard stool, alone in the darkness. She felt calmer now, her spirits restored somewhat. She realized that this was the bleakest moment, the hour of greatest darkness before the dawn. They were so close now to achieving freedom. It was almost within their hands, and she knew that the risks, the sacrifices, and the suffering were worth what they could accomplish if they did not falter now.

Israi had unleashed her worst on them. But she had not broken them yet.

Ampris's sons had a future, one she had just seen, provided she could give it to them.

She stood up and lit her lamp cube again. She went to the cooler, where the vials of stolen virus were stored, and drew out a slim tube carefully prepared by Jobul.

Calmly, her mind smooth and clear now, she poured the tube's contents into her battered metal cup and mixed it with water. She stood holding the cup a moment. It was time for the greatest risk of all. The last phase of her plan was ready to be set in motion.

Tipping back her head, Ampris drank.

In the morning she went downstairs, wondering if anyone had remained to finish their work.

Foloth was still asleep, but Nashmarl was wandering around the basement meeting room like a lost soul, restless and clearly unhappy.

"Good morning, Nashmarl," Ampris said to him.

He shot her a dark look and shame filled his eyes, but he ducked his head and turned away from her with his shoulders hunched. She sighed, wishing he could learn to make things less hard on himself. Walking up to him, she put her hand on his rigid shoulder.

He flinched, and sorrow touched her heart at his rejection.

"I'm sorry you think I am a coward," she said.

He kept his back to her. "You weren't a long time ago. Everyone says so. Why did you change?"

She sighed, refusing to prove herself to him. "There are more kinds of courage than one. Maybe you'll learn that someday."

"Foloth said you went out yesterday to fight the patrollers. Did you kill any?"

She backed her ears. "Bloodshed is not the issue in this fight, Nashmarl. We are trying to leave peacefully."

"We can't!" he shouted, whirling around to face her. "Look what they did to us. We can't just sneak away from that."

"We will go without battle," she said firmly and watched all the fire die in his face, smoldering deep with resentment. "But we will go."

"No we won't," he said, and his young voice held

disillusionment. "They're going to kill all of us because you won't let us fight. You won't let us release the virus on them. You just keep poisoning our volunteers to scare the Viis. Well, it doesn't work, Mother! It doesn't work at all."

"Nashmarl, that's enough!" Elrabin said sharply from behind Ampris.

The cub's face flushed red and he ran upstairs, slamming a door.

Ampris met Elrabin's gaze as he crossed the large empty room. He'd been outside. Soot streaked one side of his face and he had a rope slung over his shoulder.

Swiveling back his tall ears, he glowered a moment at the ceiling. "That cub needs the hide beat off him, see? He ain't got no business talking to you that way, Goldie."

"If I beat him, his opinion of me would not change," she replied quietly and hugged herself. The room seemed cooler than usual. Or perhaps there were other reasons she was feeling a chill.

Elrabin shrugged off the rope and fetched himself a cup of water from the communal pail. "I been out checking. Patrollers made more sweeps of the streets last night, but they didn't pick up much. Most folk be hiding real low now. Until the Viis start bombing or pulling 'em out of the buildings, they ought to be safe."

Ampris nodded. "We're going on with the last phase of the plan, Elrabin."

He stared at her, and his shoulders slumped. "You've taken it, then."

"Yes."

"I—I was hoping you'd back out. Figured maybe after last night you wouldn't."

"I don't quit," Ampris said quietly. "I never have."

He sighed, straightening his shoulders. "Then I need to get the Rejects in place. Ain't found Harthril yet. Figure he got killed yesterday."

She closed her eyes in regret. "Has Luax gone searching for him?"

"Yeah. This be it, I guess."

She nodded. "I need a link."

"Who you calling? The Bureau?"

"Israi."

Concern flared in his eyes, and he growled. "She's done with you. We agreed that you would—"

"The link. Please, Elrabin."

Grumbling, he fetched a hand-link for her. "You get any sleep last night?"

"A little," she said and punched in the codes. There were beeps and delays, all designed to make her traceable. Ampris kept the time running in her head, knowing she didn't have much to say, if Israi would ever get on the channel.

Finally, the Kaa's golden face appeared on the hand-link's tiny screen. Israi looked haughty and magnificent. She was wearing a collar of beautifully worked gold, and jewels dangled on little chains from each of her rill spines. Her gown was of a deep shade of purple. It made her skin glow. Her eyes held a light of ruthless triumph.

"Have you called us to surrender yourself, Ampris?" she asked.

"Yes," Ampris said. "If you will let the other abiru go free."

"Why should we do that?"

"It's me you want now, Israi. I've embarrassed and outmaneuvered you. Surely it's important for you to show the empire that a single Aaroun cannot beat you."

"We think it is the slaves who have been beaten," Israi said smugly. As she spoke, she popped a chilled plumot into her mouth and chewed.

Ampris could see the beaded condensation on the perfectly ripened fruit. The sight of it made her mouth water. How long had it been since she'd eaten anything so delicious? Their food was plain and of poor quality, carefully allotted in small portions, and designed to fill bellies rather than supply a full range of nutrients.

"You may kill the abiru," Ampris said, pulling her attention back to the matter at hand, "but you have not broken their spirit. I'm asking for their freedom in exchange for me."

Israi pretended to consider it, but already her eyes were gloating. She swallowed her mouthful and flicked out her tongue. "You put a high price on yourself, Ampris."

"I was once the pet and companion of the sri-Kaa," Ampris said with pride. "I was once the champion of the arena. Now I lead the Freedom Network. I am worth a great deal."

"Would you surrender publicly? On live vidcast?"

"Yes."

Elrabin twitched and gestured frantically, but Ampris held up her hand to keep him silent.

"And will you admit that your plague is a hoax concocted by your rebellion? Will you urge all infected abiru to turn themselves in for medical treatment?"

"I will come and tell the truth about the rebellion," Ampris said. "I will give myself up if you will let the others go."

"Very well," Israi said. She cut off sound and turned aside to consult with someone offscreen.

Elrabin gripped Ampris's arm. "What you doing?" he asked, horrified. "You're supposed to give back the viruses. That was the deal we planned. If you go in without 'em the patrollers will kill you the moment you show yourself."

The sound came back on, and Ampris shook him off. "Where do we meet?" she asked Israi.

"Get off. Get off," Elrabin muttered anxiously. "You been on too long. They gonna trace us this time."

"Where?" Ampris asked Israi.

"The Plaza of the Kaas," Israi replied.

Ampris cut off the link, but from outside she could hear the sound of approaching shuttles.

Elrabin was swearing, and she gripped him. "Get everyone out."

"Ain't many folk left."

"Get them out now. Leave the equipment. Its purpose is finished."

"But—"

"I'm going," she said, picking up her robe from the back of a chair.

He reached out and stopped her. "You wait," he said angrily. "No way you going without me. The plan was—"

"The plan—my part of it—has been changed," she said. "Pass the word to everyone. The exodus is coming. Everyone should be ready to leave at a moment's notice. Tell them to wait for the signal."

"But, Goldie—"

"Mother! A patrol shuttle is coming!" Foloth said, running downstairs, with Nashmarl right on his heels. Then Velia appeared, assisting the wounded Quiesl. Tantha limped after her, shepherding her cubs along.

Ampris stared deep into Elrabin's worried eyes. "Take care of them, my old friend. Take care of yourself."

"Wait!" he said desperately, but Ampris wrapped herself in the robe and limped down to the access tunnel.

She was surprised to see that Luthien's Kelths were still guarding it. One of them was holding a small scanner and had his ears backed. "Trouble coming in."

"We've been traced," she said. "Help Elrabin get everyone out of the building. Don't save the equipment. Don't worry about the viruses. If the patrollers break into the cooler, they'll regret it."

Nodding, the Kelths trotted for the meeting room, and Ampris went on through the tunnel.

Emerging onto the street, she put up the hood of her

robe and ducked along the back of the building into an alley. Behind her, she could hear the shuttle landing and the barked commands of the patrollers. Her heart squeezed in worry, but she kept going.

She had faith in Elrabin's abilities to get the others to safety. Her own path now lay elsewhere.

It took a long time for her to walk across the city. When she and Elrabin had first planned this, Elrabin was going to steal a skimmer and fly her to the rendezvous. But Ampris knew it was better that she go this way, alone. In these empty streets, a stolen skimmer would have been picked up by patrol sniffers right away.

The security field was firmly activated between the ghetto and the Viis districts of Vir, but Elrabin had taught all of them how to get past it. Although Ampris found her energy giving out, she kept trudging along. Very few folk were out this morning. The stench of death and smoke lay thick over the ghetto, reaching even into some of the Viis neighborhoods. Public transport was shut down, but Ampris could not use it anyway without a registration implant.

Panting and weary, she reached the Avenue of Triumph sometime after midday. Normally she would have been roasting under her long robe and hood, but right now she still felt cold. Her leg ached, and her entire body urged her to stop and rest. But there wasn't time to rest. Ampris pressed on.

She heard music ahead of her, stirring Viis military marches, along with the muted cheering of a small crowd.

As she drew closer to the Plaza of the Kaas, a handsome memorial in the city's center, she saw a moderate turnout of Viis citizens clustered around a large dais. Palace guards in green cloaks stood alert with drawn weapons. Patrollers in black body armor and helmets manned the crowd barricades. So far the crowd did not look sizable enough to cause any trouble.

Ampris looked, but saw no abiru or Rejects at all. Selected volunteers were supposed to be here, but it looked like her Freedom Network had lost hope. Her spirits sank, but she gave herself an angry shake. After having struggled so long and hard to get here, Ampris wasn't going to give up. She would see this through to the bitter end.

On the dais, beneath the floating vidcams, Israi sat with her chancellors and ministers. Ehssk the Butcher was present too, wearing a vivid coat. No doubt he was there to bolster public confidence.

Ampris hesitated a moment, feeling very tired. Her courage failed her momentarily, but she backed her ears beneath her hood and forced herself forward.

"There she is!" shouted a patroller, pointing at her.

Members of the crowd screamed and backed away from her. Others were pushed aside by the patrollers who ran forward to surround her.

Ampris stopped, her heart pounding fast, as they loomed over her, each one pointing a side-arm right at her. This, she thought, was the moment of decision. They might simply shoot her down here and now.

Quickly she lifted her head. "I have come to confess!" she called out.

Israi heard her and leaned forward to speak to one of her guards.

"Bring the prisoner here!" the officer commanded.

The patrollers closed in around Ampris. With their visors down, she could not see their faces, but she could smell the sourness of their skin. They were hostile, perhaps even a little frightened, and eager to kill her.

She limped forward, careful to make no threatening moves.

The palace guard stopped her well short of the dais and scanned her for weapons. "She's clean."

The patrollers gestured for Ampris to climb onto the dais. She hugged herself a moment, then forced herself to stand more erect as she looked at the Kaa, so resplendent in a wide-skirted gown made of cloth of gold. It was embroidered richly and glittered with costly yellow tafir jewels sewn across the bodice. She wore a gossamer-fine scarf of gold-colored silk about her head and draped across her shoulders. Her slippers were coated with jewel dust. From head to foot, she glittered with a radiance that was dazzling in the bright sunshine.

In contrast, Ampris stood there in a dusty robe of badly dyed cloth woven on Aaroun looms, a combination of imperfect handiwork and poor materials.

The council members seated on either side of Israi looked sleek, handsomely dressed, and well-fed. Ampris noticed how they all stayed behind the force field. That concerned her. She had to find a way to lure Israi from behind that barrier.

The captain of the guards saluted Israi. "The prisoner is before your majesty."

Israi did not spare Ampris a glance. She gestured gracefully. "Let her stand where she is. Ehssk?"

The scientist rose to his feet and stepped onto the circle on the dais, which activated both cams and loudspeaker. "Citizens of Vir," he said loudly, his voice carrying across the Plaza. "The so-called plague is nothing but a hoax, created by this Aaroun rebel named Ampris. No Dancing Death has reached our city. There have been no outbreaks. All Viis citizens are safe and will be kept safe. The abiru-fever affects only abiru. It cannot harm you."

A scattering of applause prompted him to bow like an entertainer. Smirking, he resumed his seat.

Ampris stared at Ehssk, feeling the fur on her neck bristle as she remembered all the degrading torture he had put her through. He was a fool and a charlatan. Under the name of research he had tormented and killed countless victims, including her newborn daughter. Ampris would never forgive him for that. She had vowed to kill him, and now he was within her reach.

But she had to put her own feelings aside and remember what she had come here to do.

Drawing in an unsteady breath, she glanced at Israi. "May I speak now, majesty?" she asked in a voice of deepest respect and humility.

"Yes, Ampris," Israi said. She was glowing with satisfaction and triumph. "We will now accept your confession."

A guard pointed at the circle, but Ampris already knew that she had to stand on it to be heard. The cams floated closer to her face, but she kept her hood in place. She was shivering now, and the robe felt good around her.

In fluent Viis, she began to speak: "The Dancing Death is greatly feared by Viis citizens, and it should be. The once mighty Viis empire was nearly destroyed by this mysterious disease, which was brought back by an explorer from a faraway world. It has decimated families and eliminated entire bloodlines. Millions of Viis died in the last great plague, and no cure was found then. No cure has been found now. Worst of all, the plague left you unable to bear and fertilize eggs with the same abundance as before."

Lord Brax leaned forward in his chair and hissed. "Sacrilege!"

Ampris ignored him. "The legendary beauty of the Viis people has also been diminished by this terrible disease. Fewer and fewer Viis hatchlings are accepted each year. More and more Rejects are pushed out into squalor and poverty, abandoned by their families because they are somehow less than perfect."

"Don't get carried away, Ampris," Ehssk said to her. "You're not here to give a speech."

She ignored him too. Unless someone shot her, she was going to keep talking. "Your scientists have given you many assurances," she said. "Your government has issued statements saying that the abiru-fever cannot harm you. But it can. The government has told you falsehoods, claiming that this is not the Dancing Death. It is. It has returned to you in a mutated, more virulent form. It struck the abiru folk first, but it will reach the Viis. It is already spreading among the Reject population, your abandoned chunen, who are dying of it without aid or care."

"Ampris," Israi said coldly, "say what you agreed to say."

Ampris stood a little straighter. "Be afraid!" she said, her voice ringing out across the Plaza to the Viis faces upturned to her. "Think how many abiru there are. Yes, the Kaa in her great wisdom has killed many of them, but there are more. Not just the common laborers that lie dead in the ghetto this day, but all the slaves in Viis households. Slaves that prepare Viis food, that tend Viis hatchlings and chunes. The most loyal, loving slave has only to give a hatchling a caressing lick, and the infection is spread. As her majesty already has cause to know."

Israi's rill stiffened and she rose to her feet. The guards started toward Ampris, who cried out, "Will you silence the truth? Do these people know that all the abiru slaves in the palace have been removed? Not one remains to serve the Kaa and her court."

Israi gestured, and the guards stopped reluctantly just short of Ampris.

"Take care," Israi whispered, her gaze flicking to the cams to show that she was well aware that today's events were being broadcast live to the entire city and planet.

The crowd had begun to shift uneasily. People were speaking to each other. A murmur of astonishment and alarm rose from them.

Ampris pretended not to hear Israi's warning. She knew the Kaa dared not cut her off at this moment. "The most rebellious, resentful slave has only to spit in the food of his master, and the infection is spread. Perhaps such a thing has already happened in your household. Can anyone watching this vidcast feel complete assurance that no slave in his employ is uninfected? The only way to stop the plague from spreading into the Viis population is to let the abiru leave Viisymel forever. We have made this offer, but the Kaa will not release us. Ask your Imperial Mother to let us go. Ask her!"

The crowd looked alarmed now. A female screamed, "My chunen are not safe. If the sri-Kaa can die, what will protect my little ones?"

They began to shove, trying to leave, but the patrollers held them in place.

"You," a guard said curtly to Ampris, "stand aside."

Ampris whirled around and met Israi's furious gaze. "What will you say to them, majesty? How will you calm them now?"

"You go too far," Israi said. "The death of our son is not a subject for your rhetoric."

"I sympathize with your loss," Ampris replied. "Ask Ehssk why he had to dissect my daughter at birth."

Israi's gaze faltered. She glanced at the scientist momentarily, and he rose to his feet. "Majesty, this accusation from a slave is too absurd. What possible—"

"Be silent," Israi said.

Beyond the dais the crowd was sounding frantic and angry now. Israi's attention moved in that direction. Her tongue flicked out.

"You will pay for this, Ampris," she said harshly and stepped out from behind her protective shield.

"Majesty, be careful!" Lord Brax called out.

But Israi walked to the circle and stood there, facing her alarmed subjects with magnificent, regal calm. Within seconds, they stopped pushing at the barricades and turned to stare at her. She gestured, and they fell silent.

"Good citizens, you have seen our mercy toward this poor deluded Aaroun, who was once dear to our heart. We raised her as a pet, and out of fond memories we allowed her to speak today, giving her the chance to confess her wrongdoing to you. Instead, she has alarmed you with lies and yet more lies."

"Majesty, take care!" called out someone from the crowd.

Her rill extended fully behind her head, Israi smiled. She glittered in the sunlight with every breath she drew. "We believe the assurances of our eminent scientists."

From his chair, Ehssk bowed very low.

"We have not removed our abiru slaves from the palace," Israi said, lying boldly. "How could we appear before you dressed and bathed and jeweled if this were true? The sri-Kaa we will not discuss, for our heart grieves too much. How many of you have lost young and tender hatchlings in their first year?" She raised the edge of her scarf to her face as though to mask grief, then lowered it. "So many things go wrong so quickly."

She paused a moment, bowing her head, and no one moved or spoke.

"Citizens," she continued, "listen not to the ravings of an ignorant savage. We say 'ignorant,' for although Ampris was given an education by us, taught to read and speak Viis for our amusement when we were young, she does not understand what she has read. She has convinced her fellow abiru that a treaty once existed between her people and ours, a treaty that promised the Aarouns their freedom."

Israi spread out her hands. "Such a treaty was signed centuries ago, but its terms stipulated that the Aarouns could not leave our service until their land became capable of supporting life again. Lord Temondahl?"

She turned to the chancellor, who handed her a holocube.

Activating it, Israi held up the image of Sargas III

before the cams, displaying it as a barren, lifeless rock. "This is the homeworld of the Aaroun race," Israi said. "We saved the Aarouns from death centuries ago, and they owe us a great debt. Yet now we are accused of deceit and evil oppression, for we will not let them return to a world which cannot support life. How many of you have stopped a chune from hurting herself and been accused of oppression when she threw a tantrum?"

Chuckles ran through the audience.

Ampris looked at them sharply, realizing Israi was a master at manipulating them.

Israi smiled. "The other abiru races also depend on us for our care of them and the meaningful employment we provide. Medical treatment has been offered to those afflicted with the abiru-fever. They distrust our mercy and refuse the treatment. What can we do?"

Her lies were smooth. Ampris glared at her, growling softly in her throat.

"Citizens," Israi said. "If you have fears about the health of any abiru you own, give them to the government. We will be importing fresh, uninfected slave stock that you may purchase for a discount in the auction."

"What about the infected Rejects?" Ampris asked loudly.

A guard struck her from behind, driving her to her knees. Israi flashed him an angry glance, and he backed off.

Gasping, feeling the world tilt and sway around her, Ampris fought to maintain consciousness. Slowly, though it took almost all her strength, she rose unsteadily once more. She was colder than ever now, despite the robe, and she forced herself not to shiver.

"The Rejects who have fallen ill are no matter for concern," Israi was saying. "We all know that they are feeble, sickly creatures from birth—otherwise, they would not be Rejects. No true Viis citizen accepted in society and of good health will ever succumb to this disease, especially if the infected abiru are quarantined and treated.''

Ampris stepped closer to the Kaa. Again a guard started to intervene, but a glance from Israi stopped him.

''Come, Ampris,'' Israi said boldly, holding out her hand. ''We cannot free your people, for they have nowhere to go. Let us care for you as we always have. Let us show you that we are merciful and capable of kindness.''

Despite the alarmed gasps of the crowd, she gripped Ampris's hand. Behind her, Chancellor Temondahl shot to his feet, and even Ehssk looked startled.

''Majesty, have great care,'' Temondahl said.

Ampris smiled to herself beneath her hood. She had been counting on Israi to grandstand.

''Ampris will never hurt us,'' Israi declared to them all, keeping one eye on the cams. ''She was once our dear companion, our golden Aaroun. The Imperial Mother fears no disease, and neither will her subjects.''

Ampris took yet another step closer to Israi, inhaling the Kaa's perfume, hearing the rustle of the Kaa's beautiful skirts, seeing how the delicate skin around the Kaa's ear canals had begun to wrinkle ever so slightly.

Facing the cams, Ampris said, ''If any historians survive to record this day, they will write of the great destruction. They will write of how Israi Kaa brought down the Viis Empire.''

Israi flicked out her tongue in anger and tried to jerk free her hand, but Ampris held it tightly and would not let go.

''You had your chance, Israi,'' Ampris said. ''You could have sent us away and lived. Now we will all die together.''

As she spoke, she shoved back her hood and stared into Israi's widening, horrified eyes. In the nearest cam's small reflecting lens, Ampris could see that her own eyes were clouded white with fever. Her tongue had begun to swell, and her skin was puffy with heat.

She lifted Israi's hand, still clasped in hers, and let the world see how violently the fever made her shake. Chills and heat alike ran through Ampris, twisting her so that she could barely stand upright. Spittle drooled from one corner of her mouth.

"No," Israi said in panic, still trying to pull free.

On the dais behind the force field, the chancellors were shouting. The guards circled, seeking an angle that would let them shoot Ampris without harming Israi.

"It can't be!" Israi shouted fearfully, her eyes wide. "It can't be!"

"Here is death," Ampris said and spit right into Israi's face.

CHAPTER TWENTY-TWO

It was as though civilization snapped. Chaos broke out in all directions. A screaming Israi reeled back from Ampris, her hands clawing at her face. Ehssk shrank away from the Kaa, refusing to touch her. That frightened the others, who gathered around her helplessly.

One of the guards shot at Ampris, but she collapsed at that moment and the shot missed her, going into the crowd, which screamed and fought to get away. The captain of the guard was shouting orders that no one heeded.

And from various points around the Plaza, Rejects came staggering out of hiding. Rejects with white-filmed eyes and swollen rills. Rejects reaching out for citizens or falling in convulsions from the fever.

Panic spread as the crowd ran in all directions. Viis citizens in colorful clothes were suddenly hitting and fighting each other to get away. Other Viis streamed out from nearby buildings, shouting and running as though they had gone suddenly crazy.

Lying on the dais while the chancellors' and guards' attention focused on the still-hysterical Israi, Ampris panted from the fever, which filled her with flames. Her skin felt like it was bursting from the heat and swelling.

"Get the Imperial Mother to safety!" someone was

shouting. "You fools, there's nothing to fear from her."

Ampris looked up and her cloudy vision cleared momentarily. She saw Chancellor Temondahl gather Israi into his arms and assist her off the dais toward the imperial litter. The guards followed, and Ampris knew this was her chance.

She had intended to kill Ehssk at this moment, but he was nowhere to be seen. Nor did she have the strength.

Revenge faded from her mind. She knew the scientist had condemned himself when he'd refused to help the Kaa.

Ampris tried to remember what she was supposed to be doing, but she could no longer concentrate. The flames were around her. She could see now that her fur was blazing. Weakly, she tried to beat out the flames, but instead all she managed to do was roll herself off the dais.

The impact of landing on the ground jolted her back to consciousness. She was so thirsty, and yet her throat was filled with sour-tasting mucus. It choked her, and she coughed, thrusting herself up on her elbows as her chest seemed to break apart.

To her right, the barricade had been torn down and trampled. She saw a shoe lying on the pavement and the crowd running now down the Avenue of Triumph. A Reject fell only a short distance from her and lay there dying.

Ampris tried to crawl to him, but suddenly hands were grasping her by her shoulders and picking her up.

She could not see, could not save herself.

"Goldie!" said Elrabin's voice, choked with emotions she could not identify. "Come on now. Can you walk? Try!"

He pulled her to her feet. She swayed, unable to see anything but shadows, hearing and feeling the flames that were consuming her. She tried to speak, but only a moan came from her throat.

Now she was floating through the air. Opening her eyes, she squinted against the blinding light and turned her head against Elrabin's shoulder. She recognized his scent. He was carrying her, his gait rough and hurried, his breath rasping in his throat.

"Too heavy," she mumbled weakly. "Hurt you."

"Never mind about me," he said in a grim, breathless voice. "Got to get you out of here. How much of it did you take?"

She sighed, and found herself freezing, shivering, and crying out in pain.

Something jolted her, and she hit her head sharply against something hard and unyielding. He'd dropped her, she thought.

But the ground dipped and bobbed beneath her.

"Just lie there," Elrabin said, panting heavily, "while I get this crate moving."

She didn't understand, but then she heard an engine sputter to life, and Elrabin saying, "Come on. Come *on.*"

And they were flying. She could hear the sound of the wind. It felt deliciously cool, and the flames went out as though snuffed.

"Elrabin," she said. Her voice sounded thick and strange to her ears.

"Hang on, Goldie. Just hang on."

The skimmer swerved violently, and Ampris moaned. They swerved again, and came to a lurching stop.

Ampris closed her eyes, sinking into the heat. The flames were back, crackling in her ears, singeing her fur. She twisted this way and that, crying out, and felt his hands grip her hard.

"How much did you take?" he asked frantically. "Goldie, Goldie, wake up and talk to me. I meant to ask you before you left. How much did you take?"

It was so hard to listen to what he was saying. She opened her eyes with a great effort and saw the snowflakes falling on a huge fire that lit the night sky. "Vess Vaas," she whispered. She was freezing, standing knee-deep in snow. Her fur felt brittle, like it might fall off. Her nose had gone numb and she could no longer feel her ears.

"Goldie, come on. Stay with me now," Elrabin was saying. His voice was so faint she could barely hear him, then suddenly he sounded very loud. "How much did you take?"

She wanted to see him, but she couldn't. He sounded so upset, his voice choked as though he were crying. But Elrabin was tough and streetwise. He didn't cry. She had to be imagining all this.

She lifted her hand, and he gripped it in his.

"Ampris," he said, pleading with her. "*Try.*"

He never called her by her real name. The fear in his voice suddenly pierced through her fog. She realized he must be asking her something important. She had to help him. He was her friend.

"Elrabin?" she asked.

"How much did you take?" he repeated. "Some of it? Half of it? All of it? Tell me!"

The answer came to her, momentarily clear. "All of it," she said.

A convulsion made her arch her back and cry out. She heard Elrabin shouting something, felt a sharp prick in her arm.

The pain stopped. Her muscles relaxed, and she dropped flat again, breathing hard. She wanted to see him one last time, but she couldn't. She couldn't.

And it was dark.

Israi reclined on a couch, surrounded by physicians, a damp cloth lying across her brow. Her magnificent gown was torn and stained with dirt. Bracelets were missing from her bruised wrists, as were some of the jewels that had dangled from her rill spines.

None of her attendants had come near her since Lord Temondahl had brought her back to the palace. She lay now in this chamber she did not recognize, with only the physicians around, prodding her and drawing blood, and felt a fear so terrible and deep she could not think of anything else.

Was she dying? Was she infected? She could not bear to ask the questions. What if she were? She looked into that abyss and her mind would not cope with the answers there. What if she were not? She closed her eyes and prayed, although she had no hope that the panoply of ancient gods would hear her. They were gone long ago, vanished into an age of myth and superstition. Israi performed the worship rituals at official ceremonies as part of her imperial duties, not out of belief.

"The Imperial Mother must lie here now and rest," one of the physicians said to her.

"No," Israi said, trying to rise. "We must know. We must have answers now!"

He pushed her down, his hand gloved, a protective suit making him an alien, shadowy figure. "There can be no answers until the tests are run, majesty. Be assured it won't take much longer."

She saw the others walking ponderously toward the door, bulky and awkward in protective suits. "Do not leave us!" she cried in fear.

"We must, majesty. The tests require our interpretation."

Breathing hard, her rill rigid beneath her head, Israi lay there and clutched the sides of her couch with both hands. She had the feeling of falling, and she wanted to wail. But her throat was already raw from screaming. She did not want to die here, alone and abandoned by her own court. They were afraid of her. Even her guards were afraid of her. Only Temondahl, the chancellor she had distrusted, had been brave enough to touch her.

Where was he now? In quarantine, having his blood

drawn? Or in the throne room, plotting with Oviel to seize her empire?

Israi tossed her head from side to side. When would she know? When would she have answers?

It seemed forever before the physicians returned. They no longer wore the protective suits. Israi sat up, staring at them, seeing their smiles, and she felt her fear fall away.

"No infection?" she asked, not allowing herself to breathe.

"None, majesty. We will keep the Imperial Mother under observation for a while longer, but—"

"Then Ehssk was right," she said, letting her mind fill with relief. "It cannot cross species."

"That is correct, majesty. The symptoms were almost identical to the plague, but it is not the Dancing Death. And your majesty is not infected."

Rage came clawing up inside Israi. She struggled off her couch, staggered, and barely kept her balance. She'd been trapped in here for hours, suffering unbearable worry and torment, cowering for her life—and all because of Ampris and her trickery.

"She is to be brought before us at once!" Israi raged, kicking at the cushions that had fallen to the floor. "If the guards have killed her, then we want to see her corpse. Now!"

"Who, majesty?" the chief physician asked timidly.

"Ampris, you fool! Who else?"

He stared at her without comprehension.

Pushing away from him, Israi clapped her hands together. "Send our servants to us. Send our attendants and our ladies in waiting. Send us Lord Nalsk."

"The Imperial Mother is overwrought and must rest," the physician said. "I can supply your majesty with a sedative if necessary."

Her rill was throbbing. She felt dizzy and unwell, and fresh fear gripped her. "Are you certain we are well?"

"Your majesty is ill, but your majesty does not have the plague. Rest and—"

"We do not want rest!" she shouted. "We want the head of Ampris!"

Suddenly she was breathless, as though caught in a vise. She stiffened, gasping for air, and the physicians surrounded her immediately. One of them snapped a bitter-smelling capsule under her nostrils, making her sneeze, and the seizure was over as quickly as it had come.

She collapsed, and they laid her on the couch again. A medication patch was placed over her heart, another on her throat. She felt the sedatives taking effect and tried to fight them. She couldn't lie here, doing nothing. Ampris had to be dealt with.

"Your majesty must rest," the chief physician said firmly. "Or we will not be held responsible for the consequences."

Through a haze, Ampris was dimly conscious of flying a long time in the stolen skimmer. She had a memory of Elrabin giving her water, which made her sick. She remembered the strong smell of fuel exhaust and a thunderous sound as though shuttles were taking off.

She remembered being jostled roughly from place to place. She remembered pain and cold and heat. She remembered Nashmarl's scent, suddenly with her as though he was close by.

Then there was nothing at all for a long time.

She awakened in a small, white place. At first she thought her vision was still clouded, but as things came into focus she realized she was lying in a narrow bunk beneath a white blanket. The walls and ceiling were white, curling closely around her as though she was lying inside a cylinder. A mask had been fitted over her nose and mouth, and a tube was feeding her oxygen. She could hear the rasp of the pump and over her head, out of her line of vision, a monitor beeped steadily.

Infirmary, she thought.

But it was very small. She eyed the curved ceiling right above her face and realized she could not sit up even if she wanted.

Not understanding anything, she tugged off the mask and tried to call for help.

Her voice did not seem to be working, but the monitor blared an alarm.

Minutes later, she heard a sound from behind her head, as though something had been unsealed, and a different kind of light spilled inside her cylinder. Her bunk was rolled out backward, and she found herself in a larger place with Jobul the medic bending over her.

The Myal smiled, and Ampris said, "I know you."

Her voice was so faint she could barely hear herself.

"Yes, of course you do," Jobul said cheerfully. He fitted the mask back over her nose and mouth. "It looks like you're feeling much better, but you must keep this on. It will help your lungs heal."

She backed her ears, trying to remember. Everything was so hazy in her mind. Thinking seemed too great an effort. "Was there a fire?" she asked.

"No. You've been ill with abiru-fever. You gave yourself too much," he said. "I distinctly remember telling you not to take more than half of what I gave you. It was best to mix all of it so that the ratios would be right, but you weren't to take it all, Ampris. That was very reckless of you."

Ampris's mind supplied her with a sudden memory of Israi's face, frozen with horror. She smiled. "It worked. Needed to be in advanced stages."

"Yes, and you nearly killed yourself. Elrabin barely got the antidote administered in time." Jobul fussed around her, taking her pulse and changing her medication patches, then smoothed her blanket. "Time for you to sleep some more."

"No," she said restlessly under the mask. "What has been happening? The ships—"

"You're on one," he said, and his voice held joy, and hope, and excitement. His eyes were shining. "We left Viisymel, Ampris. Your plan worked. We went in exodus to Station Four, with everyone milling around in confusion. The dockworkers suddenly took charge, sorting us into groups and getting us loaded into shuttles. Amazing. I think they astonished themselves at what they could do."

"I knew they could do it," Ampris said proudly.

"You've always had a bigger dose of faith than the rest of us." He cocked his head to one side. "The Rejects didn't come, so we had plenty of room."

She backed her ears. "Didn't come! Why not?"

"They backed out at the last minute. I think they were afraid we'd make slaves of them when we got to Ruu-one-one-three. Elrabin tried to talk sense into them, but they wouldn't listen. They said they'd just take over Viisymel instead."

She sighed. "Maybe they will. Perhaps it's best for them, Jobul."

"Perhaps it is." He chuckled. "The Viis were so frightened that all they did was riot and fight each other, trying to flee the city or killing each other out of what they thought was mercy. They didn't have time to worry about us."

She stared up at him, smiling at his words, yet her eyes suddenly filled with tears. It had taken so long. It had been so hard. She couldn't believe her dream had finally come true.

"Lots of ships, Ampris," he said, smiling into the distance. "Plenty of ships, just like you said. Empty and waiting for us. We're on board with barely anything except what's on our backs. I don't know how we'll colonize this planet without tools or supplies or whatever it takes to settle a new world—but we're out here in space, going just the same."

She couldn't speak now. Tears spilled from the corner of her eyes. It must be true, she thought; he sounded so happy and excited that it must be true.

His gaze dropped to meet hers, and his expression changed immediately. "Time to rest. You've gotten too excited, and now you must sleep."

She wanted to thank him for the news, but her eyes were closing. She felt herself being slid back into the cylinder, and then she knew nothing.

Released at last from three days of enforced rest, Israi met with her council. Some members were missing, but Lord Nalsk was present, and so was Lord Temondahl. Oviel, once again, stood in the back corner of the room. If he had attempted a coup during her recovery, she had not been informed of it.

"I wish to be named to the council," he said before the meeting could start. "I am part of the imperial family. I have remained here while weaker individuals fled, deserting their duty. I deserve a reward for my loyalty."

Temondahl rose to his feet. "Lord Oviel makes a good point," he said wearily. He looked very old. Like many of the others, his coat was wrinkled and in need of cleaning. Israi had never seen her council look so ill-groomed. "Loyalty is of high value these days."

Israi glared at Temondahl, but she got the point. "Lord Nalsk?"

The chief of the Bureau of Security looked immaculate as always. Israi felt certain he had not dismissed his abiru servants during the panic.

Giving her a bow, he said, "It seems a reasonable request. However, there are other matters of more pressing urgency that perhaps require the Imperial Mother's attention first."

Israi drew in a breath. She was being advised to be

cautious and not let Oviel rush her into a bad decision.

She flicked out her tongue and took her gaze from Oviel. "Yes. Let us table our egg-brother's request for the moment. Reports, please."

Temondahl puffed out his air sacs, but Nalsk spoke first: "Autopsies have been performed on the dead Rejects. Whatever killed them was not the Dancing Death. No Viis have died from it. There is no evidence of the plague at all. It was a complete hoax, from start to finish, despite the theft of the plague virus."

Israi nodded. "Where are the abiru now?"

Nalsk met her gaze. "Gone. They have commandeered the supply ships in orbit and are heading into space."

Hissing with anger, she slapped the arms of her throne and stood up. "No!"

"I'm afraid it is true, majesty."

"And who let this happen?" she demanded. "Who stood by while they disobeyed us and fled?"

"The entire city has been rioting, majesty," Nalsk replied while the others made themselves small and silent in their chairs. "My patrollers have had their hands full trying to restore order. Numerous traffic collisions, fights, looting, and mass suicides have caused great difficulties."

Israi began to pace. She was uninterested in such details, or excuses. "And the fleeing slaves?" she said. "What has been done to stop them?"

"Nothing, majesty," Temondahl said softly. "It was deemed best to wait until the Imperial Mother could make those decisions."

"Yes," she said curtly, curling her tongue inside her mouth. "They think they will head out to one of the colony worlds. They think they will be welcomed there and allowed to settle peacefully. Send word to all colony governors at once. No planet is to allow them to make orbit, on pain of reprisal. We will not allow this rebellion to spread across the empire."

"The flotilla is approaching our system," Temondahl said. "They could fire long-range weaponry—"

"—and run the risk of destroying Shrazhak Ohr or damaging Viisymel," Salteid, the new lord commander, said curtly. "There will be no warship firing heavy weapons in this system. Let the slaves pass outside the system, and we'll make short work of them."

"And if they don't leave the system?" Israi asked.

They stared at her.

"If they go to Tanvek Ohr and its jump gates? They can jump across the empire before we can catch them."

"Ships are already under orders to deploy around the second station," Salteid said. "They will not escape our system."

"At least not that way," Nalsk said softly.

"Do you think the rebels of the rim worlds are behind this—this trouble?" Temondahl asked.

Israi glanced at Nalsk, who shook his head. "No," Israi replied. "It was Ampris's doing, from start to finish."

The council members muttered in protest. "Surely no simpleminded Aaroun could have thought up so devious a plot, majesty," Temondahl said.

Israi flicked out her tongue, on the verge of assuring them that Ampris was more than capable of masterminding something this intricate. She didn't know whether to be proud of her former pet, or furious. Either way, she would not let Ampris win this game. They were not finished yet.

Hesitating, she caught Nalsk's gaze and beckoned him to her.

Together they stepped into a corner away from the others to confer.

"Majesty?" he asked.

"Quickly," she said. "Revenge upon this Aaroun has

become a matter of personal necessity. The Kaa is a warrior, and this warrior's honor has been stained by a slave."

"Understood."

"If we go after Ampris in our own imperial warship, is our throne secure in our absence?"

Nalsk flicked out his tongue, but his gaze did not drop from hers. "Probably not, majesty."

She turned away from him and returned to her throne. When Nalsk had taken his chair, she said, "No, Ampris was not working alone. She is cunning and resourceful, but she could not mastermind this without help. Tell us, council, who in this room would profit most from the death of the Kaa?"

They exclaimed in horror and automatic protest, but more than one gaze shot involuntarily across the room to Oviel.

He straightened his thin shoulders at once, his mouth falling open in outrage. His rill stiffened behind his head. "What accusation is this?" he demanded. "I've done nothing at all. I've played no part in this conspiracy."

"You protest, yet we have not accused you," Israi said silkily. "Perhaps Lord Nalsk should discuss the matter with you."

"No!" Oviel shouted. "No!"

But Nalsk stood and gestured. At once two guards flanked Oviel and escorted him out. Nalsk followed, pausing at the door to bow to Israi.

She flicked out her tongue, well-pleased with herself for having outmaneuvered Oviel. Now he wouldn't be able to cause her trouble while she was gone. In fact, she thought further, he could perhaps die under interrogation and no one would care. He was a perfect scapegoat.

"Lord Salteid," she said. "Prepare our warship. We

shall be going after these slaves personally. Ampris will not escape our punishment.''

Salteid saluted her and left, while Chancellor Temondahl did his best to protest. But Israi refused to consider staying in her palace while Ampris got away.

By evening, she was dressed in uniform and shuttling up to her ship. She came aboard to the sound of piping. The officers of her crew gave her a formal welcome. They had been chosen and awarded their rank according to their family lineage and distinction. She had no doubt that she would be well-served.

''Captain,'' she said formally as he saluted her and then bowed very low. ''Get ready for immediate departure. The slaves have a head start, but—''

''Their cargo ships are slow, majesty. They are just now reaching Shrazhak Ohr. We can overtake them easily.''

Israi flicked out her tongue and stared at the captain's green-skinned face. He looked quite sleek, but was broader in the jowls than in the brow. Standing there looking smug and handsome in his brand-new uniform, he seemed too complacent to suit her.

''Shrazhak Ohr,'' she said in astonishment. ''Can they not navigate? We believed they were heading for Tanvek Ohr.''

''Then they are going the wrong way, majesty,'' he replied. ''If I may escort the Imperial Mother to the bridge, I'll be delighted to show your majesty what I mean.''

On the way he tried to give her a tour of the ship, which had been newly fitted out from end to end upon her ascension to the throne. She had never been aboard before, but she had no interest in looking it over. She wanted only to pursue Ampris.

When she stepped onto the bridge, she saw a bewildering array of complex instrumentation banks. Shackled to a chair, a Zrhel hunched over what the captain informed her was the navigation station.

"Here are the weapons," the captain said, leading her to another station. "And here are the scanners."

A Viis ensign was bent over his instrumentation, focusing with total concentration.

The captain tapped him on the shoulder. The ensign glanced up, saw Israi, and jumped to his feet so hurriedly he dropped his headset.

She stared at him icily, not impressed. The captain glowered at him, and the ensign seemed to suddenly recall military etiquette, which forbade leaving a station in order to make obeisance to the Kaa. His rill turned bright red and fell limp over his collar.

"Activate the main screen," the captain said. "Show the Imperial Mother where the cargo ships are heading."

A blank wall section of the bridge suddenly shimmered to life. Israi saw a fascinating panorama of space, complete with stars as thick as jewel dust, streaking comets, and colored planets. She stared with awe, beginning to enjoy herself; then the view changed and suddenly she saw a grid on the screen with a cluster of crimson blips moving steadily toward another blip.

"That is Shrazhak Ohr," the captain said, pointing. "Show Tanvek Ohr's location to the Imperial Mother."

Seconds later, another blip appeared on the screen, almost in the opposite direction from where the ships were heading.

Israi flicked out her tongue. She did not understand, but she had no intention of sitting here in orbit while Ampris got away.

"Go after them," she commanded. "Now. Contact Shrazhak Ohr and inform them of what is headed their way."

The captain turned away from her and passed the order. Suddenly the calm, almost lazy atmosphere of the bridge changed to something crisp and efficient. Another ensign, also in new uniform, came and showed the Imperial Mother to her seat. She was located at the center of the bridge, almost in line with the captain. Her chair was taller than his, was much more elaborate, and was fitted with its own communications link and a master weaponry control.

Israi allowed the ensign to show her how to fasten her safety restraints. By then the ship was moving out of orbit, the main screen off again until they were on their way. When it came back on, it showed her a simulacrum of space as they slid past Viisymel's moon and headed into the system. On an upper corner of the screen, however, the scanner grid showing the direction of the abiru ships continued to be displayed.

"We can catch up with them in a day's time," the captain informed her. "Or in four hours. It depends on your majesty's pleasure."

She glared at him, deciding he was a fool. "How far are they from the station?"

"Four hours."

"Then get us there quickly. We do not want them to get away!"

He smiled. "I assure you, majesty, that they can't get away. If they attempt to jump, the station will direct them straight into the jaws of the fleet, which is waiting at the first connective. Then they will be—"

"And what if they are up to something else?" she demanded, tired of his smug assurances.

"Such as what, majesty?"

"Have you made contact with the station yet?"

"No answer, sir. Uh, I mean, majesty," the communications officer replied nervously.

Israi had the fleeting thought that perhaps as Supreme Leader she should occasionally train with her crew so that they would be used to her presence.

"Something is wrong," she said, wondering what

Ampris was up to. "We should be able to talk to the station."

"It is probably a malfunction in the station's communication equipment," he said. "They've had a lot of malfunctions lately."

But Israi refused to be reassured.

Her ship picked up speed. The four hours of travel time passed with agonizing slowness. No matter what the communications officer tried, the station did not answer his hails. "Perhaps they heard about the plague," he guessed at last. "I was stationed there for a while. We used to listen to Viisymel news. They could have picked up a vidcast and panicked. It's the only reason I can think of for them to stay off-line this way."

"What are you up to, Ampris?" murmured Israi, trying to figure out how Ampris thought. She knew the wily Aaroun must be up to another trick, but what? Did the slaves not understand that Tanvek Ohr was their only chance to escape out-of-system? Shrazhak Ohr's single working jump gate connected only to the coordinate where the fleet now waited.

"Coming into range now," the captain informed her.

Startled from her thoughts, Israi sat up straight in her chair and stared at the image of the station now coming on-screen. Shrazhak Ohr was a long, metal cylinder, suspended vertically, with docking bays encircling its top.

"Wait!" the captain said, suddenly leaning forward. "Look at that."

Israi stared at the screen without understanding. "What?"

"The jump gate is open!" the captain said.

"Of course it is, if they are going through," Israi said impatiently.

"No, majesty!" he said, pointing. "The other gate. The *old* gate. The one that's not supposed to work."

At the navigations console, the Zrhel threw back his

head, dropping feathers, and began to squawk in what passed for laughter among his people.

"Belay that," the captain ordered, but the Zrhel cackled and squawked without heeding him until someone hit him with a stun-stick across the back.

Israi stared at the screen, unable to believe what she was seeing. Yet in an instant, her mind had grasped everything. For years, the jump gate to Ruu-113 had been declared inoperable, but that must have been a lie. The Zrheli engineers had indeed sabotaged it, as had been suspected off and on, and now they were opening it for Ampris. Not for the Viis, who owned Ruu-113 and who were in dire need of its resources, but for a rabble of worthless slaves who thought they could defy the empire.

"No!" Israi screamed, furious that Ampris had somehow accomplished what Israi and her predecessors could not. "She will not have it! Captain, close in and fire at them."

"But, majesty, we're too close to the station. If we hit it—"

"The traitors are giving them Ruu-one-one-three!" she shouted. "Stop them. Even if you have to destroy the station, you must stop them now!"

On board the last cargo ship in the convoy, Ampris stared at the Zrhel female on-screen. Through a side port in the nose of the cargo ship they could all see the jump gate looming ahead. Its accelerator rings swirled in a dizzying array of colors, ever widening as it spread itself into position.

"Switch your piloting to station control," the Zrhel operative said crisply. "All ships, comply."

Over the speakers, the various ships acknowledged the order. The pilot of Ampris's ship was the last to call in. He was a rangy Aaroun with striped fur and a brown mask across his eyes similar to Ampris's. Before their departure from Viisymel, he had been a shuttle mechanic. Now he was sweating his way through trying to navigate this unwieldy ship into position.

A light flashed on the console in front of him, and he sagged with relief. "It's engaged," he said in disbelief. "I didn't think I could get it right."

The Zrhel seemed to have heard him over the open channel. She opened her beak, her eyes gleaming fiercely. "Miracles happen every day," she said. "Let us do the work now."

Ahead of them the swirling colors inside the jump gate opened to reveal the vortex itself. Ampris tried to look at it, but found it hurt her eyes. It seemed to be pulling her in, and she had to blink and look away.

Beside her, Elrabin stared with his mouth open. Velia put her hands over her eyes, and Jobul's fingers found Ampris's pulse.

"I'm fine," she said impatiently, but he went on with what he was doing.

"Ampris," the Zrhel said from the viewscreen.

"Yes?" Ampris replied immediately, managing to get her wrist away from Jobul.

"Timing is critical for passing through the gate. We have programmed it to pulse open for a limited span of time only. Pursuit ships are within range. Do you understand?"

Ampris glanced at the pilot, who sat upright with a curse. Elrabin was looking around wildly as though trying to remember which control he was supposed to operate. Finally Velia reached across him and flipped on the scanners.

A small screen in front of Elrabin showed a single ship, closing fast. He yelped. "They're right on top of us!"

Ampris turned her attention back to the Zrhel. "We understand," she said.

"You must go in one at a time," the Zrhel said. "If

anyone panics and attempts to jump line, you will destroy station control, and the gate will malfunction. It is not a question of the number of things that can go through at the same time. It is a question of mass. Your ships are each very large.''

''Understood,'' Ampris said. Her mouth was suddenly dry, and she glanced at the scanners again. At the front of the line, the lead cargo ship entered the vortex and was suddenly sucked from sight. Ampris's heart jumped. One through. One free.

''When the gate starts to close, even if you are not all through, no ship must attempt to enter,'' the Zrhel said. ''We have set the gate to destroy itself by collapsing in on its own matrix. This will prevent the Viis from ever reaching you.''

Gratitude filled Ampris. She smiled at the screen. ''You have done far more than we could have hoped for. Thank you for your assistance.''

The Zrhel nodded. ''It is now time for us to ask you for a favor in exchange.''

Elrabin glanced up in alarm. ''What now?'' he muttered.

''Of course,'' Ampris said to the Zrhel without hesitation. ''Name it.''

The Zrhel seemed to hesitate. A feather dropped off her head, floating to the desk in front of her. ''Our families,'' she said, her voice less harsh than before. ''We commandeered a few escape pods and maintenance shuttles when we took over the top of the station. We believe we can hold the Viis personnel prisoner long enough to get our families off the station. But these craft lack sufficient power and speed to enter the gate, even under station piloting control. Will your ship tow them through?''

''Of course,'' Ampris said.

''I don't know how to use the tractor,'' the pilot said, throwing up his hands.

Ampris looked at the Zrhel. "Can you give us instructions?"

The engineer nodded her head, shedding more feathers. "One moment while I call up your ship's manual."

"Hey," Elrabin said. "This Viis ship is coming right up on our tailpipe."

The Zrhel said, "We have identified the pursuit ship from its call sign codes. It is the Kaa's warship, *Imperial.*"

Silence filled the cramped flight deck while everyone stared at one another.

"Israi," Ampris said. She curled her hand around the Eye of Clarity, feeling it pulse warmly against her palm. "She is staying with this to the end."

"Going to be the end of *us,* see?" Elrabin said nervously, his ears swiveling back and forth. "I'm looking at this light that just came on. It means they got weapons locked or something, right?"

"They are not as close as they appear," the Zrhel assured them. "Just coming into range now. They will wait until they are closer, to make sure their weapons do not hit the station. Please, Ampris. Our favor."

"Yes," Ampris said, tearing her attention from the approaching warship.

"We are ejecting our small craft now. Stand by to receive instructions via computer linkup."

Lights lit up across the console in front of the pilot, who sat there helplessly, shaking his head.

From the side port, Ampris could see the escape pods bobbing forth from the hatches. She wondered how the Zrheli had managed to take over control of the station, even temporarily, and supposed she might never hear the story.

Her gaze met the Zrhel's on-screen. "And what about you?" she asked. "Are you not going to come? You said the gate was programmed."

"The Viis could break out at any time and override

our programming," the engineer replied. "It is better that we keep a skeleton crew in place."

Ampris felt her throat choke up. She knew what the engineer was saying. The Zrhel in front of her would never live to see another day. "You are very brave," Ampris said, "and I salute you."

The Zrhel opened her beak, and her fierce eyes softened for a moment. "Honor our memory by keeping the sacred places on Ruu-one-one-three protected."

"I will," Ampris promised.

Their eyes met and locked, communicating what words would have been inadequate to express.

"I have a young son," the Zrhel said. "His name is Preicet."

"I'll find him," Ampris promised her. "I have young sons too."

"Be well, Ampris," the Zrhel said. "Prosper in freedom."

Israi sat on the edge of her seat, straining against her safety restraints. "Faster! Closer!" she commanded. "Another ship has gone through."

"We'll pursue them through the gate, majesty," the captain said. He had lost his air of smugness and now looked grim and harried. "Helm, slow to quarter speed."

"No, do not slow down!" Israi commanded. "We must fire on them now."

"Majesty, if we fire weapons, we will destroy the station," he said.

"We do not care as long as they are stopped."

"Destroying the station will destroy the gate!" he said in exasperation, glaring back at her.

She blinked, startled by his defiance. Reluctantly she saw the wisdom in his words. "But they are all getting away. Only one ship is left, the one pulling the debris with it."

"Those pods, captain," said someone. "Has to be the traitors from the station."

"Or Viis personnel who have been jettisoned by the traitors," the captain said.

Israi did not care what the escape pods contained. She wanted Ampris and she was about to lose her. "They must not get away."

"No, majesty," the captain agreed. "No one is going to escape. I'm calling the rest of the fleet in. We're all going to go through that gate after them."

Israi's head was spinning as they closed in on the final ship in the line. Ruu-113 was almost considered a fable. She'd never believed in it herself, never believed it would be accessible again, yet suddenly here was the gate, open before her. All she had to do was enter. Her beleaguered Viisymel was saved after all. It could recover by drawing on Ruu-113's limitless resources. It would thrive once again, and her name would go into the Book of Greats.

"Captain!" shouted a crew member in warning.

"I see it," the captain said. "Slow engines."

"What are you doing?" Israi screamed at him. "We must follow!"

"Majesty, the gate is closing," the captain said patiently. "We can't follow."

"Closing!" She glared at the screen and saw the accelerator rings moving into position. The last abiru ship, with its flotsam of pods and maintenance shuttles bobbing behind it, was now entering the vortex.

They *were* getting away. Israi's rill stiffened. Ruu-113 belonged to *her*, not to Ampris and her rabble.

"Stop them!" Israi commanded.

"Majesty, we cannot."

She glared at the captain, whose rill began to redden. "Go after them!"

"The gate is closing," he protested. "We'll be caught in the collapsing matrix."

"You are a coward!" she shouted. "We relieve you of command! You!" She pointed at the helmsman. "Send us forward. Now!"

"Belay that order," the captain said, and the helmsman obeyed him.

Israi could not believe they would defy her. She flung off her safety restraint and hurled herself at the console. The Zrhel navigator was laughing there, his eyes quite mad.

She grabbed him around the throat. "What will make us go forward?"

Still laughing and choking, he reached ahead, and she released him. The Zrhel hit the controls, fending off the helmsman's attempt to stop him, and they lurched toward the rings. The ship plunged inside just as the implosion caught them.

Thrown off her feet, Israi heard the klaxons wailing and voices shouting in panic. The first gravitational flux hit them, rippling through metal not designed to endure such stress. Rolling on the deck, Israi heard a tremendous crack of sound. The ship shuddered in another flux, and Israi was suddenly hurled upward, her body spinning around and around in the air. Around her she glimpsed a blinding explosion as the instrumentation blew. Then she was being crushed and pulled apart by forces her body could not withstand. She screamed into infinity, until there was nothing at all.

CHAPTER TWENTY-THREE

In orbit around the green and blue globe that was Ruu-113, Ampris would not allow herself to be moved from the port screen. She constantly marveled at the planet's beauty. Transfixed, she studied the shape of the continents beneath shifting clouds. The oceans looked vast. Scans reported that the air was breathable. The water was clean and pure. Ampris barely listened to the data. The beauty of this planet alone was enough to exhilarate her. Yet now that her dream had finally come true, she found herself exhausted and spent, unable to do anything except lie by the port screen and gaze at their new world.

Foloth and Nashmarl came to sit beside her. "We'll be going down soon, Mother," Foloth said excitedly. "The pilots have all talked on the link. They think it's safe. The atmosphere and water seem to check out."

"Tomorrow," Nashmarl said. "Tomorrow we go."

Ampris smiled at him and reached for his hand, but he pulled away. They still had not talked, still had not reconciled their quarrel. There was so much she needed to say to him, and yet she couldn't reach through his stubborn barriers.

Foloth pushed his way closer to the port screen. "It's beautiful, isn't it, Mother?"

"Very," she said quietly, resting her head against the pillow.

Her concentration wandered a moment, coming back only when Foloth announced, "Someday I will rule this world."

"Kaa Foloth," Nashmarl jeered. "When I grow another leg."

"You don't know anything," Foloth said dismissively. "I can be Kaa if I want to be. Mother said we have unlimited possibilities now."

"We don't want a Kaa," Nashmarl said, his green eyes flashing with anger. "And even if we did, we wouldn't choose you."

"Cubs, please," Ampris said. They were making her head hurt. "Don't quarrel."

"I'm not quarreling," Foloth told her. "He is. Nashmarl is so immature. He doesn't—"

"I'm just as mature as you are!" Nashmarl declared, jumping up. He jostled Ampris's seat with his leg, and she winced in pain.

Foloth shoved him back. "Look what you've done! You hurt her. Get away." He shoved Nashmarl again, knocking him against the wall, and bent over Ampris. "Mother," he said in concern. "I'm sorry. Let me help you."

Although she locked her jaw to keep from crying out, a tiny whimper escaped her. The pain faded at last, leaving deep exhaustion in its wake. She opened her eyes, hearing Foloth and Nashmarl quarreling bitterly. Foloth was berating Nashmarl, blaming him, making it sound like he'd hurt her on purpose.

"Stop," she whispered, upset to see them becoming such bitter enemies. "You need each other to survive. Please, don't fight."

But they were too busy arguing to hear her. Moments later, Jobul burst in, with Elrabin on his heels.

Elrabin swore at the cubs and hustled them away while Jobul bent over Ampris in concern.

"The monitor went off, and we could hear them fighting down the corridor," he said. "Those cubs of yours—"

"Don't blame them," she said weakly, wincing as his probing touch found the pain. "So excited about planetfall."

"You're the one who's too excited," he said, applying a patch.

She tried to pull it off. "Don't want to sleep. Have to see everything."

He put the patch back on and held it in place until the drugs began to make her groggy. "Sleep now, Ampris. Tomorrow will be a big day for everyone."

Elrabin came back, panting audibly. With her eyes shut, swirling through the mists of semiconsciousness, Ampris listened to Elrabin complain bitterly about her cubs' lack of consideration.

"She's still defending them," Jobul said with a sigh. "She never changes."

"No. There ain't nothing more stubborn than an Aaroun mother." Elrabin paused, then said worriedly, "She ain't getting better, is she?"

Ampris wanted to speak to him, but she was too far away now, floating on the tide of drugs.

"She responded well at first, but there's been too much abuse," Jobul said. His voice sounded tired with resignation. "Her old wounds, the torture from the Bureau, that walk she took across the Plains of Filea to reach Vir—all of it has taken a tremendous toll on her strength. Her health is simply broken. She was in no condition to take that poison, but she wouldn't listen to me."

"Wouldn't listen to me either," Elrabin said. "Ain't—ain't there nothing you can do?"

Jobul sighed. "I can make her comfortable. That's all."

Elrabin didn't speak for so long that Ampris thought he'd left. She wanted to leave too. She wanted to go to Ruu-113. "Will she see it?" Elrabin asked, his voice choking up. "You got to make sure she gets to see it."

"I'll do all that I can," Jobul promised.

They talked longer, but by then Ampris was asleep.

When she awakened, she was strapped in a bunk on board the shuttle, and they were shuddering violently through the atmosphere.

"Good morning, Mother," Foloth said to her. Strapped in a safety harness, he grinned cheerfully at her. "Nashmarl's been sick, but I haven't."

Ampris smiled back and curled her hand around her Eye of Clarity. They bumped on down, rolled and tossed about by turbulence no one had expected. But Ampris had no consciousness of the rough ride down. She was walking far away in another vision, walking across a rolling meadow of tall grass to a knoll overlooking a valley where a prosperous town nestled. She stopped there and looked down at the inhabitants, so tiny and far away. They seemed to be going about their business in contentment. She knew without being told that these were the descendents of the people who were landing with her today. Generations into the future. People who worked and thrived and knew joy. People who did not know the meaning of the word "slave."

Standing in the clear, cool air, the sky arching over her without menace, Ampris longed to go down there and walk the streets. She wanted to see the faces and hear the voices of these people.

But when she tried to go down the hill, her feet would not move.

Sadness touched her heart, and she understood what the Eye was trying to show her. This was a future she would not live to see, except through this vision. Her work was finished, but the dream would go on. Her life had been full. She had traveled far and seen many wonders. She had known joy and she had known terror and grief. But best of all, she had lived to see this planet, and that was reward enough.

"Ampris," said a voice. Someone shook her gently.

She opened her eyes, the vision fading from her mind. Disoriented, and not recognizing him at first, she looked up at Jobul.

"Ampris, we've landed," he said.

His hand was on her wrist, and he was running a medscanner over her.

She brushed his hand away. "I want to see."

"Hey, Goldie!" Elrabin appeared and crouched beside her so they were at eye level. "We're here. You ready to see some dirt and sky?"

"With all my heart." She smiled at him, wishing she could tell him how precious he was to her. From the first day they'd met, frightened and jammed together in a holding pen at the slave auction, Elrabin had been trying to take care of her. He had brought her food that day, she remembered now, food she was too proud to eat. How angry he'd been with her for wasting it. And yet, through ups and downs, fortunes and many more misfortunes, they had remained friends. "Now, please," she said.

Elrabin laughed, avoiding Jobul's gaze, and unstrapped her.

"We'll prop you up so you can look out the port," Jobul said.

Ampris backed her ears. "Outside," she said fiercely. That one sharp word seemed to rob her of all her breath. She closed her eyes, fighting off a wave of weakness, and was suddenly frightened that she would not make it. She looked at Elrabin, pleading with her eyes, and he understood.

"Okay, outside it is."

"I don't think she should," Jobul said.

"Back off," Elrabin snarled, and Jobul stopped protesting. Tenderly Elrabin gathered her in his arms.

She started to tell him that she was too heavy for him to carry, but he lifted her easily. In startlement she realized she must have lost weight. A lot of weight.

He ducked out through the hatch with her and carried her across a torn-up clearing, stumbling a little on the uneven ground where the shuttle's landing had been less than neat. Ampris saw massive trees towering above her, their crowns impossibly high.

The air filled her lungs, and for a moment she felt strong and clearheaded. It was sweet, this air of the promised land. She smelled no pollution, no smoke, but only wood and growth and life.

Sunlight filtered through the swaying canopy above, casting dappled light across the blanket wrapped around her. Elrabin laid her gently on the mossy ground, propping her against the base of the largest tree she'd ever seen. She listened a moment, hearing the sigh of wind through the leaves. In the distance, water rushed swiftly along its course.

Relief and a feeling of well-being filled her. She smiled at Elrabin and gripped his hand. "A good place," she said.

He nodded, his eyes bright with the sheen of tears. "Yes."

"You will lead them now," she said to him, while the others gathered silently around. "You will go on, my loyal Elrabin."

"Hey, no!" he said in shock. "You can't go talking that way, see? We're depending on you—"

"Elrabin, your heart is good. You are more concerned with others than with yourself. You will lead them well."

He backed his ears, looking more upset than she'd ever seen him. Bending down, he whispered, "I ain't qualified, Goldie. You got to pick someone else. Harval, maybe."

"A dust runner? Never."

"But I never been any good at the big jobs," he said in anguish. "I ain't no fighter. Never could learn. I don't have what it takes. I got to follow, Goldie. That's what I know to do."

Ampris smiled at him gently. "This is not a time for fighting, my friend. It is a time to create a new world and new ways. Your ideas will be good ones. Have confidence in yourself."

"Mother!" Foloth said, coming over to her and kneeling at her side. He glared at Elrabin, who drew back slightly. "Jobul says that you're dying."

She looked at her firstborn cub, taking in his odd face and dark, arrogant eyes. "Yes, I am."

He blinked, going wide-eyed at that. But although he gulped a moment, he did not back away. "Then I claim your Eye of Clarity as my inheritance."

Nashmarl howled and slammed into him, knocking him away from her. "You leave her alone!" he shouted. "She isn't dying! She isn't!"

Elrabin snarled across her. "Both of you, shut up! This ain't no way to act."

Nashmarl gripped Ampris's hand and bent over it, weeping uncontrollably. "No," he sobbed. "You can't! I'm sorry. I'm sorry."

"I know," she said, stroking his arm. "It's all right."

Foloth eyed her, as composed as Nashmarl was distraught. He reached out to slip the necklace over her head.

With her last bit of strength, Ampris pulled her hands free from Nashmarl's grip and stopped Foloth. She took the Eye of Clarity from his hands, although he resisted for a moment. Prying his fingers free, she handed the stone to Elrabin.

"No!" Foloth said.

Ampris ignored her son's protests and curled Elrabin's shaking fingers around the Eye. "You have always had great courage and inner strength, Elrabin," she said. "This will help you to use those qualities, and to find new ones. It has great power. I know you will be wise enough to find it."

Elrabin's fingers tightened on hers. His ears swiveled, and his eyes spilled tears. He could not speak.

"No, Mother!" Foloth said angrily. "The Eye is my birthright. I am your son. How can you give it to this Kelth nobody? Are you trying to punish me for my Viis blood?"

Some of the onlookers gasped, but Ampris ignored Foloth. Instead she placed her hand on Nashmarl's bowed head. Her heart grieved for his anguish, spilling out now at long last. She hoped his tears would heal him, and help him. He needed so much, and she had so little time left to give him.

"My dearest Nashmarl," she said weakly, feeling very tired now. "Be strong. I have always loved you. Remember that you will always have my blessing. Whenever you need me, look inside yourself, inside your strong and tender heart, and I will be there."

Nashmarl pressed his wet face against her hand, whimpering.

She looked up at Foloth, so tight-lipped, so furious. "Foloth, I do not hate your Viis blood," she said. "How could I? It will only be a problem for you if you allow it to be. This whole world lies before you, but you must first learn how to walk in it. Becoming a Viis is not the answer for you. Viis ways cannot serve the people's needs here."

He frowned at her, puzzled and upset. Clearly he did not understand, but she had no strength left to explain. Exhausted, she leaned her head back, gazing one last time at Elrabin, her oldest and truest friend. Her eyes closed, and she entered peace.

Elrabin stared at her, lying there as though she had simply fallen asleep, and knew she was gone. He touched her hand and her face, and wept.

Behind him, one by one, the abiru people knelt also, grieving together in the sunlight of this world she had given them all.

At dawn, Elrabin carried Ampris's body to the top of a high, silent mountain rising above the landing site. Allowing no one to help him, the Eye of Clarity swinging on its cord around his throat, he buried her in a quiet place where she could always watch over her people.